Ripples On The Water

Ripples On The Water

A Novel

Jeff Morlock

To order additional copies of this book, contact:
Xlibris Corporation
1-888-795-4274
www.Xlibris.com
Orders@Xlibris.com
54263

Acknowledgements

I WANT TO thank first and foremost my wife Kathie, without whom I would never have put words to paper.

She has been and continues to be my number one fan, my constant source of support, encouragement and inspiration.

I also want to thank "The Gang" for cheering me on, and my friends Renatta, Birdie and Kay who are the other founding members in our fledgling writers group in Delano for their kind words and encouragement.

Dedication

For Janelle

Chapter 1

THE ONLY RIPPLES on the otherwise calm northern Minnesota lake was from their feet as they sat on the dock, their legs hanging over the edge with their feet dangling, toes tapping the still water. Looking out across the calm lake, the moon reflected off the water, hanging low in the sky. The stars were twinkling brightly in the cloudless sky. The only lights they could see were far across the lake, on the opposite shore, cabin lights that sparsely dotted the shoreline. They sat there quietly; he had his arm around her waist, as she rested her head on his shoulder.

"I'm going to miss you," Linda said, looking up into his eyes with small tears forming.

"I know honey, I'm going to miss you too," Tom replied quietly, kissing her on the forehead, his eyes gazing out across the lake, not really focusing on any one thing in particular.

"Isn't there a way that you don't have to go tomorrow?" she asked, sniffling a little as the tears grew and started to run down her cheeks.

"No, I told you, there isn't," he answered. "My number was picked and I have to report for duty, if I'm not there I can go jail."

"I know," she said, "I just don't want you to go; I'm afraid."

"Shhhhhhhhhhh," he said, putting his finger against her lips, "I'll be okay, I promise".

Tom lifted her chin with his hand and kissed her on the lips. He felt her shudder in his arms, he held her tight for several minutes, slowly rocking sideways back and forth.

Linda is a dark haired girl, five feet three if she's a foot, and all of seventeen years old, with fair complexion and brown eyes, and a smile that can melt any mans heart.

She is going to graduate after this next year of high school and wants to be a doctor after she goes to college.

Tom is taller at six feet even, longish brown hair and robin's egg blue eyes, and he is two years older at nineteen and his first year out of high school, still searching for some meaning to his life with no real direction or focus.

The sky began to get lighter as dawn neared. The black turned to dark blue, then to a dark orange, then purples and reds and yellows took over as the sunrise filled the sky. Tom and Linda, still sitting on the dock looking out across the lake, the sounds of birds and squirrels chirping as they woke up and began to break the silence of the morning.

"Come on," Tom said as he stood up, "I have to get going."

"I know," Linda replied, her voice quivering as she took his hand and let him help her up, "I'll drive you to the bus station, I want to spend ever minute I can with you before you go."

Tom waved and silently mouthed, "I love you," back to Linda from the window of the bus as it pulled away from the station. Linda waved with one hand as she held a handkerchief on the tears streaming down her face, whispering into the air "I love you darling," as the bus turned the corner and was gone.

Tom sat back into the seat of the bus, settling in for a long lonely ride to the airport down in Minneapolis and then off to Ft. Benning Georgia, already missing Linda, his eyes were filled with tears and he wiped them with the back of his hand.

Linda sat down on a bench and sobbed. How was she going to go on? How was she going to survive? Tom just left on a bus to the Army and she may never see him again.

The two girls were in the women's room, standing in front of the large mirror, touching up their makeup.

"Have you heard from Tom yet?" asked Janey

"No, not yet, I'm sure they are keeping him busy, with all the training and all." Linda answered

"He's been gone almost a week now, I would think you would of heard from him by now, if it were me I'd be worried." Janey pressed.

Janey and Linda have known each other as long as they can remember. They love each other and hate each other at the same time. Janey is taller than Linda, slender with long wavy red hair.

"Well, I'm not, he'll write when he can. I know he will," Linda insisted.

"Did you see Bobby in the hall?" Janey asked

"Yeah, why?" Linda replied

"Because, look at this," Janey turned towards Linda and held up a ring on a silver chain that was hung around her neck. "He asked me to go to the dance with him on Friday night."

Linda didn't say anything, she just finished touching up her lipstick, smacking her lips together before they both went back to class.

A loud voice shouted out, "All right you lousy maggots," as the overhead lights came on and an empty trashcan was kicked down the center of the giant room, certain to wake up even the soundest sleeper. "Get your lazy asses up and fall out, you got 5 minutes!"

Tom jumped out of bed and ran to the latrine. He peed and splashed cold water on his face to help wake up, then ran back to his bunk to put on his uniform, lacing his boots up, right over left, right over left. Then made his bunk as tight as he could, smoothing it over one last time to get rid of any wrinkles or lumps.

Tom fell in right next to Wayne. He was in the second row back, third from the left. That was where his spot was, based on height. When they all lined up in a single file line, with the tallest on the left. Then into six man rows, five rows deep. Tallest in one front corner, and the shortest in the opposite rear corner.

"Geeze man, how do they expect us to function on only three hours of sleep a night?" Tom asked Wayne.

"I dunno man, I dunno," Wayne answered, whispering out of the side of his mouth.

"My feet got blisters on their blisters," Tom whispered just loud enough so that only Wayne could hear.

"Raight face!" The platoon Sergeant called out in a loud commanding voice that left no question as to who was in charge. On his command they were formed up and marched out to begin their training for the day.

There was a knock on the door, Linda was sitting on her bed, her back propped up against the headboard, headphones on listening to her radio, and reading her assigned chapters for English literature.

"Yeah?" Linda replied to the knock on the door.

"Hi honey, you got some mail today," her mom said as she opened the door a crack and stuck her head in. "I think it's from Tommy."

"Mom, he's a man, he's in the Army, don't call him Tommy anymore, his name is Tom." Linda replied

"Well, I think he sent you a letter," her mom replied and set the envelope on the dresser next to the door, then left, closing the door behind her.

> My. Dearest Linda
>
> I sure do miss you. They have us up at 5 in the morning and keep us up and busy until almost midnight most nights. You wouldn't believe the crap I have to go through. The food is nasty, but by the time we get through the chow line, it tastes good because we are so hungry. Tomorrow we go to the firing range, that's gonna be awesome. I heard that we get to shoot our rifles on full auto. I hope so, we gotta carry them with us all day, everywhere we go, even to the shitter, so I hope we get to go full auto.
>
> One week down, five more to go. How are things back home? I sure do miss you. Here is my address. Sorry I didn't write sooner, but I didn't get

to the exchange to buy stamps until today. We don't get to go there until the end of our first week. That really sucks. You'd think we were prisoners here or something.

I gotta go now, lights out in ten minutes and I still have to polish my boots for inspection in the morning.

Love Tom

"I love you too," Linda said out loud to herself as she sat on her bed, leaning against the wall with a pillow propped up behind her, holding the letter pressed against her heart.

Linda sat on the seat of the school bus, gazing out the window, not really looking at anything in particular, daydreaming of Tom, and remembering the night before he left. She thought of how he had held her, how they had kissed, how he made her feel like the most important person in the whole world.

Janey lit her cigarette and peeked around the corner of the school to see if any teachers or hall monitors were coming. "Well?" she asked.

"Well what?" Linda replied.

"Are you going to the dance tonight?" Janey asked, "Mark is gonna be there, I think he likes you."

"I don't care," Linda replied, annoyed. "I'm not going to go to any dance with Mark, he's a puke, besides I couldn't, not with Tom gone in the Army and all."

"Oh Christ Linda," Janey said, "Tom's away, key word, away, in the Army. He's probably doing some girl on base anyway."

"Shut up, he is not, I got a letter from him yesterday and he misses me, he said he loves me and he has been busy, it's hard there where he is," Linda argued.

"I bet it's hard," Janey said, laughing to herself as she took a drag off her cigarette.

"What do you know?" Linda asked, angrily, "I don't see you getting any letters from anyone saying they miss you, and they love you."

"Sorry," Janey said in an attempt to calm Linda down, "I just thought maybe you might want to get out once in awhile, and do something fun with real people, instead of staying home all the time and writing to your pen pal."

"I'm going back inside," Linda said with a huff as she turned and went back inside the school.

"This is your rifle," The drill instructor said as he walked slowly in front of the platoon, holding up his rifle.

"And this is your gun," he continued, grabbing his crotch. "One is for shooting, and one is for fun."

Turning, and walking back the way he came, in front of the platoon. Like a carnival duck going back and forth, turning at one end and going to the other, turning and going back.

"When we get to the range, all eyes WILL be on me. I don't want to hear a single voice from any of you pansy assed maggots, or you will all drop and give me twenty," He barked.

"Man," Tom whispered out of the side of his mouth to Wayne, "do you think he's gonna be this way all the time?"

"Nah," Wayne responded very quietly, "I think he just wants to be sure he gets our attention, I think he'll lighten up after while."

Tom lay down on his stomach, his feet slightly apart, with his elbows spaced shoulder width apart for stability. He had his left arm wrapped through the sling and holding the fore grip on the barrel. He pressed the stock tightly against his cheek, wrapped his right hand around the pistol grip, holding his index finger on the trigger. Closing one eye he lined up the front and rear sights on the silhouette target 150 yards downrange. He took a breath, held it and gently squeezed the trigger. The barrel came up as the round went off, startling him with the loud noise and sudden jerk.

Tom slowly squeezed off four more rounds, then laid his rifle down and waited to see the results.

The target disappeared, and then it reappeared with white circles indicating where the hits were, he had two on the upper torso, two on the paper just above the shoulder and the fifth he couldn't see. "Darn," he said out loud, pounding his fist into the dirt. "Two hits, two misses, and one so far off it didn't even hit the target."

"How did ya do?" Wayne asked from the next lane over to his right.

"Not so good," Tom replied, "Two hits out of five."

"In the black?" Wayne asked.

"Yeah," Tom replied, "how about you?"

"I got three in the black," Wayne responded, "but two, I don't know where they went."

"Could of hit the dirt," Tom replied looking over Wayne's shoulder at the drill sergeant walking towards them, "shhh, here comes that hardass."

Tom sat in the shade, leaning against the barracks wall, he just finished cleaning his rifle and still needed to put it back together before he could secure it for the night and shower off.

They had been up since four thirty this morning. Starting with formation, then a five-mile run, and breakfast. Followed by classroom time until lunch, then an afternoon on the firing range, dinner and another two hours of drill practice on the parade grounds. It was hot, dirty, and windy today, causing dust and debris to blow into your eyes when lying on the ground in the dirt.

Drill practice, Tom thought was a waste of time. They all knew how to march; they had been marching as a group everywhere they had gone the past four weeks. But, drill practice was required to be perfect for graduation in two more weeks. They had to move as a group. Step as a group, so that people in the bleachers watching heard just one step instead of thirty individual steps.

After drill practice, it was individual time. That was free time for the men to write letters home, read the mail they got that day, or just relax and visit and joke around.

Tom secured his rifle, cleaned and polished his boots, and made sure everything in his locker was in order. Made sure everything was lined up perfect and in its proper place for morning inspection.

Once he was certain everything was perfect, he sat down on his bunk, and opened today's mail.

> My Dearest Tom
>
> I miss you so much. I'm glad to hear that you are doing okay, I worry about you and pray every night before I go to bed that you are safe. Last night I went to the dance at school. There was a band playing that I know you would have liked, in fact, I think they were all guys that you graduated with. I forget their names, but Janey said she knows them. You know Janey, she probably slept with them.
>
> I can't believe it's already been almost four weeks. You will be home In two weeks, right after you graduate from basic, I'm so excited. Did they tell you where you will go after you graduate? One girl I know, her brother went to Hawaii after he graduated, I hope you get sent there, then I will come see you in the spring after I get out of school for the summer, before going to college.
>
> I should go to bed now, I'll dream about you.
>
> Xoxoxoxo
>
> Linda

"Lights out!" the platoon leader shouted from the end of the hallway as he shut off the lights. Tom carefully folded the letter, put it back in the envelope and put it in his small drawer and locked it up. Then he lay on his cot, pulled the thin blanket up over him and crossed his fingers behind his head, he closed his eyes and thought of Linda, seeing her face, seeing her sweet smile in his mind, until sleep came over him.

Linda sat on the couch, sitting sideways, her arm resting on the back of the couch staring out the window. The snow was falling, it was coming down lightly in big flakes, and it looked so beautiful. Small tears welled up in the corners of her eyes. She sniffed, then lifted a handkerchief to her eyes and wiped them. Linda wanted to share this moment with Tom, but he was not here. She wanted to sit with him on the couch, in his arms and look out the window together watching the snow falling softly, quietly, together with him. It had been so long since she had seen him. She missed him so much.

She wondered if maybe what Janey had said to her might be true. What if he was with other girls where he was? What if he was sleeping around on the base? What if he did just keep her like a port in a storm? She began to sob, she told herself not to think like that, not to allow those kinds of thoughts into her head. She needed to trust her instincts she told herself. Janey means well, but she doesn't know. Janey doesn't know the love that they share. How could she? If she did, she never would have said those things.

Linda stood by the front door, looking in the mirror and adjusting her coat while she waited for Janey to arrive. It was Saturday, Linda, Janey and several other girls were going to the mall to spend the day shopping. Linda had an appointment for a facial and a manicure, while Janey had made an appointment to get her hair done. There was also a movie playing at the theater that they all wanted to see. It was a love story with Adrian Stiletto, and Mina Kurska, they were the sexiest pair in Hollywood and their newest movie was number one at the box office.

Linda sat in her seat, watching the movie, imaging herself as Mina, and Tom as Adrian. She watched as Adrian held Mina, how he looked deep into her eyes when he talked to her. She thought to herself, that's how Tom holds me. That's how he looks at me when he talks to me. Those thoughts made her happy and sad at the same time. How could she wait two more weeks for him to graduate and come home on leave? She just would, that's all there is to it she told herself. It's only two more weeks, two more weeks she said to herself quietly as Adrian kissed Mina on the lips, their kiss covered the entire silver screen.

Tom sat down on his cot and took off his boots then lay down on his back and looked at his wristwatch. "Fifteen minutes, I have fifteen minutes before formation. I can get a quick nap in," he told himself, then he closed his eyes.

Tom woke up to Wayne slapping his foot with his hat, "C'mon man, formation, let's go," He said.

Tom looked at his watch, he only had two minutes before formation, and he sighed. Holy shit, if Wayne hadn't of waken me, I would have slept right thru formation, and everybody would have ended up doing pushups until sunset. That's a good way to make enemies, that's a good way to end up hurt badly in the showers, he thought to himself.

Tom and Wayne were buddies on the buddy system. They stood side by side when the horn blew, then jumped into the pool with their clothes on and swam to the other end, then halfway back to the middle. There were ten sets of buddies in the pool, all treading water, and waiting for the next command from the trainers who were standing on the pool deck with their bullhorns.

They were instructed to remove their pants, tie the ends of the legs into knots, then bring them over their heads and down onto the water, cupping the air and making temporary flotation devices.

They then were told to tread water until the horn blew, sounding the end of water survival training for the day.

Wayne took the mop from Tom, telling him "I'll finish this, you go take care of writing to your girl."

"That's okay, I'm almost done," Tom replied.

"No, really," Wayne replied, "I'm done with my work, and besides, I couldn't have done the water survival if it wasn't for you, you helped me out and I owe you."

"We're buddies man," Tom responded, "that's what we do, I know you'd do the same for me."

"Not in the pool, not in the water," Wayne replied, "I'm scared of the water, that's why I joined the Army, not the Navy, I don't want to be on no stinkin' tin can and get hit by a torpedo and have to swim for it."

"Well, it was nothin'" Tom replied, "I'd do it again."

"I know you would, I know you would," Wayne said, "now go write to your girl before lights out, I'll finish this for you."

> My Dearest Linda
>
> I am graduating in less than a week. I know you can't come see it. But I am looking forward to it anyway. It seems like just yesterday we got our first haircut and our uniforms issued to us. I must have marched a hundred miles, done a thousand pushups and sit-ups, and shot a million rounds of ammo on the range.
>
> After graduation, I will be home for two weeks leave before I get shipped off to my duty station. I will get my orders after the ceremony on graduation day. Graduation night we are all going into town, we have to go on a buddy system so Wayne and I and a couple other guys are going to hit a few bars. We can't wait. A bunch of soldiers on the town, should make for a good drunk. We haven't been able to set one foot off the base since we got here, and beer and real food, not the garbage they serve us at the mess hall is sounding real good right about now.
>
> Anyway, I will get my flight number and times sometime next week and let you know so you can be there when I get home. I can't wait to get off the plane and see you, to see your beautiful smile, I can't wait to hold you again, it seems like forever since we last kissed. I sure miss you.
>
> All my love
> Tom

Tom folded the letter carefully and slipped it into an envelope and sealed it shut. He locked it away in his locker, and climbed into his cot. A moment later, the lights were shut off and another long day in basic training was over.

Linda and Janey were sitting at the counter at the ice cream shop when Tony and Brent walked in the door. Linda pretended not to see them and looked down at her malted as she stirred it with the long spoon. Janey looked at the large mirror behind the counter and twirled her finger in her long curly red hair and watched the two boys walking across the ice cream shop to sit with them at the counter.

"Hey Girls," Brent said as he sat down next to Linda.

"Hello hello hello," Tony said as he sat down next to Janey and leaned against her.

"Hi," Linda replied, not even looking up at either of the boys.

"Hi guys" Janey replied, leaning in against Tony, asking him, "Whatcha doing?"

"Not much," Brent said, as he reached for a menu, "what about you girls, what are you up to?"

"Hey, how come you don't ever want to come cruzin with us?" Tony asked Linda as he crumpled up Janey's straw wrapper and tossed it at her, "aren't we your type or what?"

"She's all wrapped up about her soldier boy," Janey said, "supposedly he's coming home soon and she's saving herself for him or something."

"He's graduating tomorrow, and flying home after that," Linda responded sharply, "Tom is coming home in a couple days, don't you two slugs have anything better to do?"

"Whooooooo," Brent replied, holding up his hands with his palms out, "I was just kidding around, I didn't mean nothin' by it."

"yeah," Tony said, "were just kidding around."

"She gets this way sometimes," Janey said, "she hasn't seen him in like nine weeks or something. I dunno about you, but I couldn't go that long without seeing my man."

"Hey," Tony asked, leaning in real close to Janey and nuzzling her ear "where is your man?"

"I dunno," she giggled, and winked at Tony.

"Yeah," Linda asked, "where is Bobby? you still have his ring on that chain," then she pointed to the chain around Janey's neck with Bobby's class ring on it.

Tom looked in the mirror and adjusted his dress cap, aligned his dress uniform, then walked outside to wait for formation and the march to the graduation ceremony.

The march from the barracks to the parade grounds was quiet. The only voice that could be heard was the drill sergeant calling a soft cadence. There was only the sound of one footstep at a time as the entire platoon stepped in perfect unison, they were sharp, they were precise, all the practice from the past several weeks all came down to this mornings presentation of colors at the parade grounds in front of a crowd of visitors and VIP's.

There were two rows of bleachers setup for family members, one either side of the podium stage where the commanding officer and dignitaries sat.

Tom stood motionless, moving only his eyes and looking at the crown in the bleachers and looking over at the other platoons also dressed in their dress uniforms standing in perfect formations in front of the podium stage as well.

When the commanding officer of the base finished his speech and congratulated the new graduates there was a flyover with five jets that flew in tight formation. The flyover gave Tom goose bumps and a tingling feeling down his spine.

There was an overwhelming sense of pride and accomplishment that came over him at that moment, realizing that he had completed basic training.

With a sudden cheer, all the graduates, in all the platoons on the parade field tossed their hats into the air and shouted a cheerful yell announcing they were now soldiers and no longer trainees.

Tom and Wayne sat together on the bus going into town. Columbus GA was the nearest town and it was just outside the base. They were buddies on and off the base. They were not to let one another out of their sight at any time. New graduates with a pocket full of money hitting the town for the first time in several weeks and usually getting drunk made perfect targets for local thugs. On more than one occasion a brand new graduate had ended up in an alley, beat up or mugged. With newly acquired bravery and confidence, some of the soldiers were known to try and pick up the wrong girl in a bar, only to end up outnumbered by an angry boyfriend or husband and a group of locals.

Tom, Wayne and another set of buddies got off the bus and started walking down the sidewalk. Wayne pointed to some flashing neon lights indicating a bar that featured topless dancers.

"Hey hey!" Wayne said, "lookie what they have here."

"Yeah!" one of the other buddies replied, almost running towards the bar, "let's go check it out, I could really use a pitcher of beer about now."

"Sounds good to me," Tom said, following them inside.

There was a T shaped stage in the center of the room with a brass pole going from the floor to the ceiling. There were flashing lights and loud music and a girl on the stage slowly dancing in front of a man sitting right near the stage with a pile of dollars and a drink in front of him.

Tom looked around for a table to sit at, it was dark and hard to see anyplace other then the stage.

A woman in a sheer wrap walked up the group. She had on high heels and carried a cigarette in her hand; she reached out and grabbed Wayne by the arm.

"Hello handsome," she said in a low raspy voice, obviously from spending many years smoking and drinking, "can I interest you in a private dance?"

"Not yet, we want to have some beers first," Wayne responded, smiling at her.

"Well come on in then," she said, tugging at his sleeve and leading the group to a table not far from the stage.

"We want to start with three pitchers of beer," one of the buddies in the group said to the woman as he sat down.

"I'll have it sent right over," she said as she walked away and went behind a curtain covering a dimly lit doorway.

The group of buddies drank down their beer and made many toasts and congratulations to one another, they ordered another round of pitchers and then another round of pitchers. Every once in awhile one of them would go sit at the stage and put a dollar or two up for the dancer to come and dance in front of them.

Seeing the soldiers in uniform, sitting in a circle at the table, a few girls walked over and started talking with the group. They were dancers that either just finished their dance, or were going to be up soon.

One sat on Wayne's lap and kissed him on the neck, and asked him if he would buy her a beer. He immediately raised his hand for the waitress so he could oblige her.

One of the other girls sat on the lap of one of the other soldiers and offered to do a private dance for him. He smiled and they whispered into each other's ears for a moment or two, then they got up and walked behind the curtain covering the dimly lit door.

A third girl came and sat on Tom's lap.

"Hi there," she said in a low voice, and asked "do you like what you see?" as she raised her chest and cleavage to an inch from his face.

"Yeah," Tom replied, staring at her breasts, "I do."

"Good," she said as she slowly moved her body and adjusted herself on his lap. "Buy me a drink?"

"Sure," Tom said, and raised his hand for the waitress.

The girl leaned in and then started sucking on Tom's neck.

The other guys at the table began shouting and cheering. "Goooo Tom."

Tom closed his eyes for a second, and felt her hands on his chest.

The waitress came and the girl on Toms lap turned and ordered her drink. Tom excused himself to go to the men's room. He relieved himself in the urinal and washed his hands, and then looking in the mirror saw a strange face. He was pretty drunk by now and seeing the drunken soldier in the mirror startled him. He had seen himself drunk in mirrors before, but usually in t-shirts with long hair and as a civilian. The drunken soldier in the mirror, in the disheveled uniform was not something he had seen before. He straightened his uniform shirt and tie and went back out to the table.

The girl that had been sitting on his lap was now on the stage dancing. Tom sat down and poured another beer then slouched back in his chair. Tom stared at the girl talking with Wayne, with her features and the way she wore her hair, she had a strange resemblance to Linda.

"Oh my god, Linda!" Tom thought to himself, realizing that in two days he would be flying home, in two days he would get off the airplane and see her, in two days he would be holding her, the woman he loved. He shook his head and tried to clear his mind, but she was still there.

"We gotta go," Tom said to Wayne.

"What the hell are you talking about man?" Wayne asked.

"Let's get out of here," Tom insisted, looking at the other buddies at the table, "let's go get a steak or something, I don't want to spend all of graduation night in the same dump."

"Yeah," one of the other guys said, "lets go get some decent food, we're off base, may as well get real chow somewhere, I bet we can get beer there too,"

Tom stood up, and then Wayne slipped a ten-dollar bill into the cleavage of the girl that was on his lap and stood up too.

Outside the air felt cool and fresh. They all walked down the sidewalk looking for a place to eat, staggering and laughing, bouncing off one another, doing their best to stand tall and walk straight.

Tom shut the water off and got out of the shower, grabbed his towel and went to the row of mirrors to shave for the last time before he flew home. He wiped the steam from the mirror with his towel and stared at his neck. Horrified, he looked closer.

"Shit!" he said out loud, pounding his fist against the wall.

"What's wrong?" Wayne asked from the next sink over where he was shaving.

"That girl at the bar last night gave me a hickey," Tom replied angrily, "what the hell did she do that for?"

Wayne laughed out loud, and asked, "she did what? When?"

"I dunno," Tom answered, "I suppose when she sat on my lap and asked me to buy her a beer. Glad I didn't go in back and screw her, who knows what I would have caught."

"Yeah, probably," Wayne said, smiling as he watched himself shaving in the mirror, "probably all hookers when they're not dancing."

Chapter 2

LINDA LEANED CLOSER to the mirror in her bathroom and applied the last touches of makeup before she was to go meet Tom at the airport. She slipped on her dress and shoes and grabbed her purse and ran out the door when Janey pulled up in front of her house.

"Janey, I can't believe he's coming home today, I just can't believe it," Linda exclaimed excitedly, "It seems like he's been gone so long."

"Well he was gone for a couple months," Janey said, "I wonder if he'll look the same."

"What do you mean?" Linda asked.

"Well, he may look different," Janey responded, "sometimes soldiers come home with scars or tattoos, or missing limbs or something."

"He was in basic training, not some war," Linda argued, "He's not going to have any scars or tattoos or be missing any limbs."

Janey pulled the car into a parking space, when she got out; she almost had to run to catch up with Linda as she headed for the terminal to meet the plane.

Linda was fidgeting with a handkerchief, pacing back and forth waiting for the passengers to exit the plane.

"How do I look?" she asked Janey, "tell me, how do I look? Is my makeup ok? Do you think he will like my hair? Do you think he will like this dress?"

"Calm down girl, you look gorgeous," Janey replied, grinning, "he's a man, he's a soldier coming home to see his woman. He's going to have one thing on his mind, and it's not your dress or your hair."

"Here he comes, here he comes," Linda said excitedly, as she looked at the crowd of people that were exiting the plane, she was so excited she was almost jumping up and down.

Tom came around the corner, he was standing taller and walking proud in his dress uniform, he saw Linda and their eyes locked.

When he got closer she ran to him and he opened his arms and dropped his carry on bag. She jumped up into his arms and he squeezed them around her, holding her tight, swaying back and forth. Her feet were dangling almost a foot off the ground, she shuddered as she cried, tears of joy ran down her cheeks, her mascara ran down her cheeks along with the tears. Tom turned his head and kissed her, they kissed long and deep. It felt so good to hold her he thought. It felt so good to be in his arms she thought.

After a few moments Tom set her down on the floor and wiped her cheeks with his hand. Linda looked up at him, so happy to be looking at his face again. Tom turned slightly to pick up his bags and she saw it.

"What's that?" Linda asked, in shock.

"What's what?" Tom asked

Linda reached over and moved his collar to expose the hickey.

"That!" Linda shrieked, "It's a hickey! You came home with a hickey? Oh my god, Janey was right."

"It's not what you think," Tom said, trying to defend himself.

Linda started crying, she was furious, she was hurt, she felt betrayed, she was overwhelmed with bad feelings, so many different emotions were right now swarming in her head.

"It's not a hickey?" Linda asked, sobbing, "what do I think it is then?"

"C'mon, let's go, he's no good for you," Janey said as she wrapped her arm around Linda and started to guide her away.

"C'mon Linda," Tom said, "Let me explain."

"There is no explanation" Linda replied, crying, "I know what that is, and I know how they get there, and it was NOT from me. I don't want to see you anymore, just leave me alone."

Janey held Linda in her arm as the two girls walked away and left Tom standing all alone at the airport.

Tom stood in his parent's kitchen and picked up the phone and dialed Linda's number.

"Hey Linda, it's me Tom, I've been trying to call you everyday for a week and a half now and you won't return my calls. Graduation night a bunch of us went into town and got drunk, a girl at one of the bars was flirting and gave me the hickey, but I swear, nothing happened, I promise, you have to believe me. I didn't," and before he could say another word the answering machine cut him off.

Tom picked the phone back up and dialed another number.

"Hello Janey?" Tom said, "This is Tom, you have to talk to Linda for me, she has it all wrong and won't return any of my calls. I have orders and I leave in two days and I have to set things straight with," and Janey's answering machine cut him off too.

"Damn!" Tom said, slamming the phone down.

Linda and Janey sat on the bed in Janey's bedroom. "I told you," Janey said.

"I know, but I didn't want to believe you," Linda said, her head hanging low in sadness, "I loved him so much and never thought he would do something like that."

"All guys are like that," Janey said, "that's why I don't trust them, and still fool around when Bobby is not around, I can't prove it, but he's probably doing the same thing when he's not with me, men are such pigs."

"I never want to talk to him again," Linda said, "I wasted so much time not going out, just staying home and writing to him, and reading his letters, I could have been out with Brent, or Tony, or any of the guys that asked me out, oh Janey, how could I have been so foolish?"

"Shhhhh," Janey replied, "Think of him as yesterdays news and move on, get out there and enjoy yourself now."

Tom got off the airplane and caught the military shuttle to the base. He was due to report in no later that 2200 hours and it was now 2100 hours. Tom was getting the hang of converting time. Looking at his wristwatch it was nine o'clock in the evening. The shuttle pulled up in front of a building and Tom got out and went inside carrying a large envelope with papers in it, and over his shoulder his duffel bag with his uniforms, and a small carry bag with a couple of changes of civilian clothes and his favorite sneakers.

It took just over an hour to in-process Tom at his new duty station. Ft. Sam Houston in San Antonio Texas. Then he was given a key to his room and a map of the base and told to report back in the morning for details.

Tom turned the key in the lock and opened the door. There were two beds, two lockers, two desks, two hardback desk chairs, two softer lounge chairs, two end tables and a refrigerator in the room.

One bed was made and there was a lock on one of the lockers. Tom put his stuff down on the floor and sat down on the empty bed and just looked around the room. This was his new home, for now at least.

Linda came home from school and saw a letter sitting on her dresser. She recognized the writing but not the return address. She picked it up and threw it in the trashcan, then right away pulled it out and held it for a moment; she took a deep breath and opened it.

> My dearest Linda
>
> How could things go so terribly wrong? By the time you get this I will be gone and at my next duty station, and I Don't know when I will be home again and be able to see you again. I fly out in the morning and know

I won't get a chance to see you before I leave. I tried many many times to talk to you before I left. I felt so awful that You got so upset, but you have to know that I love you.

You have to know that I would never do anything to hurt you. Yes, I did have a hickey on my neck, but it was not what you thought. I didn't even know the girl. I know that sounds bad, but a bunch of us went into town and went to a few bars after graduation. One of the places some girls came up to us and asked us to buy them drinks. One whispered in my ear that she liked a man in uniform and then gave me the hickey, it all happened so fast I didn't know what to think. I swear Linda, I didn't do anything with her. I kept thinking of you, I was thinking that in just a couple of days I was going to be home and be with you, honest, you have to believe me.

I know I can't prove it, but I am telling you the truth. You are the only one for me and I miss you so much. It broke my heart that you wouldn't see me or return any of my calls while I was home. If I don't hear from you, I'll know you threw this away without reading it, or else you read it and meant what you said about not wanting to see me ever again. I have to at least try, you mean too much to me not to. I don't know when I will see you again. But I will never stop loving you.

Yours truly

Tom

Linda finished reading the letter and held it to her breast and started to cry.

"Janey?" Linda said into the phone.

"Yeah," Janey answered, "what's up?"

"I got a letter from Tom, he didn't cheat," Linda replied, "I'm so upset right now, can you come over?"

"Sure." Janey replied, "I'll be right over, are you okay?"

"I'm mad at myself," Linda replied, "I should have at least listened to him, I should have at least let him try and explain, I was just so mad at him, I just couldn't."

"Ok, I'll be over in a few minutes," Janey said and hung up the phone.

Tom reported in at 0700 hours at the same place he in-processed at the previous night. An administrative type person sat behind the desk and looked through Tom's file, then looked up and told him that his school started in three days. That he would have some time to familiarize himself with the base and find his way around. The admin person told Tom about some good places to shop and eat in town, the Riverwalk had dozens of good restaurants and nightclubs and that he was free to go until then. All he had to do was be at the building where his class started at the date and time on his orders. Tom was suddenly lost. Two weeks ago when he was on the last base for basic training, there was no free time, there was no freedom to go into town, and each minute of everyday was planned and utilized. Now he had the rest of today and the next couple of days to find something to do, with nothing planned for him by his superiors. Tom went back to his room and arranged his closet, changed out of his uniform and into civilian clothes, then headed into town to see what it had to offer.

Linda and Janey drove into the school parking lot and Janey looked for a place to park her car. Linda reached into the backseat to get her books as Janey parked the car and shut off the engine.

Janey took one last drag off her cigarette before she got out of the car. Linda got out of the car and straightened her blouse and fluffed her hair.

"So what are you going to do about Tom?" Janey asked.

"I told you yesterday," Linda replied, "I will make him wait like you said, and then write him a short note in a few weeks."

"That's good," Janey replied.

"I'm not so sure," Linda said, "I mean, he did apologize for the mix up, and he said he didn't do anything with that girl, I want to believe him."

"Hmmpff," Janey retorted, "they all tell you what they think you want to hear."

"Well," Linda replied, "I still love him, and I know he loves me, and I have to trust him. I have to."

"You're such a sap," Janey replied, "I wouldn't even look back, I would go out with the first guy that asked me if that happened to me."

"I dunno, maybe you're right," Linda said as she reached for the door of the school.

"I am," Janey said, "see you after school."

Linda came out of the dressing room with the outfit she was trying on and stood in front of the mirror.

"What do you think?" she asked Janey.

"You look fabulous girl," Janey responded, "I know breaking up with a guy always makes me want to shop, and shopping always makes me feel better."

"Is that why you never stay with anybody very long?" Linda asked, jokingly "because you love to shop?"

"Here, try this on," Jayne said, handing Linda a leopard outfit, "this will drive the guys crazy,"

Linda took the leopard outfit and went back into the dressing room to change into it. She came out a moment later and posed for Jayne.

"Well?" Linda asked.

"You look soooo sexy," Janey answered, smiling, "I'd jump your bones if I was a guy, you have to get it, and wear it Friday night."

"What's Friday night?" Linda asked, turning and looking at herself in the mirror, "I do feel sexy in it, it feels good."

"There is a party at Nan's house, you have to go," Janey replied, "it's probably the last big one before the end of the year and we all graduate and go away to college."

Linda didn't say anything, she just raised her eyebrows and smiled, then turned on her heels and went back into the dressing room to change back into her own clothes.

Tom picked up his books, grabbed his hat and stood up to leave class.

"So what do you think of this stuff?" another soldier asked Tom, "pretty intense huh?"

"Yeah," Tom replied, "much harder than high school ever was."

"Smith, Sergeant Smith," the man said extending his hand towards Tom, "Mike, Smith, but my friends call me Smitty."

"Tom," Tom replied, shaking Smitty's hand, "Private Hanson, but I'm just called Tom."

"Nice to meet you Tom," Smitty replied, "wanna grab a beer at the club?"

"Sure," Tom answered, "I haven't found my way to it yet, where is it?"

"Over behind the PX," Smitty replied, "the O club is across the street from here, but we can't get in there, our club is probably less stuffy anyway, you know how officers are, their shit don't stink."

"So I hear," Tom replied as he pushed open the door to leave the building where class was held.

Tom climbed onto a stool at the bar, as Smitty pulled up a stool next to him and ordered a pitcher of beer.

"So you married or anything?" Smitty asked

"Nah, you?" Tom replied,

"Yep, sweet little thing I met at my last duty station, we have a little girl too," Smitty replied, looking at his watch "she's home now, probably unpacking, we just moved into base housing last week before this school started."

"Two weeks ago I was in basic," Tom said, lifting his glass of beer.

"Seems like a long time ago," Smitty responded, lifting his glass of beer, "we just got back from Panama, I was stationed down there for two years, hotter 'an hell and bugs, oh, and snakes too, my wife hated the snakes and she was from there, go figure."

"Huh," Tom replied, "wonder where I'll go when I finish here?"

"Who the hell knows," Smitty replied, "at least your stateside for now, don't get much better 'an that."

"Guess not." Tom said and raised his glass for a toast, "Stateside duty!"

"Stateside," Smitty said, as he clicked his glass against Tom's and drank down the rest of his beer.

Tom waved as Smitty drove out of the parking lot of the EM club, then he walked back towards the barracks where his room was. At the barracks, Tom opened the door to his room and saw his roommate, Specialist Terry Olson was sleeping over on his own bunk, and Tom closed the door quietly behind him and went to sit on his bed.

Tom unlaced his boots and put them under his bunk, then noticed an envelope on his desk; he picked it up and looked at it. It was from Linda. He took a deep breath then sat down to read it.

Dear Tom

    I hope this finds you doing well at your new place. I'm sorry It's taken me so long to write back to you but I had to do a lot of thinking. I really miss you a lot, but I can't see you when I want to, and I can't live with a long distance relationship, especially if there is no way to know when we will see each other again.

I don't know if I can or should believe you when you told me about the hickey you had when you were last here. Your story makes sense, but Janey said that was just too convenient and I think there may be some truth to what she said.

I wish you the best, and look me up when you come to town next. I graduate from school this Friday and then after summer ends I start college.

Fond memories

Linda

Tom folded the letter up, and stuffed it in the envelope, then folded it in half and threw it in the trash. "Damn," Tom said to himself loud enough to be heard outside his door. "Fuckin' dear john letter, that Janey is such a bitch, never did like her."

Tom pressed his hands against the window to block the glare and looked inside the car. It had cloth bucket type seats that didn't look torn up. It had a stereo, a console shifter, and a sunroof. The white writing on the windshield said Sale, but no price. Tom stood up to look around for a salesman. He wanted to take this car for a test drive. It was a used car, so he figured it was probably affordable.

Linda slipped on her new tight black pants, then turned and looked in the mirror. They do make my butt look nice, she thought to herself. Then she put on the new leopard top she had also just bought and looked at herself in the mirror. "Yes," she said to the mirror, smiling, "I never thought my cleavage could look so nice, this will turn some heads,"

Janey pulled up in front of Linda's house and honked her car horn. Linda came out the front door then walked slowly to the car,

When she opened the door Janey leaned over and said, "Wow! It looks like you got over Tom and are back on the market."

"I feel good, I feel sexy, do you think maybe I over did it?" Linda asked.

"No way!" Janey replied, "do you have a stick in that purse? You're gonna have to beat 'em off, the guys will be surrounding you like crazy, you look hot."

Tom pulled up in front of the class building and parked in the last open spot, he got out of his car and grabbed his books, he had to slam the door twice before it caught and latched, and then he walked up the stairs to the front door.

The instructor went over the last section of classroom work on advanced electronics before they broke into groups for lab assignments. Tom was paired up with two others, Sp4 Amy Guinn, and Sp4 Todd Walton for the rest of the labs.

Tom looked at Amy out of the corner of his eye when she was not looking, wondering what she looked like in real clothes, what she looked like in civilian clothes because the Army uniforms were all the same and pretty unflattering.

Linda carried a glass of beer in her hand, steadying herself with her other hand as she navigated through the crowd. She saw a spot on one of the couches and went to sit down. It felt good to sit, the heels she was wearing were new and hurt her feet, plus she had already had quite a bit to drink and was feeling tipsy.

"Hi," Tony said as he sat down next to Linda, "When did you get here?"

"Hi Tony," Linda replied, "I came with Janey, we got here maybe an hour or two ago, when did you get here?"

"I just got here a few minutes ago, "Tony replied, "I had to work and just got off, and now it's par-tay time!"

"What are you doing this summer?" Linda asked Tony.

Tony slid closer to Linda and gently placed his hand on her thigh.

"I don't know about the summer," he answered, "I'm just taking it one day at a time, and thinking about tonight right now."

Linda sank a little lower in the couch and leaned in closer towards Tony, resting her shoulder against his body.

After a half hour or so, Tony whispered to Linda, "Wanna get outta here? I got my dads car."

"Yeah," Linda replied," Let's go, this isn't my crowd anyway."

Tony pulled out from the parking space he found down a couple of houses from Nan's party and turned on the headlights.

Tony reached over and put his hand on her thigh while he drove with the other hand, he gave a gentle squeeze, feeling her firm thighs under the soft fabric. Linda scooted over towards the center of the seat and put her hand on his thigh and leaned her head on his shoulder.

"Where are we going?" she asked.

"I thought we could go park by the lake, I know a good spot for picnicking that is probably quiet this time of night," he replied, turning his head to look at her face.

"Ok," Linda said, smiling sheepishly.

Tony pulled into a spot that overlooked the lake, with the city lights and the skyline in the background. He turned off the engine, reached down to move the lever and pushed the seat back.

Linda looked up at Tony and asked, "Can we get out of the car and walk for a bit? I need some fresh air I think."

"Sure," Tony replied and they got out.

"I think I know where this is going," She said, looking out at the lake, "and I don't want my first time to be in the back seat of a car."

"Ok," Tony responded, "we can do that."

"Sure is a beautiful view," Linda said, standing against the car and looking out over the lake.

"Yep, it is," Tony said, then asked, "where do you want to walk to?"

"Oh I don't want to walk far," she replied, "I just wanted to get out of the car and take a few steps, maybe down by the lake?"

"Sure," Tony said, "ya know, it's kinda chilly, I'm going to see if there is an emergency blanket in the trunk, I can put it on your shoulders if you get cold."

"Ok," Linda replied.

A moment later he returned with a blanket under his arm, "Shall we?" he asked as he reached for her hand.

Tony spread the blanket on the ground a few feet from the shore. The sound of the waves, quietly lapping against the rocks was soothing and relaxing, Tony sat down on the blanket and patted it, gesturing for Linda to sit down on it next to him.

Tony pulled Linda close and she offered no resistance, with his fingertips, he raised her chin up, leaned in and kissed her on the lips. Her lips were warm and soft, they parted slightly and his tongue cautiously probed her mouth, exploring, tasting. She reached her arms up and wrapped them around his neck, pulling him closer to her. They lay down on the blanket and kissed passionately, their hands awkwardly exploring each other, he slid his hand up under her leopard print top and felt her soft warm flesh, then extended his fingers and brushed them across her breasts, feeling them straining against the fabric of her bra. She inhaled a deep breath of air, moaned softly and kissed him back hard. Tony lifted her leopard top with both hands and kissed her stomach, she closed her eyes and moaned softly, running her fingers through his hair. He traced his tongue up her body and kissed between her breasts. Her chest was heaving as her breathing became deeper; she lifted her bra up out of the way for him. Then Tony reached down and slid his hands inside the waistband of her pants, she raised her hips to allow him to remove them.

They made love under the stars two more times before getting dressed and heading back to the car. Neither one spoke during the drive. Linda sat right next to Tony; she rested her hand on his thigh, and her head on his shoulder and fell asleep as he drove her back home.

Tom finished calibrating the gauges before completing the lab; Spc. Guinn put the tools back in the cabinet then came back to the lab area.

"Hey, some of us are going over to the club, right after class," she said to Tom and asked him, "and I was wondering if you wanted to join us?"

"Sure, for a little while," he replied, "but I need to make it short, I gotta work on my car, stupid door won't close right."

"Great," Spc. Guinn replied, and then she picked up her books to leave and said to Tom. "Then I'll see you there."

Tom pulled up a chair at the table with Spc. Guinn and several others at the Em club. "Hey," he said as he waved and sat down.

Tom took one of the empty glasses on the table and poured himself a beer from one of the pitchers on the table.

"To the US Soldier!" he said and raised his glass for a toast.

"To the US Soldier!" they all said, raising their glasses to return the toast.

Tom walked over to Spc. Guinn and knelt down so he could be heard above the jukebox.

"Hi, Specialist Guinn," he said to her.

"Hello," she replied, smiling "You can call me Amy, it is my name, and we are out of the classroom and don't have to be so formal now."

"Okay," Tom replied, reaching to shake her hand, "I'm Tom, glad to meet you Amy."

"You too Tom," She replied as she shook his hand.

"Say, Amy," he went on, "you know Smitty?"

"Who?" she asked.

"Sorry, a friend of mine, he's in our class but different lab group. Sergeant Smith, he goes by Smitty out of uniform, anyway, him and his wife are having a little bar-b-que this weekend and he invited me, and I was wondering, or to be completely honest, hoping that you might go with me, as my guest."

Amy laughed out loud, then turned to Tom and said, "You just introduced yourself to me thirty seconds ago, and now you are asking me out?"

"Well," Tom replied, "we've talked Army stuff for a couple weeks now and I thought I would ask, besides, it's not really a date, it's just going to a friends house together. It's him and his wife, their little daughter and maybe another couple or two, I just hate to be the only single person there, so to speak."

"Sure, why not?" Amy replied, "Sounds like fun, what time?"

"Oh, I don't know, he just told me the other day, but I'll find out, he's gonna help me work on my car tonight, I'll ask him then."

Tom pulled his car up in front of the female barracks at 2 p.m. sharp and sat outside and waiting for Amy to come out. When he saw her walk out the door he barely recognized her. She was wearing blue jeans, sandals, and a tight white tank top; her hair was down and blowing in the breeze. "My god!" He told himself, "She looks a helluva lot better out of uniform than in uniform, holy shit."

Tom introduced Amy to Smittys wife and the rest of the people as his lab partner and fellow soldier. Smitty already knew her from class, not well, but enough to say hello to when she walked into his house, when he saw her, he smiled at Tom and gave him a sly thumbs up.

"I'd like you to meet my lovely wife Juanita," Smitty said to Amy as he reached out his arm towards his wife, "Juanita, this is Specialist Amy Guinn, she's in our class on base."

"Very nice to meet you," Amy said extending her hand towards Juanita.

"And this," Smitty said, as he rubbed the top of his daughters head, "is Doodles, our little ray of sunshine, can you say Hi to these people?"

"Hi," Doodles said shyly.

"How old are you?" Amy asked Doodles.

Doodles held up her hand with two fingers up like a peace sign.

"Thwee." Doodles replied.

"Doodles?" Amy asked Juanita, "Why do you call her doodles?"

"Honey," Smitty said to doodles, "go show this nice lady your room, okay?"

Doodles led the way to show Amy and Tom her room, a moment later they came out and Amy had her hand to her mouth in shock, laughing.

"What happened in there?" Amy asked Juanita.

"Well," Juanita replied, "the day we moved in here is was pretty hectic, there were men unloading the truck and she was just to quiet, when I went into her room to check on her, well, you saw all the crayon drawings on her wall, we got pretty mad, but she looked so cute there with the crayons all over the floor and her big smile, she was so proud of herself, so we just call her Doodles now."

"I love that story," Amy said to Doodles, smiling down at the little girl standing between her parents.

"C'mon," Smitty said, "beer is out on the patio in the cooler, make yourselves at home."

"Alright," Tom said, walking toward the patio, turning back to look at Amy, "think I will, want a beer?"

Tom pulled his car up in front of the female barracks.

"I'm glad you came with me today," he said to Amy, "thanks for coming."

"It was fun," she replied, "thanks for asking me, they're nice people, he seems so much different at home than he does in class."

"Yeah," Tom replied, "he's been in the army a long time, and is pretty much gung ho when in uniform and on base, outside, he's a different guy, a regular person."

"Ok, well, thanks again." Amy said as she got out of the car.

"See you tomorrow in class," Tom said, leaning over to look out the passenger window.

"Bye," Amy said to Tom as she turned to walk away.

"Bye," Tom replied and drove away.

Tom heard a noise in his room as he opened the door.

"Hey," Terry said from his bunk

"Hey, cool!" Tom said as he looked up and saw a television on top of a pile of bricks and boards and asked, "New TV?"

"Yeah," Terry replied, "what do ya think? I hate watching whatever is on down in the lounge on that TV with everybody else."

"I think it's great," Tom replied, "I agree, a TV in our room is better than the one in the lounge, we can watch whatever the hell we want to watch without having to take a vote."

Tom kicked off his sneakers, propped up his pillow and lay on his bed to watch the new TV.

Chapter 3

L INDA STOOD BETWEEN her parents for pictures; she was wearing her cap and gown for graduation. Her mom was crying, her dad was standing tall and proud of his little girl, all grown up.

Her dad reached into a pocket inside his sport coat and pulled out an envelope and handed it to Linda.

"What's this?" Linda asked as she held it in her hand.

"Open it," Her dad replied, "It's your graduation gift."

She looked up into his face as she opened the envelope, then looking down inside it saw a piece of plastic and a key.

"What? What is this?" she asked, tears forming in the corners of her eyes.

Her dad reached into the envelope and pulled the items out.

"I want you to be safe," he said, "these are keys to your new car, and this is a credit card for car emergencies only."

Linda almost jumped into her dads arms she hugged him so tightly.

"I don't want you to be stranded anywhere without a ride," her dad continued explaining after the emotional embrace from his daughter, "plus, you will need it when you go off to college in the fall, now, the credit card is for car emergencies only, like a tow or a break down. If I see one shopping trip show up on the bill I'll take it away, understood?"

"Oh thank you, thank you, thank you," Linda said, "I love you and mom so much,"

"I know, we love you too honey," her mom said as she hugged Linda.

Tom was on the perimeter road that encircled the base, he was just ahead of Amy, he was hunched over, his hands resting on his knees, catching his breath, his t-shirt was soaked in sweat and his legs ached. Every morning he would get up, dress in his gym clothes and run halfway around the base. He ran from the barracks to the front gate, then north along the fence on the dirt perimeter road to the armored vehicle maintenance area, then he would take the paved road from there back towards the theater, the mess hall, the EM club, past the PX and the auto shop building and back to the barracks. The route he took was just over ten miles and was a good workout. He ran this route then showered, had breakfast at the mess hall then went to class as part of his daily routine. This morning Amy joined him on his run, PT is a requirement and physical fitness tests are taken quarterly, with a timed two mile run, timed sit ups and timed pushups, each person based upon their sex, age, and height has a minimum amount to perform, and Tom didn't believe in minimum, he pushed himself to beat his time, every time.

Tom walked into class thirty seconds late and everybody turned to look at him.

"Sorry," he said as he sat down at his chair at the lab.

"It's okay," Sp4. Guinn replied, "we were just getting started."

"Hey man," Sp4. Walton asked, "where were ya?"

"Sorry," Tom replied, "legs cramped up on my run, had to walk part of the way, they still hurt like a son of a bitch."

"That's what happens man," Sp4, Walton replied, "when you drink to much beer the night before and then do PT, gotta drink down a bunch of water, that should help."

"Yeah, I know, but thanks anyway," Tom responded, somewhat annoyed.

Amy looked across the lab table and saw Sp4 Walton was busy paging through his notes, looking for something, then she leaned towards Tom and said quietly, "I really had fun the other day with you at your friends."

Tom turned towards Amy and smiled, "yeah, I did too."

"Maybe we can, um, grab a beer after class or something," Amy said, still too quiet for anyone else around to hear, "someplace besides the EM club, too many uniformed people there."

"Yeah, oh yeah, sure," Tom said, a big smile coming to his face, "how about today? After class today we can go somewhere, I know a place that pretty much is just locals, I hardly ever see anybody else there from the base."

"Ok, then," Amy replied, "pick me up at six?"

"Six it is," Tom said, smiling, then opening his lab book to get started with the day's assignment.

Linda hung up the phone crying, then grabbed her car keys and went out to her car and drove off.

Janey answered the front door when Linda knocked.

"That didn't take long, did you speed over here?" Janey asked.

"What am I going to do?" Linda asked Janey frantically.

"Slow down, just take a breath," Janey said, reassuringly.

"This wasn't suppose to happen, I can't be late," Linda sobbed.

"How did this happen?" Janey asked, "I mean, I know how it happened, but how? When? Who?"

"I'm suppose to go to college this fall, this can't be happening," Linda said, still crying.

"Did you buy a test kit? Have you seen a doctor?" Janey asked

"After Nan's party," Linda said, "Tony and I, we, oooh Janey, what am I going to do?"

"Have you told Tony yet?" Janey asked.

"No, no way," Linda replied.

"Ok, let's think about this," Janey said as she sat down on a chair, "first things first, being late could mean nothing, you need to take one of those tests from the drugstore, then if you are pregnant, then you gotta tell Tony."

"You're right," Linda replied, "I'm only a couple days late, but, it was my first time, and neither one of us planned for it, oh Janey, I'm so afraid, what am I going to do?"

"Let's go buy one of those tests right now," Janey said standing up and grabbing her keys, "then you'll know one way or another."

Janey read the labels on the home pregnancy tests as Linda paced back and forth in the aisles.

"Here," Janey said, "this looks like a good one, it's suppose to turn colors and tell you in just a few minutes."

"Ok, ok" Linda said, "keep it low, I don't want anybody to see me, I mean, to see me buying a pregnancy test."

"Alright," Janey replied, "I'll buy it, you just meet me at the car."

Tom turned his blinkers on to signal his turn, the road was hilly and winding and Amy didn't even see the driveway.

"Is this it?" Amy asked as she saw the rustic building with the old wooden stagecoach wheels leaning up against the building and a rusty metal roof.

"Yep," Tom said as he shut off the engine, "they have the best bar-b-que I've ever had here, and ice cold beer."

"How did you ever find it?" Amy asked, "It's so far out of the way."

"I know, Smitty and I have come here a couple of times," Tom replied, "He knows the owner, I guess they were stationed together somewhere before he retired and opened this place up."

"Huh," Amy responded, "well, it sure smells good out here, I can smell the wood smoke, I bet it smells even better inside."

"You just wait," Tom said as he opened the door for Amy.

"I'm stuffed," Tom said as he picked up his napkin and wiped his face.

"Me too," Amy agreed, nodding towards the empty plates on the table, "This was a good choice Tom, yours was way bigger than mine, I'm glad I ordered the smaller portion."

"Sure beats the mess hall, don't it?" Tom asked jokingly.

"It sure does," Amy said as she scooted her chair closer, "and I don't see anyone from the base here, I hate how everybody gossips there."

"That's why I come here sometimes," Tom responded, "I need a break every so often from the uniforms and the base so I come here, get some decent food and good cold beer, and there is no stupid jukebox in the corner blaring out top ten."

Amy slid her hand under the tablecloth and rested it on Tom's leg.

"I like being with you," she said, "I like spending time with you outside of class, you're fun."

"Thanks," Tom said, smiling back at Amy, "so are you, I mean, I like spending time with you too."

"Another round?" she asked, nodding at the almost empty glasses of beer.

"Sure," Tom replied, signaling for the bartender to bring another round of beers.

"Then I want to go," Amy said, a sly smile on her face.

"Where to?" Tom asked,

"I don't care," Amy replied, "let's just drive around in your car for awhile."

Tom smiled back, "Alright, I know some great roads that don't have much traffic."

Tom pulled out of the parking lot and headed west away from town. Amy reached over and put her hand on his thigh, Tom looked over and smiled, then reached with his right hand and stroked her hair. Amy slid her hand up along his leg and stopped when she neared his crotch and felt a firm bulge, then she slowly ran the tips of her fingers over the bulge in his pants.

Tom smiled and looked over at her, she had a mischievous look in her eyes as she smiled back at him.

"Mmm, I think you found something," he said to her.

"Just keep driving," she said, as she reached her other hand over to unbuckle his belt and open his jeans, she then lowered her head down out of view.

Tom kept one hand on the steering wheel, and ran his other hand along her body, then slid it up under her shirt and cupped her bare breast. He adjusted himself in the seat while he drove, moving back a couple of inches from the steering wheel and shifting his eyes from the road to the rear view mirror, to the back of Amy's head, doing his best to keep the car on the road.

Linda sat next to Janey at the counter of the ice cream shop, paging through a fashion magazine. The bell on the front door jingled indicating someone just entered. Janey looked up at the mirror behind the counter and saw Tony and Brent walk in. Janey nudging Linda with her elbow asked, "Did you tell him yet?"

"No, I didn't," Linda replied.

"Well?" Janey asked, "are ya gonna? cuz If he's the dad he has the right to know, after all, he's gonna have to be responsible now."

"I know, I know," Linda replied quietly, "I just don't, I don't know how to tell him, It's not something that you just blurt out."

"Hey guys!" Janey said as Tony and Brent leaned against the counter near them.

"Hi," Linda said, much more subdued.

"Hey there," Brent said, sitting down next to Janey, "what's up?"

"Hi," Tony said to Linda as he sat down next to her, "how are ya?"

Linda suddenly started to cry, Tony stepped back a second, confused, "did I say something?"

"No, it's nothing you said, so much as did," Janey said, looking at Tony.

"What's she talking about?" Tony asked Brent.

"Hell, I don't know," Brent replied, then looked at Janey and asked, "What are you talking about?"

Linda turned toward Janey, glaring at her through the tears in her eyes. "Shut up Janey, just be quiet, don't say anything."

"Whoa, what's going on here?" Tony asked.

"Sounds pretty serious to me." Brent added.

"It is," Janey responded, "Tony got her pregnant."

"Janey!" Linda sat up quickly, rigid, angered, "how could you? I asked you not to say anything."

Tony and Brent sat motionless, their mouths opened, stunned by the news, not uttering a sound.

"I'm sorry," Janey said, "I thought Tony ought to know."

Linda just turned and looked at Janey then got off her stool and ran out the door of the ice cream shop.

"Wow," Brent said after the bell on the front door stopped jingling.

"Holy shit," Tony replied, "what am I gonna do?"

"Oh shut up," Janey said to Tony, "you should of thought of that before you knocked her up."

"Geeze man," Brent added, "I had no idea you two were . . ."

"Just shut up," Janey said to Brent, cutting him off mid sentence, "just shut up, ok?"

Smitty tossed a match on the coals, igniting the lighter fluid that had been poured on them.

"Won't be long now, and the coals will be ready," Smitty said digging in the cooler for a fresh beer.

"So what's on the menu for tonight?" Amy asked Juanita.

"He's making his specialty," Juanita said, nodding her head towards Smitty, "secret spiced roasted chicken."

"Sounds good," Tom said, looking at Amy and reaching into the cooler for more beer, "want one?"

"Yeah," Amy replied.

"So what are you doing during the break between phases at school?" Smitty asked Tom, "we have two weeks you know."

"Thought I might go home," Tom responded, "been awhile since I've been up to my parents cabin, and I feel like doing some fishing."

"That sounds nice," Juanita added, and then she looked at Amy, "what are you going to do?"

"Not sure yet," Amy replied, "Tom asked me if I wanted to come with him, but I haven't decided."

"Fishing?" Smitty asked.

"Yeah, no uniforms, no PT, no bookwork or labs," Tom replied, "Just a boat on the lake, and a fishing rod in my hands." Then holding up his beer and laughing, almost as an after thought, "oh, and a cold beer, gotta have some cold ones when fishing."

Tom and Amy walked down the corridor at the Minneapolis St. Paul international airport as they came off the airplane, then they headed straight for the baggage carousel. Once they had their luggage tom looked around for the rental car kiosk and headed for it. Amy looked for the women's rest room and headed for it.

Tom rolled his window down to take a deep breath of fresh air, the smells brought back memories of childhood and summers at the cabin on lake George near Itasca State Park, headwaters of the mighty Mississippi.

"Will your parents be there?" Amy asked

"No," Tom replied, "Mom died a few years ago and dad's having a hard time with it, he started drinking a lot and now he lives with his brother out west."

"I'm so sorry to hear that," Amy replied, looking at Toms face as he drove and rubbing her hand on his leg. "Why didn't you tell me that before?"

"You never asked before," Tom answered.

"How much longer?" Amy asked.

"A couple more miles," Tom replied, "one more turn, down a dirt road, for another mile or so and we're there."

"I can't wait," Amy said, yawning, "It's been a long day and I'm tired of sitting and traveling."

"Me too," Tom replied, looking at Amy and smiling, "we're almost there."

Tom turned down a dirt road that was tree lined with tall trees with large limbs overhanging the road. The sunlight shone through the canopy of leaves every so often as they passed under.

As the road narrowed, Amy could see the turn ahead, when Tom made the turn she could see the cabin and the lake right behind it. It was, made of logs and mortar with a big stone chimney. There was a heavy wooden door in the center of the wall facing the drive, and two small windows, one on each side of the door.

Tom shut off the engine and looked at Amy.

"Well, here it is," he said, "This is the end of the road, this is my cabin."

"It looks lovely," she replied, then pointed to the red iron pump outside the back door, "is that pump one of those pumps that people buy to decorate with?"

"No," Tom said laughing, "it's real, that's where we get our water from. We also have indoor plumbing that dad put in a few years ago."

"Oooh," Amy replied.

They got out of the car and Tom unlocked the door to the cabin, and then carried their luggage inside.

Amy walked inside behind Tom, and looked around, it was small and dark, with big log beams crossing from the front wall to the back wall, and an open ceiling. There was a kitchen area in one corner, a big stone fireplace that took up almost an entire wall, and the wall that faced the lake had two large picture windows with a door between them and right outside was a porch. The floor was wood and creaked a bit when she walked across it. There was a large rug spread out on the floor. The porch was built on boulders that sat in the water and it was directly above the water.

She was two open doors, and when she looked in them she saw two bedrooms with comfortable looking beds with big fluffy down comforters on top.

"This is my favorite part," Tom said as he opened the door and walked out onto the porch, "isn't this beautiful?"

"Oh my god," Amy said, standing next to him, her arm wrapped in his arm, "the view is spectacular and the water, the water is right there, I bet if the waves are high enough they splash on the porch."

"Yeah, sometimes they do in a big storm," Tom replied.

Tom lit a fire in the fireplace and opened a bottle of wine.

"Here," Tom said, handing a glass of wine to Amy, "time to relax and unwind, tomorrow I'll take you in the boat and give you a tour of the lake, show you the different cabins and homes and who lives where."

"Thank you," Amy said as she took the wine from Tom, "that sounds like a pleasant way to spend the day."

"We'll have to go into town tomorrow too sometime," Tom added, "there's no food here, unless you like baked beans, I think there are a few cans on the shelf."

"Tomorrow," Amy said, snuggling against Tom on the sofa in front of the fire, "tonight I just want to do this, just sit by the fire and relax."

Amy woke up first and went to look out at the lake, the sun was beginning to rise and the sky was full or pink, red and purple, then turned to oranges and yellows as it rose higher in the sky and got brighter.

Tom came out and stood behind her on the porch to look at the morning sun. He wrapped his arms around her and pulled her back against him, he could hear her moan softly as she leaned back against him, leaning her head back against his chest. Tom kissed the back of her neck, and whispered into her ear, gently nibbling it, "good morning, how did you sleep?"

"Mmmmm," Amy replied, offering her neck to him for more kisses, "just fine, I slept like a log, it's so peaceful here."

"Good," Tom replied, as he moved his hands along her stomach, reaching up under one of his old t-shirts that she was wearing and cupping her breasts in his hands, "I'm glad you slept well."

Amy reached up behind her and pulled his head down to her neck.

"Oh Tom," she said as his fingers found her aroused nipples, "Mmmm, I love that."

Tom slid one hand down along the front of her body, feeling her smooth warm flesh; he slipped his hand inside the waistband of her panties. Amy began to move her hips, pushing herself back against him. She could feel him, pressing against her.

Linda and Tony were sitting in her car, waiting for the light to turn green.

"You can move in with me," Tony said, "we can live together for awhile then get married this fall."

"You don't want to marry me Tony," Linda argued, "you're just saying that, you're saying that because you're scared of being a dad."

"No, really, I'm not," Tony replied, "I mean it, you will need help with the baby, I am the dad and want to help, I want to be a part of the babies life."

"But marrying me?" Linda asked, "Are you sure? I don't know."

"Yeah, I'm sure," Tony replied, "I've liked you since sixth grade, I've had a crush on you for years, I Love you Linda, and not just because of the baby, I really do."

Linda began to cry, "Oooh Tony, that's so sweet."

There was a horn honking behind them.

"Oh geeze, sorry," Linda said, waving into the rear view mirror as she realized the light had turned green.

Linda drove her car to Tony's apartment, she wanted to look at it and give his idea some thought.

"See?" Tony said as he stood in the center of his apartment and turned around in a circle with his arms outstretched, "there's plenty of room."

"It's all so sudden," Linda replied, "so much to think about all of a sudden, so many things."

"I can help make it easier," Tony responded, "just let me try, I'll show you, marry me."

"Alright," Linda said, "maybe you're right, I don't think I can do it on my own, and I believe you'll be good to me and the baby."

"Oh I will, I will, I promise," Tony replied, "When do you want to start moving in?

"I suppose I can start anytime," Linda answered, "It's not like we have school tomorrow or anything. You have to work, but I don't have a job yet, I was going to work part time until fall when . . ." then Linda began so sob.

"Oh Linda, what's the matter?" Tony asked, brushing the hair from her eyes then wiping her tears away with his thumb.

"This fall," she replied between sobs, "I, I was suppose to start college, then, then after that go to medical school, I, I wanted to be a doctor, now that's all gone, it's all gone,"

"Aw come on Linda," Tony said, wrapping his arms around her, holding her close, "It'll work out, it'll all work out, maybe not how you planned, but it will, you'll see, now let's stop those tears and get you moved in and settled."

Linda pulled up in front of Janey's house and Janey ran out to get in her car.

"So, how did your folks handle it?" Janey asked right away.

"They are upset," Linda replied, "I know they are trying to be supportive, they say they are excited to be grandparents, but I know them, they're disappointed in me, they didn't say so, but I could see it in their eyes, they wanted me to go to school, they wanted to see me have a career and be somebody, not just having babies right out of high school."

"Were they mad?" Janey asked.

"I just told you," Linda answered sharply, "they looked disappointed, but said they were supportive, they didn't act mad, I mean, they didn't holler at me, or take my car away."

"Wow," Janey replied, "My parents would have kicked me out of the house."

"Why?" Linda asked, confused, "you are over eighteen, and already graduated from high school."

"Yeah, I know," Janey replied, "It's that whole having sex before marriage thing, they are pretty old fashioned that way."

Linda laughed, "If they only knew, you've probably done it more times than your mom has in her whole life."

"Shut up," Janey said, smiling, "and if you tell them I'll be the one that kills you, not your parents."

"I'm moving in with Tony," Linda blurted out, "and he asked me to marry him."

"You what? He what?" Janey asked, "You're kidding, right? What did you say?"

"I said ok," Linda replied quietly, "the baby is gonna need a dad, and he is the father, and he really likes me, he said he loves me."

"Geeze girl," Janey replied, "but do you love him?"

"No, not really, but I do like him a lot," Linda answered, "I think I can grow to love him, like my grandparents did, they had an arranged marriage, they didn't even know each other at first and were madly in love with each other when they both died. They were in their eighties, and I was real young, but I remember."

"When is all this taking place?" Janey asked.

"I don't know," Linda replied, "he's going to help me move my stuff right away, but I don't know about the wedding, this just came up today so we haven't made any other plans yet, it's all pretty sudden."

"I'd say," Janey replied.

Linda pulled into the parking lot of the ice cream shop. "Wanna hear something weird?" she asked Janey.

"What?" Janey asked.

"I thought I saw Tom the other day," Linda said, "a strange car drove past me on the road and it looked like Tom was driving."

"Huh," Janey replied, "he's in some other part of the country playing soldier, you have to get over him, especially now that you are carrying some other guys baby."

"I am over him," Linda insisted, "it's just that, that guy really looked like him, that's all."

Tom stood on the dock holding the rope to the boat and was waiting for Amy to come down from the cabin. He was staring off into space, thinking of the last time he was on that dock, it was the night before he went to basic training and he had spent the night on the dock with Linda, they had watched the sun rise together, sitting right here.

Amy walked up to Tom, she was wearing one of his flannel shirts and a knee length cotton skirt, and she looked at him strangely, "Hey, what's out there?" she asked, nudging his arm, "what are you staring at? Looks like you're staring into space."

"Oh, sorry," Tom replied, "I don't know, I guess I must have been thinking of when I was young and spent my summers here or something," offering to hold her hand, helping her get into the boat, he said, "here, get in."

"Why thank you," Amy said as she took his hand and climbed into the boat.

Tom squeezed the rubber ball on the fuel hose several times, pulled the choke out and grabbed the handle to start the motor and pulled, he pulled several times before it started and sputtered a moment before settling into a smooth idle.

"This is a very temperamental old motor," Tom said, gently patting the top of the old motor, "My dad bought it new when I was a boy and I've pretty much used it my entire life."

"I see that," Amy said, smiling.

Tom moved the knob and put the motor in gear, then twisted the handle and gave it gas and the old boat slowly began to move.

It was a small fishing boat; it had three hard bench seats, a set of oars for an emergency and an anchor and rope lying on the floor.

The lake was calm and smooth; Tom drove around the lake and pointed out some of his favorite houses and cabins. He told her about some of the old timers that still lived in some of them, and of others that had been built and he didn't know who owned them, he shared stories of growing up spending summers at the lake, and showed where his favorite places to fish were.

Amy turned around to face Tom, she was sitting in the center of the small boat, holding onto the sides with her hands, the breeze was blowing her hair around her face, and Tom could see she was enjoying the boat trip and the tour he was giving her. She smiled at Tom with a big sexy smile, then with one hand lifted her skirt up and showed him she was not wearing any panties.

"What a tease," He said, a big grin on his face.

"Yes sir," Amy said with a throaty laugh, "But I'm not teasing."

Tom turned the throttle as fast as the motor would go and steered the boat around a point to a quiet bay then shut the motor off and dropped the anchor. He knelt in front of Amy and placed his hands on her cheeks and kissed her, her lips were warm and soft. Then he knelt further down and lifted her skirt up and buried his head under her skirt. Amy squealed slightly when his tongue touched her, then she leaned back and placed her hands on the sides of the boat to support herself as Tom began to kiss and explored her.

Linda pointed to the corner as Tony was arranging furniture, indicating where she wanted the TV to go. She had moved all of her belongings into his apartment and was now just getting settled in.

"How does this look?" Tony asked, holding the framed picture up on the wall.

"A little to the right," Linda replied, "there, perfect, hang it there."

"Ok, right here it is," Tony replied, "I'm getting hungry, wanna order a pizza?"

"Yeah, that sounds good, I'm getting hungry too," Linda agreed.

Tony brought the pizza, a handful of napkins and two sodas from the kitchen and placed them on the coffee table in front of the sofa.

Linda held the TV remote, clicking through the channels looking for something to watch while they ate.

"Have you thought of any names for the baby?" Tony asked.

"Not really," Linda replied, "I mean, there are a few I tossed around in my head, but nothing I liked, I guess it depends on if it's a girl or a boy."

"What are you hoping for?" Tony asked, "Do you want a girl? Or a boy?"

"I kinda want a girl," Linda answered, "A little girl would be nice."

"Yeah," Tony agreed, "little girls are nice, but a boy would be good too, I could teach him to play ball and stuff."

Linda leaned her head on Tony's shoulder for a moment.

"I'm so scared Tony," she confessed, "I don't know anything about being a mom, what will I do? Do you think I will be a good mom?"

Tony put his pizza down and wrapped his arm around her, rubbing his hand on her arm. "Aw honey, you will be the best mom, I think nature has a way of taking care of that, like instincts or something, plus, your mom is only a phone call away and she was a good mom, she can help you with mom things, and I can help with the dad things, everything is going to be fine, just fine," He reassured her.

Linda opened the bathroom door, and the steam from her shower escaped into the bedroom. Tony was already in bed under the covers, the table lamp was on and he was reading a book.

Linda walked over to the bed and climbed in, beads of water still glistening on her naked body, reflected by the light from the lamp.

Tony put the book down and rolled on his side to face her, resting his head up on one hand, he smiled at her.

"What are you smiling at me like that for?" Linda asked.

"Because I have something to show you," he said as he reached under his pillow and brought out a small velvet covered box and opened it, "This is for you, this is to make it official."

"Oooh Tony," Linda said, tears forming in her eyes, "what a lovely ring, oooh, I love it, I love you."

Tony removed the ring from the box and slipped onto Linda's finger, than leaned in and kissed her on the lips.

Linda threw her arms around his neck and she kissed him back, parting her lips, their tongues touched and explored one another.

Chapter 4

TOM CLOSED THE door to the cabin and locked it, then placed the last of their luggage in the trunk of the rental car and closed it, looking at Amy.

"Well?" He asked, "ready?"

"Yeah," she replied, "the week went so fast, it seems like we just got here."

"Week?" Tom blurted out, "It's been almost two weeks, twelve days away from the base, time away from civilization does wonders, don't it?"

"I'm going to miss it," Amy said, "so I can only imagine how much you miss it, no wonder you wanted to come up here during break, it's lovely, I hope you invite me again someday," She said and winked at him.

Tom reached up and placed their carry on baggage in the overhead compartment then sat down and buckled his seatbelt.

"I love flying, but hate these stupid little seats," Tom said to Amy.

"Me too," Amy replied, giggling, "but I have more room than you do, I guess it pays to be smaller."

Tom ordered two beers from the hostess shortly after the airplane took off. Amy snuggled into her seat and leaned on Tom, resting her head on his shoulder she quickly fell asleep.

Tom smiled and kissed the top of her head, then opened one of his beers and stared out the window, watching the clouds as they drifted overhead.

Smitty stood in the waiting area and waved at Tom and Amy as they got off the airplane and walked up the ramp.

"Hey, how was the trip?" Smitty asked.

"Oh it was wonderful, just wonderful," Amy answered.

"Great, it felt good to be at the cabin for awhile," Tom responded, "I don't get there enough these days and it will be even longer before I get up there again."

"Huh," Smitty responded, then said to them, "hey! Guess what?"

"What?" Tom asked.

"Juanita's expecting again," Smitty boasted, "just found out yesterday."

"Well congratulations ya old fart," Tom said, punching Smitty on the arm.

"Yeah, tell her congratulations for me too," Amy added, "she's such a sweetheart, what does Doodles think?"

"Oh she hasn't been told yet," Smitty replied, "Like I said, we just found out yesterday."

Tom changed from a run to a fast walk, then to a slow walk as he tried to catch his breath; he stopped and bent over, and rested his hands on his knees for a moment. "Man," He told Amy, who got up early to run with him and slowed down to wait for him, "going that long without running sure takes it's toll on a guy, especially when all I did was eat and drink for all that time."

"That's not all you did," she said with a smirk as she pushed him to the side of the road, "seems to me you had lot's of exercise, just not the regular army exercises."

"You got that right I guess," He replied, reaching his hand up inside her running shorts from behind, and gently squeezing her butt cheek, "mmm, we better get going, we got class in thirty minutes."

Linda held up the maternity top for Janey to look at, "What do you think of this one?"

"It looks nice, I think you should buy that one too," Janey replied.

"So how are things with you and Bobby?" Linda asked. "I haven't seen him around much lately."

"Oh, fine," Janey replied, "he's busy, he got this job working for his uncle that takes him out of town pretty often, kinda sucks, but hey, that's life, right?"

"I guess," Linda responded, "I wouldn't like it very much if it was me."

"It's okay," Janey replied, smiling "I make do."

Linda placed the items on the checkout counter and looked in her purse for her wallet.

"Can you believe school starts next week?" Janey asked, "and we don't have to go. I have to go to work, but not to school."

"Yeah, the summer sure went fast," Linda said sadly, "I need to find a job myself, I'm not going away to college now, not like this," she said, pointing to her belly that was just beginning to show signs of pregnancy.

"Where are you going to get a job?" Janey asked.

"I don't know," Linda replied, "My dad said I can work for him, he said he will hire me to work in the office, Tony has a job, but it's just part time, he makes good money, but no insurance, my dad said if I work for him he will give me insurance, and Tony too once we get married."

"That's great," Janey said, "so why aren't you working for him now?"

"Cuz it's my dad, I don't know if I want to work for my dad," Linda answered, "I don't want to talk about work whenever I go over to their house, and that's probably what will happen."

Tom looked up when he felt someone watching him to see who it was, he had paint on his forehead and in his hair. Doodles was standing there in front of him, holding out an unopened can of beer.

"My mommy said to give this to you," she said to Tom, "she said you need to take a break, that you have worked real hard."

Tom took the beer from Doodles and rubbed the top of her head.

"So? What do you think?" he asked her, "do you think your new little brother will like the colors?"

"Yeah, I do," she said, "Will you paint my room too?"

Tom let out a laugh, "well, I dunno Doodles, your mommy and daddy just asked if I could paint this room, maybe if you ask them, they might say yes, but I don't know. Go tell your mommy I'm almost done then I'll wash up, okay?"

"Ok," she said and took off running for another part of the house.

"Hey, I really appreciate this," Juanita said to Tom as she stood in the doorway of the baby's nursery.

"My pleasure," Tom replied, "When you asked me I couldn't say no, you guys have been so good to me, you've cooked me all those wonderful meals, and Smitty helping me with my car all the time, It's the least I can do."

"Well, I really appreciate it," she said again.

"Well, you are very welcome," Tom said, getting up off his knees from painting the baseboards. "I think now it's time to wash these brushes and call it a day, what do you think?"

"I think it looks lovely," Juanita answered, "Mike just called and said he will be home in a few minutes, he's bringing some bar-b-que, so you get washed up now."

Smitty sat down at the table and poured a glass of milk for Doodles, then looked at Juanita, nodding his head towards Tom at the other end of the table, and asked, "what do you think? Did he do a good job of painting the nursery or what?"

"It's just wonderful, he did such a lovely job," she said, jokingly, "I wish you could paint like that."

Smitty laughed and swatted Juanita on the behind, then told her, "I may not be able to paint very well, but I can do other things real well, right?"

Juanita winked and smiled at Smitty, "Right big boy, you got that right."

"Hey you two, get a room," Tom said laughing, nodding towards Doodles who sat in her chair, waiting for her dinner, "there's young ears here."

Janey knocked on the door of the apartment, Tony answered it and let her in.

"Where's Linda?" Janey asked, "I thought she would be here, is she at work?"

"Yeah," Tony replied, "she's at work, it's the middle of the day."

Janey sat down on the sofa next to Tony and put her hand on his thigh, "remember that night under the bleachers at the football game?" she asked.

Tony looked at her, "yeah, I do, why?"

"Because I think of that night all the time," Janey said as she began rubbing her hand slowly up and down on his thigh.

"Me too, it was pretty wild," Tony said, "That was my first time for that, and especially with all those people around, man, it was fun and scarry at the same time."

Janey reached up and placed her hand on his crotch; she could feel him tense up. "I want to do that again, right here, right now, Linda won't be home for awhile, what do you say?" she asked as she unzipped his jeans, not waiting for an answer.

"I, I dunno, we're gonna get married," Tony protested.

"But I can tell you want it, you want me to don't you?" she asked as she pulled him out of his jeans and lowered her head, she looked directly into his eyes and wrapped her mouth around him.

"Mmmm, I guess what she don't know won't hurt her," Tony said as he leaned back on the sofa to enjoy this moment.

When Janey finished she patted him gently, he was still firm, giggling she told him, "This can be our little secret, okay?"

"Ok," Tony replied, zipping his jeans back up, "she sure doesn't do that like you do."

"Didn't think so," Janey said as she stood up and walked towards the door, "well, say hi to Linda when she gets home, I'll see you later."

Tom pulled his car up in front of the female barracks and shut off the motor to wait for Amy, he was five minutes early and knew she would not be out until she thought he would was there. Amy walked out carrying a small package and got in the car.

"Hey there," Tom said, leaning over to kiss her.

"How are ya?" Amy replied, turning her head to return his kiss.

"What's in the package?" Tom asked Amy.

"Just a little something for Doodles," Amy answered, "I was at the store and saw it and just had to get it for her."

"Oh," Tom said, "well? What is it?"

Amy turned her head and smiled and answered, "It's a little girls makeup kit, with pretend lipstick, and eye shadow, and all kinds of stuff little girls like."

"Oh," Tom said, and put the car in drive and headed away from the barracks.

Smitty stood up from the table and raised his glass of wine," To good friends, fellow soldiers, and keeping our country safe."

"Here here," Tom said raising his glass of wine to toast.

"To good friends," Juanita said, raising her glass of sparkling water.

"To good friends," Amy said, raising her glass.

"So, tell me Tom," Juanita said, "where are you going when you finish school next month?"

"Not sure," Tom replied, "I put in for Hawaii or Germany, but you never know where the Army is gonna send you."

"What about you?" Amy asked Smitty.

"Me?" Smitty replied, "I transferred here, I took this class and will be staying on here for a couple of years to be an instructor."

"Oh," Amy replied, "no wonder you asked so many questions, you were picking our instructors brains weren't you?"

"Busted," Tom said, laughing.

"Where are you going?" Smitty asked Amy.

"I'm not sure either," Amy replied, "I put in for California and Italy, I've always wanted to see Italy."

"Well," Juanita said, "you should be finding out in the next week or so, usually just before the class ends the orders are cut, right Mike?"

"Right," Smitty replied, "that's how it usually worked for me, in my twelve years in the Army, and all the classes I've been to, we get our orders just before we complete the class."

"But this is their first class," Juanita said to Smitty.

"I know, but it still works the same," Smitty said, "you should find out probably in the next two or three weeks, then you can start making plans and doing research for off base things to do."

Juanita looked at Mike and asked him, "Did you ask them?"

"No," Mike replied to Juanita, "not yet, I will now."

Tom and Amy looked at Smitty, wondering what was going on.

"Juanita and I are going away for the weekend," Smitty said, "well Doodles too, and we were wondering if you could stop by and look after the place, you know, water the plants, bring in the mail, that sort of thing."

Tom looked at Amy and then at Smitty, "Sure," he said, "no problem."

"You can even stay here if you want, help yourself to whatever is in the 'fridge," Juanita added, looking over at Mike, "right?"

"Yeah, sure," Smitty added, "make yourselves at home for the weekend."

"Alright," Tom looked at Amy and smiled, "I can do that."

"Great," Juanita said, "Mike will give you guys a key before then."

Tom opened the car door for Amy and she got in. Tom walked around and got in his side and buckled up, then started the motor.

"Why did she keep saying you guys when they asked if you could look after their house?" Amy asked Tom.

"Well," Tom said thoughtfully, "maybe because she knows it's hard for us to be alone anywhere on the base, and she is giving us a chance to spend time alone before we get our orders and go separate ways."

"She is so sweet," Amy said, "she knows that we are in love and don't get a chance to spend serious time together, at least not since we went to your cabin, and in the car a few times, but that's not real good, it's not very romantic."

Tony was sitting on the floor, reading through the directions for the babies crib, "Linda?" he shouted.

"Yeah?" she asked, poking her head in the door of the nursery, "what's up?"

"Can you find me a screwdriver?" Tony asked, "a straight flat one, I need it to put this thing together."

"Ok," Linda replied, "where is it?"

"Try the junk drawer in the kitchen," he answered, "I think I saw one in there the other day."

Amy returned with the screwdriver and sat on a stool by the door to watch.

"That looks complicated," she said, "is it?"

"Yeah," Tony replied, crumpling the sheet of paper and throwing it, "why can't they make these directions easier to follow?"

"I dunno," Linda responded, "is there anything I can do to help?"

"No," Tony responded, "have you talked to your folks about the wedding?"

"What do you mean?" Amy replied, "We talk all the time."

"It's only three months away, I know we have the minister lined up, and the hall rented, and all that, but are we going with a band or a DJ?"

"Why are you asking that now?" Amy asked, "right in the middle of fighting with the crib."

"Because it crossed my mind just now," Tony argued, "that's why, is that a problem?"

"Of course not," Linda responded calmly, "it seemed like an odd time to ask, that's all. What would you like? A band or a DJ? Because we should probably listen to some bands if that's what we want."

"I don't care," Tony said, dropping a screw on the floor.

"Know what?" Linda said, "I'm going to go into the other room, I want to finish sewing the animals for the mobile to hang over the crib when you finish it."

"Fine," Tony said, "Oh, I'm getting hungry, what's for lunch?"

Linda stood on the stool; her wedding gown was flowing across the floor. It was beautiful, with beadwork and lace trim, a long silky train, and a hand embroidered veil.

"You look lovely my dear, absolutely breathtaking," her mom said, then looked at Janey, "what do you think?"

"You will be the prettiest bride ever," Janey said.

"It feels good," Linda said, "I mean, it's not too tight and I can still move."

"For now," Janey added, "how will it feel when you wear it down the aisle and your belly is bigger than it is now?"

"It should be okay," Linda's mom added, "they stitched in some elastic on the back where the zipper is, it's suppose to allow it to stretch somewhat, it cost extra but my little girl deserves it."

"Your mom is so smart," Janey said to Linda.

Tom shut and locked the door, then turned around and looked at Amy, holding his arms out, open wide, "We are all alone now," He said.

Amy dropped her bag and almost jumped into Tom's arms, wrapping her arms around his neck, and pressing her lips against his. Tom grabbed hold of her butt; one cheek in each hand, lifting her up, she wrapped her legs around his hips and squeezed them, holding on tightly. He carried her that way to the kitchen and set her on the counter. Amy lifted up Tom's shirt and pulled it over his head, and then reached for his belt buckle, Tom began unbuttoning Amy's top, gently caressing her breasts. With one hand he reached behind her and unsnapped her bra. Amy removed her opened top and bra, while holding his face in her hands kissing Tom. Their tongues exploring each others tongues, their breathing becoming more rapid, she opened his jeans and reached her hand inside his shorts and grabbed him, he was hard and ready, she stroked him a few times before he broke the kiss and helped her remove her jeans and panties.

Amy, still on the counter spread her legs and put her hands on his waist, pulling him towards her.

Tom lifted her legs with one hand behind each knee and entered her, she was ready for him, and in one motion he was all the way deep inside, she wrapped her legs around his hips and her arms around his neck, and bit down gently on his chest as he moved inside her.

Tom hung up the phone and walked to the sofa where Amy was sitting, she was in her terrycloth housecoat, watching Tom.

"Pizza will be here in a little bit," He said as he sat down next to her and lifted her legs up onto his lap.

"I'm going to miss you when we get our orders," Amy said, with a tear in her eye, "miss you a lot."

"I know," Tom said, raising his hand up and brushing her hair aside, then wiping the tear from her cheek, "I'm gonna miss you too, a lot, but we don't have our orders yet, and we are still here now, together, tonight."

"I know," Amy replied, "it just makes me sad."

"Shhh," Tom said as he pulled her closer, holding her in his arms as she began to cry. "Come on now, we knew this was going to happen, we knew once class was done we would go different ways."

"That was before I fell in love with you," Amy said, looking up into Toms eyes, tears flowing down her cheeks, "I didn't expect to fall in love with you, I thought we would just, you know, have fun being together and doing things."

"I know, I know," Tom said reassuringly, "I didn't expect it either, maybe we will get to be on the same base someday."

"Yeah, Maybe," Amy said with a sniff as she leaned her head against his chest.

Tom held her close, caressing her arm and staring out the window, neither one said anything for a long time until the pizza guy rang the doorbell.

Linda and Janey were sitting at the counter at the ice cream shop. Linda was stirring her malted and paging through a magazine, when the little bell on the door rang indicating someone had entered. Janey looked up and gasped, "Oh, My, God," Linda looked at her, puzzled, "what?"

"It's Tom," Janey said quietly, "He just walked in the door."

Linda sat up quickly and looked at the mirror, "My god, it is him."

Tom saw the reflection of Linda's face in the mirror as he walked towards the counter and his heart skipped a beat.

Janey watched Tom walking towards them. "He looks good," she whispered to Linda, "he looks real good, he looks taller and stronger, he looks real fit."

"What am I going to say?" Linda asked Janey in a whisper.

"Hi," Tom said, looking directly at Linda, "how have you been?"

"Hi Tom," Janey said, turning on her stool to look at him.

"Hi Janey," Tom replied, not taking his eyes off of Linda, "I thought you would be gone now, off to college."

"You thought wrong," Linda said, avoiding eye contact with Tom.

"Well, um," Janey said, as she stood up and placed her hand on Lindas shoulder, "I have some things I gotta do, I'll see you later, Bye Tom, it was good seeing you."

"Yeah," Tom said to Janey with a discarding wave, then sat on the stool next to Linda, "mind if I sit here?"

"No," Linda replied, "What are you doing here?"

"I got just finished with my training and got orders to go to Kentucky, so I drove home first to pick up a few things and see the old places and people before I went, I have a couple of days before I have to report in."

"Oh," Linda replied, closing the magazine and shoving it to the side, "so how is the Army treating you?"

"It's good," Tom replied, "I like it so far, I mean, I was in basic training, then my job training, now I'm finally going to a unit to start really being in the Army. Now that all my schooling is done, it's time to go do what I've been trained to do."

"That sounds nice," Linda said, "I'm happy for you."

Tom noticed the ring on her finger and his eyes followed her arm up to her body, then he saw she was pregnant. He pointed to her stomach that was barely covered by the counter and asked her, "is that why you're not in college?"

"Yes," Linda said, finally looking Tom in the eyes, "and I'm getting married next month."

"Wow, well," Tom was shocked, then replied, "I guess congratulations are in order then, who's the lucky guy?"

"Tony," Linda said, shifting her gaze from Tom into the mirror.

"Tony? Tony?" Tom asked, "I'm surprised."

"Not that it matters anymore," Linda said, "but, that girl you told me about last time you were home, the one that gave you the hickey, what really happened? It's been bothering me all this time and I have to know."

"I told you," Tom said, looking her square in the eyes, "she was a dancer at the bar a bunch of us went into, I dunno, maybe she thought she was funny or something, but nothing happened, I was so in love with you, I couldn't get you out of my mind, I sure the hell wasn't going to have sex with her when I was in love with you."

"Oh Tom, I'm so sorry," Linda looked at Tom, "I should have believed you, I should have given you the benefit of the doubt, now it's too late."

"Kinda looks that way," Tom replied, "your letter broke my heart."

"I'm sorry," Linda responded, looking deep into his eyes, "have there been other girls?"

"What?" Tom asked.

"Have there been other girls?" she repeated herself, "you said you loved me, have there been other girls?"

"Not before you dumped me," Tom said, "but after your letter yeah, nothing real deep or serious, nothing like I felt for you, I don't know if I will ever love anybody like that again."

Linda looked away, tears running down her cheeks.

"It was good seeing you," Tom said as he stood up to leave.

"When do you leave?" Linda asked, "maybe, maybe we can meet for coffee or something before you go."

"That would be nice," Tom replied, "my dads number is still the same, he's not there, but I'll be staying there while I'm in town."

"I miss you Tom, I really do," Linda said, reaching her hand out to touch his arm.

Tom leaned over and kissed her on the top of her head, "I miss you too, and I always have, and always will. I wish you and Tony, and the baby luck."

Smitty picked up the phone, "hello?"

"Hey Smitty! It's Tom," Tom said into the phone, "How are ya?"

"Hey hey," Smitty replied, "I'm doing great, how the hell are you? Where are you?"

"I'm at my folks place," Tom answered, "figured I would drive up here on the way to Kentucky and pick up some of my things, how's Juanita and Doodles, I bet Juanita is getting ready to pop pretty soon."

Smitty laughed, "not for awhile yet, but yeah, she's ready, she wants it to be over so she can carry the little thing in her arms and not in her stomach and back, that way she can hand him off to me sometimes."

"I bet," Tom laughed.

"So have you heard from Amy?" Smitty asked, "She called here the other night."

"Yeah," Tom answered, "we talked last night for quite awhile, she seems to be settling in at her new place just fine,"

"How did she get her pick and you didn't?" Smitty asked.

"Doesn't seem fair does it?" Tom asked, "she gets Italy like she asked for and I ask for Germany or Hawaii and get Kentucky, Kentucky! What's that all about?"

"Hey man," Smitty replied, "there is something to be said about being stationed stateside, remember?"

"Yeah," Tom agreed, "Guess you're right, I just wanted to see more of the world than friggin Kentucky."

Smitty laughed hard at that, "I know what you mean man, I know what you mean, but keep in mind, you can always put in for another duty station after a year, that's what I did, it's not like you're stuck there forever."

"You're right," Tom agreed, "well, give my love to Juanita and Doodles."

"I will my friend," Smitty said, "You take care and keep in touch."

Tom hung up the phone and opened another beer, sitting alone in the quiet until long after the sun had set.

Tony walked into the kitchen and set his lunchbox on the counter.

"I heard that Tom is in town," He said.

"Yes," Linda responded, "He is, I saw him today, Janey and I were having a malted and he came into the ice cream shop."

"What did he have to say?" Tony asked.

"He congratulated us on the wedding and the baby," Linda answered.

"That was nice of him," Tony replied, "Say, after supper, I'm going over to Brent's house for awhile."

"Ok," Linda replied, turning to look at Tony, "what's going on over there? You sure have been going over there a lot lately."

"Just hanging out," Tony responded, "he bought a pool table, and some of us guys from work get together at his house and shoot pool and drink beer."

"Will you be late?" Linda asked.

"I dunno, don't wait up," Tony replied.

When she heard the knock, Janey opened the door just wide enough to see who was there.

"Hi," Tony said as she opened the door wider so he could come in.

"What did you tell Linda?" Janey asked.

"I'm at Brent's," Tony said, "with the guys shooting pool and drinking beer."

Linda loosened the belt on her robe and it fell open, exposing her naked body. Tony slid his hands inside her robe and ran his fingers up along her ribcage, then under her breasts, cupping them and circling her nipples with his thumbs.

Janey reached down and unzipped Tony's jeans then reached her hand inside his opened jeans and wrapped her hands around him.

Janey walked backwards, not letting go of Tony and sat down on the sofa, lifting one leg and putting her foot on the sofa.

Tony pushed his jeans to the floor and stepped out of them, then stood over Janey as she stroked him. Janey pulled him closer and wrapped her lips around him, taking him into her mouth, looking up at his face. Tony put his hands on her head and guided her, feeling her lips and tongue on him.

Janey leaned back and put her hands behind her head, Tony knelt down on the sofa and holding himself with his hand, he rubbed himself on her, feeling her wetness, he pushed against her and entered her. Janey let out a gasp as she felt him inside of her.

Brent shouted, "It's open" when he heard the knock on the door.

"Hey, who's got the table?" Tony asked when he opened the door and walked in.

"Bobby does at the moment," Brent replied, "but he's gonna loose it after this next shot, grab yourself a beer."

"Hey Bobby!" Tony said, "What's up?"

"Quiet," Bobby replied, as he lined up his shot on the pool table, "I'm getting ready to kick Brents ass, just one more shot."

"Hey man," Brent said, "I thought you would be here an hour ago."

"Yeah, sorry," Tony said, "I, um, had to take care of some business and it took a little longer that I expected."

"Damn!" Bobby said, annoyed, looking at Brent, "I scratched, it's your shot."

"What did I tell ya?" Brent said with a laugh, "told ya he was gonna loose."

"So how's things at home with the little woman and the baby to be?" Bobby asked as he took a sip of his beer.

"Good, real good," Tony replied, "She lets me out to play sometimes, that's how I get to come here."

"Yeah?" Bobby replied, "I promised Janey I would be home earlier than last week, geeze, she just moved in a couple of weeks ago, and you'd think we were married or something."

"Is that so?" Tony said, lifting his beer to take a sip, "I wonder how it would be if you were married?"

"Bite your tongue man," Bobby replied, "I'm not getting married, not yet anyway, too many fish in the sea."

"Oh?" Brent added from across the pool table, "I wonder what Janey would say if she heard you saying that."

Bobby shrugged his shoulders and said, "but she didn't hear me, and she's not gonna hear me say that."

"That's why I'm still single," Brent said, "no hassles, no headaches, nobody I have to promise to be home early to."

Chapter 5

TOM WAS SITTING in a big stuffed chair in the corner of the coffee shop, reading the morning newspaper and drinking his coffee when Linda walked in.

"Hi," Linda said to Tom.

He put his newspaper down on his lap and gestured with his hand for her to sit down in the chair next to him.

"Good morning," Tom said, "I was wondering if I would see you this morning or not."

Linda smiled and sat down.

"Your smile still warms my heart," Tom said, "Did you know that?"

"Thank you," Linda replied, "I'm glad you wanted to see me, I wasn't a good girlfriend before, I'm sorry I hurt you, but I thought, well, I thought you did sleep with that girl."

"Forget it," Tom said, "It's done, besides, you're getting married pretty soon, you have a baby on the way, and it looks like things have worked out well for you."

"Yeah," Linda said, "looks that way doesn't it?"

Tom looked into Linda's eyes as he brought his cup to his mouth to take a sip, and asked her, "Do you love him?"

"No," Linda replied and looked away to hide her tears, "I guess I never really stopped loving you."

Tom put his cup down and reached for her hand.

"Maybe this is for the best," he said, "maybe you will grow to love him, maybe things will work out well and you will live happily ever after."

Linda let out a big sigh, "yeah, maybe."

"Tom?" Linda looked him in the eyes and asked, "Will you take me back to your place and make love to me?"

Tom looked at her, he gazed into her eyes, then looked at her pregnant stomach, then looked at the ring on her finger, then back into her eyes, "I can't, I'm sorry, but I just can't."

"Will you take me back to your place and just hold me? Will you just hold me then?" she asked.

"Sure," Tom responded, "I can do that, in fact, I'd love to."

Tom opened the car door and offered his hand to help Linda get out of the car. Linda stood up and looked at the front of the house, the shrubs were overgrown and the once well-tended garden was now full of weeds.

"It looks so much different," Linda remarked to Tom.

"Yeah, I know," Tom replied sadly, "since mom died, dad is hardly ever here, and when he is, he is drunk and doesn't take of the place. He told me he put in my name on the title so I'll have a place to call my own when I get out of the Army, but. Well, I don't know, I might want something else by then."

"It sure is a shame," Linda replied, "your mom had this place looking so lovely, it was like a postcard."

Tom opened the door and gestured for her to enter first. He turned on a lamp on the end table by the sofa and lit a fire in the fireplace.

"So how is the Army treating you?" Linda asked, "you look good, you look like, like a poster for a recruiting advertisement."

Tom blushed, "Thanks, we work hard at staying fit, we are tested all the time so I'm always working out, can't have fat out of shape soldiers going into combat, they wouldn't last a day."

"Oh god Tom," Linda said, "I hope you don't get sent to combat, you aren't going to are you?"

"Not in the near future," he reassured her, "I'm going to Kentucky and there isn't much combat there lately."

Linda moved closer to Tom on the sofa, "Tell me I'm doing the right thing Tony."

"What do you mean?" Tom asked.

"Marrying Tony," she responded, "I feel like it's the right thing to do, for the baby and all."

"I can't tell you what the right thing to do is," Tom replied, putting his arm around her and softly stroking her hair with his hand, "It might be the right thing, but not if you don't love him, I mean, lots of women raise kids without a father, it's not easy, but you have to decide that for yourself."

"Why couldn't it be you?" she asked, looking into his eyes, her eyes filled with sadness, "why couldn't you be the father, I wouldn't be second guessing myself now."

"Because I'm not," Tom answered, "you made that decision way back when."

"I was so stupid," she replied, "so quick to judge, Janey kept saying . . ."

Tom placed his finger on her lips, "no more, it's in the past."

Amy leaned against his arm; she placed her hand on his chest and her head on his shoulder.

"Please hold me Tom," she said, "I just need you to hold me."

"Ok," Tom said, stroking her arm with his hand and leaning his head on her head, then he sighed and they sat in silence.

Linda was sitting in the chair while the hairdresser was doing her hair. Her mom was across the room hanging up the wedding dress and fluffing the ruffles out from being in back seat of the car. Janey was making last adjustments with some of the flower arrangements.

"God, I never thought I would be this nervous," Linda exclaimed.

"I know dear," her mom said, "it's normal to be nervous on your wedding day, just try and be calm, I know it's hard, but you are going to be the most beautiful bride."

Janey walked over to Linda and opened her purse, "here, this might help," she said as she reached under the counter and pulled out a metal bucket with a bottle of champagne chilling on ice.

"Oh my!" Linda's mom said as she walked over to Linda and Janey, "I like that idea, I know it'll calm my nerves."

"Mom!" Linda said, pointing to her big pregnant stomach, "I can't."

"But we can," Janey said as she popped the cork, "you can have a little bit, I don't think one glass would hurt anything."

"If I do have just one glass, I'll have it at the reception with Tony," Linda said.

"Well, fill me up," Linda's mom said as she held up an empty glass.

Tony was downstairs with Brent, already in his tux, nervously pacing back and forth. Brent opened the cooler and pulled out two cans of beer. "Here," he said as he opened one and handed it to Tony, "enjoy your last few hours of freedom."

"You make it sound so bleak," Tony said, "She's a good girl, we get along well, she lets me go out, hell, I spend lots of nights at your place, and that won't change."

"Well," Brent said, holding his beer up to toast, "here's to you and the missus."

"And the little bambino," Tony added before taking a long pull at his beer, "the driving force here, without that, I wouldn't be here."

Brent shook his head, "What did you get yourself into man?"

"Nothing I can't handle," Tony replied, "gimme another beer."

The door opened and Janey walked into the room as Tony and Brent were sitting on folding chairs, stacking empty beer cans and laughing.

"Hey guys," she said.

"Hey Janey," Tony said, "How's it going upstairs?"

"Pretty good," Janey said as she walked crookedly towards the two, "Linda's mom and I are getting drunk, Linda is a nervous wreck, and hey, it's a wedding day."

"Sounds fun to me," Brent replied, then laughed, "Tony and I are, *hic*, we are calming his nerves down here."

"I see," Janey said, "Brent, do you mind giving us a few minutes? I need to talk to Tony."

"Sure thing doll," Brent said as he stood up, momentarily loosing his balance and left the room.

"What's up?" Tony asked.

"Stand up a sec," Janey said as she sat down on the chair Brent just got up from.

Tony stood up and turned towards Janey, "Ok, now what?"

Janey reached for Tony, grabbing him by the waistband of his pants and pulled him to her, and then before he knew what was happening, she had his pants open and her hand in his shorts.

"What the?" he began to say before Janey said, "quiet, someone might hear you."

"What are you doing?" Tony asked quietly, offering no resistance to Janey.

"Come on now Tony, you can't honestly tell me you want me to stop, can you?" she asked as she opened her mouth and took him inside.

Tony closed his eyes and began rocking on his feet; he held his hands on Janeys head as she moved it on him.

The sound of knives and forks clinking on glasses filled the room. Linda and Tony stood up from their chairs at the head table and kissed. Suddenly the room erupted in cheers as everybody shouted out their approval.

Brent stood up from his seat next to Tony at the head table to make a toast, "To the bride and groom," he said raising his glass and holding it in front of him, "I have known Tony since grade school when we first played ball together in the street. His parents moved in next door to my parents, and pretty much we have been together through thick and thin since that first day. We played ball together, we learned to ride bikes together, and later we even drank together."

There was an outburst of laughter and applause, and then he continued, "When I broke my leg in sixth grade, Tony was at my house everyday, helping me with my homework. He is the brother I never had and I love him."

Tony stood up and gave Brent a big bear hug, then sat back down, Brent resumed his speech, looking over towards Linda, "and I have known this lovely girl a long time as well, I have watched her through high school, too chicken to ask her out, and we became friends too. I just want to say, I want to wish these two people, the best of what life has to offer."

There was a round of clinking glasses as everybody toasted with Brent. Then the clinking began again and Tony and Linda once again stood up from their seats at the head table and kissed, much to everyone's enjoyment.

Janey stood up from her chair along side Linda at the head table and raised her glass in front of her.

"I want to make a toast to my best friend," she began, turning to face Linda, "Linda, my best friend, my girlfriend of girlfriends, you have been there for me my whole life, whenever there was a problem, you were there for me. Whenever I had boy problems, you were there for me, I love you so much," she said as she leaned down and hugged Linda, then kissed her on the cheek, "and I know that you and Tony will be happy, that you two will have many many happy years ahead of you, and that you two will grow old together, Tony," she said turning to face him, "I know you are a good man, and I know you will take good care of my friend Linda, I wish you the best," then she turned to the audience, "to Linda and Tony, two of the most wonderful people in the world."

Tom sat on his bunk holding the remote control and flipping through the channels on the TV. Then he picked up the phone and dialed.

"Hello?" the woman's voice on the other end answered.

"Hello, Amy?" Tom said, "It's Tom."

"No, Amy isn't in right now," the woman's voice said, "Can I take a message?"

"Um, yes," Tom said, "tell her Tom called, I'm a friend of hers, we were in a class together."

"She's mentioned your name, I'll tell her you called," She said and hung up the phone.

"Thanks," Tom said into the disconnected phone.

The alarm went off, it was six thirty A.M. Tom reached over and shut the buzzer off and got out of bed. He threw on his gym clothes and went out for his morning run around the new base.

On one particular curve, he could see out over a vast valley, he stopped for a moment and stared, the view was breathtaking. There were mountains in the distance and the valley was covered in the morning fog. His mind went to the dock, sitting on the dock with the morning fog covering the lake, and Linda was by his side the day before he went off to basic training.

It seemed like a lifetime ago, but was barely a year ago. Where did the time go? He turned and began running again, his feet creating a steady rhythm as they broke the silence when they hit the ground in the quiet morning.

Tom ran harder, he pushed himself harder this morning, he wanted to shake Linda from his mind, he wanted to get rid of her smile in his head, her smell, he wanted not to think of her, not to think of her and her new husband, and their child, the child that was the glue holding those two together. They were not meant for each other, they would never last, it was doomed, but what could he do? What difference did it make to him here, to him now? He ran as fast as he could, no longer a routine jog, no longer a peaceful morning run, he was running as hard as he could, he wanted the thoughts to stop.

The emergency room was quiet when Tony helped Linda into one of the vacant seats. A nurse with a clipboard came over and sat down next to Linda.

"How long have you been having the contractions?" she asked.

"I, I don't know, awhile," Linda answered, holding her hand on her stomach, her face wincing in pain, "I know we should have come sooner, I, I just didn't think it would come this soon, I thought we could just come in and check in like we talked about."

"It's ok," the nurse said, "we'll get you checked in and get a room for you, then the doctor will be by to see you in a bit."

"Ok," Linda replied, "thanks."

"Ok, I gotta go park the car," Tony said, "I'm in the ambulance zone right now, I'll be right back." Then he kissed Linda on the forehead and left to go move the car.

Tony sat in the chair next to the bed as Linda slept, watching her. He looked down at the baby he was holding in his arms, she was wrapped snugly in a blanket and was also sleeping. He slowly rocked back and forth, naturally, without even a thought, almost as if by instinct.

"What should we call you?" he asked the baby in a quiet whisper.

Janey peeked her head in the door, "Hello?" she said, "is this where the new mom and dad are?"

"Hi," Linda said to Janey, "I'm glad to see you."

"Where is your baby?" Janey asked," Where is Tony?"

"Tony had to go to work, he was here all night," Linda replied, "but he'll be back later, the baby is down at the nursery, we can go see her if you'd like."

"Of course I would," Janey replied, "so how are you? How did everything go?"

"I'm fine, tired, it was a long night," Linda replied as she struggled to get out of bed.

"A girl huh?" Janey replied, "that's nice, I bet she's cute."

"I think so," Linda said proudly, "my mom was up here earlier, she wants me to name her after my grandmother, but Tony and I don't want to."

"Have you picked out a name yet?" Janey asked, as they walked down the hallway towards the nursery.

"No, not yet," Linda replied, "I think Tony and I will have one tonight though, we have a couple we both like, we just have to decide on one."

"What?" Janey asked, "What do you like?"

"I'm not telling you," Linda said, "not until we decide, then I'll tell you."

"Ok," Janey replied, "so when do you get to home from the hospital?"

"Tomorrow, they told me," Linda responded, "tomorrow we can all go home, it will be strange having a new baby in the apartment, but it will be nice, the nursery is ready, the crib is setup, the room has been painted, we have clothes and diapers and everything."

"Good thing," Janey replied, "because you won't have much time now to do much between feedings and changes."

Tom walked into the commander's office, standing in front if the big wood desk he. saluted and stood at attention. The commander returned his salute and instructed Tom to have a seat. Tom sat up straight in the chair, holding his hat in his hands. The commander looked through a file on his desk then put it down and looked at Tom.

"I see here that your enlistment is almost up," the commander said, "have you given any thought to reenlisting? The Army sure could use a good soldier like you. I see you have been in for four years now; you have moved up in rank as expected and have numerous awards. It would be a shame to loose you now."

"Well sir," Tom responded, "I have thought about it, I have thought about it a lot, but I want to travel more, I want to see more of the world. I mean, the Army has been good to me, it trained me, gave me a home, I really learned a lot and grew a lot in the Army, but . . ."

"If it's travel you want," the commander said, cutting Tom off in his response, "looking at your skills and history, I can personally guarantee that you can be assigned to whatever base you want. Meaning, if you request a duty station, I can see to it that you get that station."

"I will have to think about it Sir," Tom replied, "and I appreciate your helping me, but I would kinda like to go home and start a life."

"Understood," the commander replied, "and I respect that, tell you what, I'll have the retention officer contact you, he can tell you about any reenlistment bonuses you may be entitled to, talking to you like this is part of my job, and I hate to see the Army loose an outstanding soldier like you."

"Again, I thank you sir," Tom said as he stood to leave, saluted the commander with a sharp salute and left his office.

Linda sat on the edge of the bed tucking Andrea in for the night.

"Ok honey, I'll leave the night light on for you," Linda said as she kissed Andrea. "Now go to sleep, I don't want to have to come in here again tonight, you're a big girl and you can sleep in your own bed."

"K, g'night mommy," Andrea said, "love you mommy."

"I love you too darling," Linda said softly.

Then Linda stood up and left the room, closing the bedroom door behind her.

Linda looked out the kitchen window, noticing that Tony's truck was not in the driveway. It was past eleven o'clock at night and he should have been home three hours ago. He hadn't called and said he would be late, but being late was not new. Tony often came home late and more than once he hadn't come home all night.

She pulled out a tablet and a pen from the drawer and sat down at the kitchen table.

Tom closed the door of is room and sat down to take off his work boots, then he took off his uniform and tossed it on the floor in a pile. He grabbed a towel and headed for the shower.

The weather was warm, there was a nice breeze blowing, the workday was over, and Tom had a date with an ice-cold beer at the EM club.

He was getting used to California and the weather, the traffic off base he could live without, but the people seemed nice enough.

Tom toweled off and looked in the mirror, "Damn" he said to himself as he ran his hand through his hair, realizing that as he grew older, his hairline was receding and his hair was thinning.

He went back to his room and threw on a t-shirt, shorts and a pair of sandals and headed over to the EM club. A routine he had gotten quite used to.

Tom was sitting at the bar drinking his beer and watching a baseball game on the TV in the corner when he was tapped on the shoulder.

"Smitty! You old fart!" Tom said when he turned to see who tapped him. Then he stood up quickly to shake hands, "What the hell are you doing here? How are ya?"

"I thought that was you," Smitty replied, grabbing Tom in a bear hug, "I'm doing good, real good. Man it's good to see you."

"Yeah, you too, here, let me buy you a beer," Tom said, as he waved for the bartender. "So tell me, what are you doing here? How are Juanita and Doodles? And you guys had another one too just after I left . . ."

"Everyone is fine," Smitty replied, "Juanita is doing great, Doodles is in third grade now, and Danny, our son is gonna start kindergarten in the fall."

"My god, where does the time go?" Tom asked.

"I don't know," Smitty replied, "I had to come up here for a few days, seems they need my expertise for something, so I was given temporary orders to come and be an advisor for a project."

"Wow," Tom replied, "fantastic that's great."

"Yeah," Smitty said, "I wasn't too thrilled about it, but I didn't know you were here, when did you get stationed here?"

"I got here a couple weeks ago," Tom explained, "I re-upped and got a transfer here. I told I was gonna re-up, don't you remember?"

"Oh yeah, you told me all about it in your Christmas card last year," Smitty replied, "but I didn't know you would actually go through with it."

"Well, I figured if my old friend Smitty can make a career out of the Army, I could too," Tom said as he laughed and sipped his beer.

"Hey, you ever hear from Amy?" Smitty asked as he sipped his beer.

"Not much," Tom replied, "last I heard she was in Italy and getting ready to leave there and go to Germany or someplace, I dunno though, we kinda lost touch."

"Juanita and her keep in touch," Smitty added, "I guess she just re-upped and is coming stateside, but I couldn't tell you where."

"Really?" Tom asked raising his eyebrows, "stateside huh?"

"Yeah," Smitty said, "hey, listen, I have to get going, I have to meet some people in half an hour, but let's meet tomorrow and go out for dinner, okay?"

"Wouldn't miss it," Tom said with a big smile, "god it's good to see you again."

"See you tomorrow then," Smitty said, before he drained his beer and shook Tom's hand as he left.

Linda waited outside Janeys apartment for her to come out. It was raining and the rhythmic sound of the windshield wipers was hypnotizing.

Janey ran to the car and opened the door and quickly hopped in.

"What's so urgent?" Janey asked as she turned to face Linda, then saw her face, "oh my god, what happened to you?"

"Nothing," Linda said, trying hard not to break into tears.

"What happened? That bruise didn't happen by itself?" Janey argued.

"I dunno, look at me, I'm seven months pregnant and not attractive, he comes to me at night for sex and I'm to tired, he wants things done around the house and

I don't get it all done," Linda answered, "I know it's my fault, he works hard, and it's my job, and I, I . . ." she didn't finish answering Janey before she burst into tears and sobbed.

"How can I help?" Janey asked, "is there something I can do?"

"No," Linda said, "It's all my fault, he found my letters."

"What letters?" Janey asked.

"To Tom, I wrote to Tom," Linda replied, "I never mailed them, I just wrote them, then slipped them in my drawer under my panties."

"Why did you write to Tom?" Janey asked, "and what was Tony doing digging in your drawer?"

"I don't know," Linda said, "I just don't know, I don't know why I wrote to Tom, and why I saved the letters, I should have just thrown them away, and I don't know what he was doing in my drawers, he's the one that comes home late, or not at all, or smells of perfume, I just don't know what to think Janey."

"Do you need a place to stay?" Janey asked.

"No, I'll be okay, Andrea get's scared when we fight," Linda said, "But we try not to when she's awake."

"Well, if there's anything I can do," Janey said, "don't hesitate to ask, call me, day or night, promise?"

"Ok," Linda replied, "Thanks for listening, I gotta go now, I have to pick up Andrea from the sitters."

Tom pulled his car up in front of his dad's house. His dad lived here when he wasn't at his brothers house drinking. Toms uncle Jim, his dads brother never married, he lived ten minutes away from his dad and on almost any given night he would be too drunk to make it home and usually ended up sleeping on a couch at Jims. The old house never was the same after Toms mom died. He missed her.

There was snow on the ground, and the walk had not been shoveled in days. There were Christmas lights up on the neighbor's houses that lit up the night sky with all the reds and yellows, blue and greens and whites, it was almost magical.

Tom turned on the kitchen light and closed the door behind him. The house was a mess, he let out a sad sigh as he looked around then he put his luggage on his bed then began to clean up the mess. He threw away bag after bag of empty bottles, washed a sink full of dirty dishes that he imagined had been there since he was last home a couple of years ago, and hauled the trash out to the can next to the garage. He opened the garage door and grabbed the shovel and started to shovel the driveway and sidewalk.

A few of the neighbors that drove by waved or stopped their cars to say hi when they saw Tom outside shoveling the snow.

Tom walked into the ice cream shop, the little bell on the door jingled to indicate someone had entered. He walked to the counter and sat down, ordered a coffee and picked up the newspaper.

"Hello," a soft voice said from behind him.

Tom put the newspaper down and looked in the mirror. Then spun around and stood up, his arms open wide, "Linda! How are you?"

"I'm doing okay," she replied, "how are you?"

"I'm doing good," Tom said, as he wrapped his arms around her and gave her a big hug, "thought I would come home for Christmas, it's been a long time since I was home for a Christmas."

"That's nice," Linda said as she pulled away to sit down next to him and asked, "Where are you stationed now?"

"California, I'm stationed in California for now," Tom replied, and then looked down at her pregnant stomach. "Weren't you pregnant last time I saw you? I gotta stop coming home."

"Yes, I was," she replied, "we had a little girl, Andrea, she's three now, almost four."

"Almost four, wow," Tom replied, smiling, "I bet she looks beautiful, just like her mother."

"I, I tried to write to you several times," Linda said, "I started to tell you about Andrea, and about the new one on the way, and, and, I don't know, I just never finished any of them."

"Any of them?" Tom asked, confused "what are you talking about?"

"I wrote you letters, hoping maybe," Linda went on, "maybe you would be my knight in shining armor or something, I wrote and told you about Tony and I, the problems we were having, I guess it was therapy maybe, I saved them and never mailed them to you, I don't even have your address to mail them, isn't that stupid?"

"No, not stupid," Tom said, touching her arm, "It sounds sad, but not stupid. Do you want my address? I can write it down for you if you would like, I just never thought you would want to write to me now that you're married and have a family and everything."

"I know it sounds bad Tom," Linda said, "but you are the only man I trust, I mean really, I trust you more that I do Tony, my own husband, the father of my children, sometimes I just want to hear your voice, or talk to you, you know?"

"Alright, alright, I'll give you my address," Tom said as he scribbled it down on a napkin.

Linda took the napkin that Tom handed her, folded it and placed it in her purse.

"Thank you," Linda said, "you don't know what this means to me."

"You're welcome," Tom said, "I'll have to send something when the baby is born."

"That's sweet," she replied, "but it's really not necessary."

"Well, just let me know what it is," Tom replied, "I do want to know."

"Ok, hey, do you have plans for Christmas?" she asked.

"I'm hoping to see my dad," Tom answered, "haven't seen him yet, maybe I'll drop by my uncle Jims, I imagine I'll find them both there, drunk."

"I better get going," Linda said as she stood up to leave, then kissed Tom on the cheek, "I still love you," and she turned and walked away.

"I love you too," Tom replied, but she was already halfway to the door and couldn't hear him.

Chapter 6

TRAFFIC STOPPED AS reveille sounded on the base. The sun was just coming up and Tom knew it was going to be a warm day.

When the music stopped, Tom waited for the cars to pass before he resumed his morning run. It felt good this particular morning. He had just returned to California from Christmas leave at home, and the warm air in his lungs was welcoming. His morning runs were a good time to reflect and think. He worked through many of his personal and emotional difficulties while running.

The landing gear extended as the airplane readied for landing. There was a puff of blue smoke when the wheels touched the ground and the flaps were opened and the brakes were applied to bring the big olive drab military transport to a stop.

The ground crew chocked the wheels and pushed a wheeled ladder to the side of the aircraft for the passengers to exit.

The third person to exit and walk down the ladder was a woman, she was in uniform as were all the passengers and carried her duffle bag and another smaller carry on bag.

"SSgt. Guinn?" the clerk at the desk asked as he flipped through the passenger manifest in the ground floor office of the control tower.

"Yes, pvt. I'm SSgt Guinn," the woman answered," I'm reporting for duty, where is the base HQ?"

"If you ask the private out front," the clerk replied, pointing to the door, "he will drive you there."

"Out front?" SSgt Guinn asked.

"Yes sergeant," the clerk replied, "he's the duty driver today and he will drive you there."

Tom suddenly took his eyes off the electronic equipment he was working on and looked out the window of his office. A strange feeling came over him and he could not place it. His mind drifted to the cabin, he recalled making love with Amy on the front porch, he remembered driving her around the lake in his small boat and how she seemed to hang on his every word as he told her of his childhood at the lake and the stories he told of the people that lived there. The memories were vivid in their clarity. It was as if it was yesterday, her presence was so strong it was almost as if she was standing right there, in the room with him, it felt so real. He closed his eyes and cleared his mind then went back to work.

Tom drove to the EM club straight from work today, he didn't go back to his room, he didn't change out of his uniform, he just got in his car and headed straight for the club.

He pulled up a stool at the bar and ordered a beer, then reached for the bowl of pretzels on the bar closest to him.

"Buy a lady a beer?" the female voice asked as she sat right next to Tom at the bar.

Recognizing the familiar voice, Tom's eyes opened wide and he spun his stool around to look at the woman talking to him.

"Amy!" he said, wrapping his arms around her and pulling her close, he smelled her hair, "mmmmmm, I missed you," he spoke softly into her ear, still holding her close.

"I was hoping to see you here," she replied.

"How did you know I would be here?" Tom asked, loosening his hug and standing back to look at her.

"Juanita told me," Amy replied, "she said Smitty was here a few months ago and ran into you, and that you two had some beers and dinner together. When I had a chance to get assigned here I took it."

"Great!" Tom replied, "you know, I had the weirdest thing happen to me today, I was at my desk, and all of a sudden, all I could think of was you. Out of the blue I was flooded by thoughts and memories of you, it was really weird, like you walked back into my life again."

Amy smiled, "looks like I kinda did," then she asked on a more serious note, "Are you involved with anybody?"

"No, no, not at all," Tom replied, patting the bar with his hand, "I live in the barracks and spend most of my off duty time right here."

Amy smiled at Tom, and raised her hand for the bartender.

"God it's good to see you Amy," Tom said, "looks like life is treating you well, you look wonderful."

"Thank you kind sir," Amy replied, "it's good to see you too, so, tell me Tom, why is a guy like you still unattached?"

"I guess the right girls don't stick around long enough," he said, looking at Amy and sipping his beer, "there was one once, but well, we were separated by life's circumstances."

"Yeah?" Amy said, smiling at Tom, "funny thing, there was once a guy in my life too, and the same thing happened to us, we were separated by circumstances beyond our control."

"Well, I still need to unpack," Amy said, "and get settled into my room before I report to work in the morning, maybe we can get together sometime, you know, have dinner or something for old times sake."

"I can't think of anything I'd like better," Tom replied, "I'd like that very much."

"Good, me too," Amy said as she finished her beer and got up to leave.

Tom watched her leave, his eyes followed her every move until the door closed and she was gone.

Linda was in the babies room, the nightlight was dimly lit providing the only light in the room. She was sitting in the rocking chair, slowly rocking Timmy to sleep; he had a fresh diaper and had just finished being fed.

Andrea was already asleep in her room, and Tony was still not home yet. Linda had hoped that after Timmy was born maybe he would spend more time at home. Maybe Tony would show more of an interest in the children and not just come home for meals and to sleep, or for the occasional sex he demanded from her. Lovemaking stopped being part of their lives a long time ago, now Linda counted the minutes until it would end whenever he did want sex from her. Usually he would come home drunk and tell her it was time for sex, and she would lie on the bed and look at the ceiling, or lay motionless, with her eyes closed and go to a happier place in her mind until he was finished and rolled off her to go to sleep or pass out.

Linda gently placed Timmy in his crib and tucked the soft blanket around him, she kissed his little head and then went into the living room to watch TV for a few minutes before she went to bed herself.

Tony opened the bedroom door and walked in, he turned on the light and began to undress, Linda could hear him, she lie still and pretended to be asleep so he would not disturb her.

"Linda, Hey, wake up," Tony said, as he stood above her, "I want to celebrate."

"Huh? What?" Linda asked groggily as she turned to face him, her hand shielding her eyes from the light, "celebrate what?"

"I won five hundred bucks playing poker over at Brent's," Tony replied as he crawled into bed and began pawed at her, "let's celebrate."

"That's great, Tony," Linda replied, "but I'm real tired, I had a rough day today, I think Timmy is teething and wouldn't stop fussing, and I just want to go to sleep."

"You stupid bitch!" he said, slapping her across the face, "Didn't you hear me? I want you to wake up, I want to celebrate now, come on."

Linda recoiled from the pain of his hand against her face. She didn't want to provoke him any more, she sat up and held back her tears, "Ok, ok, let's celebrate, but quietly, ok? The kids are asleep."

Tom got up from his desk and walked down the hallway to get a fresh cup of coffee, he heard a familiar voice and turned. "Amy?" he asked himself out loud, surprising himself.

Amy turned and saw Tom standing by the coffee kiosk. She burst into a smile and walked towards him.

"Is this your office?" she asked, "Is this where you work?"

"Yeah," Tom replied, pointing at a doorway, "Just down the hall on the right, I have a nice little office with some repair equipment and my workbench, what are you doing here?"

"I'm going to be working here too," Amy replied, "no surprise, we were in the same class, and had the same training, makes sense we would do the same job, except I'm upstairs, they have me in a little cubby hole of an office shuffling papers until I "get my feet wet", can you believe that? Get my feet wet? I've been doing this a long time, just like you."

"Ah, the good old boy syndrome," Tom said, "It won't last long, you will prove you can do the job in no time, and end up with an office like mine. You know those guys, they don't think women belong in the Army, you earned those stripes, don't let them push you into a corner, go to the commander."

"I know," Amy replied, "I just don't want to cause waves, I just got here yesterday, I'll give it a few more weeks."

Tom finished pouring his coffee, and looked at Amy, "got any plans for after work tonight?"

"Are you kidding?" she laughed, "I just got on this base two days ago, what kind of plans would I have already? Besides, I'm waiting for you to ask me out again."

Tom stood speechless for a moment, and then replied, "um. Ok, want to go out tonight?"

"Sure," she replied, "what time and where are we going?"

"Geeze," Tom stammered, "I don't know, I'll think of something this afternoon and, I know, how about I meet you right there," he asked, pointing to the door, "by that door after work, and we'll go from there?"

"It's a date," Amy said, as she flashed him a big smile and turned to walk away.

Linda pulled her car up in front of her dads architectural firm and went inside. It felt odd to be back at work, she hadn't worked since she was pregnant with Andrea. And that was almost four years ago. Her dad walked out of his office and gave her a big hug; "So how's my little girl, are you ready to start work again? Are you sure you didn't forget how?" he asked with a tinge of sarcasm.

"I'm sure daddy," she replied, "It's not that difficult to answer the phone and scribble down some notes."

"Okay then," he said, "you remember where everything is, and I cleared my schedule for lunch, I thought you and I would have lunch together, is that ok?"

"Oh yeah," Linda replied, "that's great, I'd love it."

Linda pulled out the chair at the receptionist desk and sat down, she adjusted the chair and put her headset on.

Amy put down the newspaper and looked at Tom when he sat down across from her at the table in the mess hall, "I think I found a place," she said.

Tom put his coffee down and looked at her, "oh yeah? Where?"

"Well," Amy said, pointing to an ad in the local newspaper, "right here, it looks like a cute little two bedroom bungalow, it's only a couple blocks from the beach and the rent is not too high, wanna go take a look at it?"

"Sure, call the number," Tom replied, "see if we can look at it Saturday morning."

"Ok, I'll call today," she said then looked at her watch, "oh geeze, I'm gonna be late, I have to run, see you after work."

"Ok," Tom said, as he kissed her, "I'll pick you up after work,"

Tom enjoyed having the day off, he didn't enjoy having to work on a weekend, but the compensation day in the middle of the week was always nice. He ran some errands, went to the base barber for his bi-weekly haircut, got the oil changed on his car, went and bought a bouquet of flowers for Amy and went to the EM club for a couple of beers.

Tom was waiting in front of the office when Amy walked out; he never got tired of watching her. She smiled as she walked down the stairs to the parking lot and got into the car. Tom leaned over and kissed her on the lips, then reached into the back seat and said, "Close your eyes." He picked up the bouquet of flowers and placed them on her lap, "ok, you can open them now."

"What?" Amy asked when she saw the flowers, "what are these for? They're beautiful."

"They're for you," Tom said, "you've been back in my life for three months now and we're looking at places to rent, I think moving in together is a big step and I wanted to show you what you mean to me."

Linda rushed from her desk to the women's room, she threw open the stall door and vomited. She felt weak and clammy, and her hair was wet from sweat. She washed her face off in the sink and went back to her desk and picked up the phone, "Daddy? I'm sick and I think I need to go home."

"Ok," her dad said, "go home and get some rest then, call your mother if you want her to bring you anything."

"Thanks, but I'll be okay," Linda replied, "probably just a touch of the flu or something, maybe I'll have Tony bring the kids by tonight to see you and mom so they don't catch whatever I have."

"Ok," her dad replied.

Linda turned her key in the lock to open the apartment door. The lock was already unlocked, that was weird she thought. Tony should be at work and I know I locked the door when I left this morning, I know I did, I put Timmy down, locked the door then took the kids to daycare.

There was a noise coming from down the hallway, she saw Tony's shoes on the floor, and next to them another pair of shoes. "These aren't my shoes," She whispered to herself as she put down her purse and walked towards the sound.

Linda recognized the voices now, coming from her bedroom, she didn't believe it so she took a deep breath, braced herself for what she might see and turned the corner and stood in the doorway. Her mouth opened, she stood in shock, horrified to see Tony and Janey in bed, naked, together in her bed, he was on top of her, her legs were wrapped around him, they both looked at Linda at the same time when they heard her scream, "Tony! Janey! What are you doing?"

Tony and Janey both scrambled for their clothes and Linda stormed out of the bedroom and into the living room, she sat down on the couch and started sobbing, she gasped for air, her gut wrenched, she was angrier than she had ever been before. The betrayal was overwhelming, it was worse than anything she had experienced before in her life, worse than anything she even ever imagined.

Tony and Janey walked into the living room and stood there in silence.

"Tony!" Linda said between sobs, "How could you? We have two children, She's my best friend, why?"

"Janey?" Linda turned and said, "I thought you were my friend, he's my husband for gods sake, how could you? How could you?"

Tony began to speak and Linda held up her hand, "don't say anything, don't say a word, just get out."

Janey looked at Tony, then at Linda, "I'm sorry . . ." she began to say, then Linda pointed to the door, "get out of my house, get out of my life, I don't want to talk to you, I don't ever want to see you again, I don't ever want to look at you again, I don't ever, not ever, want anything to do with you, ever again."

"I'm sorry," Tony said, "We . . ."

Linda was glaring at him, there was no mistaking the hatred in her eyes, "Don't say a word, not a word, I put up with your beatings, I put up with you staying out late, I even put up with you not coming home, but I will not put up with you screwing some slut in our home, in my bed!"

"But," Tony argued.

"But nothing," Linda responded, shouting at Tony, "I want you out too, we are done, I'm getting a lawyer and we are getting divorced, get out of here, now!"

Tom carried in the last box from his car. "There, now all we have to do is unpack and decide what goes where."

"That's the best part," Amy said, standing next to Tom, clutching his arm, looking across the scattered boxes and garage sale furniture that was in their new living room. "Give me a couple of days," She said, "I'll have it looking like a doll house."

"A doll hose?" Tom asked, "how about just our house?"

"Deal," Amy said, looking up into Tom's eyes, and squeezing his arm.

Tom lit some candles and placed them around the room, he put them on tables and cardboard boxes that had not been unpacked yet, then he turned on some music, and opened a bottle of wine.

Amy walked out of the bedroom and saw what he had done, she cocked her head to the side and smiled at him, without saying a word, she slowly walked over to him and put her hands on his cheeks, pulling him towards her for a kiss.

"Is it any wonder why I love you Tom?" Amy said after she kissed him, "You are the sweetest man."

Tom smiled and kissed her back. Simply saying, "You make it easy."

Tom rummaged through some of the boxes in the kitchen until he found some glasses, they were not wine glasses, they hadn't bought any yet, but they would do.

Amy sat next to Tom on the floor, with their backs leaning against a wall, drinking their wine.

"Tomorrow we need to buy a bed, and pick up the sofa," Amy said, "when I bought it, they said they would hold it for us until the weekend, and tomorrow is Sunday already, besides, we need something softer to sit on."

"Yeah," Tom agreed, "the floor is going to be hard to sleep on, tonight will be okay, but I want a bed tomorrow night, it's a good thing the floor has carpet, or it would really be hard."

"Sure would," Amy agreed, "tomorrow, we will go look at beds."

Tom took the last sip of wine from his glass and looked at Amy.

"Want to go for a dip?" he asked.

"Where?" she asked.

"The ocean, the beach is only a couple of blocks away," Tom answered, standing up from sitting on the floor.

"Oooh, but it's dark out," Amy remarked, taking Toms hand and standing up too.

"I know," Tom said with a devilish smile, "no sun, usually means no other people."

Amy smiled back at Tom, and said, "Okay then, I'll grab some towels."

The moon hung low in the night sky, the small waves easily rolled up over their feet, leaving trails of sand and water as they receded.

Tom and Amy were the only ones on the beach at this time of night, it was isolated on three sides by cliffs, and the walk was littered with obstacles of boulders and felled trees.

Tom kicked off his sandals and pulled his t-shirt over his head, when he looked at Amy, she was already nude, all she had to do was slip out of the sundress she was wearing, and she hadn't bothered to put on any panties earlier in the evening.

Tom took Amy's hand in his and they ran out into the water together. They laughed and giggled like little children as they splashed one another.

Tom pulled Amy close to him and wrapped his arms around her, the salt water made their flesh slippery. He held her as she wrapped her legs around him; she seemed to float in the density of the salt water. He stopped moving and gazed into her eyes, the moonlight cast shadows on her face, her wet hair laid flat on her face, the water dripping from her nose and chin. He licked the drop of water off her chin, and then licked the salt water from under her chin and her neck. Amy leaned her head back and moaned lightly as he licked the salt water from her neck and kissed it, then gently nibbled her earlobes.

She pressed her breasts against him as she ran her fingers in his wet hair, pulling his head closer to her, loving the sensation of his warm tongue and lips on her neck.

He traced tiny kisses across her eyelids and down her nose to her mouth; she parted her lips and met him, kissing him deeply, passionately.

Tom walked towards the beach, still carrying Amy in his arms, her arms and legs still wrapped around him, still embraced in their kiss. They fell onto the wet sand; their kiss didn't break, while the waves were rolling up over their legs.

Linda put down the mop she was using and wiped the sweat from her face, she looked her mom and said, "Thanks mom, I really appreciate everything you and dad are doing for us."

"You're welcome my dear," her mom replied, reaching out and touching her on the arm, "You're our only child, and these may be our only grandchildren, we want to help you in any way we can."

"I know, and thanks," Linda said, beginning to tear up, "it's just hard, starting over like this, I know you and dad are there for me, but it's still going to be hard raising two little kids by myself."

"You just never mind," her mom replied, "you have a good job working for your father, and I will be happy to watch Amanda and Timmy when you are at work, and even at night if you need to get out once in awhile."

"Aw mom," Linda said as she began to cry, "I feel like such a failure, my marriage fell apart, maybe if I was a better . . . ."

Her mom put her finger on Linda's lips to stop her from talking.

"Shush now," her mom said, "you were a good wife, he was a horrible husband, now let's get this place of yours cleaned up so you can get your stuff moved in."

Bobby knocked on the apartment door, Linda cracked the door open an inch to see who it was, then asked, "Bobby? What are you doing here?"

"I left Janey," he replied, "When it got back to me she was sleeping with Tony, I left her. I'm sorry to hear about you two, I want you to know I feel awful."

"Thanks," Linda said, still not opening the door any further, "so what do you want?"

"I want to help," Bobby said, "I have a truck and a strong back and would be happy to help you move your stuff out of here into your new place, as far as I'm concerned, those two can rot in hell together."

"Well, I suppose," Linda said, "I could use some help, come on in, you can help my dad, he'll be here soon to help me move."

Linda pointed down the hallway to the bedroom where she wanted her dad and Bobby to carry the bed and set it up. Andrea and Timmy were sitting at the table in the kitchen while Linda's mom fixed them some lunch. They didn't completely understand what was going on, but seemed to like their new home. There was a swing set in the backyard for them to play on, they each had their own room that they would get to pick the paint colors for, and there was a TV, and food, so most of their immediate needs were met, at the moment at least.

Linda's mom took Andreas hand and her dad picked up Timmy, they had their little bags packed with pj's and some books, and a few small toys to sleep at grandma's house.

"We'll see you in the morning," her mom said as she opened the front door to leave.

"Thanks mom, thanks dad, for everything," Linda said as she kissed each one on the cheek. Then looked at Andrea and Timmy, "and you two behave yourselves, I'm going to unpack a little more tonight, then I'll pick you up after breakfast tomorrow, alright?"

"K mommy," Timmy answered.

"Ok mom, g'night," Andrea said, and then they all left.

Linda sat down on a chair and let out a big sigh.

"You gonna be okay?" Bobby asked. He was standing near the doorway and looking at Linda.

"Yeah, I think so," Linda replied, "I just feel exhausted all of a sudden."

"You haven't eaten all day, c'mon," Bobby said, "let me buy you something to eat, you need to eat."

"Thanks. But I'll fix something here," Linda resisted.

"Oh come on, I carried your fridge in," Bobby said, with a smile, "I know it's almost empty, promise, just something to eat, nothing else," he said, holding up his hand and covering his heart.

"Alright," Linda said, standing up and grabbing her purse, "let's go."

Linda closed and locked the door behind her and walked with Bobby to his truck. He opened the door for her and she suddenly felt strange. She couldn't remember the last time anybody held a door opened for her. She smiled shyly at Bobby as she got into his truck.

Tom hung up the phone on his desk and stared blankly ahead.

He didn't notice when Amy walked into his office. She stood silently, aware something was wrong. Never before did he not notice her entering the room.

"Tom?" she asked, "Tom, are you alright?"

Tom looked at her, almost as if he was looking through her, like she wasn't even there.

"Yeah," He replied, quietly, "well, no, that was my uncle Jim, my dad died this morning."

"Oh honey," Amy said, "I'm so sorry."

"I didn't know he was sick," Tom responded, "I knew he was not healthy, he hasn't taken care of himself since my mom died, but, I, I didn't think he would up and just die like this."

"What happened?" Amy asked as she walked over to Tom, she stood next to him and gently pulled his head to her breast, holding him, comforting him. "How did he die? What can I do for you?"

"Jim said he just didn't wake up, I guess he died in his sleep," Tom replied, "I have to talk to the commander about emergency leave, and go home and make funeral arrangements."

"I'm so sorry," Amy said again.

"I have to make some calls," Tom said to Amy, "I'll come find you later, I'll let you know more when I have more to tell you."

"Alright," Amy said as she kissed the top of his head and left his office.

Amy picked up the phone in her office, "hello, Juanita?"

"Hello?" Juanita asked when she answered the phone, "Is this Amy? How are you?"

"I'm fine thanks," Amy replied, "listen, is Mike around? Toms father died this morning and he has to go home and make arrangements for the funeral, and, well, I thought he could use a call from a friend right about now, he didn't say anything, but I know he's having a tough time with it."

"Aw, that's too bad," Juanita replied, "Mike will be home for lunch soon, I'll tell him then."

"Thank you so much," Amy said, "how is everything there? How are Doodles and little Danny? I bet they are getting big."

"They are doing fine," Juanita replied, "they are getting bigger every day, are you going home with Tom for the funeral?"

"I'm afraid not," Amy responded sadly, "He has to take emergency leave, and because we are not married or anything, I can't take emergency leave too. I have to use regular leave and on this short notice I won't be able to. I feel so awful, I wish I could, I want to be there for him."

"Oh sweetie," Juanita said, "that's too bad, I'm sure he will understand."

"I know," Amy replied, "but it doesn't make me feel any better, he has to go through this all by himself, it just breaks my heart."

"I'll talk to Mike," Juanita replied, "I'll tell him about Tom, don't you worry about it now, ok?"

"Ok, thanks again, bye," Amy said and hung up her phone.

Tom shut off the engine of the car. He turned to Amy in the passenger seat and said, "I'll be back next week, you have the flight numbers, right?"

"Yes Tom," Amy replied, "for the tenth time, I have the date, the time, the flight number, the phone number at your dads place, the number for the airlines to check for any changes, I'll be here to pick you up when you get back, I'm just so sorry I can't come with and be there for you, I really am."

"I know," Tom replied, "I'm sorry too, and I know you can't go, I've been in the Army long enough to know how it works, I understand, don't worry."

"Ok, I just feel bad for you," Amy said, clutching his hand.

"I'll be fine," Tom said, "really, I gotta go, see you next week," he said then kissed her quickly, grabbed his bags and disappeared into the airport.

Amy got out of the car, walked around it and got in behind the wheel and drove home in silence. She didn't understand why he was so cold, so distant; the kiss was almost mechanical, emotionless.

She knew he was hurting, she knew he was in a hurry to catch his plane, and she knew he had a lot on his mind; she just had a hard time wrapping her brain around the sudden change in him. "This is to be expected when someone looses a loved one, and I shouldn't take it personal, it's not personal." She told herself as she pulled away from the airport.

Chapter 7

TOM PULLED THE rental car into the driveway of his dad's house, now his house. He turned the engine off and sat there in the dark for several moments before he got out and went inside.

On the walls were old photographs, framed photos of Tom and his dad, one from his summer in little league baseball, another one of them, standing on the dock at the cabin, holding a stringer full of fish. There was one of Tom, in his graduation cap and gown with his parents standing at his side, big proud smiles on their faces. There was a large one over the fireplace of his parents; it was a portrait they had done many years ago, before his mom had died.

Tom looked around the house, his dad's coat was hanging on a hook by the backdoor, his coffee cup was still in the sink, a couple pair of pair of old, and well-worn shoes sat by the back door. His hat was still on the kitchen counter where he put it the last time he came home.

Tom was throwing empty cigarette wrappers and empty vodka bottles into the trash when he was startled by a knock on the door.

He turned on the outside light and opened the door.

"Hello Tom," Linda said, she was standing on the top step by the back door, looking uncertain of herself.

"Hello," Tom said and opened the door and gestured for her to enter, "how are you, what brings you here?"

"I'm so sorry, to hear about your father," Linda replied, "I was driving past, and saw the strange car in the driveway and was hoping it might be you."

"Thanks," Tom replied, "it's pretty overwhelming, I mean, it happened so suddenly, and now there's all this stuff to take care of, plus make all the funeral arrangements."

"I'm sorry Tom," Linda said again, "I really am, is there anything I can do?"

"I don't think so, but thanks," Tom replied, "want a beer?" he asked as he opened the fridge.

"Sure, why not?" Linda asked, "your dad left beer in the fridge? I thought he was a vodka man."

"No, I picked it up," Tom answered, "I figured the cupboards would be empty so I stopped and picked up some things."

"It's good to see you again," Linda said as she brought her beer to her lips, "It's too bad it's under these circumstances, but still good to see you."

"Yeah," Tom said, "you too, so how are the kids? How's married life?"

Linda paused a moment before answering, "Kids are fine, I dropped them off at my moms."

"That's nice," Tom said, "and married life?"

"We're getting divorced," Linda replied, "I have my own place now, the kids each have their own room, Andrea is doing well in school and Timmy, I was pregnant with him last time I saw you, he's in kindergarten now."

"Sorry to hear about the divorce thing," Tom replied.

"Don't be," Linda replied, "he was cheating on me, when he wasn't cheating on me, he was beating me."

"Ouch, I'm still sorry," Tom replied, "I never thought he deserved you in the first place, I don't think he ever treated you right, you never seemed truly happy."

"That's my Tom," Linda said smiling, "I never could hide anything from you."

"Listen, Linda," Tom said, "why don't you give me your number, I'll call you tomorrow, right now, well, I'm just beat and need some sleep, I haven't slept well the past two nights."

Linda stood up to leave and looked at Tom, she was biting her bottom lip, hesitating, then she finally said, "my mom's keeping the kids overnight, if it's not too forward of me, I could stay here awhile, I could, I could keep you company tonight, it wouldn't be a problem."

Tom smiled at Linda then put his hands on her shoulders and pulled her towards him, he smelled her hair and kissed the top of her head, "you don't know how long I've wanted to hear those words," he said, "but not tonight, I'm just not in a good place and I wouldn't be good company."

"But I don't expect anything from you Tom," Linda said, looking up into his eyes, seeing the sadness in them, "I can just be here for you."

"Please don't be hurt," Tom said, "it's just bad timing."

"Ok, I understand," she said as she took a step back away from him to leave.

"Thanks Linda," he replied, "I really appreciate the offer, I really do."

"Ok," she said as she scribbled down her number on a slip of paper, "call me tomorrow then, I love you Tom."

Tom smiled, "I'll call you tomorrow," he shut the door behind her and leaned his head against the door.

Tom stood in front of the bathroom mirror adjusting his tie. There was a knock on the door. Surprised, he went to open it, he wasn't expecting anybody. He opened the door and stood in disbelief, staring out the door.

"Well? Tommy my boy, aren't you going to invite me in?" Smitty asked, standing in the doorway.

"Oh, yeah, sorry," Tom said, regaining his composure, "come on in, man it's good to see you."

Smitty walked in and grabbed Tom in a big hug, "I heard about your dad, I'm really sorry."

"How did you know? How did you find me?" Tom asked.

"Amy called Juanita a couple days ago," Smitty said, "and I had to come, I just had to, you're like my little brother man."

"Well I appreciate it," Tom said, "I really do, this has been a rough couple of days. So how did you fine me?"

"Small town, everybody knows everybody," Smitty said, "I got here and just started asking around, I got the information on the funeral service from Amy, and just needed to find where you were staying."

"Know what my friend?" Tom said.

"What?" Smitty asked.

"Tonight, tonight you and me are gonna tie one on," Tom said, "we are going to get drunk tonight for old times."

Smitty let out a big belly laugh, "alright, tonight, you my friend and I are gonna commence to get drunk, plastered, shitfaced, commode huggin' drunk."

Tom gave a small sad smile, "yeah."

"But first," Smitty said, "you point the way, and I'll drive you to the church for the service, this isn't going to be easy."

Linda walked up to Tom; he was standing next to the casket, tears rolling down his cheeks. She put her arm around his waist and leaned her head on his shoulder. She took his hand as he turned to walk away and sit down for the service.

"Smitty, this is Linda," Tom said, making the introductions. "Linda, this is my good friend Mike, we call him Smitty," then Tom added, "Linda and I go way back, we sort of have a history of sorts," Tom said.

"Of sorts?" Smitty asked with a smile on his face.

"Long story for another time," Tom said then turned to walk inside for the service.

Tom woke up with a horrible hang over; he buried his head under the pillow in a futile attempt to ease the throbbing pain in his head. Smitty was already up and in the kitchen cooking breakfast. Even the smell seemed to make Tom feel even more nauseous. Tom endured the pain long enough to shout out to Smitty, begging, "Can you keep it down out there, pleeeeease?"

Smitty tapped the frying pan twice with the spatula, making an obnoxious sound and shouted back to Tom, "C'mon now, get your ass up, I thought you were tough, I thought you were a soldier, what the hell are you doing nursing a hangover?"

"Please, just kill me," Tom said as he walked around the corner into the kitchen.

"Sit down," Smitty said, "yours is almost done."

"Gee thanks," Tom said, sarcastically, "food, greasy food, just what I need, I'm gonna puke."

Smitty laughed, then said, "Know what my friend?"

"What?" Tom asked, "are you going to put me out of my misery?"

"No, bigger than that," Smitty began, "I'm getting out, I'm retiring from the Army."

"Wait a minute," Tom said, "am I still drunk? Or did I just hear you say that you are retiring? What the hell are you gonna do?"

"I have some things in the works," Smitty said, "I still have about six more months before I can retire, and I plan on firming things up by then."

"You sound so secretive," Tom said, laughing, even thought it hurt his head to do so, "firming things up, geeze, come on man, let me in, what are your plans?"

"Don't laugh, you gotta promise you won't laugh," Smitty insisted.

"Ok, fine, I won't laugh," Tom promised, "what?"

"A bed and breakfast," Smitty replied, "seriously, we found an old Victorian house, I can do all the handyman stuff and Juanita can do the cooking, we will hire some women to clean the rooms and stuff, what do you think?"

"Hey," Tom replied, "I think it's worth a shot, beats punching a time clock for someone, or staying in the Army and risk getting shot at, that's never a good thing."

"No, getting shot at is never a good thing," Smitty agreed.

Tom was packing his bags to fly back home, the funeral was over, he had gone though all his dad's personal effects and sorted them out. He had cleaned the house and taken all the things of his dads he didn't want to a charity drop off. He had been away from his Army home and away from Amy for almost a week now and was ready to go back.

Linda stood in the kitchen and looked Tom in the eyes, "I hate this," she said.

"What?" Tom asked.

"You coming into my life like this," Linda said "I tell you I love you, then you go away, I pick up the pieces and get on with my life and you swoop in and it all turns upside down again."

"I'm sorry," Tom said, shrugging his shoulders, "how am I suppose to know? How am I suppose to know if you are or are not married, if you are or are not pregnant, what's going on in your life now?"

"I'm seeing Bobby," Linda replied, "we started seeing each other a couple months ago, we are taking it slow, but I wasn't ready for you to drop in like this, damn you Tom."

Tom stood there in silence, dumbfounded, not knowing what to say. Linda wrapped her arms around him and held him tight, "I love you so much Tom, I always have, I never stopped loving you, but I can't live my life alone if you're not here in my life."

"I'm sorry Linda," Tom replied, holding her head in his hands, he could feel her trembling against him, "I really am sorry."

Amy stood at the barricade, waiting for Tom to walk off the ramp after exiting the airplane. She saw him, he was among all the other passengers walking towards her and her heart began to flutter. She started bouncing on her toes in excitement, she was so glad to see him. She could see him smile at her as their eyes met, when Tom got to her she jumped into his arms and held on tight.

"God I missed you Tom," Amy said into his ear as he held her.

"I missed you too," Tom replied, "It's good to be back."

Amy let go of Tom finally and dropped to her feet. Clutching his arm, she looked up at his face, "so how was it?"

"It was fine," Tom responded, "I'm glad it's over, I mean, I'm going to miss my dad, but I'm glad this part is done, it was hard, did you know Smitty flew up for the funeral?"

"Did he?" Amy asked, "I told Juanita about your dad, and to tell Smitty, I hoped he would call you, I guess I didn't expect him to actually go."

"Yeah, he came, he surprised the shit out of me," Tom said, "I was getting dressed for the funeral and he just knocked on the door, just like that, out of the blue, it was great, we had some nice talks, he lost his dad a few years ago too, they weren't close, but he knew what I was going through."

"That was nice of him," Amy said, as she opened the trunk of the car to put Toms luggage in.

"Yeah," Tom replied, "he was a lot of help too, he helped me go through most of dads stuff and sort it out, did Juanita tell you about the Bed and Breakfast?"

"No, she didn't," Amy replied, "what bed and breakfast?"

Tom opened the car door for Amy to get into and then walked around and got in behind the wheel.

"Smitty is going to retire in a couple of months," Tom explained, "they are going to buy this old place they found, and turn it into a Bed and Breakfast."

"Good for them," Amy said, then her tone changed and she asked, "Tom?"

"Yes?" Tom replied.

"Have you given any thought to us?" Amy asked, "To what you want to do when you retire? I know it's still a few years off, but I was thinking about it a lot while you were gone. I don't want to be apart like this again, I hated it."

"What are you talking about Amy?" Tom looked at her and asked, "You're not making any sense."

"I don't want to be apart from you anymore Tom," Amy said, looking deep into his eyes, "I want to spend my life with you, now, and after we retire, I don't just want to be in your life when we are on the same base, and then drift apart when one of us gets transferred, I don't want that anymore."

"Oh," Tom replied, turning his eyes back to the road, and putting his arm around Amy, "I've been thinking about that too a little, can we talk about it later? Huh? I'm just not ready for that today."

"Sure, we can talk about it later," Amy said as she leaned against Tom for the rest of the ride home from the airport.

Linda sat down on the sofa between Andrea and Timmy, she took each one of their hands in hers and said, "I know that Bobby has been around a lot lately, and he really likes both of you two, and I think you like him too, am I right?"

"Yeah, I like him, he's nice, he gives me piggy back rides," Timmy replied.

"I like him too Mommy, he doesn't hit you like daddy did," Andrea replied.

Linda began to cry when she heard Andreas response, she had tried to shield the kids from the abuse and violence she endured in the past, but was suddenly aware that her efforts had failed, that they still heard the shouting, they still heard the crying and slapping sounds coming from the other room, and even on a few occasions had witnessed it.

"Well, I'm glad, I'm really glad," Linda began, "because I'm thinking about some things, and he asked me, and you two, to move in with him. He owns his own house, he has a big yard for you to play in, and you will still have your own rooms, what do you guys think?"

"Ok," Andrea said simply.

"Me too, I like his house," Timmy responded.

Linda smiled and pulled both of them closer to her, "Okay then," she said, "I'll tell him we talked about it, and we all agreed that we want to make the move."

Bobby pointed to the wrench on the ground, "ok Timmy, can you hand me that wrench by the box please?"

Timmy looked around by his feet and near the empty cardboard box, then picked up the wrench, "this one?" he asked.

"Yep," Bobby said, "that's the one, just this one last bolt and I'm done."

"Yeah!" Timmy said, jumping up and down in excitement, "can you push me then? I want to swing and go real high."

Bobby laughed, "Not so fast Timmy, we need to clean up all this mess first before you can play on the swings."

"Ok," Timmy said and started picking up plastic wrappers and the sheets of paper that the directions for the swing set were on.

"That's a good boy," Bobby said as he began picking up his tools, "if you get those foam pieces, I'll finish getting my tools and the big stuff and then I can push you, okay?"

"Ok, I'll race ya," Timmy said as he scrambled to pick up all the small foam pieces as fast as his little hands could go.

Bobby came out of the garage and wiped his hands on his jeans, Timmy was already on one of the swings, pumping his legs and hardly moving.

"Are ya ready?" Bobby asked.

"Yeah, push me," Timmy replied excitedly.

"Ok, hang on tight!" Bobby said as he pulled Timmy backwards and then let him go, Timmy squealed with delight as he swung forward and then back. Each time he was at the top of the back swing, Bobby would give him a little push, and forward he would go, squealing and laughing at the top of his lungs.

"Pump your legs, pump your legs!" Bobby instructed.

Timmy folded his legs back under him when he went backwards and stuck them straight out in front of him when he went forwards.

"Like this?" he asked Bobby.

"That's right, now you got it, that's the way!" Bobby encouraged.

Linda was watching from inside the house, she was standing at the kitchen window washing some dishes and smiled, she was pleased that Bobby and Timmy were having so much fun together. It was good for both of them. Bobby didn't have any kids of his own, and Timmy's dad had disappeared from his life when he was still in diapers.

Tom closed the kitchen door behind him and sat down on the chair to take off his running shoes. Sweat was dripping from his face and his shirt was soaked. Amy was sitting at the desk in the den doing some paperwork.

"How was your run honey?" she asked from down the hallway.

"It was good," Tom responded, "I feel out of shape and I don't know if I'm gonna pass the test next week."

"That's why I got up early and ran," Amy replied, rubbing it in a little, "you like to sleep in on Saturdays, but if I don't run seven days a week, rain or shine, I can't fit into my favorite clothes, and you don't want that do you?"

"You always look good in whatever you wear," Tom said as he stood up and walked into the bathroom to take a shower.

Tom had his eyes closed as he shampooed his hair; he was startled when he felt Amy's hand touch him.

"Mind if I join you?" She asked with a smile as she stepped in and closed the shower door behind her

"No, not at all," Tom said with a pleased smile on his face.

Amy was standing behind Tom, she picked up the bar of soap and reached around in front of him and began rubbing it on his chest, while she lathered up the hair on his chest, she pressed herself against him, pressing her breasts against his back. She laid her head on his back, the side of her face resting on him, the water flowing off his head, down over her, and onto the floor. She caressed him with one hand, feeling his muscular arm, the water and soap made it slippery, her other hand holding the bar of soap inched it's way down his stomach, rubbing it back and forth of the shower, she moved her hand down farther and found he was already hard. Tom turned around and faced her, he took the bar of soap and rubbed it across her breasts, circling them, cupping one at a time and touching the nipple with the bar of soap. Amy's eyes were closed but she had a smile on her face, she was still holding onto him, gently stroking him back and forth, the soapy lather was lubricating her hand. Tom moved the bar of soap down between her breasts, and moved back and forth and in a circle on her stomach. She reached one hand up and put it behind his neck, pulling him to her for a kiss. Her other hand slowly stroked him.

Tom dropped the bar of soap, he reached down and cupped her butt with his hands, gently squeezing and pulling her towards him as he pressed against her. He met her mouth, their parted lips were wet, soft, warm, he probed her mouth with his tongue; she circled his tongue with hers. Amy lifted one leg up and hooked it behind Toms leg, grinding herself against him, she could feel his hardness pressing against her, she wanted him, she wanted him inside her, she wanted to feel him fully, totally within her.

Amy broke the kiss and turned around and put her hands flat on the shower wall, the water was beating down on her back, and running down her legs, Tom stood behind her, placing one hand on the wall locking his fingers with hers, his other hand guiding himself into her. Amy let out a gasp as he entered her, and flung her head back, her wet hair flying in the air as she pushed back to meet him.

Linda lit the candles on the table and turned out the light a moment before Bobby walked in the door.

"How was work today?" She asked.

"Fine, how was your day at work?" Bobby asked, then realized it was dark, and quiet in the house, "where are the kids?"

"They are at my moms house," Linda said, as she walked over to Bobby and helped him take his coat off, "I thought a quiet night with just the two of us would be nice."

"It sure looks nice to me," He said as he leaned in to kiss her, "So? How was your day?" he asked again.

"Good, it was good," Linda replied, with a smile, "I got a promotion at work and, and, I have some other good news too."

"Really?" Bobby replied, "congratulations on the promotion, you've worked hard for your dad, I'm happy for you, what's the other news?"

Linda reached into the drawer under the kitchen counter and pulled out a small box and handed it to Bobby.

"What's this?" he asked.

"Open it," she said, with a nervous smile on her face.

Bobby opened the box and pulled out a tiny pair of shoes, the smallest pair he had ever held.

"Ok," He said, "tiny shoes, what does this mean?"

"That means you're gonna be a daddy," Linda answered, standing behind the chair resting both hands in front of her on the back of the chair.

"A what?" he replied, with uncertainty, "are you serious? Um, that's wonderful."

"You don't sound happy," Linda said, her heart sinking.

"It's a surprise," Bobby said, "I wasn't expecting to hear that when you said you had other news, it's good, don't get me wrong, I guess I'm just in shock, that's all."

"Alright," Linda said, walking into the kitchen to bring out dinner.

"Aw, Linda," Bobby said as he walked up behind her and put his hands on her shoulders, "don't be that way, I'm happy, you just caught me by surprise that's all."

"Are you sure?" she asked as she turned to face him.

"Yes, I'm sure," Bobby said, "I'm positive."

Linda wrapped her arms around Bobby and leaned her face against his chest, "I hope so," she said quietly.

Smitty picked up the phone, "hello?" he asked.

"Smitty? It's Tom," Tom said, "how are ya you old fart? How's the B&B?"

"Tommy boy," Smitty replied with a laugh, "how the hell are you?"

"I'm good, doing good," Tom replied.

"Well that's great," Smitty replied, "retirement is great, the B&B couldn't be better, it's a lot of work, but Juanita and I both love it, plus it pays a hell of a lot more than the Army did."

"Good, good for you guys, that's great," Tom went on, "hey, I have some news for you."

"Shoot," said Smitty, "tell me what it is."

"Amy and I are getting married," Tom said in a boastful tone.

"You are huh?" Smitty responded with a laugh, "what happened? Did you finally get tired of living in sin? Or did she twist your arm?"

"Nothing like that," Tom replied, "we've been living together for almost two years now and we just decided to get married."

"Sure she's not pregnant now aren't ya?" Smitty asked, needling Tom.

"Ya know Smitty," Tom responded, "you can be a real ass sometimes, ya know that?"

"Oh come on now," Smitty replied, "I love both of you guys and I couldn't be happier for the both of you, so tell me, when is the big day?"

"Not sure exactly," Tom said, "with my parents gone, and her parents divorced when she was little, she really doesn't have much of a family you know, we figured maybe just standing up in front of a justice of the peace or something like that."

"I see," said Smitty, "then what? A honeymoon somewhere? Do you guys have a date set? Or did I already ask that?"

Tom laughed, "No, no date set yet, for a JP I don't think we need big plans, just a license and then get on his calendar."

"Tell ya what," Smitty said, "I'll talk to Juanita when she gets back from the store, but I'm sure it'll be okay. Why don't you two come here? Our gift will be a stay at our B&B, it can be your honeymoon, you can stay a week if you want, it would be our pleasure."

"Thanks my friend," Tom replied, "I wasn't expecting this, I just wanted to share our news."

"Well," Smitty said, "you shared, and now we're sharing, you just let us know when, alright?"

"Alright, hey," Tom added, "I, we really appreciate this, you didn't have to do this you know."

"I know, but I insist," Smitty argued, "plus, I know a JP, he plays poker with me, if you want, I'll talk to him for you, and you guys can have the whole thing here, ceremony, celebration, and honeymoon, it'll be great, I can't wait to tell Juanita when she gets home."

Again, Tom laughed. "OK, I have to go now, I need to run it by Amy, I'll let you know soon."

"Alright," Smitty said, "keep me posted, bye."

"Bye," Tom said and hung up the phone.

Juanita taped up the last piece of decorations on the front of the B&B. Smitty paced back and forth across the front porch like a nervous father waiting for his wife to give birth.

Tom asked Amy to look at the map. "I know we're close," He said to Amy as he looked across her arm at the map on her lap, "we just crossed the main street again, it has to be around here somewhere, what's the address again?"

"There it is!" Amy said, pointing out the car window to a charming old Victorian house, with festive decorations and streamers on the corners of the front porch, and a WELCOME AMY AND TOM banner strung across the front porch between two carved pillars, "That has to be it."

Tom pulled into the driveway of the B&B, before he put the car in park and shut the engine off Smitty and Juanita came running out to great them.

"Tommy, Amy!" Juanita shouted cheerfully as she approached the car with her arms outstretched.

Amy got out first and was greeted by an emotional hug from Juanita.

Smitty placed his hand on the door handle to open the door for Tom, "Tommy my boy," He said as Tom stepped out of the car and into a bear hug from Smitty.

Two children were standing on the porch, watching the excitement their parents were making over these strangers. Smitty looked at the two and waved at them, "Hey you guys, come say hello to your uncle Tommy and Amy."

Tom looked at the taller of the two, a girl that looked to be in her early teens and had a striking resemblance to her mother, He put his hand on top of her head and looked at her face, "Is this Doodles?" Tom asked, "Do you remember me Doodles?"

"My name is not Doodles," she replied, "It's Amanda."

Tom looked at Smitty and smiled, "Ookaay, Amanda, you sure have grown," He said, then looked at the boy, a few years younger then Amanda and held out his hand, "and you must be Danny."

"You're not my real uncle," Danny said as he shook Tom's hand.

Tom laughed, "No Danny, you're right, I'm not your real uncle, I'm just a good friend of your parents, and your sister used to call me uncle Tommy when she was little, or should I say younger?" he said smiling and looking at Amanda.

"C'mon let's get you folks settled in," Smitty said as he patted his hand on the trunk, "let me get your stuff for you."

"I'm sooo excited," Juanita said as she put her arm around Amy and began walking towards the house, "It's so good to see you two, and this is going to be our first big celebration in our new place."

"Not too big I hope," Amy replied, "I prefer something small and intimate, maybe with just you guys to standing up for us, and that's about it."

"Gotcha," Smitty said as he lifted the luggage out of the trunk of the car, "Nothing big and fancy, just a small quaint ceremony."

Tom and Amy stood side by side in a corner of the backyard. Smitty and Juanita had put up a dozen white posts, forming two lines. On the posts were strung vines with flowers creating an aisle for the bride and groom to walk down. Smitty had built a podium for the justice of the peace to preside over the ceremony from, and Juanita and the kids had set up a dozen folding chairs, also with flowered vines strung along them for the guests to sit on. The guests consisted of mainly other visitors at the Bed and Breakfast and a few close friends of Smitty and Juanita from town.

The justice of the peace stood at the podium in front of Tom and Amy while Smitty and Juanita stood by them as their witnesses.

When Tom and Amy read their vows to each other, vows that they had wrote themselves, the people in small crowd that watched could be heard sniffing as they cried. Even Amanda had tears in her eyes. Danny didn't, but nobody was surprised, as a young boy, he was more interested in the food afterwards and not the emotional part of the ceremony itself.

Smitty reached into the cooler for a couple more beers. Opening one he handed it to Tom, and asked. "So, how much longer until you retire? Have any plans yet?"

Tom looked over towards the other side of the room where Amy and Juanita, Amanda and a couple others were sitting and talking.

"I have five more years before I have my twenty, and Amy has another six months after that," Tom replied, "but I don't know what were going to do yet, we talked about going back and living in the house my dad left me, spending our summers at the lake and so on."

"What about work?" Smitty asked, "Army retirement checks are good, but you will be too young to not do anything else for the rest of your life. Any thought on that?"

"Oh, well, some, we are both certified electronics tech's thanks to the Army, maybe we will open an electronics shop, not sure yet. Hey how does this sound, T&A Electronics?" Tom replied, laughing at his idea, "you know, for Tom and Amy."

"I like it!" Smitty replied with a laugh, "can I design your logo?"

"No way," Tom replied, taking a sip of his beer, "We need to run a clean shop, no porn, for Christ sake, we can't have your ideas on display."

Smitty laughed and clinked his beer against Tom's beer in agreement, "I suppose not, but I do like the name, it's catchy."

"I kinda thought so," Tom responded.

"Wanna know something else?" Smitty asked.

"What?" Tom asked.

"You two," Smitty said, "I saw this coming years ago, part of me got nervous when school ended and you two went separate ways. Juanita told me you two would find your way back together, and she was right."

"Ya did huh?" Tom asked, smiling.

"Yep, sure did." Smitty replied, sipping his beer, "sure did."

Tom pulled the car onto the freeway and headed for home. Amy looked at Tom and yawned, then said, "I can't believe we're married, after all this time, we finally got married."

"I know," Tom smiled back at her and reached over and put his arm around her shoulders, "feels good don't it?"

"Yeah, it does," Amy replied, yawning again, "I'm sleepy."

"Here," Tom said and guided her head to his lap, "lie down and get some sleep, we have a long drive."

"Ok," Amy said as she laid her head on Toms lap and closed her eyes.

Chapter 8

BOBBY QUIETLY WALKED in the door of the hospital room, he saw Linda lying on the bed, she was asleep, and there were tubes and hoses and wires everywhere. He walked over and gently picked up her hand and held it. He wiped the tears from his eyes with the back of his other hand. He stood there for a few minutes before pulling a chair closer to her bed and sitting down.

Linda woke up and saw Bobby sitting in the chair, pulled up against her bed with his head lying on her bed, he was sleeping. She wondered how long he had been there.

She reached her hand to him, touching his hair she woke him up.

"I'm so sorry," Bobby said to Linda when he woke up and saw her looking at him.

"I lost my baby," she said and began to cry, a deep soulful cry filled with sadness and emptiness.

Bobby stood up from the chair then leaned down and hugged her.

"I know, I'm so sorry, I'm so sorry," He said, stroking her hair. "Just rest, the doctor said you will be fine, you lost a lot of blood, but we got you here in time."

Linda didn't say anything for a long time; she just lay in Bobby's arms and cried. He held her, stroking her hair, feeling absolutely helpless, not knowing what else to do.

"The kids are with your mom," Bobby said, "she said they will be up later to see you."

"No," Linda said, between sobs, "I don't want anyone to come, I don't want any visitors."

"Aw honey," Bobby replied, "but she's your mom, and Andrea, and Timmy, they want to see you, you're their mom, they're all concerned about you."

"Maybe after while," Linda said, "just not yet."

"Ok," Bobby said, whispering quietly into her ear and holding her, "anything you want, whatever you say."

Tom stepped out onto the front porch, Amy looked up at him from the porch swing she was slowly swinging in.

"Hi," he said as he walked to her and gave her a kiss.

"Hey," Amy replied, kissing him back, "so? What did you find out?"

"My extension request was approved," Tom replied, "I won't be transferring from here, I will retire from this base, next move is when I'm out, or after you retire actually."

"Great," Amy replied, patting the seat next to her, indicating she wanted Tom to sit down by her, "It will be nice to retire and start a normal life, I like the idea of living in your dads, I'm sorry, in your house and starting a small business in town, and going to your cabin in the summer, that sounds like a nice post Army life."

Tom put his arm around Amy and pulled her closer, leaning over he kissed her ear, "I like that idea too," he said, "I'm ready to be a civilian again, I had no idea when I first joined, that I'd make a career out of it."

Amy laughed and looked up at Tom, "you didn't? To tell the truth, neither did I, I guess the first time I re-upped, I was hoping to come stateside and see you again, now look at me."

"Really?" Tom asked.

"Really," Amy replied, "It wasn't a career goal, it was motivated by wanting to see you, can you believe that?"

"Huh," Tom replied, "I didn't know that."

"Well, it's the truth," Amy said, placing her hand on Tom's leg and leaning her head on his shoulder.

Bobby and Timmy were in the garage building a birdhouse to put up in the back yard. Bobby looked out the window over the workbench and saw Linda; she was sitting on a chair, staring out at the yard. Bobby looked at Timmy and said, "Ok, you just finish the roof on this, I'm going to go talk to your mother for a few minutes, ok?"

"Sure, I got it," Timmy replied and picked up the hammer.

Bobby wiped his hands on a rag and went over to sit with Linda.

"How are you doing today?" He asked.

"I'm okay," she said, without looking at him.

"It's good to see you up and around," Bobby acknowledged, "you haven't been outside the house in weeks."

"Oh, doesn't seem that long," Linda replied quietly.

"Yeah," Bobby said, taking her hand, "it has been almost a month since," and he paused for a moment, "we have to move on, we have to push ahead honey, life itself didn't end, we are all still here, you, me, Andrea, Timmy, were all still here and it's not easy for any of us."

Linda turned her head at Bobby and glared at him, "what do you know about not being easy? You weren't the one carrying the baby; you weren't the one that lost a child, what do you know? Huh? What do you know about it?"

Bobby looked down at the ground, "sorry honey, I'm sorry, I just hate to see you like this."

Linda looked back out over the yard, and stared off into space again.

Bobby looked up when he heard the tap on the kitchen window; Andrea was waving for him to come inside.

"What's up?" Bobby asked Andrea when he went inside the house.

"Mom made an appointment," she said.

"An appointment for what?" Bobby asked.

"I heard her on the phone yesterday, then I looked on her calendar," Andrea explained, "some doctor, some kind of therapist I overheard, but I don't know exactly."

"Ok, thanks for telling me," Bobby replied, "might be to help with, well, with her losing the baby."

"I hope so," Andrea replied, "she's just so sad, she needs something, she needs someone to help her through this."

"I agree," Bobby replied, "thanks for telling me, we can't say anything though, if she didn't tell us, it's private, and she's not ready to share it."

Andrea nodded "ok," at Bobby as he turned and went back outside.

Andrea heard the knock on the front door and went to open it.

"Dad?" she gasped when she saw Tony standing at the front door in the pouring rain with a bouquet of flowers in his hand, "What are you doing here?"

"I heard the bad news about your mom and her baby and thought I would stop by," Tony said, "how are you? How's my little girl?"

"I'm fine," Andrea responded, obviously troubled by the sudden appearance of her father, "You haven't bothered to contact me or Timmy in years, now all of a sudden out of the blue you stop by unannounced?"

"I'm sorry about that darling," he said "I know I haven't been the best dad . . ." Andrea cut him off in mid sentence, "you haven't been the best dad? Are you kidding me? You haven't been a dad at all! You should just go, mom won't be happy you're here."

"How's Timmy?" Tony asked, "Is he around?"

"He's not here, but he's just fine," Andrea said angrily, "he doesn't even know who you are, last time you saw him, he was maybe, six months old, you have a lot of nerve coming here like this."

"Well, can you give these to your mother?" Tony asked as he handed the flowers to Andrea, "and tell her I'm real sorry about the baby thing."

"Yeah, right," Andrea said sarcastically, taking the flowers from Tony.

"So how are things here at Bobby's house?" Tony asked, "They haven't gotten married yet, I wonder why?"

"Things are fine here, just fine," Andrea insisted, "and it's none of your business if they are married or not."

"Well it is," Tony argued, "You and Timmy are my children, and I don't like this arrangement, a lawyer friend of mine says I have a good chance of getting you back, especially if this is the household you guys are being raised in, I don't like it, I don't like it at all."

"Why are you saying this? Why are you doing this dad? Why?" Andrea asked as she began to cry.

"I'm sorry darling," Tony said, "I didn't mean to make you cry, I thought you would be happy to come live with me."

"You walk out of our lives, you don't have anything to do with us, and then you just waltz in here and expect us to want to live with you?" Andrea said tearfully, "I don't think so, why don't you just go, just go."

Andrea closed and locked the door behind her as Tony left, and then leaning against the door, she slid to the floor, cradling the flowers in her arms, crying.

Linda came out of the bedroom and saw Andrea, sitting on the floor, leaning against the door crying.

"Honey, what's wrong?" she asked.

"Daddy stopped by and brought these for you," Andrea said, "he said he was sorry for the baby."

"He what?" Linda asked angrily, "Why on earth did he do that for?"

"I guess he felt bad," Andrea said, still crying.

"But that can't be why you're crying like this," Linda replied, "What else did he say? He didn't just pop in here out of the blue like this after all these years, with flowers, say he was sorry and leave, and cause you to start crying like this, I know better."

"Nothing mom, really," Andrea insisted, "He didn't say anything."

"I'm your mother, don't lie to me," Linda said again, more sternly this time.

"He asked if you were married to Bobby yet, he said he didn't like this arrangement, he said a lawyer he knows said that he can get us back, he will get it so that we live with him, mom, Timmy doesn't even know him, can he really do that?"

"No honey," Linda said as she sat down on the floor next to Andrea and held her, "I'm sorry he upset you like that, he's just talking, I don't know what his problem is, but nothing is going to happen, you two are going to stay right here, right here with me, I promise."

Janey pushed her grocery cart around the corner of the aisle and bumped into Linda. "Oh, excuse me," Janey said, "How are you Linda? I haven't seen you around much."

"Hello Janey," Linda responded coolly, "I'm fine, I've been keeping to myself lately."

"Listen, I'm really sorry to hear about your baby," Janey said, carefully touching Linda's arm, "I really am."

"Thanks," Linda said, slowly pulling away from Janey.

"I miss you," Janey said, "you were my best friend, and I miss you, I know what I did was wrong, and I can't go back and un do it, but I would if I could."

"Well," Linda said as she began to push her cart away from Janey, "you can't can you?"

"Please Linda, please, just give me a minute," Janey pleaded, "I was wrong, I did a bad thing, but that was years ago, can't you forgive me?"

"Did you know Tony came to my house the other night?" Linda asked, "he upset Andrea terribly, after all these years, he said he was going to fight for custody, after all this time, I can't believe it."

"No, I had no idea," Janey replied, "I haven't seen Tony in several years, after that day when you walked in and . . . ," Janey paused a moment, "well we stopped seeing each other shortly after that, he started beating me, and I wasn't going to stick around for any of that crap."

"Well," Linda said, "what's done is done, I really need to get going, good bye." And she turned around and walked away from Janey, pushing her grocery cart.

Tom lie down on the bed next to Amy, she was lying there reading a book, comfortable in her panties and one of his old shirts. He started stroking her legs, feeling her soft skin as he asked her, "what would you think of taking leave and going home for a few weeks? Maybe spend some time at the cabin, maybe look into different properties for our business when we retire, and maybe put a coat of paint on the house?"

"Wow," Amy said, laughing, "sounds like you have been thinking about this a little haven't you?"

"Yeah, I have," Tom replied, kissing her on the stomach, and then looking up and into her eyes, "what do you think?"

"Well, to tell you the truth, I've been thinking about taking some leave and going away myself," Amy responded, "the cabin sounds too hard to resist, and we do need to start thinking about and looking at properties, before we know it, a year will be gone and you will be retired, although, I still have another year to go, there's no reason why you can't get started, instead of working part time here for a year. But I'm not crazy about painting the house yet, at least not until we move back and know what colors we want."

"Well don't you have an answer for everything." Tom said as he moved his hands to her sides and began to tickle her.

"Stop that!" Amy said, giggling, "stop that right now, or you'll be sorry."

"Or I'll be sorry?" Tom said, laughing, "Ooooooo, I'm so afraid."

"I mean it," Amy said, still giggling, "please stop."

"Oh, alright," Tom said as he moved up along side her, and ran his hand through her hair, "so, what do you think about my idea?"

"I think it's a good idea," Amy agreed, "when were you thinking?"

"Um, how about next month?" Tom asked, "I thought I would put in my paperwork tomorrow, for two weeks leave next month, can you do put in for yours too?"

"Sure," Amy replied, "I'll put in my request first thing in the morning," then with a deep breathy voice, she asked, "Now, where were you?"

"Right here," Tom said, as he moved back down and began kissing her on the stomach. Tracing his tongue down to the waistband of her panties, he slipped his fingers inside her panties and gently pulled them down and threw them on the floor.

Bobby got into in the passenger side of his truck and buckled his seat belt. He pointed to the street lamp in the middle of the parking lot, "Now, whatever you do, don't hit that light."

"Ok, I won't," Andrea said, nervously, then looked at Bobby and asked, "What do I do first?"

"First thing you do is buckle up your seatbelt," Bobby instructed, "then adjust your mirrors so you can see behind you, all of them."

"When do I drive?" she asked, excitedly, "when do I start the motor?"

"Hold on a second," Bobby replied, "first things first, you need to be able to see behind you, you have to see cars, trucks, children on bicycles, so adjust your mirrors first."

Andrea made small adjustments to the three rear view mirrors on Bobby's truck, then looked at him, "ok, now what?"

"Ok, Now put your foot on the brake, that's the big one in the middle," he said pointing to the brake pedal.

"Like this?" she asked as she pressed her foot down on the brake pedal.

"Yes, just like that," Bobby replied, "now, turn the key in the ignition and let go as soon as it starts."

Andrea turned the key and the engine came to life, the loud pipes from the dual exhaust startled her.

"Ok, now what?" she asked.

"Ok, now, keep your foot on the brake," Bobby instructed, "and move the shifter from the P which is park, to D which is drive, and don't let your foot off the brake yet."

"Ok move the shifter from P to D," Andrea said to herself, repeating what Bobby had just told her to do.

"That's good," Bobby said, "now take your foot off the brake, and slowly, very gently, like you want to roll an egg with your foot without breaking it, put your foot on the gas pedal and press down."

Andrea did as she was told and the truck began to move forward.

"Good," Bobby said, "Now, put your foot back on the brake."

The tires screeched, and they both suddenly shot forward when she put her foot full force on the brakes. "My mistake," Bobby acknowledged, "power brakes, all you need to do, is touch them, not step hard on them, but I think you got the idea just then."

"Yeah, I think so," Andrea replied, "that scared me."

"Startled me too," Bobby admitted, "now, again, just like before, foot on the brake, shifted into gear, move your foot from the brake to the gas pedal and slowly give it gas."

Andrea spent the next half hour starting, stopping, turning, and backing up the truck, all without hitting the street light in the middle of the parking lot.

"Ok, that's good, that's enough for your first lesson," Bobby said as he unbuckled his seat belt and walked around to the drivers door, "maybe tomorrow after work I can give you lesson number two."

"Great!" Andrea said, as she ran around and hopped into the passenger side, "I can't wait to drive again, it's really fun."

"Whoa!" Bobby responded seriously, "it may be fun, but driving is a huge responsibility, cars can be very dangerous, they can be deadly if you don't respect them."

"Sorry," Andrea replied, "I know, I have to be careful, we had drivers ED in school, and I saw all those gory films, I really appreciate you helping me, I really do."

Amy woke up first, she quietly crawled out of bed and walked into the living room of the cabin and looked out the picture window, the lake was calm and looked like glass. The sun was starting to come up and the sky this morning was one of the most beautiful skies she'd ever seen. She turned and went into the kitchen to brew a pot of coffee. Once the pot was turned on she put on one of Tom's old flannel shirts and went outside to sit on the porch and watch the sun come up.

Amy leaned back in the rocker, she put her feet up on the railing of the porch and crossed her arms, and she gazed out at the colors. The sky was a dark bluish purple, with reds turning to oranges, and oranges turning to yellows, as they got closer to the horizon and the brightness of the sun. The lake reflected the colors of the sky like a giant mirror, the whole moment was almost surreal, and it was magical in its beauty and splendor.

Amy heard the screen door shut, startled, she turned quickly to look and see who was there. Tom was standing there with a smile on his face and a cup of hot coffee in each hand. "Good morning sunshine," he said to Amy, "how long have you been out here?"

"Just a few minutes," She replied, reaching for one of the cups of coffee, "I didn't want to wake you."

Tom handed her a cup of coffee and leaned down to kiss her.

"Looks like it's going to be another beautiful day," He said, turning to look over lake, enjoying the early morning serenity, "There's no place in the world I'd rather be, no place like this."

"I agree," Amy replied, "It's so peaceful, so beautiful."

"Later this morning, I want to go into town," Tom said, "I read about a couple of properties that might be good for us and I want to take a look at them."

"Alright," Amy replied, "do you have appointments setup? Or are you planning on just driving by and looking, and then go from there if you like what you see?"

"I think I'll drive past, and if I like what I see," Tom said, taking a sip from his coffee, "then I'll call the agent and go from there, right now, I'm just getting ideas, besides, we can't do anything for another year yet."

"Ok," Amy said, stretching her leg out and placing her foot on his leg, "maybe I'll just wander around in town and browse the shops."

Tom stood up and walked towards the screen door, "I'm gonna take a quick shower, then I'll make you breakfast," he said.

Amy smiled, and then she looked back out over the calm lake and said, "Ok. I think I'll sit here awhile and enjoy the view and the silence."

Tom slowed the car down to look at the front of the building. It was old and on the main street, it had two big storefront windows and a door in between them. There was a canvas overhang and a bench out in front. The windows were dirty and there was a for sale sign taped on the inside of the window. Top stopped the car and got out for a closer look. He put his hands against the glass to shield the glare and looked inside. It had possibilities he told himself, there was lots of room where he could set up shelving for items he was working on, there was an area he could use to display items for sale, there was a counter that he could use for a cash register. And it looked like there was space in the back for a couple of desks and a workbench or two. It was dirty and cluttered with debris from whoever moved out, but it did have possibilities.

Tom got back in the car and looked at Amy, "this place has potential," he said, "make a note for this one, I like the location, great foot traffic and easy to get to, people can park on the street right in front."

Amy scribbled down some notes in the notebook she had on her lap. "Anything else?" she asked, "any idea what the price is?"

"Nope," Tom replied, "just a phone number on the sign."

"Ok," Amy replied and put her pen back in her purse and closed the notebook, "now where?"

"I think there are one or two on the next block over," Tom replied, "that I think might be worth looking at, then I want to drive by the house and make sure everything is okay there."

Amy wrote some notes in the notebook for the other two properties on the next block, and on a fourth property on the edge of town that had lots of room, but was a little expensive.

Tom pulled into the driveway of his house and shut off the engine. He sat there, quietly; tears began to form in the corner of his eye. Amy noticed the change in his mood, and looked at him, she reached up and stroked his hair. "Aw honey, I'm sorry," she said.

Tom just nodded his head, and then he wiped the tears away with the back of his hand. "It feels strange," he said to Amy, "this is the first time back since, since the funeral."

"I know, "she said softly, repeating herself, "I know."

"Last time, it was all a big blur, I think I was probably in shock." Tom continued, "now, it's just a regular walk into the house, except dad is gone, and it's mine, and he's not here anymore."

Amy sat quietly in the car, allowing Tom to work though his thoughts before he was ready to enter the house.

Amy was standing at the kitchen sink and when she looked out the window she saw a car pull into the driveway behind their rental car. A woman got out and walked towards the house, and then she paused and turned to walk towards the garage. Amy suddenly remembered that Tom was in the garage, and this woman was walking towards Tom.

Amy stood motionless for a moment then leaned closer to the window to watch the woman.

Tom stepped out of the garage and into view, the woman walked right up to Tom, she stood close to him, too close to him for Amy's comfort. The woman and Tom embraced in a hug that lasted too long for just a welcome home hug. Amy suddenly felt sick and stepped back from the window. She just witnessed her husband holding another woman and felt a sudden anger welling up inside her. This was not *her* Tom; these were not the actions from the man she married. She felt her chest tighten and her teeth clench together.

Amy looked out the window again and saw the two still talking, now Tom was sitting against the car and Amy could only see the back of the woman as she was standing near him making gestures with her hands while she talked.

Amy hesitated a moment, then opened the door and went outside.

"Tom?" she said as she walked towards the two, feigning surprise, "oh, I didn't know you had company."

"Hey honey," Tom said as he stretched his arm out towards Amy, "Linda, I want you to meet my wife, Amy, Amy, this is a dear friend of mine Linda."

"Nice to meet you," Amy said as politely as she could.

"You too," Linda replied, then smiled and said, "so you are the one that caught him huh? You're a lucky girl."

Amy walked closer to Tom and put her arm in his, "Yeah, I think so," then smiled and kissed him on the cheek.

"Linda saw the car in the driveway," Tom explained to Amy, "and stopped in, she knew dad had passed away and the house was mine and thought she would stop and say hi."

"Well that was sure nice of you," Amy replied, almost cat like.

"Tom and I go way back, we dated in school," Linda said, then laughed nervously, "but that was a long time ago, a husband and two kids ago."

"Two kids?" Amy replied, "that sounds like a handful, I bet they keep you busy."

"They sure do," Linda responded, "they're teenagers now, they grow up so fast, listen, I just wanted to stop and say hi, it was nice to meet you Amy," Linda waved as she turned to walk towards her car, then added as she opened the door, "Nice seeing you again Tom."

"You too, bye," Tom replied and waved back at Linda.

Amy turned to look at Tom as Linda backed out of the driveway. "Dated in school?" she asked, "I saw you two hugging, it sure looked like more than just a, hello I haven't seen you in awhile kind of hug."

"Oh come on Amy," Tom replied, "we dated, it was a long time ago, back before I was in the Army, way before I met you."

"I saw you two and I felt sick," Amy replied, "I didn't like it, I hated that feeling."

Tom pulled Amy close to him and wrapped his arms around her, they swayed back and forth a little bit, slowly, "You are my wife," Tom said as he kissed the top of her head, "there is nobody else, okay?"

Amy broke the hold and turned towards the house, she grabbed his hand and pulled on it, "okay, I believe you."

"Okay," Tom replied, "let's shut off the lights here and go back up to the cabin, it's a two hour drive and I'd like to get back before dark."

Tom drove in silence on the way back to the cabin, Amy looked out the window of the car and took in all the scenery. She loved the tall trees, the red barns on the farms that they passed; she even liked the smell of the cows. She liked looking at the horses, and the dirt roads that went from the paved road they were on to people's houses that couldn't be seen from this road. Tom couldn't shake the words Linda spoke to him before Amy came outside.

"I still love you, I always have, and I always will," she told him, "people come into and go out of our lives, but you are right here in my heart, you are a part of me," she told him as she put her hand on her heart. Those words kept haunting him as he drove.

He knew she loved him, and he knew deep down, that she still held a very special place in his heart, he knew, somehow that she would always be there. He was married to Amy, but something bigger than him kept her in his heart and he didn't understand it, he felt uneasy by it, Tom felt guilty for having these feelings and thoughts.

Amy is my wife. I love Amy. Tom told himself over and over again, repeating it in his mind, hoping to put away the thoughts and feelings he had for Linda.

Amy walked out onto the porch and the screen door slammed behind her. Tom was standing, leaning on the railing and looking out over the lake. She walked up behind Tom and put her arms around him, and leaned her head against his back. "Dinner will be ready in about twenty minutes," she said, "can I get you something?"

"Can you get me a beer?" Tom turned around and asked.

"Sure," Amy said and disappeared into the cabin.

When she came back out onto the porch, Tom was sitting down on the old twig loveseat.

"Here you go honey," she said as she handed him the beer and sat down beside him, then asked, "you okay?"

"Yeah," he replied, "I am, thanks, it was just awfully strange walking into that house today, it was harder than I thought it would be."

"I'm sure it was," Amy said, "I can't even imagine."

Tom ran the water in the kitchen sink to do the dishes while Amy cleared the table. "I think I'll light a fire tonight," Tom said as he shut off the water.

"That would be nice," Amy said, then she rubbed her hand on his lower back, "I like snuggling in front of a fire."

"It's been awhile since I had a fire going up here," Tom said.

"Yeah," Amy replied, then smiled and rubbed her hip against him, "A couple years ago when we were here you built some nice fires, remember?"

Tom looked back at Amy and smiled, "I sure do," he said, then flicked some suds at her and laughed.

"You!" she said laughing, and splashed her hand in the dishwater and flicked suds back at him.

Tom carried an armload of firewood in from the woodpile and closed the door behind him with his foot. "There, that should do it for awhile," he said, "I need to cut more wood pretty soon."

"I can help with that," Amy responded, "I swing a mean axe."

"Tomorrow we can chop up a pile," Tom responded, "We're not going to do anymore work tonight."

"Alright," Amy said, "then when you light the fire, I'm going to go change."

Tom was sitting on the hearth adding wood to the growing fire in the fireplace when Amy came out of the bedroom. He stopped what he was doing and looked up at her. She made his heart skip a beat. She stood in the doorway and the glow from the fire cast a soft light on her. She had changed into a slinky nightgown that made her look extremely sexy. Tom could not take his eyes off her as she slowly walked towards him.

"Do you like what you see big boy?" she asked, in a throaty voice.

"Uh huh," Tom managed to reply.

"I picked it up the other day," she said, "when you dropped me off to wander around in town, so you like it I see."

"Yes maam," Tom said, taking her hand and pulling her down onto the old bearskin rug in front of the fireplace, "I sure do, I sure do."

Amy woke up to the sudden crack of thunder, they were still on the rug on the floor, the fire had gone out and the sound of rain and the cool night air filled the room. Tom had his arm around her and was holding her while he slept. "Tom, tom," she said, gently shaking his shoulder, "let's go to bed."

"Huh?" he responded, still half asleep, "what?"

"Let's go to bed," Amy repeated, "we fell asleep out here."

"Oh, yeah, ok," Tom said as he struggled to stand up, taking her hand and walking to the bedroom.

Amy fell asleep quickly once her head hit on the pillow and she was under the warm down comforter on the bed. Tom could not get back to sleep, he pulled on a pair of jeans and a sweatshirt, went to the fridge and grabbed a beer, then went out onto the porch to sit and watch the rain. He sat in the old rocker his mom used to sit in and put his feet up on the railing, sitting in the dark, he could hear the splashing sound of the rain coming off the edge of the roof and hitting the rocks on the ground. After a few minutes he got his night vision and he could see the water just below the porch. The rain hitting the water made it look almost like the surface of the moon. In the distance, the sky would light up from the lightning of the passing thunderstorm. The distant sound of thunder echoed across the lake.

Amy woke up alone; she sat straight up in bed, looking around. She got out of bed and went out to the living room, Tom was not there, she checked the bathroom and he was not there either, she began to get nervous, unsure of where else he would be. She looked out the window and saw his feet on the porch railing and felt a sense of relief come over her. She opened the door and held the screen door so it wouldn't slam shut. Tom didn't move, he sat slouched in the old rocking chair, his head was leaned to one side and he was making small snoring sounds. Amy smiled and went back inside to grab a blanket. Trying not to wake him up, she gently covered him with the blanket, picked up the empty beer bottles on the floor surrounding the chair and took them into the kitchen. She started a pot of coffee, and then stood inside the cabin by the screen door watching Tom sleep. Realizing that she was still naked from sleeping, and making love on the living room floor, she picked a blanked up off the sofa and wrapped it around her shoulders. When the coffee was done, she poured herself a cup and went out onto the porch. She sat on the chair swing and curled her feet up under her. She listened to the rain falling as she watched Tom sleep. He looked so peaceful; she couldn't bring herself to wake him up.

Daylight broke and the rain didn't let up, the sky was a dull gray, with the clouds masking the normally majestic sunrises. Tom stirred and opened his eyes, seeing Amy on the swing, curled up in a blanket, watching him sleep.

"Good morning," Tom said, "how long have you been sitting there watching me?"

"I dunno," Amy replied, "awhile I guess, I didn't want to wake you up so I put a blanket on you instead."

"Oh, thanks," Tom said with a smile, "I love it when it rains up here."

"Why?" Amy asked.

"Because it's so relaxing," Tom explained, "the sound of it on the roof, the sound of it on the ground, the sound of it on the water, it's so rhythmic and relaxing, even the rumbling of the thunder I like."

"I find it romantic," Amy said as she got up from the chair swing and walked over to Tom, then opened the blanket, exposing her naked body to him, she threw her leg over his and sat down on his lap, she laid her body against his and put her head on his chest.

Tom raised his hands up inside the blanket and could feel her warm skin, so smooth, so soft, he began to caress her back, rubbing his hands up and down along her back. Amy moved her hips to adjust herself, when she did that, Tom grabbed her butt with his hands and gently squeezed, pulling her against him as he pushed himself back up at her.

"Mmmmm, I see you woke up in a good mood," Amy cooed into his ear.

"Whenever I wake up to you I wake up in a good mood," Tom said, as he softly nibbled her earlobe.

Chapter 9

LINDA POUNDED ON the kitchen window, trying to get Timmy's attention. He didn't respond so she opened the window and shouted out to him, "Timmy, Timmy!"

Timmy turned and looked at the house then replied, "yeah ma?"

"You need to come in and get ready," Linda replied, "your grandfather is coming to pick you up in fifteen minutes, did you forget?"

"Sorry, I didn't know what time it was," Timmy responded, "I'll be right in, I just need to pick up my stuff first."

Linda shut the kitchen window and Timmy scrambled to pick up his tools. He was in the midst of installing a five horsepower motor onto his go-cart. The go-cart frame and wheels he bought from a neighbor, and the motor he scrounged from an old lawnmower he got at a garage sale.

Timmy walked into the kitchen from the garage, letting the back door slam behind him.

"So where is grandpa taking me?" Timmy asked, "I forgot."

"I'm not sure," Linda said, "I think he just wants to spend some time with you, maybe a movie or something, I really don't know."

"Ok, I'll change real fast then." Timmy said before he left the kitchen.

Linda's dad pulled up in front of the house a few minutes later and honked the horn. Timmy quickly shouted, "bye mom," as he ran out the front door.

A moment later, Linda's dad and Timmy walked in the front door. "Aren't you coming?" her dad asked her.

"Where? I thought you were just taking Timmy," Linda replied, confused.

"No," her dad responded, "I told your mom to tell you I was picking both of you up."

"Oh, geeze," Linda replied, "No, I don't remember, can you wait while I get ready?"

"Of course, be quick, alright?" her dad replied.

"Where are we going?" Timmy asked his grandfather.

"You just wait and see," his grandfather responded, "It's a surprise."

A few minutes later Linda came out of her bedroom, she had put on a different pair of jeans, a different top, a pair of shoes, pulled her hair back and put on a baseball cap.

"So what's the big surprise?" Linda asked her dad as they drove.

"You'll see in a moment," her dad responded, proudly as he turned the car onto a small road by the marina.

Timmy looked out the window in wide-eyed amazement at all the big boats that were docked at the marina.

"Well, there she is!" Linda's dad said as he got out of the car in front of a big white boat, "this is the surprise."

"Wow!" Timmy shouted in excitement, "you bought a boat grandpa? Is this really yours?"

Linda just looked at it, and a warm smile came over her face.

"Yes Timmy," his grandfather replied, "I did, that's my boat, go ahead, climb aboard and take a look."

"I'm happy for you," Linda said to her dad as she put her arm in his and held him, "you worked so hard all your life, I'm glad to see you finally got your boat, what does mom think?"

"She loves it, she's trying to figure out a name for it," her dad said with a smile.

"I'm so happy for both of you," Linda replied, and asked, "so tell me, are you going to retire now? Are you and mom going to enjoy yourselves without working so much?"

"Well dear," her dad said with a smile, as he escorted her onto the deck of the big white boat, "the thought has crossed my mind, after all, I have a couple good architects working for me now, and you pretty much know the business end, which can free my time up."

"I still have a lot to learn," Linda rebutted her dad, "I don't think I'm ready for that yet."

"Come on," her dad said as he stepped aboard, "no more shop talk, today I want to enjoy my daughter and her son, it's too bad Angela couldn't join us."

"Yeah, well, you remember teenage girls, don't you dad?" Linda said with a slight laugh, "they kind of do their own thing."

"I suppose," he said as he fired up the twin engines.

The sun was going down when Linda's dad drove up in front of her house to drop them off. Linda looked at the front of the house, she saw the for sale sign stuck on the lawn and was overcome by a sense of horror. "Dad? Can you take Timmy with you? I need to talk with Bobby."

Her dad saw the sign too and quickly replied, "Certainly, do you want me to come in with you?"

"No," she said, her voice trembling, not even looking at her dad, "I think I can handle this, I'll call you if I need you, okay?"

"Ok," he said, placing his hand on her shoulder, "I'll be right by the phone."

Linda opened the front door slowly and walked inside. Bobby was in the kitchen on the phone, his back towards the door and completely unaware that Linda had returned. She stood in the doorway silently, watching him talk, an empty sinking feeling in her stomach, She knew something was wrong, she was glad she didn't catch him in bed with another woman, but she didn't know why he put his house up for sale and hadn't bothered to tell her about it.

Bobby felt her presence and turned to face her, then said into the telephone, "listen, I gotta go now, I'll talk to you later, yeah, bye," and he hung up the phone.

"I suppose you saw the sign in front," Bobby said quietly.

"Yeah I saw the sign in front," Linda responded, "What the hell's going on? How can you just sell your house without even talking to me about it first?"

"First of all," Bobby argued, "It's my house, not our house, we're not even married, and I don't have to check with you first."

"Oh come on Bobby," Linda replied, angrily, "we both live here, you and me, my kids, we have a life, and you don't think you owe it to me to at least talk about it?"

"Your kids, not my kids, not our kids," Bobby responded, "I don't like the fact that ever since you lost our baby, that you haven't even hardly let me touch you, for Christ sake, it's been almost three years!"

"Don't throw that in my face Bobby," Linda said as she began to cry.

"I got a job offer out of town, and, well," Bobby added, "you have to admit, we have been drifting apart lately, I guess I felt it was time for a change."

"Change?" Linda shouted, "change? You wanted change, so your idea was to sell your house and move away from me? When were you planning on telling me? Huh Bobby? When?"

"I dunno," Bobby responded quietly, "I wanted to tell you before, I wanted to talk to you about it awhile ago, I wanted to tell you before the sign went up."

"Well Bobby," Linda said as she sat down on the chair to steady herself, "I guess your little plan didn't work did it? The sign is up and you never bothered to tell me."

"I'm sorry," Bobby said.

"Sorry? You're sorry?" Linda replied, "you sure are, you're a sorry SOB for doing this, you're a sorry bastard for letting me know you don't want to be with me any longer this way."

"Maybe if you would've said yes when I asked you to marry me, what was it, four different times? But you didn't want to commit, you didn't want to get married again after Tony, well, I got news for you, I'm not Tony! I would've never cheated on you like he did," Bobby replied.

"No," Linda responded, "you're just up and moving away, and taking the home I helped make for all these years away, just like that," as she snapped her fingers, "like I was nothing."

"Sorry," Bobby responded, "It's something I have to do, if you want, I'll help you any way I can, I can help you find another place, there is still time."

Linda put her head in her hands and wept, she didn't have anything else to say, she felt wiped out, and she was emotionally drained and exhausted. How could this happen to her? She wondered. One minute she was on her dads boat, enjoying life to it's fullest, the sun was on her face, the wind was in hair, her son and her father were at the helm of the boat talking and steering the craft, and then this happens. The bottom fell out. What did she do to deserve this? Why me? She asked herself over and over.

Tom snapped to attention in front of the commanding officers desk and saluted. The commanding officer returned his salute and told Tom to have a seat. Tom sat in the seat immediately in front of the commanding officers desk and waited for him to speak.

After a brief visit, Tom again stood at attention and was presented an envelope by the commanding officer; he saluted, turned abruptly and walked out of the office.

Tom walked down the corridor to his office and began to pack up his personal items. He removed his framed certificates and photographs, wrapped them in paper and put them in a box. He gathered up all his memorabilia that he had collected and boxed it up as well. Amy peeked her head in the door and smiled, "Hey there, how does it feel to be retired?" she asked.

"I don't know, I'm still here," Tom replied, "how about I get back to you in a day or two, after I've had a chance for it to sink in a bit."

Amy laughed and replied, "ok hun, say, are you going to the club after work? They're throwing a farewell party for you, don't forget."

"Oh geeze, I forgot about that," Tom said, "I've been so busy doing my last minute paper work and all, it slipped my mind completely."

"Well," Amy replied, "now you've been reminded, I'll see you there alright?"

"Alright," Tom replied, "love you."

"I love you too," Amy said and blew Tom a kiss before she quickly disappeared from his doorway.

Amy reached over and hit the off button on her alarm clock.

She sat up and stretched before getting out of bed, and realized Tom was not beside her in the bed. She walked out of the bedroom and saw Tom standing by the kitchen counter; he was just starting to make coffee and already had everything out to make breakfast with. "Good morning soldier," Tom said happily, "how did you sleep?"

"Morning," Amy responded quietly, "I slept ok, but my head is killing me, I think I drank too much last night."

"Aaah," Tom replied knowingly, "been there."

"Yeah, I should have called it a night sooner," Amy replied, turning to go take a shower, "but I was having too much fun I guess, and now today I'm gonna pay for it."

"Sorry," Tom replied, "Will you want breakfast?"

"I don't think so, but thanks," Amy replied, and then she walked back towards the bathroom for her shower.

"Okay then," Tom replied quietly, "glad it's not me that's hung over, what a way to spend my first day of retirement, no way."

Tom poured two cups of coffee when it was ready, then sat down at the table and opened the morning newspaper, he looked up from the newspaper when Amy walked in from the bedroom, she was standing in front of him in her uniform and buttoning up her shirt. "So what do you have planned for your first day as a civilian?" Amy asked, "anything exciting?"

Tom smiled, "no, not really, thought maybe I would take a walk and go down to the beach, after I have my coffee and read the newspaper, but no big plans."

"Ok," Amy said as she walked over to kiss Tom, "I'll see you tonight then, enjoy your day."

"Thanks, you too," Tom replied, "Love you."

"I love you too," Amy replied and then left the house.

Linda stood next to Andrea and smiled, "say cheese!" Linda's dad said as he pushed the button on the camera and the flash momentarily blinded both of them. Then he pointed to Andrea, indicating he wanted her to move, "Ok, now one with you and your grandmother."

"My goodness, you look so beautiful," Linda's mom said to Andrea as she stood next to her and put her arm around her. "You look just like your mother did when she graduated from high school."

"Thanks gramma," Andrea said as she smiled for the photos her grandfather was taking.

"Say mom?" Andrea said to Linda, "I'm going to be late tonight, a bunch of us are going to a party after the ceremony, and, well, I just wanted you to know so you wouldn't worry."

"Ok, thanks for telling me," Linda replied, "I remember my graduation like it was yesterday, my how time has flown."

"Ok, well, I should be going," Andrea said, "they want us all to meet in the cafeteria before we walk to the auditorium for the ceremony, I guess the principal has a speech or something."

"Alright dear," Linda responded as she hugged Andrea, "you just be careful tonight, alright?"

"Ok mom," Andrea said as she kissed her mom back.

"Promise?" Linda asked.

"And hope to die," Andrea said smiling, then waved at Linda, her grandparents, Timmy and his girlfriend, "I gotta go, bye."

Linda sat quietly with her parents and Timmy and his girlfriend, thinking how different things were from her graduation. When she graduated, her father had given her a car and her future had looked so bright, she had plans on attending college and then medical school, she was going to spend her life with Tom, the man she was so deeply in love with, as soon as he got out of the Army, and, she was pregnant and didn't know it yet. Now, at her daughter's graduation, the daughter she had carried in her womb when she had graduated. She was in no position to give her daughter a car, she and her two children were living with her parents and she was working as an office manager at her dads architectural firm. She enjoyed her job, she loved her children very much, but life certainly hadn't turned out nearly as she had planned.

Tom took a beer out of the fridge and opened it, and then he picked up the telephone and went out onto the front step and sat down to dial a number.

"Hello?" the woman's voice answered.

"Good morning Juanita," Tom said cheerfully, "This is Tom, how are you?"

"Uncle Tom?" the voice replied, "This is Amanda, mom's not here right now, would you like to speak with my dad? I can get him for you."

Tom smiled into the telephone and replied, "Yes, thanks." Tom could hear the girl on the other end of the phone shouting, "Daaaad, telephone, it's for you."

A moment later a familiar voice came on the other end. "Hello."

"Smitty!" Tom said happily, "How the hell are ya?"

"Tom?" Smitty replied, "Is that you?"

"Yeah, It's me," Tom replied, "How are things at the B&B?"

"Hey hey!" Smitty replied, "Tommy my boy, how the hell are you? Things here are wonderful, couldn't be better, how about you? How are things with you?"

"Great, they're great!" Tom responded, "I retired, yesterday I was a soldier, today I'm a civilian."

"Well how about that!" Smitty exclaimed, then laughed, "welcome to the other side, so how's Amy? What are you doing now that you're retired?"

Tom just laughed for a moment, "well, She's good, she's good, and today is my first day of retirement, so, so far I read the paper, went for a walk on the beach, and now I'm having a beer and talking to you, so, I guess at this point, retirement is treating me pretty damn good."

"Good for you Tommy boy, good for you," Smitty replied, "hey, I hate to cut this short, but Juanita is out running errands, and one of the guests had a crisis, they dropped a diamond ring down the sink, so I have to go tear the drain apart and get it for them, ain't life grand?"

"Ok," Tom replied, "we'll talk later, I just wanted to share the news with you, good luck on that ring rescue thing."

"Alright man," Smitty replied, "take care, bye."

Tom watched as Amy got out of the car and walked towards the house. He opened the door and met her just as she reached for the knob to open it. "Hi honey, how was your day?" Tom asked as he reached his arms out for her.

"Fine," Amy responded softly, "I'm sure glad to be home."

"Yeah?" Tom asked, "why? What happened?"

"Oh, nothing happened," she responded, "I'm just used to driving in to the base with you, seeing you in the hallway at the office, having lunch with you and driving home with you, I really missed you today, a lot."

"Aw," Tom said as he pulled her close to him and wrapped his arms around her, "That's too bad."

"Yeah, I know, I hate it already," Amy replied, snuggling into his arms, "I want to retire too, right now."

Tom kissed the top of her head as they stood there in the doorway, just holding each other.

"It's only a couple more months, and it'll go by faster than you think," Tom responded, "Besides, if you retired now, what would we do? Where would we live?"

"I know, I know," Amy replied, "These things take time, I just missed you today."

"Tell ya what," Tom replied, "If you like, I can drive you in, and come have lunch with you a couple times a week, I do have base privileges you know."

"I like that idea," Amy replied, "Will you really?"

"Sure," Tom replied, "I can shop for groceries there, I can get my haircut there, I can go to the club there or the gym, just like before, but with lots more free time."

Amy went into the bedroom to change out of her uniform, Tom followed her, watching her walking from behind. She sat down on the bed to untie her boots, Tom leaned against the bathroom door watching her, he was as happy that she was home as she was, he had missed her terribly too. Amy looked at Tom and held her hand up, moving her finger gesturing for him to come over to her. Tom walked towards Amy, not sure what she wanted, then stood in front of her and looked down at her face as she sat on the bed right in front of him looking up at him smiling, not saying a word.

Amy reached up and unbuckled his belt, then opened his jeans and pulled them down to his ankles. She ran her fingertips up his legs, and slipped them inside his boxers, then pulled them down too. Tom stood there with a smile on his face and just his shirt on. Amy reached up and held him in her hands, gently caressing him, stroking him, watching him, as he got aroused.

"I've been thinking about this all day," She cooed softly as she breathed on him.

"Well," Tom replied, as he stroked her hair, "this is a very nice surprise, welcome home."

Amy looked up at Tom and gazed deep into his eyes as she kissed him gently, then took him into her mouth. She could hear him moaning quietly, she looked up and watched as he closed his eyes and a smile of pleasure came over his face.

Linda unlocked the office and went inside. She turned on the lights and started brewing the first pot of coffee for the day. There was an envelope on her desk with her name handwritten on it. She sat down at her desk and opened it. Inside there was a note and a check. Linda began to cry when she read the note.

My dearest little Linda

Life seems to have handed you a bad string of luck.

Your mother and I have given a lot of thought to this decision, and we want you to have this. It won't make up for everything, but it will help you give your children a better life. We are going to retire finally and settle in Florida, we are taking your advice, but first we are going to spend a few months in Europe, something we have always wanted to do. I know this comes as a surprise to you, but this way you can't talk us out of it. The house is yours. The business is still mine, but I'm leaving it in your hands, as of today, you are the VP and will make any and all business decisions. The money with this note is for Andrea and Timmy to go to college, we know you can't afford it, but we can and want to. We will call you when we return from our trip.

WITH LOVE, Mom and Dad

Linda folded the note up and put it back into the envelope.

"Thank you mom and dad," she said to herself, but loud enough that anybody standing within earshot could hear it.

Shortly after she wiper the tears of joy from her eyes, the phone rang and another day at the office had begun.

Tom taped the last box shut and waited for the movers to arrive. Amy was sitting at the table reviewing the moving checklist.

"Well," Tom said as he stood behind her and rubber her shoulders, "It went by pretty fast didn't it?"

"Sure did," Amy replied, "seems like just yesterday you retired from the Army, now I just retired, I'm not sure I'm ready."

Tom laughed and leaned down to kiss the back of her neck.

"Told ya," he responded, "now, let's see that list."

"I think I accounted for everything," Amy replied. "The furniture will be moved, and our personal belongings, the utilities have been cancelled, we turned in the keys for the house to the landlord, I provided a forwarding address to your, Our house, for both our retirement checks, you lined up doctors and dentists and insurance providers, I don't know what else there is to do before we leave."

"That sounds about right," Tom replied, "next week we'll look for a property for the business, the house is already taken care of, we will just need to transfer the car licenses and insurance once we get there, but we have a month."

"Wow," Amy replied, "I can't believe this day finally got here, finally, we are going to settle down like real people, no threat of being shipped out to combat, just go to work, and I can have a garden."

"Yes you can," Tom agreed, "my mom had a fabulous garden, she even won some local awards, oh you should have seen it, it was beautiful, it's all grown over now, but there is a place for it."

"You have the car hooked up right?" Amy asked.

"Yep," Tom replied, "Some clothes and personal items are in the back car, and just a cooler and snacks in the front car. When you drive, you have to take it easy, towing a car is different than driving normal."

Amy gave Tom a dirty look, "excuse me?" she said, "I was in the Army for twenty years too, I have driven all kinds of cars and trucks just like you have."

"You're right," Tom replied, "Sorry about that."

Amy looked over at Tom, he had his seat leaned all the way back and was fast asleep. She smiled and looked back at the highway and watched as the headlights illuminated the yellow stripes in the dark. She watched for road signs and tried to calculate when the next stop for gas and to stretch her legs would be. She had tuned into a talk radio program to break the silence. She wasn't really following the conversation or the phone callers, but it was enough to keep her from nodding off at the wheel.

A few miles down the road Amy pulled into a truck stop for gas. Tom woke up and was momentarily disoriented by the neon lights over the gas pumps and the semi trucks all around.

"Where are we?" he asked.

"I stopped for gas and I have to pee," Amy replied, "I think we have another three or four hours before we are there."

"Really?" Tom replied, "I'll get the gas, then drive the rest of the way."

"Ok," Amy replied, "I'll be back in a minute, I really gotta go."

"Go then," Tom replied, waving her off.

Tom filled the car up with gas and checked the air in the tires of both cars. He washed the bugs off the windshield and looked at his watch, then wondered what was taking Amy so long; she had been inside the truck stop for almost ten minutes. He locked the car door and went inside, he saw her standing by the magazine rack, paging through a magazine.

"There you are," he said as he walked up behind her, startling her, "I was wondering what was taking you so long."

"Oh geeze," Amy replied, "sorry, I was in line to buy some snacks for the rest of the drive and started looking at these, and . . ." Tom cut her off, and said, "and lost track of time, I know, easy to do when you're tired, c'mon, lets pay for this stuff and get going."

Linda was walking down the sidewalk, it was lunchtime and she had an urge for a sandwich and a malted at the ice cream shop. When she opened the door to walk in, the small bell on the door rang, indicating someone had entered. She walked to the back and had a seat on her favorite stool at the counter. She picked up the menu to see what the special of the day was when a man sat down next to her.

"Hey there stranger," Tom said, "come here often?"

"Tom?" Linda said, very surprised as she swiveled her stool around so she could hug him, "oh my god, what are you doing here?"

"Living here," Tom replied, "You met my wife Amy, well, I retired from the Army a few months ago and she retired last week, and so we moved back here. We're looking at commercial property to buy and start a business."

"Wow!" Linda replied, "that's great, so you will be here now? No more coming and going?"

"Yep, here for good," Tom replied, "So, how are you? Tell me about you and what's new."

"I'm running my dads business," Linda answered, "him and mom retired to Florida awhile back, they gave me the house and business basically, I'm still a single mom, but my kids are grown now, my daughter is in college, and my son will graduate from high school someday I hope."

"I'm recently retired from the Army," Tom replied, "but you already know that, and you met my wife, I don't have any kids, or a job."

"Boy I've missed you Tom," Linda replied, placing her hand on top of his, "welcome home, you've been gone a long time."

"Thanks, it feels good to be back," Tom said as he stood up to leave, "I can't stay for lunch, I have some errands to run, but I saw you walk in and just wanted to stop and say hi."

"Bye then, see you later?" Linda responded with a smile on her face.

"I'm sure you will, bye now," Tom said as he patted her hand, then turned and walked away.

Amy was out in the yard when Tom pulled up in front of the house. She was pulling weeds and trying to reclaim the long neglected and once beautiful garden of years gone by.

"What are you doing?" he asked Amy as he walked around the front of the car.

"Hey," Amy replied, "I want to try and get this old garden under control, but it's been neglected for a long time."

"Yeah, it has," Tom replied.

"But I'm enjoying myself," Amy replied, "It's a lot of work, but I'm having fun, how about you? Anything new downtown?"

"I found a building I want us to look at," Tom responded, "tomorrow at noon the agent is going to meet us and show us the building."

"Great!" Amy replied, "Our own little shop, it's exciting."

"Yeah, I think so," Tom agreed, "say listen, I'm going to go light some coals, I thought I would grill us a couple of steaks tonight, what do you think?"

"I think that sounds good," Amy replied, "I'm almost done here for one day, then I'll come in and get cleaned up."

Tom and Amy peeked in the windows of the empty storefront while they waited for the agent to arrive. They could see the possibilities, but also the work that would be needed. Tom liked the entrance, it looked inviting, with the recessed doorway and windows on both sides. He could buy a couple of park type benches and put out front for slow days, or for pedestrians to sit in front and relax.

The town square was right across the street, and it had a small park and picnic area, and a gazebo that was used for musicians to hold concerts during the summer.

Parking for customers was adequate.

A car pulled up and parked right in front of the building, an older gentleman with a worn leather briefcase got out and walked up to Tom and Amy.

"Good morning, Tom?" the man said as he extended his hand to shake with Tom.

"Yes, I'm Tom, and this is my wife Amy," Tom replied, shaking the man's hand.

"Nice to meet you, I'm Mr. Olsen," The man said, "please, call me Ralph, I understand you nice folks want to take a look at this fine property."

"Yes, Ralph, we do," Tom said as he looked over to Amy. "What can you tell us about it for starters, I mean, besides what we can see, what is needed that we can't see?"

"My my, Tom," Ralph replied, "you do get to the point right away, don't you?"

"I try to Ralph," Tom replied, "no sense in wasting both of our time."

Ralph put the key in the lock and turned it, opening the front door. He stepped back and gestured with his hand for Tom and Amy to enter first.

Linda looked at the clock on the wall and realized she had not had lunch yet. She stood up, grabbed her purse and told the receptionist she was going to lunch and would be back in an hour or so. She was walking down the sidewalk past the post office and saw Tom out front of his shop sweeping the sidewalk.

Linda turned and went into the florist shop. She came out a few minutes later and crossed the street and walked down to the new store in town. Tom did not see her standing there, gazing at the new look on the old building.

"It looks nice," she said.

Tom, startled, stopped sweeping and turned to look, "well, hello there, how are you Linda?"

"I'm doing good, thanks," Linda replied, "looks like you're almost ready to open your doors to the public, it's looking real nice."

"Thanks, that means a lot," Tom replied, smiling proudly, "The grand opening is next week, but I think we will open for business before that, maybe this weekend, I'm still waiting on some new test equipment so I can do repairs, but we already have the shelves stocked with things for sale, can I interest you in a new TV?"

Linda laughed, and said, "thanks, but I already have more than I need, but I know where to come if they ever break."

"Alright," Tom replied, "pass the word okay? We fix pretty much anything electronic, even your car stereo if it doesn't work. Plus, I'll install them too."

"I'll do that," Linda responded, "say, listen, I'm on my way to grab a bite to eat for lunch, care to join me?"

"Sounds tempting, but I better not, thanks though," Tom replied, "I have a lot to do in a short time, rain check?"

"You got it," Linda said with a wink as she reached out and touched Tom on the arm, "any time."

Amy arranged the flowers in the vases around the store. She setup a table near the front door that had cookies, coffee and juice on it. The front door was propped open and the huge Grand Opening banner was strung across the front windows.

Tom was busy rearranging the shelves so everything looked just so, and on his workbench all his tools were neatly arranged and tidy. Amy set a tray of mints on the counter by the cash register, right next to a basket of their business cards.

Tom held one of the cards up and smiled at himself.

"What are you smiling at?" Amy asked.

"When we first got married," Tom explained, "we were at Smitty and Juanita's B&B, and you were sitting over with all the girls talking, I was sitting having a beer, several beers actually, with Smitty and I had this idea. I told him someday, after we retire I would like to go back home and open my own business with you, and jokingly, I said I would call it T&A Electronics. Smitty had an advertising campaign right away, we were both drunk remember, and it had girls in skimpy bikinis, with T's on the tops, and A's on the bottoms embroidered on them. Hey, we thought it was funny at the time. Anyway, here we are after all these years with T&A Electronics, and it's real. I gotta call Smitty."

"Huh," Amy said, less than thrilled at the story, "all we need now is your girls in bikinis, I don't think so."

"Aw come on honey," Tom replied, "it wasn't about the girls in bikinis, that was all Smitty's idea, it was T&A, for Tom and Amy, and that's what happened. And here we are!" he said standing with his arms outstretched.

Amy smiled, "I'm proud of you, of both of us."

"Me too," Tom replied, "our own little mom and pop shop."

"Ok, here comes a customer," Amy said excitedly, pointing towards the door.

Chapter 10

TOM SHUT THE light off on his workbench and looked for the broom. He swept up the floor of the shop and walked out front to the sales floor.

"How'd we do today?" he asked Amy, as he yawned.

"Pretty good," she replied, "for our one year celebration sale it was kind of slow, but steady, you had lots of repairs I see."

"Yeah," Tom replied, "I'd just like to see sales higher."

"I know, me too," Amy replied, "tell you what, you go on home, I'll finish up the paperwork and be home in an hour or so, alright?"

"K," Tom said as he kissed her and turned to walk out the front door. Suddenly a strange feeling came over him, something he couldn't put a finger on, something he didn't recognize. He walked back to Amy and wrapped his arms around her, looking deep into her eyes, he kissed her on the lips, the held her tight. "I sure love you," he said as he let go of her.

"Well I love you too honey," Amy said with a big smile, "I'll see you at home?"

"Yeah," Tom replied uneasily, "see you later."

Tom walked the short distance to their home, something kept nagging at him, something wasn't right, he could feel it, almost like an instinct, he had no idea what it was, but something was wrong in the world, in his world, somewhere.

Amy sat at the desk in their store, she opened the drawer and pulled out the stack of books and turned on the desk light to begin the tedious accounting part of the business.

Tom walked into the kitchen, kicked off his shoes and shoved them into a corner, grabbed a beer out of the fridge and went into the living room. He turned on the TV, changed the channel, and lay down on the sofa to watch the evening news.

He thought he would relax and catch a short nap before Amy got home.

Tom woke up suddenly to the knock on the front door. He quickly stood up and went to answer it. A chill went down his spine as he reached for the doorknob.

"Mr. Watson?" the man in uniform at the door asked.

"Yes officer, I'm Tom Watson," Tom replied, "What can I do for you?"

"My name is officer James, I have some bad news for you," the officer said, "May I come in?"

"Yeah, sure," Tom replied, standing back and holding the door open for the officer, "what is it?"

"Mr. Watson," The officer began, "There's been an accident, I believe your wife has been in an accident, her car was hit by a drunk driver and,,," Tom cut him off, asking, "what? When? How? She was coming home right after me, she . . ." and he looked at his watch, it was after midnight, he realized he had dozed off for several hours, not just a few minutes.

The officer continued speaking, "and we need for you to come down and identify the body."

"Her body?" Tom asked, his voice shaking as he collapsed on the couch, "You mean she's dead? That's impossible, there must be a mistake."

"I'm terribly sorry Mr. Watson," the officer said quietly, standing in the doorway, holding and turning his hat in his hands, "I can have a car drive you if you'd like."

"No, I . . . . , give me a minute please," Tom said, still in shock.

"I'll wait until you're ready Mr. Watson," the officer said patiently, "I'll drive you, and bring you back, whenever you're ready."

Tom went into the bathroom and splashed cold water on his face, then slipped on his shoes and followed the officer out to the patrol car.

Linda rolled over in bed when she heard the phone ring and switched on the lamp. She picked up the phone, then in a sleepy voice answered, "hello?"

"She's dead, Amy's dead," Tom cried into the phone.

"Tom?" Linda replied, "Tom, slow down, tell me what happened."

"She was hit by a drunk driver, Amy, she's dead!" Tom repeated himself, crying.

"Oh Tom, oh my god, I'm so sorry," Linda replied, "Is there anything I can do? When did this happen?"

"I dunno, I left the shop and came home," Tom replied, "she stayed later to do some paperwork, it was after midnight and I had fallen asleep on the sofa, the police came and woke me up, and told me."

"Tom, you just hang on," Linda said, "I'll be right over."

"Ok," Tom replied, "you're the first person I called, I don't know why, I just did."

"It's okay Tom," Linda replied, "It's okay, I'll be over in a few minutes, let me throw something on and I'll be right over."

The sun was rising and shining in the bedroom window when the phone rang.

"Hello?" Juanita said when she answered the phone.

"Juanita? This is Tom, I have some bad news," Tom said, "Amy was killed last night, she was driving home and was hit by a drunk driver."

"Oh Tom, I'm so sorry," Juanita replied, "let me get Mike for you,"

"Tom? Are you alright?" Smitty asked as he took the phone, "I'm so sorry, what a tragedy, what can I do for you?"

The funeral procession pulled slowly into the cemetery. In front of the procession was a motorcycle escort with red flashing lights, and at least a dozen cars following it.

Tom stood quietly next to the casket, his arm outstretched with his hand resting on it. Smitty and Juanita were next to him; Smitty had his hand on Toms shoulder and his arm around Juanita. Linda stood silently next to Tom and held his hand.

Tom was amazed at the amount of people that had shown up. In the year and a half since Amy retired from the Army and the two of them had moved here and started the business, she had met many new friends. Tom was also very surprised, pleasantly surprised, if that could be possible at a time like this to see so many men and women in uniform. Several people that had been stationed with Amy and Tom over the years came to show their respects.

The honor guards, in their dress uniforms with their white gloves, folded the flag that was on top of Amy's casket into a perfect triangle, and then presented it to Tom. As they stepped back, a lone soldier in the distance played taps on the trumpet, when he did Tom began to shake and tears began to run down his face as he tried to maintain his composure. Suddenly, there was a loud crack of gunfire, and then another, then another as seven soldiers fired off a twenty-one-gun salute to the fallen soldier they had come to pay respects to. Tom began to cry uncontrollably at that point and fell into Smitty's arms.

At the church basement following the ceremony, Amanda walked over to Tom, carrying her plate of sandwiches and bars; she sat down next to him and looked at him sadly.

"Uncle Tom?" she said softly, "I'm really sorry about Amy, I really liked her."

"Thank you Amanda," Tom replied, "that means a lot, thanks."

"Oh, and Uncle Tom," She added, "you can still call me doodles if you want to."

Tom wiped a small tear from his eye as he reached out and touched her cheek, trying to smile, he said, "thank you Amanda, even now that you've grown into a lovely young woman, you will always be my little doodles."

"Okay uncle Tom," Amanda replied with a bashful smile.

"I remember watching you run around your parents house," Tom said, beginning to laugh, "You were half naked. The first time I met you, you told me you were," then he held up two fingers in a peace sign, "thwee, I'll never forget that day."

Amanda began to blush, "please uncle Tom, no more embarrassing stories like that one, ok? Promise me."

Tom reached out his hand to shake her hand, "okay, I promise."

Linda walked into the electronics shop and rang the bell on the counter. Tom walked out from the back, "Hey," he said to Linda.

"Hi, I just stopped by to see how you were doing," Linda replied. "I was on my way to lunch and thought I would stop and say hi."

"Thanks," Tom replied, softly, "I'm doing okay, business is steady, and it keeps me busy."

"That's good, I'm glad," Linda replied, "listen, I was wondering if you would like to come over for dinner sometime, it must be awfully lonely eating at home by yourself, and I am a pretty good cook."

Tom smiled, "thanks, I'll think about it."

"You do that," Linda said as she headed for the door, "remember Tom, my door is always open for you, and don't hesitate to call me, anytime, day or night if you need anything, ok?"

"Ok," Tom said, standing in the middle of the store.

"I mean it Tom," Linda said, pointing her finger at him, "you call me, anytime day or night."

"Thanks," Tom said, waving at Linda as she walked out the door then he turned and went back to his work.

Tom turned out the lights, flipped the sign on the front door around from open to closed, and locked the front door behind him as he left. It was a short walk home. He had walked it many times alone in the past six months since Amy had died. They used to drive in together most days, but he found solitude walking to and from work now. The walk was a little more than a mile and from door to door, and he could do it in a short time. Also, the walk gave him time to think and reflect, something he found himself doing more and more recently.

Tom was standing over the stove, stirring his soup for dinner when the doorbell rang. He put down the spoon and went to open the door.

"Hi, I brought you something," Linda said, holding up a basket with a cloth draped over it.

"Come in, come in," Tom replied, opening the door for her, "I wasn't expecting to see you tonight."

"I know," Linda replied, "but I was making dinner for myself and thought I would bring you a plate."

"Thanks," Tom replied, "but you didn't have to."

"I know I didn't have to," Linda replied, "I wanted to, did you eat yet?"

"No. Not yet," Tom replied, pointing towards the kitchen, "I was just making myself some dinner."

"With only one pan?" Linda asked as she walked into the kitchen, "soup? You're having soup for dinner? Oh come on Tom, you need more than that."

Linda put the basket on the table and lifted the cloth off of it, and then she went to the drawer and picked out some utensils.

"Here, sit down," she said sternly, "It's still warm, have your soup tomorrow, I brought you roast chicken, mashed potatoes, gravy, and beans, I thought you could use some comfort food, now eat."

Tom smiled as he sat down, looking up at Linda, "I feel weird eating with you standing over me like that."

"Oh, sorry," Linda said as she pulled out a chair and sat down across from him. "I suppose you already ate?" Tom asked.

"Yes, I did," Linda responded, "I guess I wasn't expecting you to eat it right now, maybe put it in the fridge for another meal, I was hoping that you already ate, it's almost eight o'clock."

"I don't have a very good schedule," Tom replied as he took his first bite, "mmm, this is good."

"Thank you," Linda replied, "I worry about you Tom."

"Me? Why?" Tom asked.

"Because I care about you," Linda replied, "I've known you a very long time, and you have been through a lot, and . . ."

Tom cut her off by saying, "I'm a big boy, Linda, really, I'm okay."

Linda looked down at the table, avoiding Tom's eyes, "I'm sorry, I didn't mean anything by that, maybe I should go."

"No, no, It's okay," Tom responded, "stay, I enjoy your company, it's been awfully quiet around here lately."

"Ok," Linda said smiling, "for a little while, but then I really should get going."

"Understood," Tom said as he ate the last bit of food that was on the plate, "mmmm, thank you, that was delicious."

"You are very welcome Tom," Linda replied, "It was my pleasure."

Tom stood up and went to the sink to wash the plate Linda brought. Linda followed him, "here, let me do this for you," she said, reaching in front of him for the faucet. They reached to turn the water on at the same time, both of their hands reaching the faucet at the same time. Tom looked down at Linda, she smiled back up at him and repeated herself a little more forcefully, "I said let me do this for you."

"Alright," Tom replied with a smile and lifting his hands away, "you win, I learned a long time ago, never argue with a woman, it's always going to be a loosing battle."

"And don't forget it," Linda said, whipping her head to the side to flip her hair out of her eyes.

Tom hopped up on the counter near the sink, "how are your kids?"

"Well, Andrea is away in school," Linda replied, "after Bobby and I split, my parents offered to pay for both of my kids college educations, she is a junior, and Timmy, well, he is having problems, I'm afraid he is going to end up living on the street. He dropped out of high school, he can't hold a job, and he won't talk to me, he just clams up. He was close to Bobby, and when he left, Timmy just kind of started to flounder."

"I'm sorry to hear that," Tom replied, "It's gotta be rough on a kid to loose a role model like that."

"It was," she responded, "and his dad was never around, he left when Timmy was a baby then popped in years later to stir up trouble, and disappeared again."

Tom shook his head, "that really sucks, have you talked to him about the military?"

"No, I haven't" Linda responded, wiping her hands and hanging the dishtowel on the stove handle, "there, all done."

"Might be good for him," Tom said, "I knew lots of guys that came from similar backgrounds, they turned out to be pretty decent guys."

"Might be an idea," Linda said quietly, "he's just so hard to reach right now, so hard to communicate with."

Tom shrugged his shoulders, "I never had any kids, I don't know what to say, maybe give him some time, I really don't know what to say."

"You don't have to say anything," Linda replied, "It's not your problem."

"Thanks for cleaning up," Tom said, changing the subject.

"It was nothing," Linda replied, "one plate? And some silver wear, and I put your soup in the fridge, big deal."

"Well, you saved me from doing it," Tom replied, smiling, "plus, I enjoyed the company."

"You're quite welcome," Linda replied, "I should be going though, I have clients coming in to the office early in the morning."

"Ok, and thanks again," Tom said as he walked her to the door.

"You're very welcome, again," Linda said with a warm smile, "I told you, call me," then she reached up and kissed him on the cheek, turned and walked out the door and into the night.

Tom unlocked the door and went inside, he flipped the sign on the door around so it said open. He turned on the lights and watered the plants. Then he turned on the radio and sat down at his workbench. He flipped through the service tags so see what he had parts for and what he needed to order parts for to do the necessary repairs. He gazed out the window for a few minutes, and then he picked up the phone and dialed it.

"Linda? It's Tom." He said when she answered.

"Good morning Tom, what can I do for you?" she asked.

"I want to thank you for bringing over dinner for me last week, and wanted to know that if, um, I was wondering, if . . ."

"Tom," Linda interrupted, "you sound like a school boy, if you are asking me out, the answer is yes."

"Good," Tom replied, relieved by her response, "I haven't asked a woman out in, god, I don't know how long, and frankly, nervous doesn't come close to describing it."

"Tom," Linda said calmly, "I told you to call me anytime, day or night, that my door is always open for you, you don't need to be nervous, we were at one time . . ."

"In love?" Tom replied before she could finish her sentence.

"Yes," Linda replied, "in love, very much in love, I never stopped loving you, I've told you that a few times over the years, so, I would love to go out with you Tom."

"Great, how about tonight? Is that too soon?" Tom asked nervously.

Linda laughed, "I'm sorry, I didn't mean to laugh, no, tonight is not too soon, I'm thrilled, tonight is fine, pick me up at when, six? Seven?"

"I'll pick you up at six," Tom said, "and I thought I would cook for you tonight."

"Ok, I'll see you at six then, bye" Linda said softly before she hung up the phone.

Linda got out of the shower and toweled off. She put on a new outfit she bought recently, a flattering skirt and top she had been hoping to wear it if Tom asked her to go out, she knew he would, and if he didn't, she was going to ask him out pretty soon. She carefully applied her make up, and put on just a hint of perfume.

Tom pulled up in front or Linda's house and got out of the car, he walked up to the door carrying a rose in his hand. He felt as if he had butterflies in his stomach and he was fifteen again when he rang the doorbell.

Linda opened the door with a big smile on her face. She had waited years for this moment, for Tom to come calling on her again.

"Hello," Tom said, holding the rose out for her.

"Why thank you Tom, come in, please," Linda said as she took the rose and held the door open for him to enter.

"Nice place," Tom said, as he walked into the front room.

"Thanks, it's been a long time since you were here last, I was still in high school," Linda said, "now it's my place, and I'm long out of high school."

"I like what you've done," Tom said as he looked around the room.

"Let me just put this in a vase with some water real quick," Linda said as she disappeared into the kitchen.

"Ok," Tom said, but she was already gone and out of earshot.

Linda came around the corner from the kitchen, Tom was watching her walk towards him like he had never seen her before, and she was at this moment more strikingly beautiful than he'd ever seen her. Linda stood next to Tom with her elbow extended for him to put his arm in, "shall we?" she said with a smile as she nodded her head towards the door.

"Yes maam," Tom said, taking her arm, "by all means, after you," he said and opened the door for her.

Tom turned the stereo down to a quieter level so the music was just in the background. He looked over at Linda; she was sitting on the sofa, watching him adjust the lights, and the music, and nervously avoiding sitting down to visit with her.

"Tom?" Linda asked, "Are you ever going to relax and sit down?"

"Yes, I'm sorry," he replied, then walked over and sat next to her on the sofa.

"Don't make such a fuss," Linda said calmly, "let's just enjoy the evening and each others company."

"Alright, you're right," Tom said, "I know, I'm acting weird, I haven't entertained like this in . . ."

Linda put her finger on his lips to stop him from talking, "I know, It's okay," she said, looking deep into his eyes, "I know."

"Would you like some wine?" Tom asked as he stood up.

"Yes, that would be nice," Linda replied.

Tom disappeared into the kitchen and returned a moment later with a couple of glasses and a corkscrew. Then he walked over to the wine rack and studied it for a moment before pulling out a bottle of red wine.

Linda held her glass up for a refill, "this is very good, I like it," she said.

"Thanks," Tom replied, before he went outside, "I need to go check the steaks, I'll be back in a minute."

Linda sat back on the sofa and put her arm on the backrest, looking around she felt comfortable, very relaxed.

Tom came back inside and grabbed the tongs, "steaks are ready, come have a seat," he said before he went back outside.

He came back in a moment later with the two steaks, hot off the grill and placed them on the counter. He went to the fridge and pulled out the two salads he made earlier, "here ya go, I made these earlier."

Tom opened another bottle of wine and brought it into the living room where Linda was already relaxing on the sofa.

"That was a delicious dinner, Thank you," she said.

"You're welcome," Tom replied, "It felt good to cook for someone else besides myself."

"Well, I must say," Linda said, as she sipped her wine, "you did a fine job."

Tom held his glass in both hands, then looked up at Linda, "I'm um, I'm taking a couple of days and going up to my cabin, and I was wondering, if maybe you might want to drive up one day."

"Oh?" Linda replied, "when?"

"I'm leaving tomorrow," Tom answered, "I was wondering if you might like to come up say, this weekend for an afternoon or something, I might be able to catch some fish and do a fish fry for you."

"I'll have to check my calendar," Linda replied, "but that would be nice, maybe I can make it up there Saturday."

Tom smiled at Linda, "I would like that, a lot."

"We'll see," she said, sliding closer to Tom.

Tom brought his mouth to hers, gently brushing his lips against hers, feeling their softness, their warmth. He paused a moment, smelling her perfume, then pulled back a bit.

"I don't know if, I," he hesitated, "I really like you, I, I,"

Again, Linda pressed her finger against his lips to stop him from talking. "Tom," she said, looking straight into his eyes, "It's okay, really, when you're ready, I'll be here. I'll be here for you, I'm not going anywhere."

Tom relaxed a bit, but felt a sense of awkwardness and embarrassment.

"Listen," Linda said as she stood up, "It's been a very lovely evening, I've enjoyed it more that you know. I should be going though, and I will think about this weekend and driving up to see you, promise."

Tom stood up with Linda, feeling like a bumbling teenager, "alright, thanks for coming," he said.

Linda smiled and put her hand on his face, "I enjoyed every single minute, every, single, minute," she said as she kissed him goodnight.

"Oh, geeze," Tom said, suddenly realizing that her car was not here, remembering that he had picked her up and now had to drive her home, "I need to drive you home."

"Yeah," she said, as they both burst out laughing.

Chapter 11

TOM WAS OUTSIDE the cabin splitting wood, there was a large pile of wood that he had to split, and another large pile he had spent the day splitting and needed to stack. A small trail of smoke was rising from the chimney and the smell of wood smoke made him feel good. He heard the noise of gravel crunching under the tires of the car coming down the narrow drive. He turned around to see who it was then he saw Linda's car. His heart skipped a beat and a smile crossed his face. He swung the ax one last time and stuck it into a log, then took off his gloves and walked to meet her. Linda smiled and waved as she pulled into the parking spot behind the cabin and saw Tom walking to meet her.

"Hey!" Tom said as he waved back, "I'm glad you could make it."

"How could I resist an invitation to a place like this?" she responded with her arms outstretched, looking around, "plus, I really wanted to see you again."

"I'm glad you came," Tom replied as he closed the car door for her and opened his arms, cocking his head and smiling.

Linda walked slowly towards Tom, smiling back at him, and then stepped into his arms, feeling him holding her, she held him back and they stood that way for several seconds, silently, just holding each other.

Finally she let go and stepped back, pointing at the pile of wood, she said, "looks like you've been busy."

"I have been," Tom acknowledged, "I went out fishing first thing every morning and have plenty for dinner, and I also did a bunch of other stuff around here that needed taking care of."

"Let me get my bags," Linda said, "then you can show me around, I forgot what it's like up here it's been so long."

"Your bags?" Tom asked in surprise.

"Yes Tom," she replied with a smile, "I'm not going to drive back tonight, at least, I hadn't planned on it."

"Ok then," Tom said with a smile as he opened the trunk and carried her bags into the cabin.

Linda stood in front of the picture window, looking out over the lake, "can we go down to the dock?" she asked.

"Sure," Tom said, opening the door.

They walked down to the dock and out on it, Linda slowed down and gazed out across the water, then she stood there, looking out across the lake. She put her arm around Tom's waist and stood close to him, "This is lovely," she said.

Tom put his arm around her shoulders, holding her near him, "yes, it is, I love it here."

Linda turned and put her hand on his chest, "I know," she said, "this is where we spent your last night before you went into the Army."

Tom lowered his eyes, meeting hers as she looked up at him, he leaned down to kiss her, his mouth met hers, their lips parted, their tongues met each others, their tongues danced and explored, tracing across each other, tasting, feeling the warmth and moistness. Tom brought his hands up to Linda's head, holding it as he kissed her. Linda raised her hands up to Toms face, running her fingers along his chin and cheeks, feeling his closed eyes with her fingertips, the running them through his hair, kissing him back. They pressed their bodies against one another as they kissed. Tom broke the kiss first and held Linda's head against his chest, his strong arms, holding her close. Both of them were breathing hard, the moment seemed to sweep them away in passion.

"God I've missed you Tom," Linda said, her head leaning against his chest and whispering, "so much."

"Let's go inside," Tom said, softly, "I want to make love to you."

Linda turned and took his hand as they walked back up towards the cabin.

Tom closed the door behind them as they entered the cabin. Linda turned around and looked at Tom, "not yet," she said with a smile, "I would like to go take a bath first, do you mind?"

"Um, no," Tom said, then he asked her, "do you need a towel, here let me get one for you." He went to the closet in the spare bedroom and came out with an over sized terry cloth towel, "here," he said simply as he handed it to her.

Tom heard the bath water running in the bathroom and went outside to carry in some wood to make a fire with. He stacked some wood in the fireplace and lit a fire. Tom was nervous, anticipating what was to come, he walked in circles for a moment, pacing, before setting out some candles and lighting them. Tom knocked on the bathroom door and asked Linda, "Would you like me to open a bottle of wine?"

"Sure, that would be nice," she replied, "you can bring my glass in here if you want."

Tom almost dropped the bottle of wine on the floor as he tried to uncork it. He fumbled with the corkscrew for a moment before getting it to work. He poured two glasses and carried them to the bathroom, he held them both in one hand so he could turn the knob and open the door with the other hand. Tom stood still for a moment, staring at Linda. She was lying in the bathtub, bubbles covering the surface of the water, her arms were resting on the sides, shiny and wet from the water, and her hair was wet and tied loosely on the top of her head. Linda had lit some small candles herself and placed them around the bathroom giving the room a soft warm glow. She sat up a bit and reaching her hand out for a glass of wine. The water level was at mid breast, with her shoulders above water and the bubbles surrounding her breasts.

Tom handed her a glass of wine, gazing at her for a moment before speaking, "my god you look good," he said.

Linda smiled as she took the glass from Tom, "thank you," she said, "I bet I look a mess with my hair up and everything."

"Oh no," he replied, as he sat down on the toilet seat, "you look beautiful, you really do."

"Well, thank you Tom," she replied as she sipped her wine and slid back down into the water so just her neck and head were above it, "as long as I look good to you, that's all that matters right now."

"Well you certainly do," he replied.

"I'm ready to get out," Linda said, pointing to the towel folded on the vanity, "Can you get the towel for me? I can't reach it."

"This one?" Tom asked, reaching for the towel, "sure."

He stood up and picked up the towel, when he turned to hand it to her, she was already standing, her nude body glistening from the bath water. She gave Tom a big smile as she stepped out of the bathtub. She didn't reach for the towel, so Tom wrapped it around her, and began to dry her off. She put her hands on his waist and watched his eyes as he dabbed the water off her face, then off her neck. She watched his face as he toweled off her breasts, carefully dabbing the drops of water and not just rubbing the towel across her. She held her arms out, one at a time as he toweled them off, then she smiled at him as he toweled off her stomach. She turned around so he could dry off her back and kept her eyes fixed on his face, fascinated by the love in his eyes. She turned her head away, and closed her eyes as he toweled off her back, dabbing her shoulders and down the center of her back, then dabbing softly around her round butt. She heard his knees crack as he kneeled down on the floor and began to towel off her legs, running the towel down the outside of one leg, then back up the inside, pausing at her upper thighs. Linda parted her legs slightly so Tom could dab her with the towel, then he went down the inside of the other leg, to her foot and back up the outside. Dropping the towel on the floor, Tom placed his hands on her hips and kissed her, he held his lips on her round butt for a moment before standing up.

Linda turned around to face Tom, taking his hand in hers, "I don't want anymore wine right now," Linda said, looking into Toms eyes. Tom could see the love in her eyes; he could see the hazy look of lust, and the want she was feeling inside for him.

Tom turned and with her hand in his, led her to the bedroom.

Linda lay down on the bed, and looked at Tom as he knelt then laid down next to her. He placed his hand on her cheek and brought his lips to hers. Linda was waiting, her lips were parted, and her eyes fixed on Tom's eyes as their lips met. It was warm and soft, he softly squeezed her upper lip with his lips, then traced his tongue along the inside of her top lip, he could feel her tongue touching his, softly exploring his as he probed her mouth.

Linda soon began to breath more rapidly as she became excited, Tom was breathing faster too as their kisses became deeper and more passionate. He could feel her hands pulling his shirt out from inside his pants, she was tugging at it until it came out, then she slid her hands up under his shirt, feeling his warm flesh. Tom ran his hands down her body, caressing her, feeling her naked skin as they continued to kiss.

Tom sat up and pulled his shirt over his head, not stopping to unbutton it, he just wanted it off, now.

Linda began to kiss his chest, running her fingers through the hair. Tom slowly moved his hands from her shoulders, down her arms, then up along her sides, stopping to cup her breasts, and rubbing his thumbs back and forth across her hardening nipples.

Linda reached down and unbuckled his belt, then fumbled with his zipper as she opened his jeans. Tom stood up from the bed and removed his pants and boxers, then knelt on the bed between Linda's legs, taking one leg in his hand, he brought her foot to his mouth and kissed her toes, one at a time, taking each one into his mouth when he kissed it. He looked up at Linda, her eyes were closed, she was no longer watching him, she had a smile on her face and she was caressing her breast with one hand. Tom traced small wet kisses up along her leg, stopping behind her knee to lick and kiss it. Then he kissed wet trails up along her inner thigh, he could see was slowly stroking herself and he kissed the back of her hand, causing her to moan softly. She moved her hand and he kissed her, slightly parting her moist lips with his tongue, then he kissed her other thigh and continued tracing his wet kisses down towards her other knee.

When Tom got down to her other foot, see she was slowly moving her body, she had begun to write her hips, she had one hand caressing her breasts, and she was stroking herself again with her other hand. Tom moved up alongside her, and placed his hand on her breast, then kissed her on the stomach. She let out a small gasp and a quiet moan. Tom was excited by her response to his touch. He traced more kisses and gentle nibbles up her body to her breast; she took her hand and held his head to her as he took her breast into his mouth, circling her nipple with his tongue.

Linda pulled Tom up closer to her, she kissed his mouth, full and deep, she held his head in her hands as she wrapped her legs around him, squeezing him, pulling him to her, grinding herself against him. Tom reached down between their bodies, and guided himself, as he pushed into her.

"Oh, god," Linda shouted out loud, then, biting down softly on his neck, she reached her hands down to his butt, pressing it to her, pulling him deep inside her.

Tom dropped on top of her, exhausted, then rolled off of her to one side. Laboring to catch his breath, he caressed her with his hand and kissed her neck, whispering in her ear, "you are wonderful."

Linda turned to face Tom, she held his face in her hands and kissed him softly, "I love you Tom."

"I love you too," he replied, wrapping his arms around her and holding her close, holding her tight. H could feel her trembling as he held her in his arms. He looked down and saw her crying, he wiped a the tear from her eyes as his eyes met hers, "are you okay?"

"Yes," she sniffed, "I'm fine, just fine."

"You sure?" he asked. "Oh Tom," Linda replied as she buried her face in his chest, getting as close to him as she possibly could, "I have waited my whole life for this night, for this moment, for you."

Tom was speechless, he held her head, and ran his fingers slowly through her hair and kissed the top of her head.

Linda woke up, she was still in Tom's arms, he was sleeping softly, waking up when she moved, "did I fall asleep?" he asked.

"I think we both did," she replied, smiling up at him, and then she said, "I'm chilled."

"I am too," he agreed, "I'll go stir the fire and throw another log on it, ok?"

"Yeah," she said, kissing his chest and moving away from him as he stood up.

Linda walked out of the bedroom wearing a big fluffy robe.

Tom looked at her and smiled, his eyes gazing up and down her body, "you planned for everything I see."

"I told I wasn't planning on driving home tonight," she replied with a grin.

Tom stood up from the fire, his jeans were on, but he hadn't bothered to buckle his belt or put on a shirt before he came out to tend to the fire.

Linda went into the kitchen and came out with two glasses and another bottle of wine, "how about a nightcap?" she asked.

Linda snuggled up against Tom on the sofa, the fire was blazing in the fireplace, and the only sound that could be heard was the crackling of the wood as it burned.

"This is nice," Linda said quietly, almost as if she was speaking to herself.

"Yes, it is," Tom said, agreeing with her as he put his arm around her and rested his hand on her shoulder.

She laid her head on his shoulder and stared into the fire.

The sun was shining into the bedroom window, when Tom opened his eyes; he looked down and saw Linda's head, resting on his chest, her arm draped across his body as she slept. He gently stroked her head, causing her to stir. She woke up and looked up at him, her eyes squinting from the bright sunlight.

"Good morning," Tom said.

"Hi," she said back, with one of the most beautiful, most loving smiles he had ever seen.

"How'd you sleep?" he asked.

"Like a log," she replied, as she moved up alongside him, "I slept very sound, once we went to sleep."

"I'm glad," Tom replied, reaching to kiss her.

He felt her hand on him as they kissed, he cold feel himself getting aroused again by her touch. Linda smiled at him, then she lifted up the covers and her head disappeared under them.

Linda waved at Tom as she drove away from his cabin. He waved back and suddenly felt emptiness, all alone. He put his gloves on, picked up the axe and began to split the rest of the wood on the pile into firewood.

Linda drove back home, she drove in silence, and her mind racing with the recent memories of the short time she just spent with Tom. It was only one night, and yet it seemed like so much had happened in that one night. She didn't want to go back home alone; she wanted so badly to call him, to hear his voice. Tom didn't have a telephone at his cabin so she couldn't call him and hear his voice. She drove thirty five miles down the road before she stopped for gas, then she turned the car around and headed back to the cabin, back to Tom, back to the man she had loved since she was a young girl, to the man she had loved her entire life.

Tom swung hard, the axe came down and the log split in half, with tiny splinters of wood flying in all directions. He put the ax on the ground and leaned it against his leg as he wiped the sweat from his forehead and neck. He split a few more logs before putting the axe down and taking a break. He took off his gloves and went inside the cabin, opened the fridge and took out a cold bottle of beer and held it against his face. It felt good. He opened the beer and walked down to the dock, standing there, he looked out over the lake. He began to daydream; memories of Amy came back to him, of their time up here, of the tour he gave her around the lake and how they made love in the boat. Then his mind wandered to the night before he went into the Army, of how Linda and he had spent the night on the dock and watched the sunrise together. He thought of this morning with Linda, and yesterday and last night with her, a smile came to his face. He knew he had loved Amy, he had spent many years with her, they were happy together, but something was always missing. At that moment, Tom realized it was Linda that he had been missing; it was Linda that he was truly one hundred percent in love with, and had been for as long as he could remember. Amy and the other women in his life were just filling a void. He swallowed hard at that thought. The feelings he had were bittersweet, he was sad and happy at the same time. Tom sat down on the bench at the end of the dock. He put one foot up on the dock post and rested his beer in his hand on his knee. There was a creaking sound; it was the sound of someone walking on the old boards of the dock. Tom turned around to see who it was.

"Linda?" he said, as he quickly stood up.

"I couldn't leave," she said as she walked towards him, "I just had to come back."

"But, I thought," Tom began to say. Then Linda put her arms around his neck and kissed him, she pressed her lips against his, and she opened her mouth and probed his mouth with her tongue.

Linda broke from the kiss and said, "I don't ever want to leave you, I don't ever want to be away from you again Tom, I've waited my entire life for you and I'm not going anywhere without you, not ever."

Tom wrapped his arms around her and lifted her up, returning her kiss, he held her for several minutes, locked in one of the most passionate kisses either one of them had ever experienced.

"I love you so much Linda, I don't want to loose you," Tom said, whispering into her ear as he held her tight, "not ever again."

Tom took Linda by the hand as they walked back up to the cabin. Tom lit another fire and took off his sweatshirt. Then he turned to look at Linda. He saw her looking back at him, a big smile on her face, she appeared as happy as he did at this very moment.

"I'm not going home until tomorrow," Tom told Linda, "I want to spend one more night up here before I go back to work."

"Then I won't go back either," Linda replied, "if that's okay with you."

"If, that's okay with me?" Tom chuckled, "Of course it's okay with me, you just made my day when you turned around and came back, you don't know how glad I was to see you."

"Then it's settled," Linda said as she took off her sweater and threw it on the back of the chair, and walked towards Tom, "I'm staying the night."

Linda reached out and grabbed Tom by the belt, pulling him closer; she unbuckled his belt, and opened his jeans. Tom lifted her top over her head and threw it on the floor. She slid her hands inside the waistband of his boxers and slid them off, as they dropped to the ground, Tom reached behind her and unhooked her bra, he slid the straps down off her shoulders and let it fall to the floor. Linda unbuttoned his shirt, beginning at the bottom button and working her way up, while Tom slipped his hands inside the waistband of her pants sliding them over her hips and letting them drop to the floor. Linda stepped out of her pants as they lay in a pile around her ankles. She took his hand and pulled him with her as she led him to the bedroom.

When Linda woke up, she was lying in bed on her side, Tom was behind her and his arm was reaching over her, his hand cupping her breast, their knees were both bent as they were snuggled close together, she could hear him, snoring softly in her ear. She could feel his warm body pressed against hers, from her head all the way down to her feet. It felt so good, it felt perfect and she never wanted this moment or this feeling to go away. She smiled to herself and moved her hips a little as she snuggled back against him, closed her eyes and drifted back to sleep, feeling safe in his arms.

The smell of frying bacon that was coming from the kitchen woke tom up. He sat up and looked at his watch, realizing he hadn't slept this late in a very long time. He got up and pulled on his jeans and threw on a t-shirt and went out to the kitchen. Linda heard him and turned, she was in her big fluffy robe again, holding a spatula in one hand and her other hand resting on her hip.

"Good morning sunshine," she said, with a very happy smile.

"Good morning to you too," he said as he reached his hand around her waist and kissed her.

Linda set the plate of toast on the table and sat down across from Tom. He already had a mouthful of eggs and just smiled at her.

"I see you're hungry this morning," she said with a wink, "I wonder why."

"You almost wore me out," he said with a smile, "I'm not used to this much sex, I think I'm getting old."

"I wanted to talk to you about something Tom," Linda said with a serious note in her voice.

"Ok, go ahead," he said, putting his fork down and giving her his full attention.

Linda folder her hands in front of her and rested them on the table then looked Tom square in the eyes.

"Before you went into the Army, we had made plans," Linda began.

"Yeah," Tom replied, not exactly sure where she was going with this.

"Please, just listen and let me finish," she replied, "before you went in, we had planned on getting married, then you came home on leave, and we, well, you know what happened, we've both been married and had lives between then and now. And, well, I want you to know that, um, that the answer is yes."

"Answer is yes?" Tom asked, confused.

"Oh my god, I feel so embarrassed," Linda replied, bringing her hands up to hide her face.

"Linda, I don't understand, what are you talking about?" Tom asked, sincerely, reaching across the table to touch her hand.

"If you still, after all these years, if, Tom, I still want to be your wife." Linda blurted out, but not very gracefully.

"Oohh," Tom said, smiling, "you had me scared there for a moment, I had no idea what you were talking about, and you sounded so serious."

"Tom," Linda said, dropping her hands from covering her face, "I am serious, this is serious to me."

"Alright," Tom replied, "can we go sit on the sofa and talk about this?"

"Yeah," Linda replied, "I really want to."

The front door of the store opened and Tom looked up from his workbench. He didn't recognize the young man that walked in. His arms were empty so he wasn't bringing anything in for repair.

"I'll be right with you," Tom said loud enough so that the young man looking around the store could hear him.

"K," the young man replied.

Tom walked out to the front to greet the young man.

"Good morning, how may I help you?" he asked.

"Are you Tom?" The young man asked.

"Yes, I'm Tom and this is my store," Tom said, "and you are?"

"I'm Tim," The young man answered, "Linda's son."

"Oh Timmy," Tom said, extending his hand, "nice to meet you."

"I prefer Tim," Tim replied, shaking Tom's hand.

"Ok, Tim it is," Tom replied, "So, how can I help you."

"I'm looking for a job," Tim said, "and my mom said you might have something for me."

"Well, gee, Tim, I don't know," Tom replied quietly, "this is just a small store, what do you know about electronics repair?"

"Nothing," Tim said honestly.

"Nothing? Hmm," Tom replied, "well, that's what I do here Tim, I sell and fix electronic items."

Tim lowered his head and stared at the floor.

"I can learn," Tim replied, "maybe there is something I can do."

"Tell ya what," Tom replied, "maybe there is something, I can use someone to sweep the floors and keep the shelves looking nice, maybe make some pickups and deliveries, how does that sound?"

"Great!" Tim said excitedly, "I can do that, and learn more by hanging out and watching."

Tom smiled, "It can only be part time, a couple hours a day after school, you are still in school, right?" Tom asked, already knowing the answer.

"No, I quit school, I hated it," Tim answered.

"Oh," Tom replied seriously, "I don't know then, I'm going to want someone I can count on, someone that follows through on what is put in front of them, and not following up with school is a big red flag for me."

"Oh," Tim said, "does that mean that I can't work for you then?"

"Sorry son, I'm afraid so," Tom replied, "As both an employer, and a friend of your mom, I need to, well, sort of look out for everyone's best interests, my interest is a reliable employee, your moms interest is a stable future for her son."

"You sound just like she does," Tim said, as he turned and walked out the door.

Tom stood there in the center of the floor for a moment, wondering if he did or said the right things, second-guessing himself. He had just in a way, lectured a boy he had never met before, just because he was in love with his mother. "When did life get so damn complicated?" Tom asked himself out loud.

Tom locked up the shop for the night and decided to stop by the local bar for a drink on the way home. He walked in and saw some people shooting pool while others were sitting at a couple tables scattered around the darkly lit room. There was a TV in the corner above the bar with a football game on it. Tom walked up to the bar climbed onto an empty stool and ordered a beer.

"Tom?" he heard a woman's voice ask.

Tom turned around and saw a vaguely familiar face, "Yes," he said.

"Tom is that really you?" she asked again.

"Yes, do I know you?" Tom asked, looking at the woman.

"Yeah Tom, It's me, Janey," she replied, reaching out and lightly touching him on the arm, "you remember me don't you Tom?"

"Oh, Janey," Tom replied, taking a sip off his beer, "It's been awhile, I didn't recognize you."

"Buy me a drink?" she asked, sitting down on the stool next to Tom.

"I suppose," Tom said, signaling for the bartender.

"So what are you doing back here?" she asked, batting her eyes, "you sure are looking good these days, looks like life has taken good care of you."

"Thanks," Tom replied, politely asking "what's new with you?"

"Oh not much," Janey replied, "I haven't seen you in here before, where have you been hiding?"

"I moved back, geeze, a couple of years ago," Tom replied, looking up at the TV, "I started my own business."

"I never see you around," Janey replied, "you should come in here more often, I'm here almost every night, maybe if you came in more," she winked and nudged him with her shoulder, "we could get together sometime."

Tom looked at her as he drained his beer, "I don't come in here very often, in fact, this is the first time since I moved back."

"Well don't be a stranger Tom," Janey said, gently moving her finger up and down his arm, "really, you should come here more often, I'd really like to see you."

Tom stood up to leave and looked at her, "I don't think I'm going to make a habit of coming in here, I try and keep myself busy."

"Aw Tommy," Janey said, "don't leave yet, let's have another drink hun."

"I don't think so," Tom said as he turned and walked out the door.

Linda was setting the table for dinner when Tim walked down the stairs from his room, "Hey, who's coming for dinner?"

"Why do you ask that?" Linda asked.

"Because you usually set two places at the breakfast bar for us," Tim replied, "and tonight you are setting four places, are grandma and grandpa in town?"

"No," Linda replied with a smile, "your sister is coming home from college for the weekend, and, I invited a special someone to dinner, that I want you two to meet."

Tom stood at the front door, a bouquet of flowers in his hand, hesitating a moment before ringing the doorbell.

Linda opened the front door when she heard the doorbell; Tim was in the dining room, standing by the doorway with a cookie in his hand. Andrea was upstairs unpacking her bag for the weekend.

"Tom, please come in," Linda said, standing back, moving her arm in a sweeping motion, indicating for Tom to enter the house.

"Tom, this is my son Tim," Linda said, waving her arm for Tim to come closer.

"Tim, I want you to meet Tom," Linda said, as she introduced them to each other.

"We already met," Tim said.

Tom, nodded his head in agreement.

"You did? When?" Linda asked.

"Tim came to my shop looking for a job," Tom answered.

"Really?" Linda turned and asked Tim in surprise, "when?"

"The other day," Tim replied, "but he didn't have anything for me."

Andrea walked into the room at that minute, changing what had suddenly become an uncomfortable moment.

"Oh, Andrea, I would like you to meet Tom," Linda said.

Andrea walked over to Tom and held her hand out.

"Tom, this is my daughter Andrea," Linda said, "she's home from college for the weekend."

"It's a pleasure to meet you Andrea," Tom said as he shook her hand.

"I want to know more about this job thing," Linda said, looking directly at Tim.

"I just went there and asked if he had anything for me," Tim replied.

"Why did you go to his shop?" Linda asked.

"I heard you talking about him on the phone to grandma," Tim explained, "and, well, I figured if I told him I was your son, maybe he would hire me."

"What an idiot," Andrea said to Tim.

"Shut up," Tim replied to Andrea.

"Stop it, both of you," Linda said, sternly, "I invited Tom here tonight, and I want this to be a nice evening, for all of us."

"I'm sorry," Andrea said, and then asked, "Is there something I can help with in the kitchen mom?"

"No dear, I think I have everything under control," Linda answered, "but in a bit I can use your help."

"I was just trying to get a job," Tim said, "you said I need to get a job if I'm not going to go to school."

"Yes," Linda replied to Tim, "I know what I said, but I would rather you finished school, and then get a job, it's going to be real hard to get a good job if you don't finish high school."

"I can find a job," Tim insisted.

"How about we talk about this later," Linda said to Tim.

"I told him I had something for him," Tom said, "but not if he wasn't going to school."

Linda turned and looked at Tom, "you did?"

"Yes, I did," Tom responded, looking at Tim, "I told him I needed someone I could count on to finish a task, and dropping out of high school is not finishing a task."

"Whatever," Tim said rudely, as he left the room.

"I'm so sorry," Linda said to Tom, "this is not how I had the evening planned."

Tom chuckled, "oh forget it, he's young, I was that way too once, and I've had a hundred just like him fall under my responsibility in the Army,"

"Yeah, maybe," Linda replied, "but this is my home, you are my guest, and he is my son, and, this is not the Army."

Tom just smiled and Linda, and patted her behind as he followed her into the kitchen.

"He's had a hard time the past few years," Linda began to explain.

"I know," Tom replied, "you told me all about his dad leaving when he was a baby, and about pretty much being raised by Bobby and then him walking out of his life too."

"What am I going to do?" Linda asked Tom sadly.

"Nothing much you can do," Tom replied, "he's going to have to make his own decisions, and when he falls on his face a few times, hopefully, he'll smarten up, but he has to find his own way."

"You make it sound easy to just watch him fall," Linda said.

"I never said it was easy, I said he has to find it on his own," Tom said, "tell ya what, maybe after we tell them the news, maybe he'll look differently at me and listen to what I have to say."

"Or maybe not," Linda replied.

"Or, maybe not," Tom agreed, "but, I can help out, he does need a male figure to look up to, and I'm not planning on going anywhere, he'll see that I'm here long term and won't walk out on you."

"God I hope so," Linda said, holding Toms hand, "he sure needs something."

"I can be here," Tom said, "the rest is up to him."

Chapter 12

THE MOOD AT the dinner table was quiet, nobody had spoken for a few minutes and the only sounds that could be heard were the clinking of utensils on china.

"Tom and I have some news," Linda said, breaking the silence, "we're getting married."

Linda and Tom shared the history they shared, from dating in high school, to staying in contact off and on during their marriages. How Linda had been with Tom at his fathers funeral, how they had never fallen out of love after all this time.

"That is so romantic," Andrea said with a big smile on her face, "I knew he was special, since you started dating him again I've seen a change in you, you're much happier."

"How did you know?" Tim turned and asked Andrea.

"Mom and I talk," Andrea replied, "she told me about Tom a couple of months ago, I knew this was going to happen, I just knew it, I'm so happy for you mom."

Tim rolled his eyes and shrugged his shoulders, "whatever."

Tom put both of his hands flat on the table and looked at Tim.

"Tim, I know I'm not your dad, and I never will be, but after your mom and I are married, I want you to know, I want you to be able to come to me for anything."

"Like a job?" Tim snipped.

"I already told you about that," Tom responded, "that won't change, but I'm here long term, I'm not going to leave you like your dad and Bobby did, I give you my promise. I'm here to stay."

Tim just looked down at his plate quietly, without responding.

Linda closed the door behind her as she stood on the front step with Tom.

"I think it went okay," Linda remarked.

"Me too," Tom agreed with a smile.

"Are we still on for tomorrow?" Linda asked, wrapping her arms around Tom's neck and rubbing her nose against his nose.

"You betcha," Tom replied, running his hand down her back and cupping her butt, "until tomorrow."

Linda responded to Toms kiss, kissing him back. Someone passed the house in a car and honked the horn as they stood out on the front porch kissing like two teenagers, sneaking away to make out.

Tom was installing the last repair part in the radio for a customer when the front door opened. He looked at his watch. It was five minutes before closing time and he really just wanted to close up on time and spend tonight with Linda.

He looked up from his workbench and saw Janey standing in front of the counter. She was wearing heels and a long coat that was buttoned up the front.

"Hi Tom," she said.

"Hello Janey," Tom responded, "can I help you with something?"

"As a matter fact you can," she replied, walking towards him, "you can show me around your little store here."

"Alright," Tom responded, "I was just about to close for the night, but I suppose I can show you around, as you can see this isn't a very big store."

Tom showed her the items on the shelves that were for sale, and he showed her his workbench where he did repairs for customers.

"Do you have an office?" she asked, "I want you to show me your office."

"My office?" Tom asked, "Alright, this way," he said, turning and walking down a small hallway between the restroom and the utility room.

"This is it," he said as he flipped on the light switch and turned around.

Janey had unbuttoned her coat and pulled it open, she wasn't wearing anything under it, she was magnificent for a woman of her age, it was obvious that she had spent countless hours working out and taking care of her body. She still had the body of a thirty year old.

"What the?" Tom said, when he saw her holding her coat open for him, making sure he knew that she was naked under her coat, "what are you doing?"

Janey walked right up to Tom and pressed her naked breasts against him, she reached down and grabbed his belt buckle and began to unbuckle it.

"Hey, wait a minute," Tom protested, "what are you doing?"

"What do you think I'm doing Tom," Janey asked as she quickly unzipped his jeans and shoved her hand inside the waistband of his jockey shorts.

"Hold on," Tom said, grabbing her arms, "I'm getting married to Linda, I'm not going to do this."

"I can make you forget all about Linda," Janey said in a low whisper, as she put her mouth to his ear, "she can't do you like I can."

"Wait a minute," Tom said, pushing Janey away abruptly, "I don't want you, now, or ever, I don't want anything to do with you."

"I've never been turned down by a man, or a woman," Janey said defiantly.

"Well, now you have been," Tom said as he zipped his jeans back up, "I want you to leave, now, and I don't want to see your face in here again."

Janey pulled her coat shut tight, overlapping it, she held it closed with clenched fists, not bothering to button it back up.

"You'll be sorry Tom," Janey spit at him, "I promise you, I can make your life miserable."

"You already have," Tom said as he escorted her to the front door and almost pushed her out, "next time you try something like this, I'll have you arrested."

"You haven't heard the last of me," she shrieked as Tom closed the door behind her.

Tom opened the door when Linda arrived, he was not smiling like usually did when he saw her.

"What's wrong Tom?" Linda asked.

"Janey," Tom replied, "she came to my shop just before I closed today, and . . ."

"And what?" Linda asked with sudden urgency, "what Tom?"

"She asked me to show her around, I didn't think anything of it," he began to explain, "when I showed her my office, I turned around and she had taken off her coat, Linda, she wasn't wearing anything, nothing, then she tried to have sex with me."

"And?" Linda asked, hesitantly.

"And nothing!" Tom replied, "I shoved her away, then she made all kinds of threats."

"God I hate her," Linda replied.

"Honest, I didn't do anything, she came after me," Tom said, defending himself. "She's not right."

"She screwed my first husband, in my bed!" Linda said as she began to cry, "why is she doing this?"

"I don't know," Tom said reassuringly as he wrapped his arms around Linda, "but whatever it is she's doing, it's not going to be with me, I hold her responsible for you dumping me way back when."

"Oh Tom," Linda said, scrunching his shirt in her hands, "why is she doing this to us?"

"I don't know," Tom replied, "I really don't know, but as long as you know what happened, which was nothing, she has nothing to hold over us, she's just a twisted soul."

"Promise me Tom," Linda said, looking up into Tom's eyes, "promise me you will never cheat on me, and promise me that you will never leave me."

"Linda," Tom said softly, as he gently lifted her chin with his finger and softly kissed her lips, "I promise, I promise you with everything I am, that I won't ever leave you, I will never cheat on you, I promise you that."

Tom stood on the dock and threw a stone out across the lake. Throwing it low, he got it to skip three times before it sank.

"I really want to thank you for coming up here and being my best man," Tom said, "this is home for me, it has fond memories for Linda too, and we thought it would be the best place for our wedding."

"Tommy my boy," Smitty replied, putting his arm around Tom's shoulder, "I wouldn't miss this for the world, Amy, bless her soul, was wonderful, she was a good woman and a good wife for you. I remember you talking about Linda before you even met Amy, and I don't think you ever shook her, you two belong together, it's my sincere honor to be asked to be your best man, and that comes from the bottom of my heart."

"I know it does," Tom said, "And I really appreciate it."

"Good," Smitty replied, with a squeezing one-armed hug, "now, where is the beer?"

Tom nudged Smitty, just enough to knock him off balance, causing him too fall into the lake.

"It's in the fridge ya old fart," Tom replied, laughing loudly.

"I'll get you, you just wait," Smitty said as he splashed his arms in the water.

"You and what Army?" Tom asked, still laughing, "come on now, you can stand up, the water is only four feet deep right there."

"It is?" Smitty said, realizing it wasn't very deep after all, then straightened out his legs and stood up, "Oh, how about that."

"C'mon, let me help you out," Tom said, extending his hand to help Smitty out of the water.

"Here, help me with this!" Smitty said, grabbing Tom's hand and yanking it, pulling him into the lake with him.

Linda and Juanita stood on the porch of the cabin, leaning against the railing, holding their glasses of wine and watching the two old friends laughing and splashing each other in the lake.

"He sure likes Mike," Linda said, smiling at Juanita.

"Yeah, he sure does, and Mike really likes him too," Juanita replied, "and Tom really loves you too, I've know Tommy for way too many years to admit, and I have never seen him this happy."

"Really?" Linda replied, "I met Amy a couple of times before she was killed, and she seemed very nice."

There was an awkward silence on the porch for a moment, before Juanita responded, "Amy was nice, they were good together, but I don't think Tom was ever as happy with her as he is with you, I think she filled something he needed at the time, and his heart was, well, in a way, this is going to sound silly."

"What?" Linda asked, turning to face Juanita "is there something I should know?"

"No Linda," Juanita said, reaching over and touching Linda's hand, "I think in a way, his heart was always waiting for you, and now, he's with you and he's complete, look at him," Juanita said with a warm smile, pointing at the two grown men at the end of the dock, laughing and splashing like little children in the water.

Tom was adjusting his tie in front of the mirror when he heard a knock on the bathroom door. He opened the door and saw Tim standing there.

"Yeah?" Tom asked.

"Can I talk to you?" Tim asked Tom.

"Yeah, sure, what is it?" Tom asked as he put his hand on Tims shoulder as they walked out onto the porch.

"I've been thinking," Tim replied, then stopped speaking.

"About what?" Tom asked, "do you want to tell me later after the ceremony?"

"No, I want to tell you now," Tim replied, "Um, I want to come to work for you."

"Tim, we've had this talk," Tom said, "you know what I expect of someone that works for me."

"I know, I know," Tim replied, "that's what I want to tell you, I want to go back and finish school, and then come and work for you, I can do it, I know I can."

Tom pulled Tim closer to him and gave him a hug, "I'm proud of you son, I really am," Tom said, then asked, "have you told your mother yet?"

"No, not yet," Tim said softly, "I don't know how, it's not a very good subject around our house."

"Well, I think you should tell her," Tom said, "I know she'll be very pleased, trust me, she'll be happy to hear that."

Tom stood under the arbor that was decorated with vines and had flowers weaved into it. Next to him was Smitty, both standing proud in their suits and ties. Tom stood motionless, with the exception of his smile and tears of joy, as he watched Andrea and Tim walking down the makeshift aisle carrying a bouquet of flowers. Behind them, was Linda, with her mother holding one arm, and her dad holding her other arm.

Tom and Linda walked down to the dock, it was after midnight and the bonfire on the other side of the cabin was still going. Andrea and her date were picking up their stuff to head back to town. Tim had crawled into the back seat of Linda's parent's car, as they got ready to leave for the trip back to town. The rest of the guests and friends had left an hour or two ago. Smitty and Juanita were sitting on the ground, leaning against a log watching the fire. They had a blanket draped over them and were quite content just being outside, under the stars, in front of the fire, and away from their bed and breakfast for a few days.

Tom lifted Linda's top up over her head, exposing her naked breasts, he then kissed her neck, and at the same time cupped her breasts in his hands. Linda held his head, moving her head back to allow him better access to her neck. She loved it when he kissed her there. Tom ran his fingers across her nipples; they were erect in the cool night air. Without pausing, he pushed her pants down and she wiggled out of them as they fell to the ground. Tom stopped and took off his shirt and his jeans as quickly as he could. Linda stood there, naked, in front of him in the moonlight, he couldn't believe how happy he was, nor how lucky he was, she was now his, that after all this time, after all these years, they were finally married to each other. Tom jumped in first, followed by Linda, squealing when she hit the water.

Linda swam over to Tom quickly and wrapped her arms and legs around him, holding on tight. Tom loved the feel of her wet naked flesh; his hands seemed to slide up and down her body with ease. He slid his hands down and held her butt, helping to hold her up. Linda parted her lips and kissed Tom full on the mouth, her tongue probing, exploring his mouth. Her kiss was both sensual and aggressive. Tom responded by kissing her back, his mouth locked onto hers, their two tongues almost wrestling, entwined and probing, exploring each other mouths. Linda could feel Tom, he was getting extremely aroused, and she could feel him pressing against her. She squeezed her thighs together, holding him between them. Neither one wanted to wait another minute; Linda reached down into the water and guided him into her. With her legs wrapped around his legs, she took him all the way inside, grinding herself against his body. Tom spread his legs apart so he wouldn't fall over, then he pushed back at her, meeting each one of her squeezes and grinds with his thrusts. Linda stopped kissing Tom and gently bit him on the shoulder to prevent herself from screaming out loud. Her hands were on his back as she began to buck against him, harder and faster. Tom held onto her butt, holding her against him, he didn't want to loose this. He braced himself, thrusting, pushing back, and meeting her as they climaxed at the same time. It was fast, the excitement of being in the lake, at night, with people nearby, possibly hearing them, or even perhaps walking up on them was exhilarating and they were both extremely turned on.

Tom climbed up the ladder, and onto the dock first, then helped Linda out of the water, they got dressed, giggling like teenagers, and then walked back around the cabin to what was left of the dwindling bonfire.

Tom climbed down off the ladder and wiped his hands on his pants. Painting was not one of his favorite things to do, but the old house had needed a new coat of paint for years. Tom stood back and gazed at the house, admiring his work before putting the ladder away and washing out the roller and brushes that he used. Tim was on the other side of the house cutting the lawn. Tom wanted everything just right before he put the house up for sale.

It was a nice house, a solid house, and it was full of his childhood memories. Tom had grown up in this house, and except for his time away in the Army, had never lived anywhere else. He had watched the small maple tree in the front yard grow. The tree he had planted when he was six years old, was no bigger around than a pencil and a foot tall when he had planted it. Now, it was two feet around and gave shade to most of the front yard.

Linda had put her house up for sale a week earlier. Their plan was to sell both houses, and buy one that they had found and both loved, just outside of town.

"Oh Tom," Linda said, when she came outside after hearing the ladder being put away, "you sure did a good job, it looks beautiful."

Tom smiled and kissed her on the forehead, "Thanks, I'm glad that's done, I hate painting trim, especially when up on a ladder."

"Well, you sure did a good job," She replied, slapping him on the butt with the dishtowel she had in her hand, "lunch is almost ready, tell Tim, then come in and get cleaned up."

"I'll get you for that," Tom said with a laugh, as he pretended to chase her into the house.

Tim walked around the corner of the house pushing the lawn mower. He pushed it into the garage and put it in the corner where it was stored, then looked at Tom and said, "I'm done."

"Good," Tom said, "your mom came out a minute ago and said lunch was almost ready, so I guess you timed that pretty good."

"Yeah, I guess so," Tim replied.

"So what do you have planned for this afternoon?" Tom asked.

"I dunno," Tim replied, "I thought I would pick up Sue and we would go do something."

"Aaah," Tom said with a smile, "how are things with you two?"

"Pretty good," Tim said quietly, "she's nervous."

"Nervous? About what?" Tom asked.

"About me joining the Army," Tim replied, "I told her I was joining after I graduated from high school and try to figure my life out, and she thinks I should just go to college like Andrea did, especially since grandpa already put money away for me to go."

"Well?" Tom responded, "what's wrong with that?"

"I don't just want to go to college," Tim replied, sitting down on a lawn chair in the garage, "I want to do more, I want to travel, I want to experience life, not just bury my nose in books for four years."

"Sounds like you've given this some thought," Tom said as he hopped up on the workbench in the garage.

"I have," Tim replied, "ever since I met you, and from the things that mom has told me, well, I've changed, I went back to school, you gave me a job and I haven't missed a single day. I want more, I want to join the Army, it's what I want to do. I can always go to college while I'm in the Army, or after I get out."

"Have you told all this to Sue?" Tom asked, "maybe if you explain it the way you explained it to me it might help."

"Well, not exactly," Tim replied, "I kinda mentioned it, I said I wanted to join the Army, but I guess I didn't tell her the rest, maybe I should huh."

"Yeah," Tom said with a smile, "maybe you should, you have to do what your heart tells you to do, and, if she's the one, she'll understand and respect your decision."

"What if she doesn't?" Tim asked with wide-eyed fear, "what if she doesn't want me to join even after I explain it all to her?"

"Well son," Tom said, stepping down from sitting on the workbench, "that's something that I can't answer for you, now come on, lunch is probably ready now."

"K," Tim said getting up from the lawn chair, "I sure hope she understands, because I really like her."

Tom smiled and put his hand on Tim's shoulder as they walked towards the house, "let's go eat some lunch."

Tom sat down at the table for lunch, Tim sat across from him, and Linda was putting their sandwiches on plates when the phone rang.

"Want me to get it?" Tim asked.

"No, I'll get it," Linda said, then quickly put their plates on the table.

"Hello?" she said as she picked up the phone.

"Really? That's great! Ok, see ya in an hour, bye," She said and hung the phone up. "Guess what?" she said excitedly to anybody that would answer.

"What?" both Tim and Tom said at the same time.

"That was the real estate agent," Linda said as she sat down at the table, "there's an offer coming in on my house, he's going to meet us over there in an hour."

"Great!" Tom replied, reaching over and touching her hand.

"That's cool mom," Tim replied, "that's great, so now you guys are going to buy that place you looked at?"

"That's the plan," Linda said to Tim, "now we just need to sell this place."

"Not really," Tom replied, "I don't owe anything on this place, and we can afford that one with the sale of your place."

"Wow!" Tim responded, "Do you mean we're moving to that one just outside of town? The one with the pool?"

"Yep," Linda replied, "that's the one."

"I'll talk to him when we get over there," Tom said to Linda, "and have him list this house right away."

Linda unlocked the office and walked inside. She turned on the lights and put the coffee on to brew. She sat down at her desk and was going through her messages for the day when the receptionist came in and poked her head in the door.

"Hi Linda, sorry I'm late," she said.

Linda looked at her watch and shook her head, then replied to the receptionist, "Cindy, it's two minutes after, in my book, that's not considered late."

"Alright, thanks," Cindy said with a smile then went to the front desk to begin her day.

Cindy buzzed Linda an hour later and said there was a delivery for her. Linda got up from her desk and went to the front of the office and stopped in her tracks. There was a beautiful bouquet of flowers on the receptionists counter with a note attached. Linda looked at Cindy and pointed to the flowers, "these?" she asked.

"Yes," Cindy said with a big smile, then she winked, "it's from your husband, you must have done something good last night."

"Oh you," Linda said, pretending to slap her from across the counter, "it's none of your business what I did last night."

Linda and Cindy both broke out laughing for a moment, before Linda took her flowers back to her office and Cindy returned to work.

Tom pushed the sofa into place as Linda pointed to where she wanted it. "There, I like it right there," she said, placing her hands on her hips and cocking her head at an angle making sure she liked it where it was, "yep, right there."

Tim walked in the door carrying a box, "this is the last of my stuff off the truck," he said, "can I go in the pool after I put it in my room?"

"Sure," Linda replied, and then turned to Tom and asked, "what do you think?"

"I don't have a problem with it," Tom replied, "First swim on the first night at our new house, why not?"

"Alright!" Tim said excitedly and bolted up the stairs to put his stuff in his room.

Tim shouted down from upstairs, "I'm gonna call Sue, alright?"

Tom looked at Linda and they both smiled, "all right son," Linda said, shouting back up the stairs to Tim.

"I'm glad they worked that out," Tim said as he put his arms around Linda's waist, "joining the Army is important to him, and he really wanted her to be okay with it."

"I know," Linda replied, snuggling in against Tom, "now I'm going to worry about my baby."

"He doesn't leave for another month," Tom said, kissing Linda on top or her head, "he'll be fine, it'll be good for him, I'm so proud of him for getting his act together."

"Me too," Linda replied, turning her head and resting it on Tom's chest, "I was really worried and scared for awhile, I didn't know which direction he was going to take, I thought for sure he would end up jobless and wandering the streets."

"I think he will be just fine," Tom assured Linda, "he has a good head on his shoulders."

Tom put on his magnifying glasses to see the small circuit he was soldering on the radio he was repairing. He heard the front door open and looked up to see who it was. He smiled and stood up when he saw Linda walking across the room towards him, "Well hi there," he said walking around the end of his workbench opening his arms to greet her, "what brings you here?"

"I missed you," she replied, "I thought we could have lunch together."

"That's a good idea," Tom said, removing the funny looking magnifying glasses from his head, "I'd love that, what do you have in mind?"

Linda walked back to close the door and locked it, not saying a word, and then she flipped the sign around from open to closed. She turned to Tom and smiled as she slowly walked towards him, keeping her eyes locked on his, she began to unbutton her top, giving him a sexy smile as she did so. Tom watched her, enjoying the little strip tease show she was performing for him right there, right in the middle of the store. When she got to him, her top was unbuttoned exposing part of her breasts, she took his hand and led him back to the office.

"I think I'm going to enjoy my lunch today," Tom said as he followed Linda back to his office.

Once in the office, Linda turned to face Tom, she was still holding his hand. She brought his hand up and placed it on her breast, then reached down and unzipped his pants and reached her hand inside.

Tom caressed her breasts; he leaned down and took one nipple into his mouth, and circled his tongue around, teasing it.

Linda closed her eyes and leaned her head back and let out a soft moan. Tom put his hands on her waist and lifted her up onto his desk, then he walked around to sit in his chair, he rolled his chair in close between her legs and lifted up her skirt. Linda placed her hands behind her on the desk and leaned back on them. She watched as Tom's head disappeared under her skirt, then she could feel his fingers, gently moving her panties to the side, she felt his tongue, and then she closed her eyes again and leaned her head back to enjoy his skills.

Linda reached up to kiss Tom before she stepped out the door to walk back to her office. She had a bounce in her step and a smile on her face as she swung her purse and walked back to work. Tom watcher her walking away, he loved watching her, it didn't matter what she was wearing, or what she was doing, she was in his life, she was with him, and he knew that he had to be the luckiest guy in the world. He never seemed to be able to spend enough time with her. He smiled to himself and returned to his workbench to finish the repair he had started before Linda came in for lunch.

Linda hung up the phone and called for Tom, he came in from the backyard where he had been skimming leaves off the pool.

"What's up honey?" he asked Linda.

"Andrea just called," Linda said, as she sat down in the chair by the table.

"And?" Tom responded.

"She tried to call earlier but the line was busy," Linda said.

"Ok," Tom replied, "I know there has to be more to it, what did she have to say?"

"My baby is getting married," Linda said, slowly turning her gaze towards Tom, "she's getting married."

"Really?" Tom asked in surprise, "to who? I didn't know she was serious with anybody."

"I guess she is," Linda said, dumbfounded, "she hasn't told me either, she said she's been seeing a guy on campus and they're getting married, Tom, my daughter is getting married, and I don't even know who this guy is."

"Wow," Tom said as he sat down next to Linda and took her hand, "kinda sudden isn't it? When? I mean, when are they getting married? We are going to meet him first, aren't we?"

"I sure hope so," Linda responded, in a state of shock, "I can't believe this, why hasn't she told me about this boy? I'm her mother, how can she just get married? Just like that? I don't understand."

Tom sat silently, stroking Linda's hand, watching her eyes sadden, as they seemed to look far away at nothing.

Tim walked in the door at that moment. Not noticing the silence in the room, he reminded Tom and Linda, "tomorrow I need to be at the airport at seven, I can't be late, Sue wants to come with when you take me."

"Alright," Tom responded, "we'll get you there."

Tim noticed his mom was behaving strangely, she didn't even notice when he came into the room, and didn't respond when he told them about getting to the airport, "Mom?" he asked, "you alright?"

"Andrea just called," Tom replied, "she just told your mom that she's getting married, it caught her by surprise, and it really stunned her."

"She what?" Tim asked suddenly, "What did you say? Andrea is getting married? To who?"

"We don't know," Linda responded quietly,

"Wow," Tim replied, not knowing what else to say at the moment, "that's a shocker, I never thought she would spring something on you like that."

Sue knocked on the front door, the sun hadn't come up yet and Tom was still in the shower. Linda was in the kitchen and still in her bathrobe cooking eggs. Tim was pacing like an excited father waiting for his wife had given birth to a baby. Tim opened the door and smiled nervously, Sue entered and kissed him.

"Good morning," Sue said to Tim, "how'd you sleep?"

"Hey," Tim replied as he kissed Sue, "I don't think I got much more that two or three hours, I kept tossing and turning."

"I wouldn't think so," Sue said, "I know I wouldn't if I was hopping on a plane and flying off to Army boot camp first thing in the morning."

"Yeah," Tim replied, taking her hand and walking into the kitchen where Linda was just finishing the eggs.

"Good morning Sue," Linda said, "did you have breakfast yet?"

"Good morning," Sue replied, "actually, no, I didn't, but you don't have to make anything for me."

"Oh don't be silly," Linda replied with a smile, "have a seat, I'll just give you Tom's, he's still in the shower, I'll just make him fresh eggs when he gets out of the shower."

"Thank you," Sue said to Linda as she sat down at the table, sitting in the chair right next to Tim so she could hold his hand while they ate.

Tom walked into the kitchen and stood behind Linda, wrapping his arms around her waist, and kissed her on the back of her ear, whispering softly, "good morning sweetheart, sure smells good in here."

Linda leaned back into Tom's arms, and turned her head slightly, "good morning to you too, your breakfast is almost done, can you finish it up so I can go get showered?"

"You bet," Tom said as she handed the spatula to him.

"Good morning Sue," Tom turned and said, "you're here bright and early this morning."

"Good morning," Sue replied to Tom as she sadly gazed into Tim's eyes, "I couldn't miss this, I couldn't forgive myself if I didn't see Tim off at the airport today."

"How was it for you Tom?" Tim asked, "What was it like before you went in the Army? Were you nervous or scared?"

Tom chuckled a little, "well Tim, it was a long time ago, but I don't think I sleep a wink the night before I went."

"Ok, because I really didn't either," Tim said, "so it's normal then."

"Yeah," Tom agreed, "I think it's normal, don't worry, they throw a lot at you at first, and it's overwhelming, but it's nothing you can't handle, I know you'll do fine."

Tom took the egg out of the frying pan and put it on a plate just as Linda walked into the kitchen from taking her shower.

"Perfect timing," Tom said, holding the plate out for her, "hot off the stove."

"Thanks hon," she said, taking the plate from his hand and kissing him then sitting down with Tim and Sue to eat her breakfast.

Linda put her arm around Sue, as Tim blew a kiss and waved his final goodbye from the door of the airplane before stepping inside.

Tom put his arm around Linda as both women wept. Small tears formed in Tom's eyes as well.

"He'll be just fine," Tom said, trying his best to reassure Linda and Sue. "He'll write to you in a couple of days, and it'll be important for him to hear from home. Take it from me, some days letters from home are what keep you going."

"Ok," Sue replied, "I'll write every day. I'll start tonight and then send a whole bunch once I get his address."

Tom gave Sue a warm smile and gently patted her on the back, "that's nice, that'll mean a lot to him."

"I miss my boy child," Linda said, sniffing, and wiping tears from her eyes. "It's silly, his plane hasn't even left the ground yet and I'm standing here blubbering like a fool."

Tom smiled and said, "I'm gonna go grab a soda, anybody else want one?"

"No thanks," both Linda and Sue answered.

Tom held Linda's hand as they walked down the sidewalk. It was evening and the sun was just going down. Children were out playing ball in the street, a dog was trying to chase the ball, barking, ready to catch it in the event one of the children dropped it by mistake. They walked over to the main-street and up to the corner where the ice cream shop was; Tom opened the door and held it for Linda. The tiny bell on the door rang when it was opened, indicating someone had entered the store. Tom placed his hand on Linda's lower back, assisting her onto one of the stools at the counter. He sat next to her and opened up his menu, then closed it right away and put it back in the holder.

"I know what I want already," he said to Linda, leaning close to her and leaning his shoulder against hers.

"You do huh," she replied, "what are you going to have?"

"My favorite," Tom replied, "a hot fudge malted."

"Mmmm, that sounds good," Linda said, looking, and seeing his smile, "can I share? I don't want a whole one."

"Sure," Tom responded, with a small laugh, "Somehow I knew you would ask that, I'll ask for two glasses."

Tom took the long handled spoon and dipped it into the malted, then raised it to Linda's mouth for her to have the first taste. When he pressed it against her lower lip, she opened her mouth and reached her tongue out slightly to taste the cold ice cream.

Her eyes opened wide, as her tongue touched the cold chocolaty ice cream that Tom was holding at her mouth.

Linda laughed and brought her hand up to catch the drop of ice cream as if fell from the edge of the spoon.

Tom stuck the spoon in the malted again then he put it in his own mouth this time.

"Mmm, mmm, mmmm, mmm, mmm," Tom said, licking his lips, "these are as good, no, they're better than I remember they were."

"Tom," Linda said, looking up out of the corner of her eye, "they are the same as always, true, they are very good, but they've always been this good."

"Oh," Tom said quietly, looking back at her out of the corner of his eye, "guess I just must me mistaken then or something, all I know is it sure tastes good today."

Linda leaned her head on his arm, saying to him, "you crack me up."

Tom just looked straight ahead at the mirror on the wall, watching Linda's reflection and smiled warmly.

"Want some more?" Tom asked as he scooped another spoonful out and began bringing it to Linda's mouth.

"Ok," she said, nudging him with her elbow, looking down at the malted in a glass in front of her, "don't you think I can eat on my own with my own spoon without your help?"

"Hey!" Tom said in a mock defensive tone, "just trying to help."

Tom patted Linda's butt as she walked out the door of the ice cream shop in front of him. She held out her hand for his as she began walking down the street to go back home. Tom took her hand and brought it to his lips to kiss it. A few doors down he let it go and put his arm around her shoulder as they walked down the sidewalk, stopping to look into the different store windows along the way.

Linda stopped abruptly and touched the window of the pet store, inside was a small cage with kittens and next to it another small cage with two puppies. "Aw, Tom," she said, pulling at his hand, "look, aren't they cute?"

Tom looked in the window of the pet shop and smiled, "yes honey, they certainly are cute."

Linda tapped on the glass and made little faces at the kittens, they just ignored her, then she stepped in front of the puppies and tapped on the glass. The puppies stood up on their hind legs, their front legs trying to climb up the side of the cage they were in and yelping at Linda. Tom laughed, he thought it was comical how Linda tapped on the glass and made little faces and noises, trying to talk to the puppies, and they tried and tried to climb out of their cage, crying and yelping at Linda, almost like they had their own secret conversation going.

Tom gave Linda's hand a gentle tug, pulling her away from the pet shop window. Linda wrapped both of her arms around Tom's arm and leaned her head against his arm as they walked. Tom kissed the top of Linda's head and grinned at the world, happy to be walking, happy to be alive, happy to be with the love of his life.

Linda held up a dress and looked at it, "what do you think?" she asked, "Should I get this one?"

"I think you should," Andrea responded, "It looks good, go try it on."

"I want to look nice for your wedding," Linda replied as she opened the door to the dressing room, "I'll be right back."

Linda handed the clerk her credit card, then she turned and watched Andrea hold up and look at different purses. Linda smiled to herself, wondering where the time went, wondering how her little angel had grown up so fast. Pleased, and thankful, that she grew up healthy and into such a beautiful woman.

Linda took her receipt and picked up the bag with her new dress, and went to walk out if the store. Andrea walking alongside her said, "I can't wait for you to meet Jerry, I hope you like him, he's really a great guy and I really love him."

Linda put her arm around her daughters shoulder and smiled reassuringly, "I'm sure I will dear," Linda remarked, "If he makes you happy, that's all that's important."

"Oh mom," Andrea said as she leaned in against her mother, "he does, we get along so good together."

"That's good," Linda responded, "too bad Tim can't be here, I know he would want to meet Jerry too."

"Yeah, I know," Andrea acknowledged, "but we didn't want to wait, Tim will meet him, just not this time."

"Hey," Linda added, "your grand parents will be here tonight, they should be here in time for dinner. When I told them, they said they wouldn't miss your wedding for the world."

"Oh good," Andrea replied, "I know it's happening real fast and all, but we just couldn't wait any longer."

Linda burst out laughing, she stopped walking and turned to face Andrea, "couldn't wait any longer? Andrea my dear child, if you hadn't of waited this long, you would've told us you got married already, instead of telling us that you're going to get married, I mean, this is all pretty sudden don't you think?"

"Yeah, but we love each other and want to get married right away," Andrea replied, "besides mom, you always told me not to put off until tomorrow what I can do today, remember?"

"Well, yeah," Linda replied, "but I didn't mean something this big, wow."

"Mom, I have to tell you something," Andrea said quietly, lowering her eyes from her moms, "promise you won't get mad?"

"I'll do my best honey," Linda replied, "but I can't promise how I'll react."

"Fair enough," Andrea agreed, "The reason we're getting married so quickly is, um, mom, I'm pregnant."

"Oh, dear," Linda responded, her eyes open wide in surprise.

"Mom, it's okay," Andrea said, "it's not like you and dad, we have been together for almost a year, we were talking about getting married, before we found out, we just, we just moved up the date, that's all."

"Oh my baby," Linda said as she hugged Andrea, "I guess I'm happy for you, really."

"Thanks mom," Andrea said, patting her mom on the back while she returned her hug.

Chapter 13

TOM SAT NEXT to Linda on the edge of the bed; Linda held a photo album of Andrea and Tim when they were young children.

"This is when Andrea had her fifth birthday party," Linda said softly, "wasn't she cute?"

"Yes," he said, looking closer at the photo, "she looks like her mommy."

"Oh, and this one," Linda said with a smile, "I think she was about ten here, this is when she was into climbing trees, she was such a tomboy when she was young."

Tom chuckled and rubbed his hand on Linda's back, caressing her. "You did a good job, you raised two very fine children."

"Thank you," Linda replied, leaning against Tom, "I did my best."

"What's this?" Tom asked, pointing to a photo.

"Oh my god," Linda said laughing, "That must have been Halloween or something, she was dressed as a punk rocker, almost looks like she's a walking dead or something doesn't it?"

"Sure does," Tom agreed, then changed the subject. "I like Jerry, I think it went well tonight, Andrea seemed nervous, but it's got to be hard to bring your boyfriend, or soon to be husband home to meet the family and all."

"Yeah, I like him too," Linda agreed, "I think he'll be good for her."

Tom stood on the dock and cast his line out, then sat down on the bench to wait for a fish to bite. The wind was picking up a little and the clouds were rolling in across the lake. He could smell the rain in the air, it was still a ways off, but it was coming. Tom knew from growing up on this lake that fishing was usually the best just before a storm approached. He didn't know why exactly, he knew there was some scientific reason for it, but all he knew, or even cared, was that before a storm, the fish would bite, and that meant fresh fish in the frying pan.

Tim walked out onto the dock and sat down next to Tom on the bench.

"I wish I could have been here for Andréa's wedding," Tim said to Tom.

"I know you do," Tom replied, "she would have liked for you to have been there too, but, well, they don't let you out of basic training for a wedding, it's hard enough for a funeral, but not a wedding."

"Yeah, I know," Tim said, "but I still wish I could have been here ya know, it would have been nice. Is Jerry a nice guy?"

"Yes," Tom replied, "he seems like a very nice guy, granted, we only met him a couple days before their wedding, then they left right afterwards to get back to school, so I really don't know him very well."

"But he seemed nice, right?" Tim asked.

"Yes, he seemed nice, I think he's a stand up guy," Tom answered quietly, "turns out they've been together almost a year, the things you find out."

"I feel different now," Tim said to Tom.

"Different? How?" Tom asked.

"I dunno, it's weird, so much happened in basic, I learned so much, I think I really grew up," Tim began, "and when I got home yesterday, my friends all seem so, I don't know, I can't explain it."

"Exactly like they were when you left?" Tom replied.

"Yeah! That's it," Tim agreed, "like they are stuck in some time warp or something, still doing the same thing, partying, hanging out, just like in high school."

"I know what you mean," Tom said as he began reeling in his fishing line.

"Was it that way for you too? I mean, when you came back from basic," Tim asked.

"Pretty much," Tom said as he cast his line out again. "I think it's going to rain real soon, how about making sure all the car windows are shut?"

"Ok," Tim responded, "say, want me to bring you down a beer?"

Tom looked up at Tim and smiled, "yeah, sure, that would be great, bring one for your self too."

Tim came back a few minutes later with two beers and handed one to Tom.

"It's nice to see you back and doing well," Tom said, holding up his beer to toast with Tim, "Thanks for the beer."

"Thanks, and you're welcome," Tim said, touching his beer against Tom's, "so how many fish have you caught so far?"

Tom reached down and hoisted up the stringer that was tied to the dock, "looks like enough for dinner, I could use some help cleaning 'em."

Tim looked at Tom with a grin and shook his head, "I had to ask didn't I?"

Tom laughed, "I guess so."

Tim sat back and sipped on his beer, gazing out over the lake, the sky was getting darker and rain could be seen in the distance. "I can't believe I made it through basic, the next two weeks before I have to report for school will go fast," Tim said.

"Yep, it will past quickly," Tom agreed, "Tell ya what, I'm going to pull my line in now, why don't you go tell your mom and Sue that the fish will be cleaned and ready to fry," then he looked at his watch, "in say, forty five minutes."

"I'm on it!" Tim said, jumping to attention, and doing a playful salute, then turning and running off the dock towards the cabin.

Tom started a fire in the fireplace while Linda began frying the freshly caught and cleaned fish for dinner. Tim and Sue were out on the porch, sitting on the swing together watching the rain and enjoying one another's company.

Tom, satisfied the fire was burning well enough, went into the kitchen of the cabin; he put his hands on Linda's shoulders and began to rub them.

"Mmmm, I'll give you thirty minutes to stop that," she said as she moved her head from side to side, allowing Tom better access to the base of her neck.

"Want me to take over?" Tom asked, "I do fry a pretty mean fish ya know."

"No thanks," Linda replied, "I'll fry the fish, you just keep doing what you're doing, it feels good."

Tom looked out the picture window and saw the backs of Tim and Sue's heads on the swing. Then he dropped his hands down along Linda's sides and reached around in front, reaching up and cupping her breasts, "What did I find?" he whispered softly into her ear, gently nibbling her earlobe.

"Tom, stop it!" Linda said, giggling, "I'm trying to cook here, can't you see?"

"I can see," Tom said, caressing her breasts, "you don't use these to cook with do you?"

"No," Linda replied, bringing one hand up to hold Tom's hands firmly against her breast, "I don't use them to cook with, but you are distracting me, and I might burn the fish, how will you explain that one? Huh?"

"Fine," Tom said, removing his hands from her breasts and slapping her on the butt, "I'll set the table then."

"Thank you," Linda responded, "that needs to be done too."

Tom went to add another log to the fire while Tim and Sue washed up for dinner. Linda was putting the last of the food on the table when they all heard a crack of thunder and saw the bright flash from the lightning at the same time. The cabin shook it was so loud and close. At that moment the power went out and the cabin went dark except for the glow from the fireplace.

"Ok," Tom said calmly as he opened the pantry door, "everybody just sit down, I'll get the flashlight and dig out some candles, we'll have a candle light dinner."

"yeah," Linda said, "except instead of violin music in the background, we have thunder and rain."

"Want me to sing?" Sue asked, trying to create some humor and hide her fear, "I can sing for us."

"That won't be necessary," Tim responded, patting Sue on her hand, then reaching for the platter of fish, "we can see the food, let's eat."

"Tim!" Sue said, clearly annoyed, "can't you wait? Look, Tom's lighting candles, it'll only take him another minute."

"Sorry," Tim said, folding his hands on his lap and sticking out his bottom lip, looking like a little school boy that was just punished.

"Go ahead," Tom said, lighting the last candle and placing it on the table, "we can start, look, there's plenty of light, just don't open the fridge."

Linda looked around the room of the cabin, seeing a dozen or so candles placed all around the room. She smiled and cocked her head, "Tom, it looks lovely, you made it look so nice in here, thank you."

Tom leaned down and kissed Linda on the side of her cheek before sitting down himself, "You are quite welcome my dear," he said, smiling.

Tom and Linda sat on the porch swing of the cabin, slowly swinging back and forth. The rain was still falling and the smell of wood smoke that came from the fireplace, combined with the smell of rain in the air smelled good.

Tim added another log to the fire and stirred it, while Sue toweled off the last plate from dinner and put it away in the cupboard.

The storm had passed, lightning could still be seen in the distance and the quiet roll of distant thunder still echoed across the lake.

Tom had his arm around Linda, his hand slowly stroking her arm; Linda was leaning against him, her feet tucked under her as she snuggled against him.

"I love it here," Linda said quietly, "I love the sound of the falling rain, it is so relaxing."

"Me too," Tom agreed, "It's good to have Tim home, him and Sue sure get along good, I wonder if they will end up together."

Linda looked up at Tom, "Oh, I think so," she said and smiled, "I see a lot of us in them."

"You do?" Tom asked.

"Oh sure," Linda replied. "I just hope they don't go through years of pain and heartbreak like we did."

"Yeah," Tom said, sighing, "things sure didn't go like we wanted them to when we were young, did they?"

"No, they sure didn't," Linda responded, reaching her hand up and placing it on Tom's chest, gazing into his eyes with a look that left no question as to how deep her love for him was, "but I did get two wonderful children, and, in the end, you and I did end up together."

Tom smiled at her, then he kissed her forehead, at the same time pulling her closer, "Yes, we did, and I plan on growing old with you now, I think the best is yet to come."

"Aw," Linda said softly, kissing his chest then burying herself into his arms.

Tom just grinned happily and stared out across the lake, watching the lightning in the distance as the storm moved farther away.

Linda put her arm around Sue and waved at Tim as he boarded the airplane. Sue waved with one hand and with the other she held a handkerchief to her eyes, wiping away her tears. Both women were crying and hugging each other. Tom waved and put his hand on Linda's shoulder, "Ok girls," he said, sounding reasonable, "let's go now, he's on the plane and we can't see him anymore."

"Can we wait a few minutes?" Sue asked, sad eyed with tears running down her face, "can we wait until his plane takes off?"

"Sure we can," Tom said and went to stand by the window to watch the ground crew prepping the airplane for departure. Tom hated these kinds of moments. He knew that Sue and Linda wanted to hang on to the moment as long as possible. He remembered the exact thing happened when Tim took off for basic training just three months ago. "Oh well," Tom said to himself, acknowledging that women are different creatures than men are, and that they will more than likely do the same thing again next time, and the next time, and the next time that Tim flies out. As long as he is in the Army and flying someplace, they will hang on to the minute and be teary eyed. He also knew that, next time, he would be here with them, he would reassure them, he would comfort them, he would do the same as now, except maybe not recommend that they leave until after the airplane has taken off and far out of eyesight. Maybe even then, he will watch and wait quietly until they mention they are ready to leave. That would be the safe choice, but Tom knew himself, and he will again, probably before they're ready to leave, suggest leaving, and again he'll face two crying women who are not yet ready to go.

"I think I see him," Tom said, waving at a hand waving from the tiny window of the airplane, "See him? He's in the fourteenth window back, can you see him?"

"Is that Tim?" Sue asked, waving rapidly, almost as if she were trying to put out a fire.

"It looks him," Linda replied, waving a smaller, more dignified ladylike wave towards the person waving from the airplane, "it's kind of hard to tell though, the windows are so small and I don't have a good view."

Linda picked up the phone, "hello?" she answered.

"Hello, mom?" the voice said, "It's me, Tim."

"Tim? Are you all right? What's wrong?" Linda asked, panicking, "what happened? Where are you?"

"Mom, mom, it's okay," Tim replied, "I had a layover, remember? And well, due to a snowstorm, I'm stuck in Denver overnight, the airline is going to put everybody up in a hotel, but I just wanted to tell you I'm fine."

"Oh Timmy," Linda said, her tone obviously relieved, "you had me worried sick."

"I'm sorry mom," Tim replied, "I didn't think. When we got off the plane and were told that the airport was closed down from the snowstorm, I just wanted to call and tell you. So you wouldn't worry if you saw it on the news or something."

"Well, thanks Tim," Linda replied, "I guess I appreciate that, but you did scare me, I thought something bad had happened to you, I wasn't expecting to hear from you for a few days. Have you called Sue yet? Want me to call her?"

"No mom," Tim replied, "It's alright, I already talked to her, but thanks. Oh, I gotta go now, the shuttle to the hotel is getting ready to leave, Love ya, bye," Tim hurriedly hung the phone up before Linda got a chance to respond.

"Bye, I love you too," Linda said into dead silence, and hung up her phone.

"Who's that?" Tom asked when he walked into the room and saw Linda standing by the phone, her hand still on the receiver and looking upset.

"That was Tim," Linda responded, "he's stuck in Denver for the night, his layover got delayed by a snowstorm so he called to tell me.

"Oh," Tom replied, "everything alright?"

"Oh, yeah," Linda said, "he just scared me at first, but everything's ok."

"Ok," Tom replied, not a bit concerned, "those things happen all the time, I'm going for a walk, want to come with?"

Linda looked at Tom from across the room and smiled, "yeah, I would love that," She said.

Tom stood up from his workbench and stretched, his body ached from sitting on the stool, hunched over making repairs. He walked to the front of the store and went outside. He gazed up and down the street and then sat down on the bench on the sidewalk in front of his store. The sun was bright and the sky was blue, small clouds, high up in the sky slowly drifted by. Tom sat down and put his arm across the backrest of the bench and crossed his legs. It was a beautiful day and he was glad to be alive. Some people honked their horns and waved as they drove past. He smiled and waved back at them. For some reason Tom turned his gaze up the street and saw Linda, she was walking down the sidewalk towards him and he smiled, he could see her smiling back at him. It struck him as odd, he seemed to have a radar or something and could pick up on her presence, even from a block away he just knew inside that she was there and coming his way, it was uncanny he thought. Whatever it was, he was happy that he had this mysterious ability. Or was it just coincidence? It couldn't be, it happened too often.

Tom stood up and started walking towards Linda, he could see her smiling, her head cocked to the side, even the way she carried herself he could see how much she loved him and how happy she was that he loved her. Even with the sunglasses blocking her eyes, Tom knew the look in her eyes. It warmed his heart.

"Hey there!" Tom said from two doors away, raising his arms to meet her.

"Hi honey," Linda replied, swinging her purse, almost childlike, "I thought I would come see if you have time for lunch."

"With you?" Tom replied, wrapping his arms around Linda, "I always have time, why didn't you call first?"

"It was such a lovely day," she replied, "I thought I would take a walk, it's okay isn't that I just walked over?"

"Oh of course," Tom responded, "I didn't mean it like that, normally you call first. I guess if you had called, I was outside and would have missed it anyway."

"Oh?" Linda asked, "What were you doing outside?"

"I swept the sidewalk," Tom replied, "I sat on the bench and watched the clouds drift past, I waved at people driving by, I was just outside enjoying the day, I don't do that often enough I don't think."

"Good for you," Linda said, as she kissed Tom, then turning, she took his hand and began walking back towards his store, "let's go lock up and grab some lunch."

"Sounds like a great idea," Tom said, holding her hand as they walked down the sidewalk back to his shop, smiles on both of their faces.

Tom flipped the sign in the door around to read closed. He shut off the lights and locked the door.

"Ok, now where?" he asked Linda.

"The diner?" she replied, shrugging her shoulders.

Tom took a sip of his iced tea and looked at Linda, she was looking at him as though she had something to say, he recognized that look in her eyes.

"What's up?" he asked.

"Andrea called me this morning," Linda replied, "She wants to bring the baby and come stay for awhile."

"Oh, that's great!" Tom said happily, "It'll be good to see them, we haven't even seen the baby yet, what's her name again?"

"Sunrise," Linda said, "Her name is sunrise, but, Tom, she wants to stay awhile."

"Sunrise?" Tom asked, "how could I forget a name like that?" then it dawned on him, "awhile? What does that mean?"

"Seems that they are having, how do I say it, domestic problems? So she wants to stay with us until her and Jerry work through them."

"Oh," Tom said quietly, digesting that new information, "she knows that she won't fix anything by running doesn't she?" Tom inquired.

"Honey," Linda responded, looking sadly into his eyes, "I don't know, I just know she is my baby and needs our help right now."

"That's fine," Tom replied, "she can come, she is always welcome, her and little sunshine,"

"It's Sunrise Tom, please try and remember that," Linda said sternly.

"Oh, sorry, Sunrise," Tom replied, looking at his glass of tea.

"Thank you," Linda said, reaching across the table and placing her hand on Tom's, "it means a lot to me, and to Andrea, it really does."

"When is she coming, did she say?" Tom asked.

"Yes, she will be here for dinner tonight," Linda replied, "I'll make up the guest room for them after work."

"Don't worry," Tom replied, gently squeezing Linda's hand and smiling at her, "It's pretty quiet today, I'll just go home after lunch and do it, you have more on your plate at work than I do today."

"Aw," Linda said, cocking her head and smiling at Tom, "I really appreciate that, I sure do love you."

"I love you too," Tom said, winking at Linda, "I'll go home and get the guest room ready, then go back to the store for a couple of hours, I'll just pick you up after work, okay?"

"Okay," Linda replied, "I hope she's okay, she sounded so upset on the phone this morning."

"I'm sure she'll be fine," Tom replied, "sometimes a cooling off period is good, but she will have to go back and face him, they'll have to work this out, but until she's ready, I get to spend time with our new granddaughter."

Linda saw a twinkle in Tom's eye when he mentioned he would get to spend time with Sunrise. At that moment, more than anything, she wished that she would've had the chance to raise children with him. She felt deep inside that he would've been a wonderful father, and that he'll be a loving grandpa. She saw how he was with her two grown children.

Tom put down his newspaper and answered the telephone, "hello?"

"Tommy my boy!" the voice on the other end said.

"Smitty ya old fart!" Tom said, laughing into the phone, "how the hell are ya?"

"Doing good, I'm doing good," Smitty replied, "how are you? How's life treating you?"

"Can't complain," Tom replied, "I'm married to the best wife in the world, my business is doing well, my granddaughter is here with me, I'm babysitting today while Linda and her daughter are out doing girl stuff, life is good. So what's up?"

"Well, Doodles is getting married and," Smitty replied, "She wants to know if you and Linda would like to come."

"No shit?" Tom said, "Doodles is getting married? Well how about that, of course we're coming, I wouldn't miss it."

"Good, talk it over with Linda," Smitty replied, "I'll have Juanita mail you folks an invitation, and in the meantime, I'll book you a room here at the B&B."

"Alright, can't wait," Tom said enthusiastically, "It'll be good to see you guys again."

"Yeah, same here," Smitty said, "hey guess what? Danny will be home for the wedding, I can't believe he's been gone almost fours years already, boy, where does time go?"

"No kidding?" Tom replied, "So he didn't make a career out of the Army like his dad did after all did he?"

"No, I guess not," Smitty replied, "but that's okay, now his mother won't be up worrying about him when she watches crap on the news about soldiers dying and stuff, Tommy, It's a different Army now, we never really saw any of the shit, today, young men are going and dying everyday, I'm glad he's getting out, I really am."

"Good for you, good for him," Tom responded, "we're going through that now, Linda's son Tim was just home on leave a month or so ago, and he still has a couple of years ahead of him. I reassure Linda that he'll be fine, he'll be okay, but you and I both know, any day he can get the call and get shipped out, and then, well, you watch the news."

"Yeah" Smitty agreed quietly, "all we can do is cross our fingers and pray for them to come home safely, and hopefully in one piece."

"Amen," Tom responded, "well, give my love to Juanita for me, and tell Doodles we'll be there, okay?"

"Will do," Smitty responded, "ya gotta go so soon?"

Tom laughed into the phone, "you just wait ya old fart, wait until Doodles has kids, and you baby-sit, I tell you, this short call has been a luxury for me, but she's fussing now, and I probably have to change her diaper, and feed her, but hey, I wouldn't trade it for the world. Oh, there she goes, gotta run, good talking to you."

"Yeah, you too," Smitty said as they both hung up their phones.

Tom sat in the chair for a moment, his mind racing with memories of when Smitty and him would go out drinking, shooting pool and coming in late. Of all the times Smitty would help him home because he had too much to drink. How Juanita had made family dinners and invited him to join them.

Sunrise let out another cry from upstairs in the guestroom, Tom stood up quickly and ran up the stairs to pick her up, and pat her back gently. With Sunrise in his arm and her head on his shoulder, Tom suddenly knew exactly why she woke up and was crying. He laid her down on the changing table and removed her sleeper, when he opened her diaper he saw her surprise for grandpa.

Tom removed the dirty diaper and carried it at arms length with one finger and a thumb, not really wanting to touch it in the first place. He quickly dropped it in the diaper pail and closed the lid. "Whew" he said out loud, fanning his hand, trying to get rid of the smell.

Sunrise lay on her back on the changing table, looking up at Tom and smiling. She made some little noises, Tom knew she was talking to him, but had no idea what she was saying, and the noises she made were far from words. Those would come later.

Once she was in a fresh diaper and her pink and white sleeper with the little animals and letter print, Tom carried her down stairs and sat down in the rocker on the front porch. He held her, rocking back and forth. All was well in Tom's world at that moment.

Tom explained as best as he could to Sunrise what the birds were when they flew down and landed on the lower tree branches, singing and chirping. Sunrise looked at Tom and just made her little noises, and smiled when he ticked her tummy.

Andrea tucked Sunrise under the blanket. She had fallen asleep easily tonight. She looked so peaceful in the crib, her eyes closed, with her little fingers on her little hands, clenched making little fists.

Linda and Tom were walking up the sidewalk, holding hands, returning from their evening walk.

"Mom, Tom," Andrea began, "I want to thank you guys for everything, Jerry is coming in the morning to pick us up, we're going back home."

Tom stood quietly, waiting for Linda to respond.

"Oh, I'm so happy for you, for both of you," Linda replied, hugging Andrea tightly.

"Is everything okay?" Tom asked, "I mean, did you two work everything out?"

"Yeah, thanks," Andrea said, standing on her tip toes to kiss Tom on the cheek, "You guys are wonderful, I don't know what I would have done without you."

Tom smiled and hugged Andrea, "glad we could help," He said.

"We talked for a long time," Andrea said, as they sat down on the front porch, "we both were at fault and we both realized that, well, that bringing a child into the world is a bigger responsibility then either one of us imagined, and we both, with your help, have a lot to learn and we both have to work at it constantly."

"Wow," Tom said, both amazed and proud of the wise words that just passed Andrea's lips.

"Oh my baby," Linda said, walking over and hugging Andrea again, "I'm so proud of you."

"Thanks again," Andrea replied, "I love you both, both of you really helped a lot."

Linda carried Sunrise to the car and strapped her into the car seat in the backseat of the car. Andrea hovered behind her, watching carefully, not wanting anything to happen to her baby.

Tom chuckled and looked at Jerry, "the way Andrea is watching over her, you would think Linda's never strapped in kid a before."

"She's a good mom, and she told me how good you two were to her," Jerry said, offering his hand to Tom, "and I want to thank you."

"You're welcome," Tom replied, shaking Jerry's hand, "We enjoyed having little Sunrise here, and we're glad you two patched things up, take it from me, marriage is work, it takes a lot of work, every day."

"Really" Jerry asked, "you and Linda seem so, you look like everything is perfect, I don't believe that you two have to work at it."

Tom smiled and looked Jerry square in the eye, "We both came from previous relationships, we were both sort of set in our own ways, and believe me, we still have to work at it, but, when you love each other like we do, even the work can be pleasant."

Tom held Linda's hand as they waved goodbye to Andrea, Jerry and Sunrise as they drove away.

"They're good kids," Tom said, raising his arm up to put it around Linda's shoulder. He could hear her sniffling. He pulled her closer then reached his free hand up and wiped away her tears.

"I'm worried about them," Linda said, leaning against Tom, feeling his strong loving arms embracing her.

"Aw honey," Tom said, "They'll be fine, they're young and still have some growing and maturing to do, we all went through those times, remember?"

"Yeah, I know," Linda replied, "but it wasn't easy, there were lot's of rough spots."

"Look at it this way," Tom said, turning to walk back into the house, taking Linda by the hand, "They're crazy about each other, they both love and cherish that little baby of theirs, they both know it's going to take a lot of work, that's the hard part I think, knowing it takes work. Lot's of people think it'll be easy and then at the first sign of trouble they quit. These kids are smart and I truly, with all my heart, think they're gonna make it, I really do."

"Oh Tom," Linda replied, putting her arm around his waist, and hooking her thumb on his belt, "I sure hope so, it would kill me to see her go through what I went through."

Tom smiled and nodded, then opened the front door for Linda, patting her butt as she walked in the door ahead of him.

Tom peeled potatoes for dinner while Linda made a salad. Linda had put a chicken in the oven earlier and Tom had baked a pie earlier in the day. Tom washed his hands off then he went to put on some music. Linda smiled when she heard the music come on in the house, she turned to put the salad in the fridge and was startled. Tom was standing right behind her, silently watching her, she had no idea he was there.

"Oh geeze Tom!" Linda shrieked, hitting him on the chest with her fist, "don't scare me like that."

"I'm sorry," Tom said while laughing, "I didn't mean to scare you, I thought you knew I was standing here, didn't you hear me crunching on this carrot?"

"Noo, I didn't hear you," Linda said, shutting the fridge door, "if I heard you do you think I would have gotten scared?"

"Sorry," Tom repeated himself, shrugging his shoulders.

"Ok," Linda said, standing on her toes to kiss Tom.

"Tell ya what," Tom said, after she kissed him, "I'll light some candles and put them out on the table for dinner, how does that sound?"

"Sounds good," Linda replied, smiling and turning her head. She looked up from the sink and saw Tom's reflection in the window, and then she turned around to watch him. Linda stood in the kitchen and watched Tom, leaning back against the cabinets with her arms crossed in front of her. Tom was bobbing his head back and forth, playing an imaginary guitar along with the music and sort of dancing as he went around the room lighting the candles. Oblivious to the fact he was being watched by Linda, he was happy in his own little world at that moment, enjoying life, enjoying his music, everything was perfect right then and there.

Tom slid his plate to the side and refilled their wine glasses, and then he lifted his glass and looked at Linda.

"To my lovely wife, to a wonderfully blessed marriage, to my best friend, and a very good life," Tom said, and then he touched his glass against Linda's glass.

"Aw, you're so sweet," Linda said, gazing into his eyes, "To us," she added as she clinked his glass with hers.

Linda shook Tom's shoulder, "Tom, Tom, wake up, wake up, please,"

"Huh? What's up?" Tom asked groggily, as he opened one eye and looked up at Linda. She was standing at the edge of the bed, her eyes were red from crying, her hair was messed up and she was extremely upset. "Honey?" he asked, quickly sitting up, instantly wide-awake.

"It's my mom," Linda said, sobbing, "Tom, my mom died."

Tom stood up faster than he had ever stood up before, he wrapped his arms around Linda and then she broke down crying.

"When? How?" Tom asked, "I didn't even hear the phone ring."

"Dad called a half hour ago," Linda replied between sobs, "you slept, right through it, I was in the kitchen making coffee and it only rang once, Tom, my mom died."

"I'm so sorry honey," Tom said calmly, holding his hand against the back oh her head as she cried, then moved aside to help her, "here sit down."

"What's dad going to do? He's all alone now," Linda asked, then looked around the room, "where's the phone? I have to call the kids and tell them."

"Shhh," Tom said, holding her, "In a minute, I want you to get your composure first, I can call them if you like."

"No, I have to call them," Linda insisted, "I need to call my children."

"Ok, Ok," Tom said, standing up to go find the telephone, "I'll get it for you, then you have to tell me what happened."

Tom returned a moment later with the telephone, "here honey."

"Thanks," Linda said, still sobbing but not quite as bad.

Tom saw that Linda was trembling and having difficulties dialing the number.

"Here," Tom said, taking the phone from Linda, "I'll dial then you can talk, who do you want to call first?"

Chapter 14

TIM STOOD AT the front of the church, he was wearing sunglasses and stood straight and tall, proudly in his Army dress uniform. Some of his friends were standing near him in a small circle, talking. Andrea walked up the sidewalk; she was dressed all in black and also had on dark glasses, behind her was Jerry carrying Sunrise. Andrea stopped when she got to Tim; he turned from his friends and hugged Andrea. They hugged for a long minute before either one of them spoke.

"Mom's inside," Tim said, and then looked at Tim, "is this your little girl?"

"Yes, this is Sunrise," Jerry said to Tim, extending his free hand, "I'm jerry, we haven't met yet, I'm really sorry about your grandmother."

"Thanks," Tim said, shaking Jerry's hand, "nice to meet you, hell of a place to meet my brother in law and my niece for the first time, a funeral."

"Yeah," Jerry replied softly, and then asked, "So you're in the Army huh?"

"Yes sir," Tim replied proudly, then saw Tom motioning for him, "oh, looks like it's time to go inside."

"Yeah, I think so," Jerry agreed, hoisting Sunrise up and adjusting her in his arm so he wouldn't drop her.

Linda poured some iced tea and brought the tray out onto the front porch. Tom was sitting on the swing, holding Sunrise above his head and gently wiggling her. Sunrise laughed and giggled. Tom laughed back and made silly baby noises, which made her laugh and smile even more.

Andrea was sitting in a chair next to her and Jerry sat on another chair, holding her hand. Tim stood leaning against the post near the steps leading down to the sidewalk.

"Iced tea anyone?" Linda asked as she set the tray down, and then went to sit next to Tom on the swing, "I'm glad all of you could make it, especially you Tim."

Andrea and Jerry nodded their heads in agreement, not saying anything.

"I had to Mom," Tim replied, "grandma was important to me, to all of us, we lived with her, she helped you raise us, how could I not come home?"

Linda smiled at Tim, "well, I'm really glad you did, and grandpa was glad too, even though he doesn't say it, I know he's glad."

"How is grandpa?" Andrea asked, "He didn't talk to me at all."

Linda looked down at the floor; Tom put Sunrise on his lap then put his free hand on Linda's hand. She began to explain; "he doesn't remember much anymore, he's real sick, I don't think he'll be with us much longer, your grandma took care of him."

Linda began crying, "Your grandpa isn't the man you kids knew, he doesn't even recognize me anymore and I think we'll have to move him into a home now that grandma is gone."

"That's so sad," Andrea responded, "he was always so healthy, so strong, it's hard to see him like this."

"He started showing signs right around the time of your wedding," Linda replied, "but tried to cover them, now, now he doesn't even know where he is anymore."

"I don't ever want to end up like that," Tim said, "I want someone to just shoot me."

"Tim!" Linda said angrily, "don't even talk like that."

"I don't mom," Tim replied, "I don't want to go out like that, like a vegetable, I don't."

"Tim!" Linda repeated herself, "I said don't talk that way, I don't want to hear it, not now, not today, just stop."

Tom looked at Tim, he didn't say a word but Tim could read the look in his eyes and stopped talking before he said another word to upset his mother.

Andrea stood up and took Sunrise from Tom's lap, "I think I'm going to see if she needs to eat."

"Good idea," Jerry said, standing up and following Andrea into the house, "I'll help."

"I'm sorry mom," Tim said, apologizing, "it's just that last time I saw grandpa, he was great, he drove, we went fishing, he was strong, he was the grandpa I knew, I don't know this guy. How do I talk to him?"

"You just do," Linda replied, "you just talk, don't expect an answer or any response, just do the talking and pray that somehow he hears and understands you."

Tom put his arm around Linda, patting her shoulder, "It's real hard for your mom to watch," He said to Tim.

Tim made a grimaced face and nodded his head, trying to understand how it must be for his mom.

Tim put his empty glass down on the tray then reached over to touch Linda's hand, "I'm going to go out with some friends tonight before I fly back tomorrow, okay?"

Linda smiled a sad smile, "okay honey, I'll see you in the morning."

Tim kissed her then turned to go inside the house.

"I don't know what's got into him," Linda said.

Tom shrugged, "I don't know, say, listen to this, I thought about going up to the lake and doing some fishing this weekend, what do you say?"

Linda looked up at Tom, "Oh honey, I can't, I think I better start looking for a home for dad, maybe think about selling their retirement home and boat and moving him to a good facility, I hate the thought of that, but, well, now that mom's gone, *sniff,* I think now it's time."

"I agree," Tom said, "do you still have the name of their neighbor down there? Maybe he can help find a good agent to help sell it."

"Yeah, I think so," Linda replied, "maybe I should just go down there myself, they have so much stuff to go through, I should try and find all the legal papers and stuff."

"Tell ya what," Tom said, "I'll call some of my customers, and tell them I will be closed for a few days and that I won't be able to fix the things they dropped off. I'll fly down with you and help."

"Could you?" Linda asked, looking into Tom's eyes, as a sigh of relief passed her lips, "Oh that would be great."

"Of course I will," Tom said, gently squeezing her with his arm.

Smitty stood at the front of the room and raised his glass, "To my little baby and her new husband, I have watched you grow and blossom into a fine young woman. I am happy to see you with such happiness and love in your life, and to my new son in law. I know you will be good to my little girl, and if you aren't," he paused a moment and smiled, "I know where you live."

The friends and guests laughed and raised their glasses to the toast made by the father of the bride.

"And," Smitty added, "as long as I'm up here, I want to thank everybody for coming today, I know some of you traveled far for this festive occasion, and I, we, really appreciate it. I want to welcome and thank one of my dearest and oldest friends Tom, and his wife Linda for coming."

Tom stood up at that moment, and raised his glass of champagne, "I want to thank you for inviting me, and I wouldn't miss Doodles wedding for all the money in the world." Tom sat back down as people clinked glasses and looked up at the wedding party at the head table. Amanda began to turn red, embarrassed and blushing. "Uncle Tom," she shouted out from her seat.

"Oops, sorry about that Amanda," Tom shouted back. Guests began to laugh. Amanda whispered something into her new husband Ron's ear, then he smiled and laughed, then looking out across the crowd to Tom he held his glass up, as if he was doing a private toast.

Tom raised his glass up and smiled back at him.

Juanita tapped Tom on his shoulder; he looked up at her and smiled.

"My turn," she said and reached her hand out.

Tom stood up and took a quick sip of his beer, and then he followed Juanita out onto the crowded dance floor.

Linda sat back in her chair and watched. She was glad to be sitting this one out. Her feet were beginning to hurt. The heels she was wearing looked nice, but they were very uncomfortable, and she was more comfortable wearing sneakers or sandals.

"Who is that over there?" Tom asked Juanita, as he pointed to an attractive girl sitting by herself.

"Her?" Juanita asked, looking in the direction Tom pointed. "That's Becky, she's Danny's girlfriend," Juanita replied.

"Oh, where's Danny?" Tom asked, "isn't he here?"

"He's here, maybe out having a smoke or something," Juanita replied.

Tom kissed Juanita on the side of her cheek and thanked her for the dance then went back to sit with Linda.

"That was lovely," Linda said, touching Tom on the arm, "you two dance good together."

"Not as good as we do," Tom said, leaning in and softly kissing Linda on the lips, "You are my favorite dance partner any day."

Linda smiled and batted her eyes playfully at Tom, "keep that up, you just might get lucky tonight."

Tom chuckled, "I hope so," he said, and then looked around the room,

"I'm ready to leave pretty soon, how about you?"

"Anytime you're ready honey," Linda replied, taking a sip of her drink, I don't know anybody here except Mike and Juanita, and they are pretty busy with their family and their local friends.

"Ok, we'll leave in a few minutes then, I'm getting tired too," Tom replied, "I'll go find Smitty and say goodbye, say, have you seen Amanda lately?"

Linda sat up straight and looked around the room, "No, I haven't come to think of it, I haven't seen either one of them for awhile," She replied, then whispered into Tom's ear with a giggle, "maybe, they already left to go start their honeymoon."

"Ya just never know," Tom said, standing up, taking Linda's hand, "okay, let's go say goodbye."

Tom watched himself in the bathroom mirror as he brushed his teeth. He had undressed and washed his face off. His mind though of what was to come. Linda had been teasing him in the car all the way back to the B&B from the wedding. She had nibbled on his ear while he drove; she had rubbed his thigh and caressed the bulge in his pants, as he got excited. She had opened her blouse and exposed her breasts, teasing him the entire drive. A few more brushes and then a quick rinse and spit, then he would open the door and see her, lying on the bed, waiting for him, wanting him. Just a couple more seconds, he was ready.

Tom smiled his biggest smile as he opened the bathroom door and stepped towards the bed. Linda was in bed, but she was under the covers and already fast asleep. Tom cocked his head and smiled a small smile, then walked over and snuggled the blankets around her, kissing the top of her head. She didn't move a muscle. Her eyes were closed and she had the most beautiful peaceful look on her face as she slept. Tom walked around to the other side of the bed and crawled in, he laid there on his side, resting his head on his hand and watching her sleep for several minutes before drifting off to sleep himself.

Linda took the mail that the receptionist handed her and leafed through it quickly. She made some notes on her calendar then picked up the phone and dialed.

"Tom's electronics, may I help you?" Tom asked.

"Hi honey it's me," Linda replied, "I need to talk to you, want to meet for lunch?"

"Um, sure," Tom responded, "It can't wait until tonight I take it."

"Well," Linda replied, "it probably could, it's not really urgent, but I, well, it's . . ."

"Honey," Tom said, interrupting her train of thought, "not a problem, I'll pick you up in, say fifteen minutes? It's almost lunchtime anyway."

"Thanks," Linda replied, "I really appreciate this."

Linda was waiting in front of her office when Tom pulled up in the car. He got out quickly and walked around to the sidewalk.

"Hey, what's so important," Tom asked as he kissed her and opened the door for her, "is something wrong?"

Linda got in and buckled up, and waited for Tom to get in the drivers side.

"Tom," she said, "I want to sell the business."

"What? Why?" he asked, surprised.

"I have enough money, and now that dad is, well," she began, "he has no input any longer, from selling their retirement home and his boat, I have a nice nest egg put away, he set money aside for him and mom in case one of them got sick, thank god, and well, I want to sell it. One of the architects that worked for dad, and then worked for me when dad stepped down has expressed an interest in buying it."

Tom sat there, listening, as she talked, he hadn't even started the car engine yet.

"Ok," Tom replied, "sounds like you've given this a lot of thought. If it's what you want, then I think you should do it."

"Yeah," Linda said, "I think I want to, I just wanted to talk to you about it first."

"Honey," Tom said, reaching over and touching her face with his hand, "you don't need to talk to me first, you can do whatever you want to do with your dads business."

"I just wanted to talk to you first," Linda replied, "It's a big step and, and I just wanted to discuss it first, I wanted to see if you think I'm doing the right thing or not."

"Honey," Tom said, holding her chin in his hand and turning it so he could look into her eyes, "whatever you decide to do is fine, I'll support your decision either way. If you do sell it, you'll have more time to do what you want to do for yourself, and, you will have the means to do it with."

Linda smiled at Tom, "thanks for listening and supporting me," she said, "it means a lot."

Tom smiled back at Linda, "that's what I'm here for, now, let's go eat some lunch."

Linda smiled and nodded her head, then tapped the top of his hand.

Tom turned the key in the ignition and started the engine. He looked at Linda, then put the car in gear and pulled away from the curb.

Andrea knelt down to tie Sunrise's shoe, "there you go now, go give grandpa a big hug," she said, then patted Sunrise on the head.

Tom moved to the edge of his chair and held his arms open wide, "come here," he said with a big smile, "come to grandpa, that's a good girl."

Linda stood behind Andrea, watching Sunrise waddle across the room, her little butt distorted by the diaper inside her pants. She took tiny steps, carefully placing each foot firmly on the floor before taking the next step. When she got closer to Tom, she began to smile and drool, her steps got faster and she fell forward, forgetting to move her back foot forward first. Tom laughed hard, a deep belly laugh as he watched Sunrise scramble to get back up and walk the remaining few steps to grandpas open arms.

"Hey! She did it!" Tim shouted from the kitchen. He was leaning on the breakfast bar watching, holding his beer in both hands, and laughing, "she walked all the way across the room all by herself, how long has she been able to do that?"

"Just a couple of days," Jerry replied from the sofa, where he was watching the whole event unfold as only a proud father could.

"That's great," Linda said, clasping her hands together at her chest, smiling at Tom, "did you see that? Did you see how she walked across the room to you grandpa?"

"I sure did," he said, sweeping Sunrise off her feet and up into the air in one smooth movement, "I sure did see my little goomba walking to see grandpa, all by herself," then he lowered her and kissed her on her bare stomach, causing Sunrise to giggle.

"I'm so glad everybody is here," Linda said as she turned to go back into the kitchen, touching Tim's arm as she walked past him, "it's been a long time since everyone was home at the same time for Thanksgiving."

"Sure has been," Andrea added, "I don't know when the last time was."

"Me neither," Tim said, standing up and turning around to lean back on the counter, "It's been awhile, I think it was before I joined the Army and before you went to college Andrea."

"I think so," Linda replied, "and we were all at . . ." then she stopped talking and began to cry.

"Oh mom," Andrea said as she walked across the kitchen to hug Linda, "I know it's hard, this is the first Thanksgiving since both grandma and grandpa passed away," Andrea looked straight into Linda's eyes, "but we're all here."

Linda hugged Andrea for a long minute in the center of the kitchen, "Oh my baby, I'm so glad you are here, all of you."

"How is she doing?" Jerry asked Tom, still sitting in the living room, a short distance from the kitchen; "it looks like she's having a hard time today."

Tom leaned back in his chair, rocking back and forth with Sunrise standing on his lap. She was playing with his hair and smiling at him.

"She has her good days and her bad days," Tom replied, "she has really been looking forward to today, all week long, she's really happy all you kids could make it this year."

Jerry nodded his head and looked down at the floor, then took a sip of his beer, "it's gotta be hard, both of my parents are here, well, not here, they are in Iowa, but they are still alive, and you two are here, I can't imagine what it's like to loose a parent, and both in one year, ouch, that sucks."

Tom looked over at Jerry, "yeah, it does."

"Tom?" Linda called out from the kitchen, where she was standing in front of the oven.

"Yes dear?" he replied from his chair in the living room.

"Can you come take the turkey out?" she asked.

"I can get it mom," Tim said, "I'm right here."

"I'll be right there," Tom said at the same time, standing up and putting Sunrise on the floor.

"Gotta go cut the turkey pretty soon," Tom said to Jerry as he rubbed his hands together, "It smells good already, I can't wait to eat."

Tom picked up the bowl of mashed potatoes and put some on his plate, "thanks for saying grace Jerry, that was very nice," Tom said.

"So how is work going?" Linda asked Andrea.

"I quit," Andrea replied with a smile, "Jerry is doing very well at his job, and we can afford it, so I quit so I can be a stay home mom."

"Well good for you," Linda replied, "that's just great, I'm happy for you."

"I'm working for Tom," Tim added, "I started last week, I figured I've screwed around long enough after getting out of the Army, I'd better get a job."

Tom laughed, "screwed around long enough?" he said, then added, "you were hardly out of the Army a month before you started work."

"From working everyday in the Army, a month off is a long time, I'm not used to that anymore, I don't know how I didn't work and it didn't bug me before I joined."

"Because you hadn't grown up yet, that's how," Andrea added, taking a sip of her wine. "You grew up when you were in the Army, it was good for you."

Jerry just smiled, then turned to feed a spoonful or mashed potatoes to Sunrise, who was seated in a high chair between him and Andrea, with food that almost covered her entire grinning little toothless face.

"I'm just glad that everybody is home this year," Linda said, choking up with emotion.

"I agree with your mother," Tom said, "It's really good to have everyone here today."

Chapter 15

THE FRONT DOOR of Tom's electronics opened and a tall burly man with graying hair and beard walked in.

"Where is the owner?" he demanded.

"He, he's not here," The woman in her early twenties replied, "can I get the manager for you?"

"I want to speak with the owner," the man said again, pounding his fist down on the counter.

Tim walked out from the office in the back of the store.

"I can take this," he said to the woman who was beginning to get flustered by the seemingly upset customer.

"Hello sir, my name is Tim and I'm the manager, how can I help you?" Tim asked, extending his hand to the man.

"I would like to speak with the owner," the man insisted.

"I assure you sir, I can help you with whatever you need in this store," Tim said, very professionally.

"Where can I find the owner?" The man asked again.

"Sir," Tim insisted, "The owner is not here, I'm the manager and I assure you, I have the authority to make whatever decisions are necessary to satisfy your problem."

"That I highly doubt young man," The man replied, then put his arm on Tim's shoulder and turned him sideways as they walked towards the back of the store. "I apologize," the man said, "I was hoping Tom would come out from in back, he and I are old friends and I wanted to surprise him, where can I find him?"

"Well," Tim said, pausing, "I really hesitate to tell you where he is, I mean, I'm sorry, but I don't know you."

"You're Tim, right, his step son?" The man asked.

"Yes," Tim replied cautiously, not sure who this guy was or how he knew who he was.

"And you are?" Tim asked.

"Has he ever mentioned the name Smitty to you?" the man asked.

"You're Smitty?" Tim replied, suddenly standing straight and tall, extending his hand again, "geeze, yeah, he's talked about you, lot's of times."

"Sooo?" Smitty replied, "Where is he?"

"He's not here, he's up at the cabin," Tim explained, "him and my mom are there pretty much all the time, he comes in once in awhile, but I run the place now."

"I know where it is, we were there years ago," Smitty replied.

"I think I met you a long time ago," Tim replied.

Smitty smiled and placed his big hand on Tim's shoulder,

"Keep up the good work kid, and don't tell Tom I'm in town, I want to surprise him."

"Oh man," Tim replied, "I think he'll be surprised, I won't tell him, I promise."

"Thanks," Smitty replied, "I better gas up the car first, then I guess we'll drive up to the cabin and surprise him."

Tom sat on the bench at the end of the dock, watching his bobber, waiting for it to disappear under the water, letting him know he had a fish on. It required patience, but Tom had nothing urgent to attend to and had plenty of time to watch and wait.

The sun was dropping down behind the trees as evening was approaching. Tom stood up and reeled in his line. The bobber hadn't disappeared, but he'd been fishing long enough for today and wanted to go back up to the cabin, light a fire in the fireplace, and be with his wife.

He laid his fishing rod down on the bench and walked back up the hill towards the cabin.

Linda opened the door just as Tom reached for the knob, startling him.

"Hi, I was just going to come down and see you," Linda said, smiling at Tom.

"I called it a day," Tom replied, putting his hand on her waist and kissing her on the lips, "thought I would come up and see what you were up to."

"I just finished tidying up the kitchen," Linda said, returning his kiss, "so, are you hungry?"

"Yeah, I think so," Tom replied, "want me to light the grill?"

"In a minute," Linda replied, "why don't you sit down for a minute first?"

Tom chuckled, "Honey, I've been sitting all afternoon, my butt is sore from sitting, fishing is hard work."

"Yeah, I know how that is," Linda said, playfully hitting his arm, "all that walking up to the fridge for a cold beer, then sitting on the bench watching the bobber and girls go by in boats, I know how hard that can be."

"Well, it's a tough job, but somebody's gotta do it," Tom replied, wrapping his arms around her from behind, cupping her breasts with his hands and rubbing his whisker stubble on her neck.

"Oh Tom, stop it," Linda said, laughing, "I have an idea, why don't you go get washed up, get that stinky fish smell off you and I'll light the grill."

"Yes dear," he replied, patting her butt as he turned to go inside the cabin.

Linda put some charcoal briquettes on the grill, squirted some lighter fluid on them, then lit a match and threw it on, watching the flame slowly grow until all the briquettes were flaming. She picked up an arm full of firewood from the woodpile and carried it into the cabin and put it on the stack of firewood that was already next to the fireplace. Then she pulled two wine glasses out of the cupboard and opened a bottle of wine.

Tom opened the bathroom door and stepped out, holding a towel to his head, the steam following him from the shower.

"Aaahh, much better," Tom said, as he stood in the doorway, toweling off his graying and receding hair, "I even shaved," he said, smiling.

"Well good for you," Linda said with a smile, "so did I."

Tom walked over to her, and touched her face with his hand, "you do a better job shaving than I do, you're much smoother than I am. You'll have to teach me your trick."

Linda hit him on the shoulder, "don't be silly, you know exactly what I mean."

Tom glanced over at the fireplace and saw the stack of wood he carried in earlier had suddenly grown.

"Did you bring in wood?" he asked, surprised, pointing to the stack of firewood, "I don't remember it being that high."

"I did, right after I lit the grill," Linda said, standing straight with her hands on her hips, "now you won't have to, all you need to do is grill the steaks, I made the salads when you were fishing and I threw some potatoes in the oven."

"Wow!" Tom said, cheerfully, "you have been busy, thanks I appreciate that, all of it."

"You're welcome," Linda replied, "I even poured us some wine."

"Oh my goodness," Tom replied, "I better go get dressed then, so I can relax with my baby," then he turned and went into the bedroom to get dressed.

Linda was sitting in her chair in front of the fireplace, her reading glasses sitting low on her nose and paging through a magazine while Tom put the last dish away in the cupboard,

"There, dishes are done," he said, folding the dishtowel and slipping it in the handled of the oven. A flash of light outside caught his eye and he turned to look out the window over the sink.

A car pulled into the driveway and turned off the headlights.

Tom stood still, watching the strange car that just pulled onto his property, not knowing who it was or why they were there. He knew he was not expecting anybody, and the way it was parked, he couldn't see the license plates to see where it was from.

"Are you expecting somebody?" Tom asked Linda from the kitchen.

"No, why?" she asked.

"Because somebody just pulled in and I don't recognize the car," Tom replied, "I wonder who it is."

"I don't know," Linda said, putting her magazine down and taking off her glasses, then walking into the kitchen to look out the window with Tom.

Tom watched as two shadowy figures got out of the car and began walking towards the cabin. There was a vague familiarity to the shapes and the way they walked, but Tom couldn't place them, not yet.

"I should have fixed that yard light," Tom said, annoyed at himself, "I can't tell who it is, and they're walking up to the cabin."

Tom looked at Linda. She just stood there, looking at him, looking nervous.

"Who is it?" she asked.

"I don't know," He said, turning and reaching for the knob to open the door. Just as he reached for the door, a heavy knock pounded on it. Tom opened the door and stood staring, motionless.

"Well Jesus Christ," Tom said, quickly opening the screen door, "what the hell are you doing here? Come in, come in."

"Who is it?" Linda asked, noticing the change in Tom, the sudden excitement and cheer in his voice.

"Oh my god, It's Smitty and Juanita," Tom said, answering Linda, then gave Smitty a big bear hug, "what the hell are you doing here? What a surprise?"

"Hi!" Juanita said in a high and cheerful voice, as she embraced Linda.

"Oh my god," Linda said, "It's so good to see you, what brings you guys up here?"

"How did you know we were here? How did you find us?" Tom asked, "geeze, ya old fart, it's sure good to see you, come in, sit down, want a beer?"

"I gotta tell ya," Smitty said as he sat down on the sofa, "I think I scared the shit out of some poor little girl at your shop."

"Oh, how's that?" Tom asked, opening a beer and handing it to Smitty, while Linda poured a glass of wine for Juanita.

"We stopped at the shop first thing when we pulled into town, right," Smitty began, "and I walked in, my chest all puffed up like a pissed off customer and demanding to speak to the owner."

"Who was it?" Tom asked, sitting back and sipping his beer.

"I don't know, a short blonde about yay high," Smitty replied holding his hand out about shoulder height as he sat in the chair, "she got so flustered, I swear, she was ready to pee her pants, then this guy walks out from somewhere, said he's the manager and he told the blonde girl he was going to handle the situation."

"Oh my, that must have been Tim, he's my son," Linda said, holding her hand to her mouth, waiting to hear what was coming next from Smitty's story.

"Yeah," Smitty said, "then when he kept insisting you were not there, and that he was the manager and in charge, I took him aside and told him who I was, you should have see him, he turned all sorts of colors. He went from nervous and white, to red and embarrassed, it was funnier than hell."

"Oh Mike, you were so mean to those poor kids," Juanita added, slapping him on the arm, "he came out to the car and laughed about it halfway up here."

"Sorry," Smitty said, turning to Tom, "I was hoping to get you to come out of the back room or something."

"Poor thing," Linda said, referring to Tim, "I wonder what he thought?"

"Hey," Smitty said to Linda, "he did good, he was very professional and didn't back down, not one bit."

Tom shook his head and laughed, "what a shit, now I have to give them all a hazardous duty bonus for dealing with you."

"Looks like your store is bigger now than last time we were here," Smitty acknowledged.

"Yes, it is," Tom explained, "when Amy and I started it, it was just the two of us, then when she died, I didn't do much in the lines of growth, I just worked it, made enough to put food on the table ya know, then Tim worked for me awhile before he joined the Army. I ran it as a small shop, doing mostly repairs and some sales, just sort of plugging along. When Tim got out of the Army, he came back to work for me again. I tell you, after just two years, he is now managing the place, I have two girls working the floor, sales have quadrupled, he manages it and does repairs, I pop in once in awhile and do paperwork and make sure it's still there, but pretty much, he runs the show."

"Wow!" Juanita said, "that's great, so you two basically have retired again?"

Linda looked at Tom and smiled, "yeah, pretty much."

"Hey," Tom added, smiling back at Linda, "we worked hard for many years, it's about time we slowed down, and had time for ourselves."

"What about you guys?" Linda asked, "So, what brings you two up here? How's your B&B?"

"Kinda the same thing here," Smitty said, "Amanda and her husband run most of the day to day operations, and Danny, well, he is living with his girlfriend and playing music, he has a band, but he comes around pretty often and chips in."

"So you two retired, again?" Tom asked, as he stood to throw another log on the fire in the fireplace.

Smitty looked at Juanita, "yeah, I guess you could say that,"

"We want to travel and see the country, this is the first place we came, and we wanted to see you two without a wedding or a funeral bringing us together."

"Aw," Linda replied, touching Juanita on the knee, "how sweet."

"Great!" Tom responded, "well, welcome to our cabin, do you have any plans?"

"Seeing you, fishing, drinking a few beers, catching up," Smitty said, finishing his beer.

"Maybe tomorrow we can get some fishing in then," Tom said.

"I can take you into town," Linda said to Juanita, "I know a few fun shops we can go to. I just know you'll love them."

Juanita smiled and nodded, "ok, sounds fun."

Juanita covered her mouth as she yawned.

"Here," Linda said as she stood, "let me get you fixed up in the guestroom, I bet you're tired from driving."

"Yes, I am," Juanita said, standing up and following Linda from the living room.

Smitty pulled two cigars from his shirt pocket and held them up, looking at Tom, "One of our guests gave these to me, they are genuine Cuban he told me, and exceptionally good, care for one?"

"Don't mind if I do," Tom said smiling.

"Honey?" Tom called out from his chair to Linda in the guestroom.

Linda poked her head around the corner, "what?"

"I'm going to step outside for a cigar with Smitty," Tom said to her, "we'll be back in a few minutes."

"Ok," Linda said, nonchalantly, as she went back about her business helping Juanita get settled in.

Tom and Smitty walked down the path to the dock, then out to the end and sat down on the bench.

"Sure is nice up here," Smitty said as he dug in his pocket for his lighter, "it's so quiet and peaceful," then he looked up, "Christ, look at all the stars, I don't know if I've ever see so many."

Tom smiled and looked up as well, "no city lights to interfere."

Smitty lit his cigar then held the lighter up to Toms cigar, Tom sucked in on it until the tip glowed red. Then he nodded and said, "thanks."

"Tom, I gotta talk to you," Smitty said with seriousness.

"Yeah? What's up?" Tom asked, relaxing on the bench and enjoying the cigar and the evening with his dear old friend.

"It's Juanita," Smitty said, beginning to choke up.

"Hey, what's going on?" Tom said, turning to face Smitty, "something wrong?"

"Tom, she's got cancer, she's dying," Smitty said, his voice cracking.

"Oh geeze man," Tom replied, putting his hand on Smitty's shoulder, "I'm sorry to hear that."

"We've gone to a dozen specialists," Smitty explained sadly, "it's too far along, it's everywhere, and they really can't do anything for her at this point, maybe if we caught it sooner . . ." he trailed off, not actually speaking so much as thinking to himself.

"Is there anything I can do man?" Tom asked, rubbing Smitty's shoulder.

"She followed me all over the world Tom," Smitty said, "she's been the best wife a guy could have, all my years in the Army, she followed me around from base to base, setting up house, then packing it up to move again, never complaining. It just isn't fair."

"Sure isn't," Tom agreed, "god, I'm so sorry, how's she doing with this? She didn't let on anything was wrong."

"Oh, she won't," Smitty said, sitting up straight and turning to look at Tom, "that's why we're here, we left the B&B with Amanda and her husband. We're traveling around the country, seeing everything she wants to see before . . ." he stopped again and lowered his head into his hands.

"Oh man," Tom said, rubbing his friends back, "how, what did they, when is, how much longer?" Tom tried to ask, not knowing exactly how to ask what he wanted to ask but didn't want to hear the answer to.

"Less than six months, Tom, my sweetie has less than six months, not even a year left, what am I going to do?"

"I don't know what to tell you," Tom said, shaking his head and shrugging his shoulders, "I don't know."

"She won't even see her grandchildren," Smitty said, "Amanda just found out that she's pregnant, and I don't think Juanita is going to be around when the baby is born."

"God I'm so sorry Mike, I'm so sorry," Tom repeated himself again, "do the kids know yet?"

"Yeah," Smitty replied, "They've been kept up to date on everything. It was their idea for us to travel and see the country. It's something she's always wanted to do. Damn it Tom, it just isn't right, she has to die before I could get around to taking her to see the country, what was wrong with me?"

"Come on, get hold of yourself Mike," Tom said, "it's not your fault, how were you to know?"

"I'm her husband," Smitty insisted, "It's my job to protect her, it's my job to take care of her, I should have taken her on more trips, we should have traveled more when we were younger and healthier."

"Mike, mike, come on man," Tom said, "your life played out how it was suppose to, you did travel, you saw the world together, you raised a family, you defended your country, raised two fine children. You started and ran your own business for years, don't beat yourself up, you two had a good life. Be happy for what you did, what you accomplished, don't get mad at yourself for what you didn't do, come on."

Linda poured herself a cup of coffee and sat down at the kitchen table. The sun was coming in the picture window of the cabin, filling the room with light.

Tom was out back splitting firewood, and she could see the backs of their heads as Smitty and Juanita sat and spoke to each other quietly on the porch swing.

The back door opened and Tom walked in, carrying an arm full of freshly split firewood.

"Hi hon," Linda said as he walked past her on the way to the fireplace to stack the wood.

Tom stacked the wood then came back and poured himself a cup of coffee and sat down with Linda.

"It's a horrible thing about Juanita isn't it?" Linda said to Tom.

"Sure is," Tom replied, "sometimes life just isn't fair, she's so full of life, I just don't understand."

Before Tom could respond, Smitty and Juanita walked in the front door off the porch.

"Hey," Tom said, nodding his head.

"Got any more coffee?" Smitty asked, rubbing his hands together.

"Sure, let me get you a cup," Linda said as she began to stand.

"No, no, I can get it," Smitty insisted, "you stay sitting, "I know how to pour a cup of coffee."

Juanita smiled at Linda and said to Smitty, "me too dear."

Smitty opened almost every cupboard door before he found the cups.

"You know," Juanita said teasingly, "I bet Linda could have told you were the cups were if you just asked, instead of looking in every door."

Linda held her hand over her mouth as she began to chuckle.

Tom looked up at Smitty as he sipped his coffee, and nodded his head to the side, "she's got a point man."

"Shut up, both of you," Smitty said, his smile barely visible behind his big grayish white beard, "I needed the exercise anyway, and I didn't want to be a bother to your wife Tom."

"Right," Tom said, shaking his head and looking at Juanita, joking sarcastically, "like I believe that for a second."

"I thought you two were going fishing today?" Juanita said, changing the subject.

"Oh, yeah," Tom said, looking up at Smitty, who was still standing in the kitchen, "soon as we finish our coffee, right?"

"Good," Linda responded, looking at Smitty, "because your wife and I have some serious shopping to do."

Juanita sipped her coffee, giggling quietly to herself.

Tom held the boat as Smitty climbed out and onto the dock.

"Wow," Smitty said, "what a day, I don't know if I've ever caught this many fish, tell the truth, I don't remember ever in my life fishing like this and enjoying myself so much, thanks man."

"Hey," Tom responded, "I enjoyed it too, we needed fish for dinner and we worked hard for them."

Smitty let out a loud laugh, "Well, if sitting in a boat with a cigar and a good friend, downing beers and catching some fish is work, I had the wrong career."

"I guess so," Tom agreed, "wouldn't it be great to get paid to do this?"

"Sure would," Smitty said, agreeing, handing Tom the stringer and his fishing rod.

"Just leave the rod in the boat," Tom instructed as he took the stringer of fish from Smitty's hand, "now we better get these cleaned and on ice."

"I wonder if the girls are back yet?" Smitty asked.

"I doubt it," Tom replied, "knowing Linda, and the shops she likes, we may not see them for a couple of days."

"That bad huh?" Smitty asked, laughing and putting his hand on Toms shoulder as they walked up the path to the shed to clean the fish.

Tom heard footsteps outside the shed and turned to look, he saw Juanita standing there, smiling.

"Hey," Tom pressed his finger into Smittys' ribs, "look who's here."

Smitty straightened up from leaning over the cleaning table and turned around to face his wife, in his hand he held a filet knife and a fish head. "Ew," Juanita said, wrinkling her nose and looking completely grossed out.

"Oh, sorry," Smitty said, throwing the knife and fish head down on the table, then grabbing a rag and whipping his hands off, "Hi there, how was shopping?"

"It was nice, we went to this real fun store and I bought a dress, what do you think?" she asked as she held as she turned around and modeled it for him.

"Looks nice on you, I like it," Smitty said, leaning in to kiss her.

"No way!" Juanita said, stepping back a step and holding her hands up to block him, "you stink like dead fish."

Tom laughed, "That's what happens when you catch and clean them, the smell just kinda follows."

"Well, hurry up and get them cleaned, and come inside," Juanita said, turning around and walking away towards the cabin.

Linda waved at Tom from the door to the cabin and smiled, Tom smiled and waved back with a filet knife in his hands.

"Looks good on her," Tom said, referring to the new dress Juanita was wearing.

"Yeah, it does," Smitty said quietly, "she sure puts on a good face doesn't she, I couldn't do it, nope, if I was dying, I don't know what I would do, but I don't think I could cover it that well."

"Maybe she's made her peace," Tom suggested, "I mean, she has a strong faith. Maybe she's made her peace and is okay with it."

"Do you really think so?" Smitty stopped cleaning the fish he had in his hand and asked Tom.

"I don't know, it sounded good," Tom admitted, "I don't know what to say, I just know some people are more afraid of death than others."

"Yeah, I know," Smitty said as he resumed cleaning the fish, "it sure makes you realize your own mortality, that's for sure."

"No shit," Tom said, "none of us knows how or when we'll go, just one day our number is up and that's all there is to it."

They cleaned the rest of the fish in silence, each one lost in his own thoughts.

Tom pulled the car into the driveway; it had been a long quiet drive back to town from the cabin. The past couple of days had been serious and somber. Tom knew the next time that he would see his friend would be to bury his wife. He was terribly saddened and troubled by that realization.

Linda knew Tom was bothered and tried her best to leave him alone with his thoughts. She knew that he had been friends with both Smitty and Juanita since his early twenties, and that was a long time ago.

Linda used the time to catch up on her reading, she had a couple of books she had started and never finished, she would pack them and bring them with to the cabin, just in case it rained and turned out to be a good day to curl up in front of the fire with a book.

"I'll get the door," Tom said quietly as he got out of the car.

Linda got out and grabbed her purse and another bag and followed Tom into the house.

Tom carried the last bag into the house and Linda closed the door behind him.

"What can I do for you honey?" Linda asked, "you look so sad, I'm sorry about Juanita, I know how much she means to you, both her and Mike mean a lot, I know."

"Thanks, but there is nothing you can do," Tom said, walking past her with the bag to put it in their bedroom.

Linda stayed in the kitchen and put away the few food items they had brought back from the cabin with them.

Tom came out of the bedroom and walked up behind Linda, he wrapped his arms around her waist and leaned his head on the back of her neck and began to cry, "promise me something," he said, "promise me you will never die on me, I couldn't live without you."

Linda felt tears coming to her own eyes as she reached up and patted his head, "aw honey."

"She was like a sister to me," Tom started to say, "I spent many many nights at their house, I can't begin to count all the meals she cooked for me, she was the sister I never had. I can't imagine what Mike is going through."

"This is really getting to you honey," Linda turned around, and held his face in her hands, whipping the tears from his face with her thumbs, "you are calling Smitty Mike, I don't know if I've ever heard you call him by his real name."

Tom looked into her eyes and nodded, holding back more tears, trying to stop them from coming.

"All you can do is be there for him," Linda said, "That's all you can do."

Tom slipped on his shoes and then stood up and reached for the knob to open the kitchen door. Linda walked around the corner in the kitchen from the hallway. She had on her housecoat and held her hand to her mouth as she yawned.

"Morning hon, where are you going so early?" she asked.

"Oh, good morning," Tom replied, "I thought I would go out for a walk, I couldn't sleep any more."

"Want me to come with?" Linda asked as she rubbed her eyes, "or would you rather be alone?"

"No, that's okay," Tom replied, "I didn't want to wake you, but if you want to come, I'll wait."

"Ok," Linda replied, "let me throw on some clothes real quick, I'll be right back," then she disappeared back around the corner.

Tom walked over to the sink and looked out the window. The sun was just rising above the trees and he could see the birds outside the window, pecking at the bird food he had put in the feeder.

Linda took Tom's hand, holding it and swinging her arm back and forth with each step taken as they waked along the road. Tom stopped walking and pointed to a deer running across the field, it was several hundred yards from them, and Linda had to squint with her eyes to see it. They watched it running along the old rail line until it reached a small grove of trees where it stopped, then looked around before it lowered it's head to eat.

"It's amazing how graceful they are," Linda remarked with a smile, as she watched it from a distance, "absolutely beautiful."

"Yep," Tom agreed as they began walking again.

The morning sun began to rise higher in the sky as they walked along the road, stopping every so often to watch different animals going about their business of gathering food and hunting, of making nests and scurrying about.

"I need to call Sue when we get back to the house," Linda said, "her baby is due any day now and I just want to check in and see how she's doing."

Tom nodded his head, "I was thinking about her this morning too, It's hard to believe that she's due already, it seems like just yesterday they told us she is pregnant," Tom said, "where does the time go?"

"I know," Linda replied, putting her arm around Tom's waist and leaning her head against his arm, "I guess we're just getting old."

"Who's getting old?" Tom argued with a chuckle, "I'm not, I think it's a conspiracy, I think someone comes in and tints our hair at night and puts achy powder in our food so our joints will ache, and I think someone comes in and lowers the floor when we sleep too making it harder to bend over and pick things up, but I don't think we're getting older, nope, I don't."

Linda laughed and squeezed him with her arm that was around his waist, "you just go ahead and think that honey," she said, "I'm sure that's what it is, what else could it be?"

"Maybe I should go into the shop today," Tom said, "give Tim some time to spend with his wife, pretty soon their whole house will be upside down. Once the baby comes nothing will be the same anymore."

"That would be nice," Linda said, "I bet he'd really appreciate that. He does spend a lot of time there, and I think he would like it if you went in and told him to go home."

"Yep, I think I'll do that," Tom replied, "after our walk, I'll get cleaned up and go in and tell him to go home and stay with his wife until the baby is born, I can handle the shop for a few days, after all, It is my store and I started it, I can handle it."

"I'm sure you can dear," Linda replied, "I'm sure you can."

Tom sat on the stool at the workbench, leaning back with his arms crossed, he watched the two girls stocking shelves and talking back and forth. He watched as one helped a customer and the other busied herself, tidying up behind the counter. A warm feeling came over Tom as he watched the business he had started several years ago, he was pleased as he watched one of the girls answer the phone and make some notes. Tim had done a fine job, Tom was proud of him. He had come to work for Tom shortly after he got out of the Army and after just a few years had grown the small one person operation to a business that now employed three people on the sales staff, a second person repairing customer items and Tim himself, doing repairs, ordering supplies and inventory, managing the store and doing the bookwork. Tom's name was on the building, but now he could see that it was Tim's passion that drove the company. Tim had worked hard building it up to what it was today.

"Mr. Watson?" one of the girls in the front of the store said, holding her hand over the receiver of the telephone, "phone call, line one."

"Ok," Tom said, "thank you."

Tom picked up the phone and pushed the button that was lit up.

"This is Tom," he said, then his voice changed dramatically, "what? When? How big? Ok, I'll be right there."

Tom hung up the phone and grabbed his coat, then headed for the front door of the store. He stopped and looked at the girls standing behind the counter, "I'm going to the hospital, Tim's wife just had a baby girl, I'll be back in a couple hours."

Tom opened the door slowly and peeked into the hospital room.

Linda was standing near the bed holding the newborn baby. Sue was lying on the bed with Tim sitting on the edge holding her hand.

"Is this the right room?" Tom asked as he opened the door further and walked in.

"Hi honey, look at your new grand daughter, isn't she sweet?" Linda said, gently rocking the little bundle of baby and blanket back and forth in her arms.

"Hi there," Tom said as he leaned down and kissed Sue on the forehead, "how did it go?"

"It went good, but I'm awfully sore," Sue answered, "and I'm tired, I didn't get much sleep last night."

"I suppose not," Tom said, with an understanding smile, "and how's the new proud poppa?" he asked as he reached out to give Tim a hug.

"I'm fine, I'm tired too, but not as tired as Sue is," Tim replied, looking over at Sue, "I had a nap awhile ago when she was resting and they had the baby down in the nursery."

Tom walked over to Linda and put his arm around her shoulder. He kissed her on the lips and then lifted the blanket up so he could see the babies sleeping face.

"Aw," Tom said, gazing at the new little baby girl, "isn't she cute, she looks just like her momma."

"Her name is Carolyn," Linda responded, smiling up at Tom.

"Carolyn?" Tom replied, "that's a nice name, Carolyn, aren't you a cutie," he said, gently touching her little nose with the tip of his finger.

"We named her after my grandmother on my mom's side," Sue explained.

"That's nice," Tom replied.

"Isn't it?" Linda said, agreeing.

"How's the store?" Tim asked.

"What?" Tom asked in mock annoyance, "your wife just had a baby, what are you doing asking about the store? This isn't the time to talk shop kid, it'll be there when you get back, right now, just enjoy this time, they grow too fast not to."

"Thanks," Tim said, adjusting himself on the edge of Sue's bed, lifting one leg up and twisting sideways.

Chapter 16

TOM CARRIED TWO glasses of wine out to the front porch where Linda was sitting on the swing.

"Here you go," Tom said, handing her a glass of wine.

"Thank you," Linda replied, moving her feet so Tom could sit next to her.

Tom sat down on the swing and Linda moved closer to him.

"Sure is a lovely night," Linda said, sipping her wine.

"They don't get much better than this," Tom agreed as he took a sip of his wine, "any evening that I'm able to sit with you is a wonderful evening in my book."

"Aw," Linda said, looking up at Tom's face, then she reached her hand up and touched his cheek, and kissed him softly on the lips, "you say the sweetest things honey."

Tom smiled at Linda, and then put his arm around her and pulled her close to him, "that's because I love you, and they are true, everything I say to you is true."

Linda tilted her head and smiled up at Tom, "god I love you Mr. Tom."

Tom chuckled softly, "I love you too Miss Linda," and kissed her on the top of her head, holding his lips on her for several seconds.

Linda put her glass down on the table near the swing then reached up and held her hand against Tom's cheek and kissed him, she pressed her warm lips against his. Tom parted his lips and touched hers with his tongue, tracing along her lips as she opened them.

Tom broke the kiss reluctantly, "hold that thought!" he said as he reached over to put his wine glass down on the table near Linda's.

"Ok," Tom grinned, "where were we?"

"Right here," Linda smiled and said as she closed her eyes and moved towards Tom to receive his kiss.

Tom lay on his back with his head on the pillow and looked up at the ceiling. Linda was lying next to him, her head on his chest with his arm around her and his hand stroking her warm skin. She listened to his heartbeat, it was still rapid, but it was slowing down.

"That was fantastic," Linda said, running her fingers through the graying hair on his chest.

"Yeah, it was," Tom said, catching his breath, "you are fantastic, that was great."

"We are good together aren't we?" Linda said, kissing his chest.

"We sure are," Tom agreed, stroking her hair and moving it out of her face with his other hand so he could look into her eyes.

Sue walked up the sidewalk. Carolyn held her mother's hand with one hand as she walked next to Sue and carried her stuffed bunny under her other arm.

"Happy Birthday," Linda said, greeting them from the steps on the front porch, "I can't believe she is already a year old."

"Can I help her walk?" Sunrise asked as she came out of the house, letting the front screen door slam shut behind her, "I'll hold her hand and walk real slow, please?"

Sue strapped Carolyn into her highchair and pulled it up to the table. Tom helped Sunrise onto her chair where a booster seat was in place, ready for her to sit on.

Linda carried a cake into the dining room and it had a big number one candle that was lit in the center of the cake.

Tim stood behind Carolyn with his arm around Sue. Across the table and behind Sunrise stood Andrea and Jerry, holding hands and watching the look on Carolyn's face as the cake and burning candle was set down on the table in front of her.

Tom stood back from all of it holding his camera and taking as many pictures as he could.

Sue helped Carolyn blow out the candle and then everybody sat down for cake and ice cream.

"Grampa, guess what?" Sunrise said.

"What goomba?" Tom replied, his face inches away from Sunrises face, looking intent.

"I went to school today grampa," She explained.

"You did? No way, that's for big kids," Tom said, smiling and gently pinching her nose.

"Grampa, I'm five, I go to kindergarten and I even rode a bus," Sunrise replied.

"Wow!" Tom said with a chuckle, "so, tell me goomba, what did you do in school today? Did you learn anything or do you have to go back?"

"Grampa," Sunrise said very seriously, "I have to go back, you know that, I have to go every day."

"I know honey," Tom said, rubbing his hand on the top of her head, "grampa was just teasing you."

Sunrise looked at Tom, then put a fork full of cake into her mouth and started to chew, before she finished chewing, she returned to her conversation with a mouth full of cake, "we got to use finger paints today granpa, I made a house."

"A house? Wow! Good for you," Tom replied enthusiastically.

"And I painted mommy and daddy and a tree and a sun and a dog," Sunrise said, describing her finger painting in detail with enthusiasm.

"A dog? You even painted a dog?" Tom asked, with exaggerated facial expressions.

"Yes grampa, we don't have one, but daddy said we're getting a dog so I made one in my picture," Sunrise explained.

"Well, how about that," Tom said as he stood up, "grampa needs to help grandma in the kitchen, you eat your cake now like a big girl."

Tom scooped up some ice cream into a bowl and stood in the kitchen, leaning against the doorjamb watching the goings on in the dining room. He watched Linda fussing over her grown kids and her grand children and he smiled to himself. She had so much love for her children, and watching them all interact the way they were warmed his heart. He wondered what it was like when Tim and Andrea were young like Sunrise and Carolyn, he tried to imagine a much younger Linda fussing over her two children, serving them dinner and getting their breakfast ready as they hurried to eat and dash out the door to school in the morning. Not having any children of his own, at least that he raised from birth, he didn't have any of his own memories to reflect back on. Andrea and Tim were his stepchildren. They were adults when he met them. Andrea had already graduated from high school and was away in college, and Tim had dropped out of high school and was floundering, looking for direction. Tom truly enjoyed the moments he had with the grandchildren, he was grandpa to them and he had watched them grow from birth. Only a year for Carolyn, but it was a start and there were more to come, and he looked forward to those years coming.

"Tom," Linda said, waving her hand, motioning for him to come to her, "quick, get a picture of this."

Tom leaned over the table with his camera and took a photo of Carolyn feeding herself her cake. There was frosting in her hair, frosting on her nose and frosting on her cheeks. Her smile was bigger than life itself, she was so happy. She even had crumbs of cake in her ear, and all down the front of the frilly white top she was wearing special for her first birthday. Tom pushed the button on the camera a dozen or more times. There was no way he was going to miss this shot. He took several pictures, and even some backup pictures in case some didn't turn out. A photographer, he was not, a very happy and proud grandfather that wanted to capture every moment, every event, every silly little thing he was.

Tim picked up the telephone, then put his hand over the receiver and called for Tom.

"It's for you," Tim said, silently mouthing the words to Tom across the word and holding up the telephone.

"Hello?" Tom said as he took the phone into the kitchen where it was quieter so he could hear better.

"Tom? Hi, this is Amanda," the woman's voice on the other end said.

"Amanda?" Tom asked, puzzled.

"Yes, Amanda, Tom, don't you remember me? Doodles?" she said, trying to get Tom to recognize her.

"Oh for heavens sake, how are you?" Tom said, finally recognizing the woman on the other end of the line.

"I'm doing fine thanks," she said, "listen, I've been trying to find your number for weeks, digging through my dads stuff . . ."

"Is everything alright?" Tom asked, interrupting her.

"Dad died," she said quietly, starting to cry into the telephone.

"He had a massive heart attack and was gone before the paramedics even got to the house," she explained, "I'm sorry uncle Tom, I know you would have wanted to be here, but I just now found your number, I swear, I've been looking and hunting for weeks trying to find it so I could tell you."

"Oh Amanda, I'm so sorry to hear that," Tom responded, "I would have been there right away had I known, how are you doing? How is Danny? I know you two were close to your dad."

"I'm fine thanks, Danny is having a hard time," she replied, "I think he wished he had more time with dad before . . ." she trailed off, her emotions preventing her from speaking.

"I understand," Tom replied, "it's rough, I was away when my dad passed, and I still miss him and wish I spent more time with him towards the end, especially knowing now, that you don't get another chance once they go."

"I know you were good friends, he talked about you all the time," Amanda said, "he was so happy that you and Linda came when mom died, that was important to him, I think more important than any of their other friends."

"She was like my sister Amanda," Tom replied, "there's no way I wouldn't have been there."

"I know he appreciated it," Amanda responded.

"Can I do anything for you?" Tom asked.

"No, but thanks," Amanda replied, "I just had to tell you and I feel so bad it took so long, but . . ."

"It's okay," Tom said, interrupting her again, "don't beat yourself up, okay?"

"All right uncle Tom," Amanda replied.

"That's my Doodles," Tom said, "try and think of it as, your dad went to be with your mom, he missed her so much and wanted to be with her."

"I know," Amanda responded, crying softly into the telephone, "but now they're both gone, "I just miss them, both of them."

"Listen," Tom said, "I want you to feel free to come stay with us, tell Danny too. If you want a little vacation, come up here and we'll go to my cabin, do some fishing, you know, if you want to get away, I want you to feel free to call me. Anytime, okay?"

"Okay, thanks, I'll tell Danny too," Amanda said.

After a few more minutes, Tom hung up the phone, he stayed in the kitchen and stared out the window, blocking out the noises of Carolyn's birthday party coming from the dining room.

"You okay?" Linda asked, putting her hand on Tom's shoulder and gently shaking him, "Tom?"

Tom shook his head and turned around to face Linda, she could see he had tears in his eyes and they were still red and puffy.

"Yeah," he said, trying to hide his grief from her and holding back his sadness, "I'm fine."

"No," Linda replied, "I know you Tom, I know better than that, who was that on the phone? What's the matter?"

"That was Amanda, Smitty's daughter," Tom began, choking up, "Mike died a couple of weeks ago, and . . ."

"What?" Linda asked, holding his face in her hands, "when? How, why didn't anybody tell you before this?"

"Amanda said she's been looking though his stuff for a few weeks," Tom replied, "trying to find my number, she said she just found it, that's why she didn't tell me sooner, she felt bad."

"Aw, I'm so sorry," Linda said, standing on her toes to kiss Tom, "I feel so bad for you, and for his family."

"Yeah," Tom said, "me too."

Tom wiped the last tear from his face then went and splashed cold water on it from the sink, "I think we better go back and join the party," Tom said.

Linda smiled a sad smile and took Tom by the hand, "Yeah, everybody will be gone in another hour or so, then we can talk about it."

Tom nodded and followed Linda back into the dining room where there was lots of laughter and life taking place for Carolyn's first birthday party.

It was a bittersweet moment for Tom, he was watching this innocent young child having her very first birthday, laughing and smiling and wearing almost as much cake as she had eaten, and also absorbing the news that his best friend had died.

Linda opened the fridge and took two beers out and opened them, she carried them out to the garage where Tom had been spending a good deal of his time lately and handed him one.

"She sure is pretty," Linda said.

"Thanks," Tom replied, taking the beer that Linda handed him and sat down to take a break.

"I can't wait to see her in the water," Linda said, "I've never seen anything so beautiful, so sleek and smooth."

"I need to finish sanding this coat," Tom said, running his hand along the bottom of the cedar strip canoe he was building, "then apply another coat of poly, I think three or four more coats and then she'll be ready."

"What about the seats?" Linda asked.

"Well, I'm glad you asked," Tom said with a smile as he took a sip of his beer, "after I finish all the coats of varnish and poly on the bottom, I'll flip it right side up and work on the inside. I was wondering if you could sew some seat cushions, I thought of weaved cane seats, but I think I want something softer to sit on, something with padding for these old bones."

Linda smiled, acknowledging she understood completely what he was referring to when he talked about his old bones.

"I could probably do that," she responded, "as long as you tell me how big you want them."

"Oh, I'll make the seat frames," Tom said, "and have you sew some seat cushions to go on them."

"Ok, well, when you get to that point, just let me know," Linda said, running her hand along the smoothly sanded wood, "you're sure doing a good job honey, I'm impressed."

"Thank you," Tom replied, "that means a lot to me, I hope to have it done soon, I'm anxious to bring it to the cabin and take it out on the lake, early in the morning, with the fog lifting and the sun just coming up, the lake will be smooth like glass."

"Sounds like a wonderful plan," Linda replied.

Tom nodded, "yep," then stood up from his stool, "ya know what honey?"

"What?" Linda asked, watching him get up, and listening to him groan as he moved slowly.

"I think I'm going to call it a day," Tom said, making agonizing faces as he reached for the light switch, "semi retirement and working all day like that, all hunched over takes it's toll. I'm not as young as I used to be."

Linda smiled and opened the door, "no honey," she replied, "we sure aren't as young as we used to be."

Tom shut out the light above the workbench in the garage and lovingly patted the upside down canoe with his hand as he walked past it on the way to the door.

"You're right," Tom said, smiling, turning back to look at the canoe, "I am doing a good job, I'm proud of my project."

Linda put her arm around his arm as they walked around the house to the kitchen door.

"I need to go to the market and get some things for dinner," Linda said as they walked into the kitchen, "want me to pick anything up for you?"

Tom, thought silently for a moment, "no, not that I can think of, want me to come with?"

"You want to?" Linda asked, surprised, "that would be nice."

"Sure," Tom replied, "let me finish my beer and get cleaned up."

Tom walked behind, pushing the cart as Linda looked at her grocery list and put items in the cart. Tom stopped to talk with the butcher and looked at some fresh steaks in the meat cooler.

"Linda? Is that you?" Tom heard a voice ask, it came from around the corner so he couldn't see the face, but the voice sounded vaguely familiar.

"Yes," Linda said, turning to see who was calling her name, her face temporarily flushed with anger when she saw the person calling her name, "Janey," She said calmly.

"Oh my god, it's so good to see you," Janey said walking closer to Linda with her arms outstretched for a hug.

Linda stood still, not wanting to see or speak with Janey, but feeling trapped and unable to avoid this moment. Janey wrapped her arms around Linda and Linda just stood there, stiff as a board, not returning the hug.

"I haven't seen you around in ages," Linda said when Janey took a step back, "where have you been?"

"I just moved back," Janey said cheerfully, "I've been in Florida, but I got homesick, and, well I just decided to move back, aren't you glad to see me?"

Tom walked around the corner at that moment and froze in his tracks when he saw Janey standing there. She looked much older, her skin was tan, but very wrinkled and dried looking, her hair was almost white, and she was so thin she looked sickly.

"Janey," Tom said politely as he walked past her to put the package of steaks in the cart. He didn't stop and visit, he grabbed the handle of the cart and began to push it, looking at Linda, "I'm going to keep shopping, come find me."

Linda nodded at Tom and then looked at Janey, "no, I guess not, you stole my husband and I'll never forget it."

"Oh Linda," Janey said, with a practiced pouting look, "that was so long ago, why can't you forgive and forget already? Besides, you're much happier now than you ever would've been with what's his name."

"This is true, but you were my friend, I trusted you, and you hurt me, you betrayed me Janey," Linda replied, "didn't we have this same talk last time I saw you? In fact, I think it was here in this store too."

"Oh I don't know," Janey said, waving her hand as if to wipe away the entire conversation, or at least the topic, "anyway, I hope we run into each other again."

"Right," Linda said, turning to go find Tom.

"And say Hello to that handsome husband of yours for me, will you?" Janey said with a mischievous grin.

Linda spun around quickly and walked right up to Janey and pointed her finger at her, almost touching her face, "You stay away from Tom, so help me Janey, if you . . ."

"Or you'll do what?" Janey asked sarcastically, interrupting Linda before she could finish her warning, "you couldn't keep your first husband away from me, how are you going to keep this one away? You don't have what I have darling, men can't resist me, they never could."

"Maybe not when we were young," Linda replied angrily, "but now, look at you, you're a wrinkled up old lady, you got nothing, nothing!"

Janey stood there dumbfounded, her mouth hanging open, shocked that anybody had said that to her as Linda turned and walked away. Linda disappeared around the corner of the aisle, holding her head up proudly.

Tom watched Linda walking towards him, a small smile appearing on her face.

"Is everything alright?" Tom asked, reaching out to touch Linda's arm, "I didn't want to hang around, I don't have any use for that bitch."

"Tom," Linda said with mock surprise, "why I'm shocked at you, I never thought I would hear you say that about anybody."

"Yeah, right," Tom said, challenging Linda, "you know better than that, you know what I think about her, so, how did it go?"

"It went fine, better than fine," Linda said with a relaxed smile, "I think I finally put her in her place after all these years."

"Oh?" Tom replied, "Do I even want to know what you said? Or is it too hard core for my ears?"

Linda put her arm around Tom's waist and they began to walk towards the checkout counter, "let's just say, I don't think she'll be calling me to come over for tea anytime soon," Linda said as she began to laugh.

"Alright then," Tom replied, "maybe I should have stuck around and watched that cat fight, sounds interesting."

"What kind of steaks did you get?" Linda asked, changing the topic.

Linda carried the life jackets down to the dock; following behind Tom as he carried the canoe he built on his shoulders, preparing to launch it for the first time.

"I hope it floats," he said from under the canoe as he stopped to flip it over and set it into the water.

"I don't have any doubts," Linda replied, "I just know she's going to float."

Tom gingerly set the end of the canoe into the water and edged it in until the entire canoe was floating on the water. He knelt on the dock, holding onto the side and looked up at Linda with a huge proud smile, "hey! It floats."

"I knew she would," Linda replied, almost giddy with excitement, "here," she said, dropping the life jackets, "I'm going to go grab the paddles."

"Ok," Tom said, adjusting himself so he could sit on the dock with his feet resting on the floor of the canoe. He looked out across lake, thinking of all the hours he had spent working on this project, wondering all the while if it would even float once he had it completed. Now it was finished, it was in the water, and best of all, it was floating. Now just a few more minutes, and he would be in back and Linda would be in front, and they would push away from the dock and see how it handled.

"Sorry," Linda said when she returned to the dock with the two paddles, "I had to pee."

Tom smiled and reached for her hand, "here. I'll help you get in, now remember, this will tip over much easier than the fishing boat, so you have to sit very still and keep your center of gravity very low."

"Ok," she replied, slowly getting in and sitting down immediately on the seat.

Tom handed her a paddle, then he got in and sat down, pushing the canoe away from the dock. It felt good; he was very happy and proud to dip the paddle in the water to make his canoe move forward for the very first time.

"This is nice," Linda said as the canoe glided silently across the water. They stayed near the shoreline on the maiden voyage, saving a longer trip for another day. They paddled along for a while, passing several cabins and homes on the lake, waving back at neighbors that waved at them from their docks or lawns.

"I'm going to head back now," Tom said, "the wind is picking up and I want to get off the lake before the waves get any bigger."

"Whatever you say honey," Linda said from the front of the canoe.

Tom held onto the dock, steadying the canoe so that Linda could climb out. He handed her his paddle then climbed onto the dock, he lifted the canoe up out of the water and laid it upside down on the dock.

"Well I think that was a success," Tom said proudly as he stood up.

"I think so," Linda said in agreement, "I couldn't believe how smooth and quiet it was, it was like floating on air."

"It was nice wasn't it?" Tom replied, reaching for the paddles that Linda was holding, "let's put these away for today," he said as he put his arm around her shoulder as they walked off the dock and up the path towards the cabin.

Tom leaned the paddles up against the wall in a corner inside the shed. He grabbed the axe and his gloves and walked towards the woodpile.

"I'm going to split some wood for the fire, I'll be in soon," he said to Linda as she reached for the knob on the backdoor to go inside the cabin.

"Ok," she replied, "I'll start dinner then."

Tom closed the door behind him as he made his last trip in from outside carrying the firewood he just split. He stacked a few small pieces and lit them, adding some kindling to help it start faster.

"Dinner's almost ready," Linda said from the kitchen, "by the time you get washed up it'll be done."

"Ok," Tom said with a groan as he stood up from kneeing on the floor, "maybe I should get myself a wood splitter, my back is always sore when I'm done."

"If you need one honey," Linda said, standing in the middle of the kitchen, holding a hot pad in her hand and watching Tom, moving slowly with his tired old muscles, she tilted her head to the side, "aw honey, you work too hard."

"Guess I'm not as young and nimble as I once was am I?" he said with a smile as he walked into the bathroom to wash up for dinner.

Linda sat down next to Tom, sitting across from him she felt as if she was too far from him, she liked being closer. She blew out the match after she lit the candles on the table.

"There," she said with a smile, "how's that?"

"Looks nice, romantic I think," Tom said as he reached for her hand, "you make things so nice, I'm so lucky to have you for my wife." Then he brought her hand to his lips and kissed it.

"Thanks honey," Linda said with a warm smile, "I enjoy it, I love the way you truly appreciate the things I do, I really do."

Tom refilled their wine glasses then set the empty wine bottle down on the floor next to his chair.

"Tomorrow I want to get up early," Tom said as he lifted his wine glass up, "and hit the water early."

"Alright," Linda said, "before the sun comes up?"

"Well, maybe not before it comes up," Tom decided, "but early, before the fog lifts and before it starts getting wavy."

Linda nodded her head and sipped her wine, "I like that idea," she said, "I would love to go with you."

"I hope so," Tom said, smiling at Linda, "I can't share that magical feeling with you if you're not with me, there's nothing like being on the lake as the fog lifts. The water is still calm, it looks just like glass, and you can sit there and watch the world wake up."

Linda smiled and raised her glass, holding it up in front of her, "tomorrow, to smooth waters, and bright beginnings."

"To tomorrow," Tom said as he touched his wine glass against hers.

Tom opened his eyes and saw the faint early morning light coming in through the bedroom window, he reached over to touch Linda, but found only an empty spot where she had been. He sat up and placed his feet on the floor to get up out of bed. He could hear Linda in the kitchen; a moment later he smelled the smell of fresh coffee brewing.

"Good morning," Tom said as kissed the back of Linda's neck.

"Oh, hi," She said, turning around to face him, she wrapped her arms around his neck, "how'd you sleep?"

She kissed Tom on the lips, her lips were soft and warm and he loved her kisses.

"I slept good," he replied, "I always seem to sleep good here, I think it's the fresh air or something."

"Here," Linda said, turning and reaching for an empty cup, "I made some fresh coffee."

"Thanks honey," Tom replied, patting her butt and reaching for the sugar on the counter.

Tom followed Linda outside to the front porch and sat down on the swing. Linda sat next to Tom and curled her feet up under her.

She held her cup in both hands, gingerly taking small sips, blowing the steam as she brought the cup to her lips.

"Mmmm," Tom said as he rested his cup on his knee, still holding the handle with his hand, "you make good coffee honey."

"Thank you," Linda said, looking at him out if the corner of her eye.

"After our coffee, I want to hit the water," Tom said, gazing out over the calm water on the lake, "while it's still smooth."

"Ok," Linda replied, "you said that last night."

"I know," Tom replied, "I'm just telling you again in case you forgot, or changed your mind and wanted to stay here."

Linda turned and looked at Tom, a serious look coming across her face, "are you kidding? No way! I'm going with."

Tom chuckled a little, "alright then, I guess it's settled."

"You're right mister," Linda said, blowing on her coffee, "it's settled then."

Linda dipped her paddle into the water, creating a very small sound as the water made a tiny splash. The canoe glided across the smooth water, silently, almost effortlessly. Then when she lifted it out of the water and reached forward to start her next stroke, the water dripping off the tip of the paddle made another noise. The only noises they heard were the soft splashes as their paddles slipped into the water, and as the drops hit the water from the paddles before they slipped into the water again.

"Isn't this peaceful?" Tom asked from the back seat of the canoe, his voice just above a whisper.

"I love it," Linda replied, turning her head sideways and whispering back at Tom.

"Shhh, stop paddling for a minute," Tom said softly.

"What? Why?" Linda asked as she rested the paddle on her lap.

"Look to your right," he said, as he rested his paddle on his lap, the canoe was still gliding, but beginning to slow down. "On the bank, see the deer?"

"Oh wow," Linda said quietly, staring at the deer at the lakes edge.

One of the deer, a male with a large set of antlers stood cautiously, watching the strange object floating past on the water in front of him. The others, three smaller females stood nearby, two had their noses in the water, their ears flicking and tails nervously twitching. The other female stood a few feet from the water, her head was down but her eyes and ears were on the canoe.

"Aren't they beautiful?" Linda remarked. Turning sideways, she lost her balance for a second and quickly grabbed the sides of the canoe. The paddle hit the side of the canoe and made a noise t hat echoed off the quiet lake. She looked up and saw a raised tail flashing as the last deer quickly disappeared into the trees.

"Where did they go?" she asked.

Tom smiled, "they got scared and took off. It sure don't take much."

"They were so beautiful," Linda said, talking a little more excited and a little louder than before.

"They sure are," Tom replied, "you won't see them in the middle of the day, not like that anyway."

Tom secured the canoe to the rack he built on the side of the shed.

"Ready?" Linda asked, as she closed the trunk on the car.

"I think so," Tom replied, "I want to take one more look around first."

Tom came around the corner of the cabin, brushing his hands on his blue jeans, Linda was already in the car waiting.

"I had to put my axe away," Tom said as he got into the drivers seat of the car, "I almost forgot about it, can't have it rusting on me, I use it too much."

"I was wondering what you were doing," Linda said as she reached for and buckled up her seat belt.

Chapter 17

TOM STOOD BACK to admire his work. Standing on the front porch, holding the paintbrush in his hand he smiled.

"Linda?" he shouted from the front porch.

"Yes?" she replied, as she came out of the house, holding the screen door in her hand to keep it from slamming, "what do you want?"

"Well, what do you think?" Tom asked proudly, nodding towards the swing he just painted.

"About what?" Linda asked, looking towards the swing.

"The swing!" Tom replied, "I just painted the swing, what do you think?"

"Oh," Linda replied, "It looks nice," she said as she turned towards the door and reached for the knob.

"Huh!" Tom said, pretending to be hurt by Linda not noticing what he just did.

"Oh come oh sweetie," she said, turning back around and touching his face with her hand, "I was just kidding, it looks lovely, it was looking pretty faded and beat up, I'm glad you painted it."

Tom grinned like a proud little boy that was just acknowledged for a major accomplishment.

"That's better," he said, then he looked around the porch, "can you think of anything else that needs painting?"

Linda chuckled, "no honey, I think that's it for today."

Tom picked up the paint can and rags he had strewn about and went to wash up.

Tom stood up from his chair when he heard the knock on the door.

"You expecting anybody?" he asked Linda.

She looked up from her chair next to his where she had a blanket on her lap and was reading a book, "No, not that I can think of," she replied, "maybe it's a salesman or something," she said as she picked her book back up and went back to reading.

Tom opened the front door, and was taken back with surprise.

"Well hello!" he said as he opened the door, "come in, come in. why didn't you just come in? Why did you knock?"

"We wanted to surprise you," Andrea said as she hugged Tom at the front door.

"Who is it dear?" Linda asked from her chair in the living room.

"It's the kids," Tom replied, calling out to Linda in the other room, "Andrea, Jerry and Sunrise stopped by."

"Well for heavens sake," Linda said as she walked up next to Tom and held out her arms for Sunrise, "what brings you guys over tonight?"

"Well," Andrea began, "it's your anniversary tomorrow, and we wanted to bring you something."

"Come take a look," Jerry said, waving his arm for Tom and Linda to follow him as he stepped down off the front porch.

"I hope you like 'em," Sunrise said cheerfully, doing her best not to let on what the surprise was.

Jerry had parked the car in the driveway so it couldn't be seen on the road in front of the house if Tom or Linda were to look out the front window.

Tom stopped dead in his tracks when he walked around the house and saw the car in the driveway.

"Oh . . . my," Linda said, holding her hand in front of her mouth.

"Well?" Jerry asked, standing at the side of their car, holding his arm up pointing to two shiny bicycles on a bicycle rack on the roof of the car.

"Do you like 'em grampa? Do you like 'em grandma?" Sunrise asked excitedly, jumping up and down.

"Yes, we sure do my little goomba," Tom said as he rubbed the top of Sunrises head, "we sure do."

"You really didn't have to," Linda said, as she put her arm around Andrea's waist, "weren't they expensive?"

"Mom," Andrea replied sternly, "you know better that that, don't question a gift."

"But . . . ," Linda started to say before being interrupted by Jerry,

"It was Tim's idea," Jerry began to explain, "we all talked about it and agreed."

"Actually, I think Sue came up with the idea," Andrea said, correcting Jerry.

"You're right, it was," Jerry replied, "anyway, we were all together a few weeks ago and talking, and, well, we decided to get you guys bikes, we know you like to get out of the house, and . . ."

Andrea added, "you can see more on a bike faster, and it's easier than walking, besides, I think you would look really cute in those little outfits."

"Little outfits?" Tom replied laughing, "I don't know about that, riding a bike is one thing, god, I haven't been on a bike in years, how about you honey?" he asked, turning towards Linda.

"I, I don't know, I used to ride a lot when I was younger, but gosh," she said, "that was years ago."

"Ok," Jerry added, "maybe not the little outfits then but, well, we all hoped you could use these and maybe even get to enjoy them."

Linda wrapped her arms around Andrea's neck, "thank you so much," she said.

Andrea and Linda both began to cry, smiling and laughing.

Tom shook Jerry's hand, then embraced him in a bear hug and patted his back, "thanks son, what a wonderful gift."

"You're welcome," Jerry replied with a smile and turned to remove the two bicycles from the roof rack.

"So you like 'em don't you!" Sunrise said, holding her hands behind her back, and swaying back and forth sideways.

"You bet goomba," Tom said as he lifted her up, "oh my god, you sure are getting big, pretty soon I won't be able to lift you anymore."

"Daddy said I can bring my bike over and go for a ride with you sometime," Sunrise said, then, looking at Jerry she said, "didn't you daddy."

Jerry chuckled as he lowered the second bicycle to the ground, "yes honey, I did," He said to Sunrise.

Tom sat on the bench at the end of the dock, holding his fishing rod in his hand and slowly lifting the tip up and lowering it back down. He heard the dock creaking from someone walking on it. He turned his head to see who it was.

"Hi honey," he said to Linda as he slid sideways on the seat, then patted it with his hand, "have a seat."

"Any luck?" she asked, as she cast her line out into the lake.

"A little," he replied, "kinda slow today, I think the storm last night scared them away for a couple days."

"That's what you said," Linda replied, leaning back on the bench.

"What time are the kids coming?" Tom asked.

"They should be here for dinner," Linda replied, "Tim told me Carolyn is working and they'll be up after she gets off."

"What about Andrea and Jerry?" Tom asked.

"I expect them any minute," Linda replied, "that reminds me, I should go make up the bedroom for them, I almost forgot."

"Is Sunrise bringing her new boyfriend?" Tom asked.

"I don't know," Linda replied, "I don't think she's coming up this time, she doesn't really like to travel while she's pregnant."

"Oh, I guess not," Tom said, nodding, "wait," he said.

He reeled in his fishing line and put his rod in the holder attached to the bench, he held out his hand, "help me up please."

Linda reached out her hand and let out a soft grunt as she helped Tom stand up.

"There ya go," she said, patting him on the arm.

"Thanks hon," he said as he patted her softly on the butt, "it's rough getting old, these old bones don't work like they used to."

"Tell me about it," Linda replied, turning her head back and smiling at Tom, "mine aren't much younger than yours are."

Tom kissed Linda on the cheek then took her hand as they walked up the path towards the cabin.

Tom held the door to the cabin open for Linda so she could enter first. He followed close behind her, almost stepping on her heels with his feet.

"Let me help you," he said as he grabbed onto her sweater and helper her take it off, then he hung it on the hook by the back door.

"Thanks," she replied, as she twisted the cold water tap on the sink, "want me to make a fresh pot of coffee?"

"That would be great," Tom replied, "I think I'd like a cup."

Tom sat down on the sofa in front of the fire, Linda sat next to him stared into the flames of the fire.

"I like to look at the fire," Linda said without turning her eyes away from it, "it's mesmerizing how the flames flicker and dance."

"I know," Tom replied, rubbing his hand on her back, "It's easy to get lost in your thoughts staring at the fire, I find myself daydreaming a lot when I watch it, who needs a TV when there's a fire in the fireplace."

"I'm glad we don't have a TV here," Linda replied, "I would never go out and enjoy the outdoors if there was one here. It's funny how we tend to live different here than we do in our house."

Tom sighed and sat back on the sofa, "You're right, I never gave it much thought."

"Are you going to get Tim to split wood for you?" Linda asked, "I don't want you to hurt yourself, your leg has been giving you troubles lately."

"Oh hush," Tom replied, "I'm still capable of splitting wood, I'm not that old."

"Now Tom," Linda argued, "if we did all the things we used to do, because we thought we still could, we would end up in the hospital in no time flat, besides, remember what the doctor told you."

"Oh that's crap," Tom argued, "If I quit doing do all the things he told me to do, I wouldn't ever do anything. No, I'm going to do what I can as long as I can."

"Stubborn stubborn man," Linda replied, sitting back on the sofa and putting her hand on Tom's leg, "I don't see why you don't let Tim split wood for you when he's here, give him something to do, and there will always be more to split after he leaves."

Tom slowly stood up from the sofa and walked into the kitchen to refill his cup of coffee.

"Want another cup?" he asked Linda.

"No thanks, I'm fine," She replied, "maybe turn on the outside light, Andrea should be here any minute."

"That's what you said an hour ago," Tom replied as he poured his coffee, his hand shaking a little.

"Well, I thought they would be here by now," Linda responded, "I wonder what's taking them."

"Never mind," Tom said as he heard a car and looked out the window, "they're pulling in the driveway now."

Linda braced herself on the arm of the sofa as she stood up. She walked into the kitchen to greet the visitors.

Tom opened the back door and watched as Andrea and Jerry removed their bags from the trunk of their car.

"I thought Sunrise was coming with them," Tom said to Linda as she stood next to him, watching out the door.

"So did I," Linda replied, "I guess not."

"Hello there!" Andrea said as she noticed Linda and Tom watching from the kitchen door.

"Hi," Linda replied to Andrea, "how was your drive?"

"Not too bad," Jerry answered, "we off to a got a late start and stopped to eat, hope you didn't wait for us for dinner."

"No," Tom replied, "We figured you would eat before you got here, you usually do."

Linda nodded her head, agreeing with Tom, then asked, "Where is Sunrise? I thought she was coming with you."

"Mom," Andrea said with a smile, "she's coming up, but she has a surprise."

"Andrea," Jerry said quickly, "you weren't suppose to tell."

Andrea looked over at Jerry as they reached the door to the cabin, "she's my mother, I'm not going to keep a secret from her."

Linda's eyes perked up, "what's this?"

Andrea stopped and hugged Linda when she stepped inside the cabin, "you have to act surprised when she gets here."

"Alright," Linda replied "I'll act surprised."

"What's going on?" Tom asked as he shook jerry's hand, "what's the big secret?"

"Hey Tom," Jerry replied, returning Tom's handshake, "Sunrise has this boyfriend, right? Well, anyway, I guess they are getting serious, and . . ."

"And she wants you to meet him," Andrea interrupted, "they will be up tomorrow morning."

"Oh my," Linda replied.

"My little goomba," Tom said, "I guess she's all grown up now."

"Yes she is," Andrea said as she gave Tom a kiss on the cheek, "so how are you guys?"

"We're doing good," Linda replied, "we took Tom's canoe out on the water this morning, oh, Andrea," Linda said, touching Andreas arm, "you should've seen the deer, they were right near the edge of the water as we paddled up close, they were so beautiful."

"Yeah, until they got spooked and ran away," Tom said with a laugh, "your mother sure handles a canoe paddle well, I think she's a natural, she sat up in front and paddled like a pro."

"Really mom?" Andrea asked.

Linda stood proudly with her hands on her hips, "I did, Tom taught me how to paddle, and, well, I think I did a good job, I tell you, the canoe he built is so smooth on the water, I couldn't believe it."

"Come in you two," Tom said as he slowly walked towards the living room and sat down in his chair.

"We're going to put our stuff away first," Andrea said as she walked towards the guest room, "but we'll be right out."

"Can I get you kids something?" Linda asked from the living room.

"No thanks mom," Andrea said from the guest room where she was quickly unpacking her bag.

The back door opened and Tim stuck his head inside, "anybody home?" he asked, as he stepped inside to the kitchen.

"In here," Linda said loudly from her chair in the living room.

"Sorry we took so long," Tim said as walked over to Linda and leaned down to kiss her on the cheek, "how ya doing mom?"

"Fine, I'm fine," Linda replied.

"Where's Sue?" Tom asked from his chair.

Tim stood up and looked at the back door, "well, she was right behind me," he replied.

Sue walked in a moment later, "Tim, did you see the sky?"

"No, why," he asked as he reached his hand out to Tom.

"Howdy, how's things up here?" he asked, shaking Tom's hand.

"It's beautiful, no clouds and the stars are real bright," Sue said as she walked over to greet Linda and Tom.

"How's the store?" Tom asked Tim as he shook his hand.

"Store's good Tom," Tim replied, "I wanted to talk to you about that."

"Oh?" Linda replied, turning her attention to Tim and Tom

"Nothing bad mom," Tim turned and replied to Linda.

"Tom, I want to talk to you about buying the business from you," Tim began, "but let's not talk about it tonight."

Tom's raised his eyebrows and nodded his head, "ok, we'll talk about it tomorrow."

Sue looked at Tim, "let's get unpack so we can sit and relax."

"K honey," Tim replied, picking his bag up off the floor and following her into the other guest room.

Linda looked at Tom and reached her hand over and laid it on his arm, "did you hear that?" she asked, "Tim wants to talk to you about buying the business, what are you going to say?"

"I, I don't know," Tom replied, "I haven't given it much thought, I suppose maybe I'll sell it to him, I mean, I haven't worked there a day in years, he runs it and has for quite some time. What do you think I should do?"

"Honey," Linda replied, cocking her head and smiling at Tom, "that's your baby, you started that up before we were married, you'll have to decide that on your own."

Tom sighed and sunk down in his chair, "I just don't know what to do," Tom admitted, "He's worked hard for me, for so long, I hate to take any money from him."

"Sleep on it honey," Linda said, patting his arm, "you don't have to decide tonight, wait until tomorrow, see what he has to say."

"You're right," Tom said, reaching over with his other hand and patting her hand that was on his arm.

Linda smiled at Tom, "I'm glad they're here."

"I know, me too," Tom replied, smiling back at her.

Tim was the first one to come back into the living room of the cabin from unpacking. He threw a fresh log on the fire and stirred it, "There, it was looking kinda small," he said, standing up and brushing the dirt off his hands.

"Thank you," Linda said to Tim.

She looked over at Tom and noticed his head was leaning to the side and his mouth was partway open. She smiled and pointed to the blanket next to his chair, "Tim honey, can you throw that on Tom, he fell asleep in his chair."

Tim picked the blanket up and lovingly placed it over Tom, touching the sides and folding the top down so it was at the middle of his chest.

"How's that?" he asked Linda.

"That's good," she replied, gently lifting one corner up and adjusting it slightly, "thank you, he won't sleep long, but he falls asleep often in his chair now."

Tim nodded, "ok."

Tom opened his eyes and looked up at the ceiling, the noise of someone splitting wood outside woke him up. The drapes were drawn, but the sun was still coming in around the edges. Tom sat up and rubbed his eyes, he was confused, the splitting sound was too rapid for just one person splitting wood, but there were no other sounds, no gasoline engines that run one of those mechanical splitters. And Tom didn't know anybody that could split wood that fast, not for more than a couple swings of the axe anyway.

Tom crawled out of bed and put on his blue jeans and a flannel shirt, he slipped on an old pair of loafers and walked out into the living room. He smelled the coffee brewing and walked into the kitchen.

Linda, Sue, Andrea and Sunrise were all sitting at the table having their morning coffee and talking. They stopped talking when they saw Tom, walk around the corner into the kitchen.

"Good morning honey," Linda said with a smile.

"Good morning," the rest of the women said as soon as Linda did.

"Good morning honey," Tom said as he leaned down to kiss Linda.

"Good morning girls, how is everyone today?" he asked as he looked at the group.

"Oh Sunrise!" he said, noticing she was sitting at the table with the other women, "Hi there, when did you get in?"

"We got here about an hour ago," She replied, standing up and walking over to give him a hug, "how are you grampa?"

Tom returned her hug and replied, "I'm doing just fine, not moving as fast these days, but I'm doing fine."

Linda sat in her chair, holding her coffee cup with both hands, her elbows on the table and the cup near her chin, she watched Tom hug Sunrise and she smiled.

"Grampa," Sunrise said, taking his hand and leading him towards the back door, "I have someone I want you to meet."

"Is that who's making all the racket out there?" he asked jokingly as he nudged her arm with his elbow.

"No grampa," Sunrise replied, looking up into Tom's aging face, "he's someone special and he means a lot to me, I want you to meet him."

Tom looked back at the women around the table, they were leaning in towards one another, holding their hands over their mouths and whispering, Linda had a big smile on her face and Andrea and Sue were laughing. Tom wondered what was going on, what all the secrecy and laughing was about, but quickly shrugged it off as just women being women.

Sunrise opened the door and reached up and held her hand over Tom's eyes, "K grampa, take my arm now and don't look."

She guided him out the door and down the three steps to the ground. Tom concentrated on his footing, and let Sunrise guide him outside. Tom suddenly noticed that the sound of axes splitting wood was gone and he could hear the soft sound of the breeze and singing birds. He also heard the soft rumbling voices of men and feet shuffling and of shoes in the dirt walking towards him.

"Ok, grampa," Sunrise said as she removed her hand from in front of his eyes. He squinted his eyes briefly; the bright sun was hard on his eyes after being closed shut while walking out the door.

"Hey Tom," he heard Tim and Jerry say as they waved at him, they were standing by the wood pile with gloves on and axes in their hands.

"Grampa," Sunrise said in a very cheerful voice, "I want you to meet Gary."

A tall young man standing near Sunrise, also holding an axe, he was wearing one glove and holding the other in his gloved hand, extending his hand to Tom, "nice to meet you sir, Sunrise talks about you all the time, she really thinks highly of you."

"She does huh?" Tom replied, looking at Sunrise with a smile and shaking Gary's hand. Gary shook with a firm grip that impressed Tom, "well Gary, it's nice to meet you too."

"What's going on out here?" Tom asked, turning his attention to Tim and Jerry.

"We split some wood for you," Jerry replied first.

"Yeah, Gary helped us," Tim added, "and we split at least two cords, should be enough to last you awhile."

"Don't you think?" Tim turned to Jerry and asked.

"I hope so," Jerry laughed.

"Me too," Tim replied with a laugh, "my back is killing me, I'm not used to this kind of work."

"Nice meeting you sir," Gary said with a wave as he walked back over towards Tim and Jerry, slipping on his other glove, "I think you guys are getting old, let me show you how it's done."

Tim winked at Jerry, "he'll show us how it's done, like we never split wood before."

Gary lifted the axe aver his head and swung it down hard and fast, with a sharp cracking noise that echoed out over the lake, he split the piece of wood into two smaller pieces of wood for the fireplace.

"Now that's how wood is split," Tom said with a chuckle, "in my day, I used to split wood like that, but not anymore, not like that."

Gary stood proud and smiled at the other men; he put another piece on the chopping block and proceeded to split it in half.

"Wow guys," Tom said with a tear in his eye, "I really appreciate this, you know, you didn't have to come up here and split all this wood for me."

"We know," Tim replied, taking his gloves off, "it's something we wanted to do, we are able to so we did."

"That's right," Jerry added, shrugging his shoulders, "you and mom have done so much for us and the kids over the years, what's a little bit of work?"

Linda sat next to Tom on the front porch of the cabin. Sunrise and Gary were sitting on the bench at the end of the dock, they were sitting arm in arm and she had her head resting on his shoulder, every so often Tom could hear laughter being carried up by the wind from the dock.

"He seems like a nice young man," Linda said to Tom, as she laid her book on her lap and looked into his eyes, "I remember when we sat on the dock and laughed like that, we still do."

Tom smiled and patted her hand lovingly, "yes we do honey, yes we do."

"It sure was nice of those boys to split all that wood for you wasn't it?" Linda asked.

"Huh?" Tom asked.

"I said," she repeated herself, "it sure was nice of those boys to split all that firewood for us wasn't it?"

"Oh, yeah," Tom replied, "it sure was, they sure split a lot of wood, did you see it all?"

"Yes dear," Linda said with a smile, "I did see it."

Tom stood in the driveway of their house, watching two squirrels chasing each other up and down the tree; they went around the trunk of the tree and then raced back up and disappeared among the branches.

He couldn't see them any longer, but he could still hear them chattering.

"Ready?" Linda asked as she walked out the door and pulled it shut behind her.

"I'm ready," Tom replied, pointing up at the tree, "I was just watching those two squirrels chasing each other, I wonder who finally won?"

Linda held out her hand and Tom reached out and took it with his hand, he turned when she was next to him and began to walk.

"I don't know honey," she replied, "Do you think they were racing or playing tag?"

Tom chuckled, "ya know, I never gave it that much thought, but they were sure busy and seemed to have a lot to say to one another."

"Kind of like us huh?" she replied with a smile, gently tugging his hand.

"Kind of," Tom replied back, letting go of her hand and holding out his elbow. Linda put her arm through his and put her hand in her coat pocket.

Tom stopped at the end of the driveway, and looked both ways.

"Malted?" he asked Linda as he looked towards town.

"Sure," she said with a smile and took a step in that direction.

Tom switched places with Linda so that she was on the side of him furthest from traffic.

It was late morning when they got into downtown; it took longer to walk downtown from their home now than it did a few short years ago. Neither Tom nor Linda walked as fast as they used to. Ten years ago when they first moved to this home on the outskirts of town, it was a paved country lane with only a half dozen or so houses between the city limits and their house. They used to walk from the front door of the house to the front door of Tom's electronics shop in just under half an hour. It was a brisk walk, but they enjoyed the scenery and the chance to visit without the distractions found at home. Today, the walk takes just over an hour and is no longer done briskly.

"Wow," Tom said as he stopped and looked at the sign above the door. The sign read Tim's Electronic sales and service. "It looks different."

"Yes it does," Linda said as she stopped along side Tom and looked at the new sign, "I guess that it's one thing to talk about it, and know about it, but another thing to actually see it."

"It feels strange," Tom replied, "I'm used to seeing my name up there, I mean, what, twenty odd years it was there, now I look at it for the first time and my name isn't there."

Linda pursed her lips and nodded, "I know honey, I guess it's an end of an era."

"Yeah," Tom replied quietly, "an end of an era."

The front door of the store opened and Tim stepped out and waved his arm at Tom and Linda, "hey there, come on in, please come inside."

Tom looked at Linda then stepped towards the door with Tim waving and welcoming them inside.

"I was hoping you two would come by and see what's new here," Tim said proudly, "as you can see," he said, holding his arm out and turning in a slow sweeping motion, "I've made a few changes, I moved the customer counter over to the side, I added displays here in the center of the store, and I added a workbench and hired another repair guy."

"Very nice," Linda said then looked at Tom, "don't you think so Tom?"

"Yes, oh yeah," Tom agreed, "It looks very nice, I like what you've done, I hardly recognize it now, it's a far cry from when I first opened the doors more than twenty years ago."

"Tom," Tim said, reaching out and touching Tom on the forearm, "this is your doing, you were my inspiration, you started all this, I just made changes and updated it, hell without you and your vision, it wouldn't be here and I sure as hell wouldn't be here. It's because of you Tom that I turned my life around, and look, here I am."

Tom held his head up, proud and high when he heard Tim talking like that. It made him feel good.

"Well son," Tom said, putting his hand on Tim's shoulder, "you done good, you made me proud, and I have to admit, when I saw the new sign above the door, it took me by surprise, it was hard to see the change, but deep down, I'm glad it's been changed, and it has your name on it, it's yours now."

"Thanks Tom," Tim replied, "that means a lot to me, it really does."

"We won't take any more of your time," Tom said as he turned and reached for the door and winked at Tim, "we have a date and we're heading downtown for a malted."

Tim smiled and opened the door for them, "ok, stop in anytime, anytime."

"Bye now," Linda said as she kissed Tim on the cheek, "you and Sue are still coming for dinner tomorrow, right?"

"Of course," Tim replied, returning Linda's kiss, "see you tomorrow mom."

"See you tomorrow," Tom said, waving from the sidewalk.

"See ya," Tim said to Tom, waving from the door of the store.

Tom held the door open at the ice cream shop for Linda to enter first, the tiny bell on the door rang, indicating someone had entered. Tom looked up at the bell as it rang, wondering how old it was and how many times it had rang, indicating someone had entered or left. Turning his attention back to Linda, he patted her on the butt as she walked in the door in front of him. She turned her head sideways and smiled. She loved it when Tom touched her, especially after all these years, it warmed her heart. It was those little things that made her feel truly loved by Tom.

At the counter, Tom took her hand as she climbed up onto the stool. Tom sat next to her and asked right away, "Know what you're going to have?"

"I'm not sure yet," Linda said as she picked up and opened the menu, looking to see if there was a special today that she wanted to try.

"I know what I want," Tom said, folding the menu closed and laying it down on the counter next to him, "I want the hot fudge, I think that's my favorite."

"I knew you were going to pick that," Linda chuckled

"Oh yeah?" Tom asked, "and how did you know that?"

"Because you always order that," Linda replied, looking at him out of the corner of her eye, "I can't remember the last time you had anything different here."

"Oh," Tom said, looking up at the ceiling and rolling his eyes, "I'm that predictable am I?"

"Yes hon," Linda said, leaning her shoulder against his arm, "I think so."

"Hmmm, well," Tom said grinning, "I think I'm still going to have that, may as well stay with it if it works."

Linda shook her head and smiled, not saying a word, and put her menu in the rack behind the napkin holder.

Chapter 18

THE SUN WAS beginning to set as they reached the sidewalk that led up to their house. Tom was tired from the walk and was starting to favor his left leg.

"Are you alright dear?" Linda asked, concerned as she noticed the change in his walk.

"I don't know," Tom replied, "my leg sure hurts, it started awhile ago."

"I noticed you favoring it," Linda acknowledged, "you started doing it a few months ago, more so when you get tired, maybe you should get it checked out."

"I think so," he grimaced, "it really has gotten worse lately, but I didn't want to complain, I thought it would just get better with some rest."

"I think we need to make an appointment for you," Linda said, taking his arm in her hand, "want me to call the doctor for you?"

"Thanks honey," Tom replied and slowly climbed the three steps to the front porch, "I think I'll sit down and rest a bit out here."

"Ok, here," she said and propped a pillow on the swing for him to lean back against, "I'll go make a pot of coffee and look up the doctor's phone number."

"Thanks hon," Tom said as he sat down, then he reached out and grabbed her hand with his, "what would I ever do without you?"

Linda smiled and shook his hand gently, "I'll be back in a few minutes."

Linda held the door of the clinic so Tom could walk out behind her. He walked awkwardly, trying to get used to his cane, practicing what he just learned, step with his good leg, and move the cane and other leg together as if they were one.

"This is going to take some practice," he told Linda as he walked with her towards the car.

"I know it will," she agreed, "but I think it'll help you, it'll take some weight off your bad leg."

"Guess I can't chase you around very well now can I?" Tom said jokingly, "You'll have to give me a head start."

Linda laughed out loud and put her arm around Tom's waist and gave a little squeeze, "I'll make sure I'm easy for you to catch."

"Whew," Tom replied, "I was worried for a minute."

"I bet you were," Linda said, stopping at the car.

Tom opened the passenger door so Linda could get in, then he walked around the front of the car to the drivers side, noticing the whole time that she had not taken her eyes off of him.

Tom leaned down and pressed his face against the drivers window, flattening his nose against the glass, looking across the inside of the car and saw Linda laughing at his childish antics.

Tom opened the door and tossed his cane into the back seat of the car, then climbed in and buckled up his seatbelt.

"Sometimes you can be pretty silly," Linda said to him, placing her hand on his leg.

Tom opened a bottle of wine and set it down to breath while he got two glasses and set them on a tray. Linda placed some cheese slices she just sliced up on the tray and arranged some crackers around the edge.

Pleased with the presentation of their snack, he picked up his cane and walked out to the front porch, stopping to hold the door for Linda as she carried the tray out behind him.

Tom sat in the rocking chair on the porch and laid his cane down beside him.

Linda set the tray down on the table between the two rocking chairs and sat down on hers. Tom poured the wine and handed Linda a glass. Raising his glass towards Linda, "to a wonderful and blessed life, and to the future, where the best is yet to come," Tom said with a smile.

Linda, cocked her head and smiled, then clinked her glass against Tom's, "to us," She said, "the best is yet to come."

They each took a sip of their wine, then Linda set her glass down on the tray and picked up a cracker, "how can it get any better than this?" she asked Tom.

"I ask myself that every day," Tom replied with a loving look, "and yet it does, each day it just gets better and better."

Tom and Linda sat in their chairs quietly, watching the sun setting across the open area across the street from their house.

There were trees blocking the view of the sunset for many years. Now the trees were gone and it was a beautiful sight, the sky was a pale blue, turning to purples and oranges and reds, with sharp yellow almost white streaks shooting up from the horizon.

In a few months, the views would once again be blocked by the housing development going in.

"Hello Mr. And Mrs. Watson," a child shouted out as he rode past their house on his bicycle. Tom and Linda waved, but he was gone before they could verbally respond. Which was better, Tom thought. He couldn't recall the name of this particular child, nor from which house on the street he even lived in. Funny, Tom thought to himself, a few years ago, they had deer running through their yard. Now they had neighborhood children. The deer were much quieter, but the children could be hired to help out by cutting the lawn and doing other odd jobs.

Linda stood up quickly and went inside when she heard the phone ringing. The screen door slamming shut behind her, the sudden loud noise surprising Tom and making him jump in his chair.

A few moments later the porch light came on a second before Linda came out and stood in front of Tom. The sun was now well below the horizon and the sky was getting darker, the evening air was cool and crisp.

"That was Andrea," Linda began, "she's at the hospital, Sunrise just had a baby boy."

"They did huh?" Tom looked up, squinting his eyes at Linda, all he could see was the shadow of her face, outlined in the porch light hanging from the ceiling just behind her, "seems like only yesterday we were at their wedding, my, where does the time go?"

"His name is Hunter," Linda said as she sat down in her chair, "I think that's a nice name, what about you?"

Tom shrugged his shoulders, "I guess so."

"Oh come on," Linda said, "show a little more excitement will you, he's our first great grandson, that's a big deal."

"I am excited," Tom said, turning in his chair to look at Linda, "I am, really, I just never hear that for a name before. Do you think I'm old fashioned?"

Linda smiled at Tom, "no honey, I don't think you are old fashioned, I just think we come from a different generation with different names, look at Andrea, she named her lovely daughter Sunrise, nobody in our generation would have ever thought of that for a name, now almost anything is used, even made up names."

"Guess you're right," Tom replied, reaching for his cane, "I think I'm going to go inside."

"Me too," Linda replied, "It sure cooled off in a hurry, I wonder if there's a storm front blowing in."

Tom opened his eyes and looked at the clock on his nightstand. His eyes quickly opened wide when he realized he had slept in later than usual. He sat up and rubbed his eyes, then picked up his cane and slowly walked into the bathroom to take a shower and wake up.

Linda was sitting near the kitchen table, her chair pushed back and away from the table as she held the newborn baby on her lap and made faces and noises to it.

Tom heard the strange noises his wife was making as he got closer to the kitchen, and then he heard the muffled voices of Sunrise and Gary. He suddenly knew what the strange sounds were, smiling inward, he knew that shortly he would be making similarly silly noises and faces and holding the newest addition to the family.

"What do we have here?" Tom asked, announcing his entrance to the room, his eyes focused on the baby on Linda's lap, "A miniature goomba?"

Sunrise smiled and reached her arms out to Tom for a hug, "good morning grampa, isn't he cute?"

Tom gave Sunrise a one armed hug while leaning on his cane with his other, "I don't know, I haven't had a chance to see the little guy yet."

"Grandma, show Hunter to grampa," Sunrise instructed, "he hasn't seen him yet."

"Isn't he precious?" Linda asked Tom as she held him up carefully, one hand under his padded butt and the other carefully cradling his head, "just look at his little nose."

Tom walked over and looked at the baby, then reached out and touched his nose with his fingertip, "you look just like your daddy don't you." Tom said to Hunter, more of an observation than an actual question and not really expecting a reply back.

"Hello Gary," Tom stood up and said, almost an after thought, "you two sure did make a beautiful baby here, can't wait for my turn to hold him."

"Here, have a seat," Sunrise said as she pulled out a chair and moved it closer for Tom to sit on, "I'm sure grandma will let you hold him pretty soon."

"Thanks," Tom said, sitting down next to Linda and leaning over to touch the little fingers on Hunter's hand.

"Listen," Sunrise said, her hand on a cloth bag made with a blue elephant print, "everything you'll need is in the bag right here on the counter, we won't be gone long, and thanks again you guys."

Tom sat up; looking confused and asked, "what's going on?"

"Gary and I are going to a movie," Sunrise replied, "Grandma suggested it and said you guys would watch Hunter."

Tom quickly looked over at Linda who was smiling and nodding her head in agreement, "that's right dear, we're babysitting today, isn't that wonderful?"

"I, I, guess so," Tom replied nervously, looking up at Sunrise, "I haven't watched a baby since you were a baby, and that was a long time ago."

Linda chuckled, "It's okay, you two go on, go have fun, we'll be fine, just fine."

"Thanks grandma," Sunrise said as she kissed Linda on the cheek.

"Thanks, we really appreciate this," Gary said with a wave as he opened the door for Sunrise.

"It'll be fine," Linda repeated herself reassuringly to Sunrise while she elbowed Tom in the side, "he's all talk, he actually does a great job, now you two don't worry."

"Will I get to hold him?" Tom asked with a laugh, looking over at Hunter who was now sleeping on Linda's lap. Tom lifted his hand up and waved in a form of dismissal, "go now, we'll be fine."

"When did all this secret planning take place?" Tom asked Linda after the door closed and Sunrise and Gary had left.

"Actually, just this morning" Linda replied, it's alright isn't it?"

"Oh, of course it is," Tom said, touching his hand to Linda's face, "what else was I going to do today? Build a house?"

"Thank you," Linda said, leaning her face into Tom's warm hand.

"I just hope I'll get a chance to hold the little bugger," Tom said with a grin as he rubbed his finger under Hunter's chin, "I hate to wake him up. Babies always sleep so peacefully when they're little like this, don't they?"

"Because they don't have a care or worry in the world," Linda replied, not taking her eyes off of Hunter.

Linda woke up when Tom stopped the car, "are we here already?" she asked, still sleepy.

"Yep," Tom replied with a chuckle, "you dropped off to sleep almost as soon as we pulled out of the driveway, and slept all the way."

"I'm sorry," she said, rubbing her eyes and adjusting her car seat back into an upright position, "I guess I was tired."

"I guess so," Tom said, "give me a minute to get out and I'll open the cabin."

"Ok," Linda replied, "I'll gather the stuff from the car, can you pop the trunk?"

Tom turned the key in the door and pushed the door open, he noticed a light on in the living room and paused for a second.

Linda walked up behind him, noticing that he had opened the door but not entered and asked, "What's wrong?"

"There's a light on," Tom replied, "I don't remember leaving a light on, in fact, I remember checking before we left last time to make sure all the lights were off and both doors were locked."

"Are you sure?" Linda replied, putting her hand on his back as she looked around him to see inside the cabin.

"Yes, I'm sure," he replied, annoyed, "wait here," he instructed and stepped into the cabin, walking slowly, holding his cane in both hands as a weapon.

"Tom, be careful," Linda said softly, as he went inside. She held the door open so it would not slam shut and make any loud noises.

"Linda, come here," Tom shouted from the living room.

Linda quickly entered the cabin; curious as to what Tom saw so that he called for her instead of coming to the door to get her.

"Would you look at that," Tom said, pointing above the fireplace mantle. Perfectly centered was a large framed portrait of all the children, grandchildren, and one great grandchild. All captured in a permanent smile.

"Oh my god," Linda said with her voice quivering as she pointed her finger, "look, what does the card say?"

"I dunno," Tom said, reaching for the card tucked into the corner of the matting of the framed portrait.

Linda looked around the cabin and noticed other items that were not there before. New matching quilts on their worn old chairs and out on the porch, right in front of the window were two log rocking chairs.

"Oh Tom," Linda said, tears forming in the corner of her eyes pointing around to the new items, "look at all these things, what does the card say?"

Tom opened the envelope and pulled out the card, then opened it and read it to Linda.

Dear Mom and Tom

We got together and decided to give this to you for your anniversary. (It takes less energy to enjoy than the bicycles) We look good don't we?

You two are a perfect example of what love is. You show it to us and to each other daily. We only hope to have half the love that you two share, if any of us has half that much in our marriages, we will be blessed and lucky.

If you look around the cabin, we left a few other things for you too.

We hope you enjoy them as much as all of us did giving them to you.

We will get together when you get back to town, but we wanted something there, from all of us when you got there so you will know that even when we are not together, we are with you.

Love
Andrea, Jerry, Tim, Sue,
Carolyn, Sunshine, Gary, and Hunter.

"My goodness," Linda said as she sat down on her chair, "how nice."

"They certainly are thoughtful, and wonderful, those kids," Tom said as he sat down in his chair and gazed up at the portrait.

Linda woke up first, to the sound of a squirrel making a chattering noise in the tree right outside the bedroom window. She put on her housecoat, and went into the bathroom. She looked at herself in the mirror. It was hard getting older, where she once had smooth soft skin, she now had wrinkles, her beautiful dark hair was now gray and thinning, and she no longer stood straight up like before. Her posture was degrading; she now stooped over with the obvious signs of age. She brushed her teeth and went into the kitchen to put on a pot of coffee. She didn't hear Tom as he walked into the kitchen; the soft thumping of his cane on the wood floor was drowned out by the sound of water running in the sink.

"Good morning," he said as he put his hand on her hip and kissed the back of her neck.

"Oh my god!" Linda said, as she jumped from being startled, "you scared me, when did you get up?"

"Sorry about that," Tom replied, "I thought you hear me come in."

"Well, I didn't," She replied, her hand on her chest, catching her breath, "you're going to give me a heart attack sneaking up on me like that."

"I didn't sneak up on you," Tom said, defending himself, "and I said I'm sorry."

Tom opened the cupboard and pulled out two coffee cups, "is the coffee done yet?" He asked.

"Not yet," Linda replied, as she opened the fridge to get the cream for her coffee.

"Ok, then I'm going to get dressed," Tom said as he turned and walked out of the kitchen.

Linda poured herself a cup of coffee and walked out to the front porch. Leaning against the railing on her elbows, she could look straight down and see the water, motionless against the rocks. No boats were on the lake yet and the water was still calm, so calm it looked as smooth at glass.

She raised her cup to her lips, blowing softly at the rising steam from the hot coffee. Out of the corner of her eye she saw a sudden movement and turned her head to see what it was. A chipmunk darted in and out of the rocks, following the shoreline looking for scraps of food to eat or take back to his nest. Pausing every few feet to sit up and look around for signs of danger, ears alert and tail twitching nervously.

Tom walked out of the cabin and onto the porch, his back pushing the door open as he held his cane in one hand and his coffee in the other.

"Another absolutely beautiful morning," Linda said, acknowledging Tom's presence.

"I see that," Tom replied, as he sat down on one of the new rocking chairs from the kids, "hey, this is nice."

Tom finished his coffee and put his cup down, then using his cane for support, stood up, "I'm going out to the shed for awhile," he said, picking up his empty cup.

"You sure have been spending a lot of time out there," Linda replied, "what do you do out there anyway, do you have a girlfriend out there that I don't know about?"

Tom turned and smiled, "you'll see," then opened the door and went inside the cabin.

Tom applied another coat of varnish to the board on the workbench and wiped his hands off on a rag. Looking up and out the window, he saw Linda walking towards the shed. Tom opened the door and walked out of the shed to meet her, "Hi honey," he said as he greeted her.

"Hi, I thought I would come and see if you wanted some company," Linda said as Tom quickly closed the door behind him.

"How about a walk?" Tom asked as he reached his elbow out for her to hold onto.

"Alright," Linda said, looking at the closed door to the shed, then, turning and putting her arm inside his arm, she began to walk with him, "where are we going?"

"I don't know," Tom replied, "how about out to the road and back?"

The walk down the dirt drive to the paved road was a half-mile, a short easy walk in years past, but a good walk that took some time now as age set in. Their walk now was more of a shuffle, no longer the long strides of youth, or even the not so long strides of middle age.

Slowly walking down the side of the dirt drive, arm in arm, Tom walked with his cane for support, and Linda leaned on Tom for support.

Every so often, they would stop and rest, using the break to watch the local wildlife. Still untouched by developers, the land around the cabin held numerous kinds of birds, rabbits, deer, fox, raccoons, and many other smaller animals that shared the woods.

A hawk flew overhead, with wings barely moved, as it appeared to float on the air currents, looking down for prey. On the side of the road, Linda watched butterflies fluttering their wings as they moved about the wildflowers. Their vibrant colors always amazed her, how they were so delicate and beautiful.

Tom stopped at the edge of the paved road; they stood there a moment, resting, before turning and heading back towards the cabin.

Tom opened the door for Linda and held her hand as she walked up the steps into the cabin. Tom followed her into the cabin then headed straight for the sofa, "I'm going to take a quick nap hon," he said to Linda as he lay his head down on a pillow and put his feet up.

"Ok," She replied, "I'm going to read for a bit then lay down myself."

Linda threw a quilt over Tom on the sofa before she sat down in her chair to read.

Linda opened her book and began to read, after only a few moments, she glanced over at Tom and smiled, he was fast asleep already.

Tom woke up from his nap and saw Linda still in her chair, her book on her lap and her eyes closed, he struggled a little to get up off the sofa, then put the same quilt she had put on him, over her while she slept in her chair. He leaned down to kiss her on the forehead but stopped short, not wanting to wake her up.

He closed the door of the cabin quietly behind him as he went back out to work in the shed.

Tom sat down on his stool and picked up a cloth to buff the surface, taking great care not to make any smudges. He rubbed and buffed and didn't notice Linda walking towards the shed from the cabin, he heard the door open and quickly threw a cloth over his project.

"Hi there," Tom said, turning on his stool to face her, "how was your nap?"

"It was nice," she replied, "thanks for covering me up. I must have fallen asleep while I was reading."

"You're welcome," Tom replied, turning on his stool back towards his workbench, "come here, I want you to see this."

"What is it?" Linda asked, "Is this why you've been spending so much time out here?"

"Yep," Tom replied, lifting up the cloth, revealing the board, "ta-dah!"

Tom had spent not only hours, but also days working on his project. A plaque with the edges all hand carved to look like it was a hundred years old. In the center, he hand carved the words, "Welcome to our little piece of heaven," He had painted the carved words, and then he stained the surrounding board and applied several layers of varnish.

"Oh my, Tom," Linda said with a gasp, "It's beautiful."

"I'm going to hang it over the door," He said proudly, showing off his work, "so everybody can see it when they walk in the door."

"Oh Tom, that is wonderful," Linda said as she leaned down to kiss him, "It is, isn't it? This is our little piece of heaven isn't it?"

"I think so," Tom agreed, "and you are my angel from heaven."

"Aw," Linda replied, a small tear forming, "you love me today like you did when we were first together, it hasn't faded a bit."

Linda wrapped her arms around Tom's neck and she held tightly. Tom reached up and put his arms around her waist, holding her tight. "Nope, it hasn't faded a bit."

Tom rinsed off the soap on the last pot from dinner and put it on the counter. Linda put away a dish then picked up the pot and with the dishtowel in her hand she dried it off and hung it up on the pot rack hanging from the ceiling.

"Can we go down to the dock before you light a fire tonight?" Linda asked Tom, "I want to watch the sunset over the lake."

Tom raised his eyebrows, "sure hon, whatever you want, let me grab a sweater first, it gets cool down at the water in the evening."

"Thanks, can you grab mine too please?" she asked.

Linda held onto Tom's elbow as they walked down the path to the dock, stopping to step down on each step. The old wooden dock creaked as they walked on it. Tom sat down on the bench at the end of the dock and took off his shoes and socks.

"What are you doing?" Linda asked.

"I'm taking my shoes and socks off. I want to dip my feet in the water."

Linda nodded her head, "sounds like a good idea, I think I'll take mine off too," she said, and sat down on the bench next to Tom and slipped off her shoes too.

She held her feet in the air and wiggled her toes, "feels good don't it? The fresh air on my feet, I don't know when the last time I was outside barefoot."

"Sure does," Tom said, standing up from the bench.

Tom helped Linda get up from the bench then took three steps to the edge of the dock and slowly sat down on the dock, his bones creaking as he lowered himself down. Sitting on his butt on the edge of the dock, he hung his legs over the edge and touched his feet to the water. The late evening lake was calm. Like the early morning, it was smooth like glass. A small ripple went out from where his toe first touched the water. Looking up at Linda and raising his hand, he smiled at her invitingly, "come on, I'll help you."

Linda took his hand and slowly lowered herself until she was sitting on the dock next to him. She lowered her feet into the water and tapped her toe playfully on the top of the water, causing little ripples to form and move away.

Tom put his arm around her waist and pulled her closer. Linda reached over and took his other hand in hers, holding it with both of her hands, she leaned her head on his shoulder.

As quiet as the setting sun, they sat on the dock together, still madly in love with each other, watching another day come to an end.

The End